PENGUIN BOOKS

Emma Heatherington is the international bestselling author of fifteen novels, including the Amazon UK Top 10 and US Kindle hit *The Legacy of Lucy Harte*, as well as *Secrets in the Snow* and *The Promise*.

Her novels are set in Ireland, each exploring life-affirming issues combined with heart-warming love stories. Emma's distinctive style, full of poignancy and warmth, has developed a loyal and ever-growing fanbase.

This Christmas

Emma Heatherington

PENGUIN BOOKS

PENGUIN BOOKS

UK | USA | Canada | Ireland | Australia
India | New Zealand | South Africa

Penguin Books is part of the Penguin Random House group of companies
whose addresses can be found at global.penguinrandomhouse.com

Penguin
Random House
UK

Published in Penguin Books 2023
002

Copyright © Emma Heatherington, 2023

The moral right of the author has been asserted

Typeset in 10.4/15 pt Palatino LT Pro
by Integra Software Services Pvt. Ltd, Pondicherry

Printed and bound in Great Britain by Clays Ltd, Elcograf S.p.A.

The authorised representative in the EEA is Penguin Random House Ireland,
Morrison Chambers, 32 Nassau Street, Dublin D02 YH68

A CIP catalogue record for this book is available from the British Library

ISBN: 978–1–804–94185–0

www.greenpenguin.co.uk

For my darling Aunty Eithna.
Thank you for everything, especially Christmas 1991
and all you did for us in those early years without
mummy xxx

this
Christmas

Ten Days to Christmas

Chapter One

Rose

I can't take my eyes off him.

I know it can't be Michael, but I keep moving closer and closer towards this stranger as happy holiday music fills the air.

I remind myself to breathe as I cross the hotel lobby to where he's addressing a small group of men by the polished mahogany bar. His friends don't notice me as they marvel at his every word, smiling and laughing at his never-ending charm.

His dark hair peppered with grey at the sides, the way he talks with his hands. I can hear his infectious laughter now as my mind goes into overdrive. I can see the outline of his profile, so confident, commanding the floor as cheesy festive music bellows out of the in-built hotel speakers.

I'm right behind him. My hands are shaking. Before I can say anything, he turns around.

'*The* Rose Quinn?'

He has a charming smile.

My heart hits the floor.

'Brian Jones,' he says, extending a hand to greet me. 'I'm married to Alice.'

His hand is silky smooth, not rough and weather-beaten like Michael's was. I take it politely as my eyes widen and I fake a wondrous smile.

'Yes, Alice, of course. She's been a great addition to the team.'

'And is already fitting in well with her colleagues. I've managed to blend in here with some other abandoned husbands and partners.'

My pulse throbs in my neck. I could easily be sick. This has never happened before.

While Michael has rarely left my mind the past few years, I've never drifted into a cloudy haze like this where I imagined I'd seen him again. But it's almost Christmas, and that's when his loss always clutches at my throat more than any other time of year, threatening to stop me in my tracks once and for all.

'I was just about to greet everyone in the City Suite,' I announce, my voice a stark contrast to the raw torment I'm feeling. 'Please make your way next door. You can bring your drinks, of course.'

I'm shaking inside, yet my outward confident demeanour will never give me away. I've worked hard at that.

The man's wedding ring glistens on his finger, clinking against his glass as he raises it and nods.

'We'll be right there,' he calls as I walk away with a wobbling lip and a thumping heart. I feel his eyes bore into me with every step I take. 'It's going to be a wonderful evening.'

4

I approach the City Suite of the bustling hotel, greeting my staff and their guests on the way with a smile, air kisses and compliments I truly mean despite my sadness. They're an adorable bunch, and they deserve a night like this. It's the least I can do.

You look stunning, Mia. I adore your dress.

Have some champagne, Luca. No, of course your outfit isn't too much, darling. It's Christmas.

It's so lovely to meet Simon at last, Nico. You've told us so much about him.

More shaking of hands, more air kisses, more compliments follow.

Everything in this hotel screams festive, from the savoury canapés to the mulled wine, and the over-the-top decorations that greet me at every turn. Tall, sparkling trees twinkle against the navy walls, familiar music fills the air and hotel staff don bright red Santa hats as they happily top up our glasses. The mood is bouncy, it's happy. But I can't wait for this night to be over.

I stop in the doorway of the City Suite where my colleagues and their guests are now waiting for the formalities to be over and the real party to begin, which is exactly when I plan to make my discreet escape home.

I've promised Carlos I'll hang around for one dance, fake a few more jovial conversations, and then it will be over to him to entertain the masses for the rest of the evening.

I take a deep breath. I smooth my polka dot skirt and petticoat down past my hips, feeling proud to be wearing

an outfit I sewed myself. I flick back my dark, curled hair
and pull out my compact mirror to quickly touch up my red
lipstick.

I'll get through this. I'm Rose Quinn, CEO of Activate
International. I can do this. I clink my glass to get everyone's
attention, immediately soothed by the array of familiar faces
who turn towards me.

'Merry Christmas everyone!' I announce with a beaming
smile. 'Thank you all for making the effort to be together
tonight to celebrate the end of another wonderful year.'

My small group of colleagues burst into applause as I take
up a central point in the hired hotel function room.

'Let us raise a glass,' I suggest, 'to another twelve months
that once again proves that we're the most creative, the most
passionate and the most talented digital marketing team in
Ireland.'

'Hear, hear!' Carlos calls out to me. His jovial stance and
flamboyance fill the room as always. After almost three years
in partnership with him, I'm glad to have him to focus on to
keep my mind steady.

'Online is a fast-moving, forever changing industry, but,
as always, we at Activate will remain miles ahead in a global,
digital world – one where we'll continue to move forward at
a pace our competitors can only watch from afar.'

My stomach is in knots. I see the man who looks like
Michael in the corner of my eye, but I keep going. I keep
smiling.

'Here's to another bumper year, where we will continue
to nurture and encourage every individual in our growing

team. I am immensely proud of what we have achieved and continue to achieve. I am inspired every day by the dedication, creativity and passion that every single one of you brings to our small but vibrant agency. So, here's to Activate. Here's to the future. Here's to you.'

More applause. More clinking of glasses.

I've almost convinced even myself that I've got my shit together.

I have a job to do here in Dublin. It's the one thing in life that I do very well.

It's the one thing I can't afford to let go, no matter how much I'm grieving sore.

'What A Speech! What a speech! Seriously, you rock, my darling.'

'Bet you say that to all the girls,' I tease, taking an espresso martini from Carlos. We touch glasses in celebration.

Now that the formalities are over and after a quick freshen up in the bathroom, I'm slowly coming back to myself after my earlier wobble, but the escape door is never far out of my sight.

I fix Carlos's oversized collar which is sticking up at the back of his neck. He is dapper in his yellow paisley shirt and clashing orange dicky bow. Even on dreary Mondays he wouldn't look out of place at any fancy do, despite working in a slightly cramped but chic office in inner city Dublin. He's ten years older than my thirty-six years, but it's a running joke how I can't help but mother him.

'I don't say that to everyone, and you know it,' he says, leaning in to give me a kiss on the cheek before adjusting his round, black-rimmed glasses. He smells like spiced wine. 'You're my bestie. Now, are you OK? As wonderful as you were just now, I'm just checking.'

Carlos never misses a trick.

'I was thrown off course ever so slightly by my mind playing games earlier, but I'm fine now.'

'Rose? What happened?'

I shake it off, knowing I'll tell Carlos about my fleeting moment of madness eventually.

'It's silly. Honestly. Just a bit of a wobble. So, tell me all about your festive plans. Are you looking forward to taking some time out? I can't wait to just switch off and do nothing.'

Carlos raises an eyebrow.

'Hmm, OK. You can let me know when you're ready. Now, please tell me you've reconsidered my offer to join us for Christmas. My dad's bought an extra cheeseboard and new wine glasses – *crystal* wine glasses – in case you change your mind. And he's finally invested in Scrabble. An all-new limited edition.'

We walk towards a high table with tall stools by the window. I claim it quickly by setting down my silver beaded handbag, which belonged to my late Granny Molly in the 1960s. Like most things I own, it's been on this earth for a lot longer than I have.

'That's so, so sweet of him,' I tell Carlos as we slide onto a stool each. 'But you know I'm only faking this for tonight. I can't do Christmas just yet.'

'But Rose—'

'I mean it, I can't,' I explain for the umpteenth time.

'But why punish yourself like this?' he whispers. 'Haven't you suffered enough?'

'I can't face it yet,' I whisper in return. 'Tonight is as good as it gets, Carlos. Then my plan is to have *no* plans, just like before. I'm taking some extended leave from tomorrow and when I come back after all the fuss is over, I'll be fully recharged and refreshed to pick up again.'

He scrunches up his face, his brown eyes glistening with concern. His glasses are steaming up with the heat, so he takes them off and buffs them up as he speaks.

'No one would expect you to be so hard on yourself like this, Rose,' he reminds me, his brow creased with worry. 'And don't say you have George. He doesn't count.'

I sip my cocktail and glance around to make sure none of our staff members are within earshot. Thankfully they are mostly now singing into champagne bottles while swaying arm in arm in time to the festive music. For a flickering moment I wish I was that age again, that *happy* again. Fearless and carefree, the world my oyster.

As far as anyone else in our small but forceful agency is concerned, I'm leaving the fast-moving city life this Christmas to spend time with my ageing parents and doting sister up north where I come from. They believe this is what I've done for the past few years since I first arrived in Dublin with a rescue dog, a smashed-up heart and just about enough strength to land a job where I've managed to work my way up to the very top in a relatively short space of time.

'George will be with me wherever I go and whatever I do,' I say, managing a smile for my business partner. 'He is excellent company.'

Carlos rolls his eyes.

'He prefers meaty chunks in jelly to a fancy turkey dinner,' I continue. 'He doesn't get drunk, but still sleeps most of the day. My George is an *ideal* Christmas companion.'

'So, you aren't tempted to ditch him and jet off somewhere hot for a change, then?'

I put my hand to my chest in mock horror.

'Me and George are a team, Carlos. A package. We're a—'

I'm about to say 'a family', which makes my stomach twist when I think of my actual family up north, who I only wish I could celebrate Christmas with like I used to.

'Have you called your mum yet to tell her you're doing it alone again?' asks Carlos, reading my mind, it seems.

'No.'

'Sarah?'

I shake my head.

'Are you going to?'

I shake my head again.

'Oh, Rose.'

'I can't tell them yet,' I say, dropping my voice down as low as I can beneath the irritating seasonal music. The raucous laughter in the air which would, in days gone by, be treacle to my soul, is now only a reminder of how miserable I am inside. 'I dread the disappointment in my mother's voice when I tell her I want to spend Christmas alone again. But I need to, Carlos. I have to.'

He looks away. I know what he's going to say.

'You do realise that when you finally do decide to spend Christmas with your whole family again, it might be too late. You know as well as I do that life can change in the blink of an eye.'

I pause. My stomach drops at the thought.

'I get that, Carlos. I totally do,' I sigh, feeling a confession coming on. 'Don't get mad, but I had this crazy fantasy moment where I thought I saw him earlier. It was just someone who looked like him. I knew that, but—'

Carlos goes to interrupt but I talk over him.

'Look, I know it's stupid and sad before you say so. I knew it couldn't be him, yet I couldn't stop myself from having a closer look.'

'Was that your wobble earlier?'

'Yes,' I nod, feeling my eyes fill up.

'I'm so sorry, babe,' says Carlos. 'And it's not stupid or sad. It's heart-breaking. I'm sorry.'

My throat dries up. It's almost time for me to get out of here.

'I was *this* far from totally humiliating myself when the man turned around and – oh Carlos, am I losing my mind? It was the new girl Alice's husband. But for just one second, just one glorious second, I let myself imagine he wasn't gone at all.'

I bite my lip and look away. I won't cry tonight, no matter how emotional a few cocktails can make me feel. I have sobbed my lungs out to Carlos behind closed doors over losing Michael, but there's no way I'm breaking down in front of everyone here.

11

'Oh Rose, you're killing me,' Carlos replies, slipping off his stool to be closer to me. 'But you're doing so, so well. One step at a time, remember? I know how hard it was for you to come here tonight and put on such a brave face for everyone.'

I scan the room. My team mean the world to me. As painful as this is, there's no way I could have let them down by not showing up to thank them for another amazing year in business. I promised myself I'd put on a front for them, even if it means dancing and smiling when I really feel like curling up into a ball and pretending Christmas isn't happening at all.

'And if you really believe that being on your own at Christmas helps you get through the season,' Carlos says, 'then I won't try to convince you otherwise. But don't feel you have to, darling. You won't always have to.'

'I know, I know,' I manage a smile. 'Maybe this will be the last Christmas I feel I have to spend alone.'

Carlos nods and clasps my hand. He has the type of face you'd love to paint, all angles and corners with glasses that probably cost more than my entire outfit.

I can tell he wants to change the subject to make me smile again. I can tell by how he has gone from looking deeply concerned about my grief to swaying and clicking his fingers as the sound of Mariah Carey belts out around us.

'You requested that song, didn't you?' I ask him, crinkling my nose as a genuine grin sneaks up on me.

'Never.'

'Bit insensitive, don't you think, considering the lyrics? All I want for Christmas is you?' I can't help but laugh, even though inside I want to cry. 'I bloody hate this song.'

He puts his hands up and bops along in time to Mariah, stepping from side to side as he clicks again.

'Just one dance like you said you would? Then I'll pretend you got some mysterious tummy bug and had to slip off, just like we promised.'

'OK, OK, I hear you,' I reply. It may be the most dreaded time of year for me, but I've a business to run and bills to pay, which often means putting my own sadness on pause when it's called for. 'Just one dance and then I'm out of here.'

His eyes light up. My own eyes catch the Michael look-alike who stands holding a pint in one hand, the other in his pocket. I feel his gaze on me, but I ignore it. I may be sad and lonely but I'm not of the mindset to flirt with anyone, never mind a married man.

We push our way through the glittery revellers who sing along as they dance like no one's watching. And then I dance too.

My body moves, but inside I'm a mess.

All I want for Christmas is to be my real self again, but even Christmas can't make that wish come true.

George, a huge mound of black and white fluff, all slobbers and a panting tongue, greets me at the door of my city town-house when I get home. Despite my weary head and heart, I manage to indulge him before I even take my coat off.

I bend down and ruffle his ears, and he almost purrs in response.

'Let's get you a nice treat, eh?'

As far as Christmas parties go, apart from the Michael moment almost causing me a panic attack, tonight was a roaring success. I managed to bluff my way around, or else dodge, enthusiastic questions about how I'm going to spend my extended break this year before slipping off early with just enough buzz from a few drinks which I hope will help me sleep.

But now that I'm home, with two whole weeks of annual leave ahead of me, the reality of being alone for Christmas hits me once more.

What *am* I going to do for two whole weeks while the rest of the world parties like it's 1999? And it's ten days to go until the 'big day' itself. Why didn't I just smother myself in work like I usually do?

I used to love this time of year.

My humble childhood is peppered with memories of huge family gatherings in our crumbling old farmhouse, Dad stoking up the fire in the living room and Mum singing badly as she peeled sprouts and carrots.

My job was always Chief Decorator: I took charge of the tree and made sure every room in the house felt festive, taking great pride in laying the main dining table. I was meticulous with my handmade efforts ever since I was old enough to use glitter and glue. In fact, I remember winning a prize at school for a centrepiece which was a pretty, frosted wooden log with a red candle in the middle. I ran home that day and placed it on our table set for dinner which was bursting with love.

My sister Sarah and I would make hot chocolate on Christmas morning and bring it to our farming neighbours. In fact, we'd carried on this tradition into adulthood back when, no matter where we were in the world, we'd always find our way home in time for Christmas Day.

But not any more.

Since I lost Michael, I've spent the past few alone with the TV off, my phone on silent and only alcohol and old George to numb the pain. It's like I'm facing a brick wall too high to climb over, and I can't even bring myself to try and knock it down. Michael's mother, Evelyn, goes numb at this time of year too, I've been told. I did visit her after the accident, but she was too far gone to reach and my guilty conscience made it too hard to try to change her. She shut herself off from everyone after his death, unable to lift her head or open her door to anyone, even to me.

Especially to me. I fear she blames me as much as I blame myself.

So now, as soon as the very word 'Christmas' is mentioned, the fear and guilt that sticks inside me like wet dough becomes suffocating. No matter how much I want to, I just can't go home.

I can't do it. I don't deserve to.

I kick off my high heels and slump onto the sofa where George joins me, snuggling in as he always does.

'I think I did a good job tonight, George,' I tell my one true companion. 'And now it's just me and you, old pal. Me and you with the curtains shut and with books and boxsets to keep us entertained.'

I should probably go to bed but instead I switch on the TV only to be greeted by a chirpy, attractive woman on a beach. She's dressed in a bikini and a Santa hat and she holds a delicious cocktail as she gushes about winter sun holidays.

Could *I* jet off to the sun like Carlos suggested?

No. I would feel bad about leaving George behind, though the idea of packing up and heading off does have a strong appeal right now.

We *could* go somewhere closer, couldn't we? I might not be able to just jump on a plane with a rescue dog who tends to pee on strangers' legs, but I could go somewhere else in Ireland, just for a change of scenery.

And now I'm crying.

I miss Michael's touch, and how safe I felt in his arms, his wise words that were always so poetic and reassuring. I miss how he used to whisper to me as I fell asleep, even if it was just for a few snatched hours before he had to leave me again for his work that took him all over the world.

He would tell me what to do for Christmas if he could.

'Where could we go, George?' I ask the sleeping dog beside me. He has the grace to cock up one ear at the sound of his own name even if he is lost in the land of slumber. 'I bet you'd love a new beach to explore at this time of year, wouldn't you? Or a forest to run around in? Somewhere we could shut off but still feel like we're doing something for Christmas rather than lying around cooped up here? Somewhere like . . .'

A vision of a familiar cottage comes to my mind. It calls to me like an old friend, luring me closer, telling me I'd be happier there than here on my own in Dublin.

But no . . . I couldn't.

I close my eyes to blank it out, but the image gets stronger. I know this cottage. I know it very well. I picture the secluded surroundings, the thatched roof that oozes tradition, its red front door through which I'd step into a cocoon of safety and joy. I can already feel the heat of the blazing fire. I can smell the smoky turf burning, its familiarity and warmth that hangs in the air.

Within seconds a burst of curiosity has me looking it up on my phone as if fate has taken over and I've no longer any self-control.

And there it is, right before my eyes, in all its glory.

Seaview Cottage: a cosy, pet-friendly hideaway, right by a pocket-sized luscious green forest but not far from the Atlantic Sea . . . Situated near the most idyllic picture-perfect village you could ever find, with chocolate-box surroundings and warmth like no other. Close to Fanad Lighthouse, sandy beaches and so much more. Comfort, seclusion and peace guaranteed.

My heart clenches when I see it and my weary mind is flooded with warm memories of days gone by when I'd spend stretches of summer there, hearing tales from my Granny Molly of her childhood days.

But then I read the small print.

'Seaview Cottage is closed for Christmas,' it says on the Airbnb page. 'Sorry for any inconvenience. See you in springtime.'

Typical.

There are hundreds of similar properties scattered all over Ireland, so I search and search through various websites, but each 'dog friendly' one I try is booked up, which makes my whimsical decision to just 'get away from it all' at the last minute suddenly feel farcical. It's the most wonderful time of the year, after all. Or at least it is for everyone else.

I go back to the picture-perfect Seaview Cottage and stare at the screen again. It captivates me. It sneaks under my skin. It offers me a hug from afar.

'Seaview Cottage is closed for Christmas,' I read it aloud, so those last three words can sink in, but no, it's not happening.

'Rules are made to be broken, old George,' I tell my sleeping dog. 'And my motto has always been, "If you don't ask then you don't get."'

I might sorely regret this in the morning, but there's an urgent fire in my belly now. I want to go there more than anywhere else in the world. Seaview Cottage is far enough from my home village to stay out of the way of my family, yet near enough for a car journey to see them if I'm brave enough to make the trip with cap in hand at the last minute.

I could walk in the forest and on the beach with George. I could visit the nearby lighthouse and soothe my weary soul with its stunning views. I could have frothy hot chocolate in the cute little place that serves up the best pancakes with maple syrup and berries. I could bring bundles of books to read by the roaring fire. I could take some much-needed time out from the smog of the city to clear my mind, and who knows, maybe this will be the last Christmas I feel like

I should be alone? Maybe this is exactly what I need to do this year.

Before I can think too deeply about it all, I quickly scroll through my phone where I find an email address I haven't used in a very long time. George groans beside me. I'm not sure if that's a good sign or a bad one but I take it as a vote of encouragement. Then, without thinking any further on the subject, I begin to type.

It's me, I write, even though I know it's a bit late to be corresponding with anyone right now, especially out of the blue like this.

Look, I know this is crazy, and that you're closed at this time of year for rentals . . . I also know I'm putting you in a very awkward position in more ways than one by asking . . . but I need to get away and there's nowhere else available as I've left it totally last minute.

I pause, and then I just go for it.

Please can I stay in the cottage over Christmas? From tomorrow?

If you say yes, I'll be eternally grateful. I promise you won't even know I'm there. But if you say no, I will totally understand.

Anyhow, I hope you're all OK and have a great Christmas either way. Love always. Rose

I press send and feel a rush of heat through my veins. I hug George closer and shut my eyes tight, urging myself not to hold on to the sliver of hope he'll say yes.

He might just ignore me. I wouldn't blame him if he did. In fact, I'm pretty sure I wouldn't be wanted there, not in a million years.

I take George outside for a pee. I boil the kettle. I pop in some toast. I walk back into the sitting room and before I sit down, my phone bleeps. I catch my breath. I'm almost afraid to check. Could it be him? Has he replied to me already?

He has.

Wow. This is unexpected, he writes back. I was just about to fall asleep, but I'm glad now that I checked the phone first.

It is unexpected to *me* too, as is his friendly, speedy reply. My eyes fill up.

I read on . . .

I'll leave the key under the mat for you but don't tell anyone, OK?

And please drive safely, Rose. It gives snow by tomorrow evening. I'll try to see you if I can get to the cottage without anyone noticing. Oh, and don't tell a soul you're coming here. Please. Not a soul. I'm looking forward to seeing you again. It's been way too long.

Am I crazy? One minute I think I'm seeing Michael in a hotel lobby and next I'm asking to stay at Seaview Cottage for Christmas over three hours away when it's threatening to snow.

'George, come here to me. We're going to the most special place in the whole world,' I tell my dog as I stare wide-eyed into space and let it sink in. George whimpers back as if he understands. 'I'm not sure I deserve this, but he said yes.

He said we can go to Seaview Cottage for Christmas. Oh, George.'

With a fresh wind in my sails, I quickly type back a response before he has the chance to change his mind. My fingers move like lightning, tears rolling down my face.

I'll keep out of everyone's way. No one will know I'm there, I promise.

Thank you so much. It will be just me and my dog. Did you even know I have a dog? We have so much to catch up on, but only if you want to, of course. I'll see you tomorrow, I hope. Oh, I can't wait. You've no idea how much I need this. Well, maybe you do. Anyhow, thank you. Thank you!

I'm going to Seaview Cottage for Christmas. I won't believe it until I get there.

Nine Days to Christmas

Chapter Two

Charlie

'I'm going,' I say out loud to absolutely no one listening. 'No matter how many times she calls me to convince me otherwise, I'm going.'

So now I'm talking to myself. Wonderful.

Helena has already sent me a grand total of five messages this morning from the new phone I bought her as an early Christmas present.

Six, if I include the meme she sent of a cute cartoon puppy in a Santa suit with giant eyes crying up into the camera lens. I do my best not to encourage her by replying, but a claw of guilt tugs at me from the inside, reminding me I'm all she has.

I push back my overgrown hair, which according to Helena makes me look like a seventies rocker. I'm never quite sure what way to take that. As much as I do love her, the way she has an opinion on absolutely every move I make can be a hard pill to swallow.

What are your plans today? she messaged at 6 a.m. before I'd barely opened my eyes.

Did you sleep well? I didn't.

Are you still leaving today, Charlie?

It won't feel like Christmas without you.

That one stung, I admit, but there's no going back now. I am leaving. In fact, I'm leaving in the next few seconds if she'd only stop messaging me so I can go.

It took me a long time to make this decision. Now my bags are packed, the car is filled with fuel and Max is all set for the journey. Helena knows how to press my buttons, so I must be assertive and maintain my stance.

I still can't believe I'm doing this, but I am.

I glance around the house I once loved with all my heart and remind myself that this – a Christmas alone – is essentially my fault. Just like me, my home has lost its soul and is an empty shell of its former self. The living room which was once bursting with colour and festive cheer looks as bare as the trees that stand in the front garden through the window outside, huge weeping willows grey and stark, and for the past two years I've lost interest in making it look or feel any more homely.

It's now meticulously clean and white inside, with nothing out of place. No plastic toys scattered on the floor, no tiny trainers in the hallway, no muddy pink wellington boots by the back door. No mac and cheese to serve up on demand, or Cheerios for breakfast. My house serves its purpose as a place of work with a home office in the spare room, and a place to eat and sleep, but that's as far as it goes.

It doesn't feel like a home any more. There are photos of Rebecca everywhere: on the table in the entrance hallway; on the living room mantelpiece; on the dining room walls. They capture so many stages of her young life. Her first Christmas on Santa's knee looking more terrified than anything. Her first ride on a mini rollercoaster where *I* look more terrified than anything and she is ecstatic with her arms in the air. Her first day at school where her schoolbag looks like it might tip her over. My gaze falls on a picture of her horse-riding with Helena on a beach near the Giant's Causeway . . . so many memories, frozen in time and enough to break my heart every time I glance their way.

I stare into the empty corner where a Christmas tree used to stand so proudly at this time of year, full of decorations made with tiny hands and surrounded by a rainbow of red, green, gold and silver presents all waiting to be torn open on Christmas morning.

Even the television set haunts me. I close my eyes, picturing her in cosy pyjamas with festive slipper-clad feet dangling off the edge of the armchair as she watches re-runs of everything from *Home Alone* to *Elf* to *The Snowman* on repeat.

Right, that's it. I need to go.

My phone bleeps. Helena again no doubt but I don't have time to check. I don't have time, yet I do check. I always do.

Charlie, I got a new green velvet dress for Christmas Day but I'm not so sure about it. If I send you a photo, will you tell me the honest truth? Have you left yet?

I count to three before messaging her back.

Yes, send me the pic and I'll give you my honest thoughts when I get to Donegal. I'm leaving now.

I *am* leaving right now.

I really don't want you to go, she replies.

I put my hands to my head and sit down for just one moment to think it all through again.

She is the one person in the world who needs me now. Now that my daughter is off playing happy families with her mum and new stepdad in another country, this is it. Just me, Helena and Max against the world.

But it's not enough. How can it ever be enough?

I lean my face into my hands and close my eyes, but every time I do I see Rebecca's tear-stained face at the airport when we were forced to say goodbye six weeks ago.

She didn't want to leave me. I didn't want her to go. Am I doing the same thing now to Helena? Am I causing the same pain to her that's been inflicted on me by leaving her at Christmas?

Oh Rebecca. How can I get through the holidays without you?

This isn't right. I could punch something. This isn't Christmas. This is purgatory. What do I do?

Maybe I need to stay and face up to the fact that this is the way it's going to be from now on. Me, Helena and Max in this white-walled, love-starved corner of Belfast where I feel like I'm pleasing everyone but myself as bloody usual. A life where I live in this torment, knowing I can't be a real father to a child that's thousands of miles away, on the other end of a phone, yet smile and put on a brave face for everyone else to see?

No. I can't stay here. I can't spend Christmas here without my daughter.

Max is in the car waiting. I blow out a long breath, grab the car keys and shut the door behind me before I let Helena change my mind. I need a break. She knows I need a break. I need to do this for my own sanity. I'm already hanging by a thread.

'County Donegal, young Max,' I say to my seasoned friend who at six years old – actually, forty-two in dog years to give him his dues – is probably the only thing keeping me functioning these days. Well, Max, Helena and the twelve clients who tell me their problems every week and remind me that even though my own world has been tipped on its axis, I still have a whole lot to live for.

I may not have Rebecca to take to see Santa, or to open presents with, or to sing cheesy carols with, or to watch on with pride from a packed audience full of smiling parents at the school nativity, but I can and I will get through this.

It's not Christmas without her, so I need to do what I need to do to get over this first Christmas without my baby girl. I need to forget it's even happening.

Max jumps up onto his hind legs and looks out the window.

'And don't even think about doing your usual trick and disappearing on me when we get there, OK?' I tell my bouncy springer spaniel. 'It's one thing roaming around the fields at home, but this is brand-new territory for us both. I promised you'd be on your best behaviour, you hear?'

Max's brown and white tail is wagging like a pendulum on speed. I reach across to pat his downy coat as we make our way out of the city and onto the motorway that will take us west in the direction of Donegal to the 'secluded retreat' where I plan to do nothing but wallow in the silence of my own misery, walk a beach or two and hopefully let the sounds of silence be my only friend. It will be like Christmas doesn't even exist when I get there, and that's exactly what I'm hoping for.

Chris Rea sings on the radio about driving home for Christmas, and since I'm driving *away* from home for Christmas, I flick stations immediately.

Frosty the Snowman? No thank you. I flick again. Michael Bublé?

'No, no, no, I'm not in the mood for you, Mr Bublé, no offence.'

I hit Classic FM, confident I won't be force-fed festive offers from an orchestra or quartet, but a few seconds later I realise they're performing *The Nutcracker*, so I hit Bluetooth and kick off my own playlist, which is what I should have done in the first place to spare me from Christmas cheer.

It's lashing rain outside. I've the wipers on full blast and as I cruise along, Max snoozes while I do my best not to overthink the fact that this is the first Christmas in all my thirty-seven years that I'll spend totally alone.

Charlie Sheerin, therapist and life-fixer for all, is running away from his *own* life for two weeks in the hope that it might give him some direction on what to do next.

Over halfway into my journey, I stop at a huge supermarket where I'm nabbed by carol singers rattling their charity buckets at the doors.

'Cheer up, it's Christmas, darling,' an older lady says. I could say so much in return but I know she means well. My furrowed brow and determined stare, no doubt, say it all.

I throw in some loose change, then grab some groceries and wine for my solo stay, doing my best to push past trollies as shoppers panic-buy and stock up on ridiculous amounts of food as if the end of the world is coming.

'Bah humbug,' I say to the cashier who flashes me a hearty smile as she scans each item, then laughs so hard that her whole upper body jiggles.

I didn't think it was *that* funny.

'Oh, I feel exactly the same,' she replies mid-giggle, as if I've broken some secret seal. 'I'm so glad you said that. Bah bloody humbug. Bah humbug!'

And then she whispers.

'What a load of over-hyped nonsense! Loathe entirely! My children call me the Grinch!'

She is still laughing when I lift my bags, which makes me smile too, and when I get back to the car to load up the boot, I pause to remember how previous trips to the north-west coast of Ireland were once so different.

They weren't last-minute Christmas escapes like I'm doing now. They were summer holidays filled with a million childlike questions like *Are we there yet? Can we please get ice cream on the way?*

The music was never my choice in those days, but I secretly loved it. A bucket and spade were used as a drum kit to chant along to in the back seat, with Rebecca telling me to sing louder and louder.

Do the funny voice again, Daddy! Sing just one more time.

I feel my skin tingle at the thought of how much I miss her. Every single minute of every single day, I miss her so badly.

'How about a cheery rendition of "The Wheels on the Bus", Max?' I ask my dog who doesn't seem too bothered with what season it is, or that Rebecca is no longer here to make it magical again. 'Let's pretend we're going on our summer holidays and the sun is shining instead of this miserable sleety rain.'

And so to pass the time I sing it, loudly beating my hand on the steering wheel as I drive.

The wheels on the bus go round and round.

My stomach is going round and round too, but the journey goes smoothly. My mind eventually stops galloping through a journey of regret as we pass through tiny villages and towns decked out with fairy lights in windows. Umbrella-wielding shoppers criss-crossing the street laden with too many bags, dodging cars eager to get through.

We drive on long stretching roads with overtaking lanes and green fields that go on for as far as the eye can see. The sat nav takes us along some scary hairpin bends and narrow roads where approaching the crest of the hills and valleys is like taking some crazy gamble of roulette, and even though it's miserable outside, everyone drives slowly and with consideration. They even wave as they pass.

This is what I love about Donegal. The friendly wave of a stranger, the sheep dotting the rust-coloured mountains that line the roadsides. The vast skies that meet forty shades of green. The sense of freedom and wide-open spaces with the sea in the distance.

This is a place called Fanad Head – the very place I've longed for. I feel my shoulders relax already.

'Uh oh, someone's in trouble,' I say to Max when I come across a car with the bonnet raised on the narrow roadside moments later. I'm glad for once it's not me, especially not in this cutting cold weather. It gives snow later too. Sleet, then snow, then more snow for the next few days.

I wonder at what age do you start becoming obsessed with weather forecasts? Am I having some sort of mid-life crisis by trying to pretend it's not Christmas and watching weather forecasts like my dad used to do?

I slow way, way down to see a lady holding a huge yellow umbrella in one hand as she peers into the engine, one high-heeled boot behind her pointing in the air, the other performing a very impressive balancing act.

I should stop. It's too dangerous on these narrow roads to pull over, but there's no way I can pretend I didn't see it and drive on.

And that's when I hear a familiar voice from the past in my head.

Keep driving, Charlie, for goodness' sake. You don't always have to be the Good Samaritan for everyone. Mr Good Looking,

Mr Always Charming, Mr Can't Mind His Own Business. No wonder we're always running late. It's not your business.

And so I do what I always used to do.

I ignore it.

I indicate left and slowly pull in behind the parked car. I grab a raincoat from the backseat and drape it over my head. I lock the doors, just to make sure Max can't escape on to the winding road, then jog in the pouring rain to the other car.

You can't fix everything and everyone, Charlie. Focus on what matters most for once in your life instead of trying to change the world.

'Can I help?' I call out through the pelting rain as I hold the coat above my head for shelter, but the person doesn't hear me at first. 'Hello?'

She turns towards me, slightly flustered but with a look of sheer determination on her face, which is smeared with oil on both cheeks – a stark contrast to her red lipstick, puffed out green dress and blue mackintosh. Her look, all big hair and vintage statements, would be better suited at a fancy party, not stuck on a roadside in rainy Donegal.

'Not a good day for car trouble,' I say, feeling stupid as soon as the words come out.

'There's never a good day for car trouble,' she says, screwing the oil cap tight with one hand and balancing the huge golf umbrella in the other. 'I think the alternator is on the way out, but it's just as well I stopped as it needed an oil top-up too. Not exactly what I bargained for on my way to—'

'Sorry?' I call out through the rain, unable to catch the end of her sentence.

'Nothing,' she replies, louder this time, and as if she's already said too much. I can see the tip of the famous lighthouse in the distance. I've only been here a handful of times, but that sight never fails to light me up inside.

The woman looks me in the eye for the first time. She blinks back stray raindrops that fall from her eyelashes onto what can only be described as a beautiful face. Aside from her cheeks being streaked with oil, she looks pristine for someone who has been caught off-guard in such a downpour. She's like a burst of rainbow colour on a grey day, but at the same time she has a confident glare that could easily cut you in two.

'A blessing in disguise, then,' I say, feeling a bit foolish now.

'Sorry?'

'The car trouble.' I shuffle, my boots squelching in the puddles. 'Hardly ideal and quite dangerous in this weather.'

She looks at me like I've just sprouted horns.

'Anyhow, you've got it all under control,' I say quickly, wishing for once I'd listened to the voice in my head to keep going and mind my own business.

'I sure do,' she tells me as she whacks down the bonnet and puts a hand on her hip to make her point, no doubt staining her expensive-looking coat as she does so. 'You thought I needed help to fix a car because I'm a woman, didn't you? Was it the lipstick or the heeled boots?'

She laughs but it's more in mockery than in humour. I stutter a response. My too-long hair is now sticking to my face and my cheeks burn in a way they haven't done since I was a schoolboy.

'Gosh, no,' I eventually manage, pulling the hood of my navy raincoat over my head. I may not have oil on my face or clothes but I'm sure I'm a sodding mess by now in my old jeans and grey T-shirt. I see her glance at the tattoo sleeve on my left arm, tilting her head to the side as she does so. 'I didn't think that for a second. I only stopped to see if—'

'Well, thank you, but I've got it all sorted,' she tells me, wiping her hands on a tissue while balancing the yellow umbrella on her right shoulder. 'OK, I'd better get going. I've got somewhere to be.'

'Have a nice time wherever you're off to.'

I told you so, I hear the voice from Christmas past say. *How embarrassing. When will you learn? You can't save everyone, Charlie. Save it for the day job, for goodness' sake.*

I pull out from the roadside, glancing back at the woman as she gets herself together in her own car. Then I venture on towards the lighthouse and the nearby village where I hope to find a fortnight of solitude and silence.

I need this even more than I realised.

When my friend Niall told me this hideaway cottage in Donegal was secluded, he certainly wasn't joking.

I'm doing my best to follow the sat nav, which no doubt has taken me on an 'extra scenic' route, but I certainly didn't expect it to be quite so remote.

It's Donegal, I remind myself. When they say it's remote, it's remote. I've passed acres of fields in every shade of green,

I've driven along rocky mountain roads that would take even the most cynical breath away, and I've checked and double-checked that I'm on the right path.

After winding roads which seem to last forever, views of the sea that I can only imagine would be heaven on a clear day and a stray sheep that causes an emergency stop, I find myself passing through a very cute little village with just a few pastel-coloured buildings, a thatched-roof pub with a restaurant, a café, a craft shop plus a very ornamental church which has an outdoor manger, all of which is looked upon by a perfectly plump pine Christmas tree.

'Civilisation at last, Max,' I say to my sidekick who has been remarkably calm throughout most of our journey, except for his tendency to bark for an unknown reason every time we hit a junction. 'Ah, this is exactly what I dreamed of.'

We take a right turn out of the village and onto a narrow country lane which becomes thinner and bumpier by the second. We cross over a cattle grid and past some hawthorn bushes until into our view comes what will be our home for the next two weeks. I put my window down for just a second to see if I can hear the sea which looks like a dark blue blanket in the distance.

I can. My heart lifts at the prospect of it all.

The cottage has whitewashed walls with corners that curve at the edges, jade-green sash windows, a thick thatched roof that looks like a bad haircut just like the pub down the road, and a bright red door that gleams from its centre.

There's a small dark grey van parked outside which I assume belongs to Marion, the owner who agreed to meet me here this morning to talk me through a few 'quirks' of the cottage, which I'm told has stood here for three generations. I'm a little bit late, probably due to my attempt at helping a stranger, but not late enough to be too apologetic. I've learned enough in life to realise that these things happen. A few minutes either side of an agreed time isn't worth sweating about.

I park up, thankful that the rain from earlier has subsided even though huge, cauliflower-shaped clouds hang low, threatening to burst their banks with snow, and then I leave Max in the car to go to greet my host.

'You must be Charlie! Welcome to Seaview Cottage,' she calls to me when she opens the red front door. 'Come in, come in. Let me show you around. Thank goodness I lit the fire earlier. You're soaked through, my love.'

I walk up the narrow gravel pathway that runs between two wild gardens on either side to meet my host. Judging by the smell of freshly baked bread and a crackling turf fire which fills my senses, she has been hard at work for my arrival. She is ruddy-faced with neat, bobbed silver hair. She wears a thick woolly jumper and a hearty smile that oozes warmth, which makes me feel at home instantly.

'It's Marion, isn't it?' I say and she nods. I extend my hand but she awkwardly offers an elbow touch instead. 'You've no idea how much I'm looking forward to some time out here, just me, Max and the sweet sounds of nature. Thanks for squeezing me in.'

Marion looks very pleased with herself to own a place that ticks all the boxes I have in mind.

'Well, Niall did give you a glowing review,' she tells me. 'I hope you're doing OK? It's not easy, I suppose. You've been through the wars, but you're lucky to have a lifelong friend in Niall. He's a very pleasant lad.'

My jaw drops just a little as I wonder what else Niall has told her to convince her to let me stay. Just like the woman with the broken-down car earlier, I notice her checking out my tattooed arms, my dishevelled mop of hair and rather casual attire. A T-shirt in this weather is far from ideal.

'Yes, Niall and I have been buddies since our first day in playgroup, and that wasn't today or yesterday.'

'You're not what I expected, I have to say,' she quips, and I raise an eyebrow.

'I hope that's a good thing?'

'Yes,' she says with a twinkle in her eye. 'Yes, it is. Niall said you were quiet and unassuming. I just had a different image in my head which reminds me how we shouldn't jump to conclusions, but it's a good thing, yes.'

'Er, thank you . . . I think.'

She tucks a lock of silver hair behind her ear and holds my gaze just a second too long.

If I was on my usual form, I'd enjoy the possibility that she's flirting with me. Maybe I don't look too scruffy after all.

Marion springs back to life and leads me into the kitchen where I see a deep white Belfast sink, painted blue kitchen cupboards and, just as I'd thought, a tray of warm, freshly baked scones on a checked tea towel upon the table.

It's like something from a movie.

'This is . . . wow. This is cosy.'

'It is,' she says, squeezing her hands together as she admires her handiwork. 'And it's not everyone I'd allow here off season, but when Niall told me all about you, I just couldn't say no.'

'Oh?'

'But never mind all that. Now, let me run you through what you need to know for your stay. It's an old cottage but all its faculties are working apart from a few quirks I mentioned to you on the phone,' she continues. 'For example, the back door needs a mighty tug to get it shut but I'll show you how. There are some hiking boots and a rucksack in the back porch if you fancy a ramble. There's a hot tub out the back. Oh, and the heating . . . well, you need to press the heating button at least three times to get it going. If that doesn't work just give it a thump.'

I raise my eyebrows.

'Not too much of a thump, but you know what I mean, I hope,' she says, glancing at my arms again. Her eyes linger again, longer than they probably should. 'OK, yes, where was I? Oh yes, the garden. There's a little gate at the bottom of the garden that leads into a wonderful forest walk which is a delight at this time of year. Now, the garden is secure, but there are a few gaps in the hedge that could be negotiated with a bit of exploration, so mind the dog if he likes to roam.'

'That he does.'

'And the shower might run cold if you don't – oh. Hang on a second,' she says when we hear a car arrive outside. 'Are you expecting company?'

Her neck cranes towards the front door.

'No chance,' I reply, too busy eyeing up the forest that runs along the back of the cottage to care much. With the sea at the front in the distance and a forest at the back door, this is a little slice of heaven. 'Company is the last thing I want, to be honest.'

The sound of a car door closing sends Marion scurrying down the wooden floor of the hallway, wiping her hands on a tea towel and muttering as she goes.

'Well, I certainly wasn't expecting anyone. This is a dead end but maybe it's someone who's taken a wrong turn. That happens sometimes.'

I follow her, realising I probably should in case this uninvited guest is some sort of threat, but before she gets to it, the red door opens from the outside and we're met by a red-haired man with a very impressive matching bushy beard.

He is slightly stooped over, as if he is carrying the weight of the world on his shoulders, and his attire makes me feel like I'm impeccably turned out in comparison.

'Marion?'

'Rusty?'

'What's going on?' he asks, walking inside as if he owns the place. I quickly cop on that, actually, he does own the place.

He wears a heavy khaki coat, a blue checked shirt and baggy jeans that have seen better days, but his face, which I'd guess is close to sixty years old, is in a puzzle. He stops dead when he sees me, and then looks at me with a blend of confusion and despair.

'What on earth are *you* doing here?' Marion asks him through gritted teeth and a polite fake smile. 'It's off season, Rusty!'

'It's my cottage – I didn't think I needed an appointment?'

'It's *our* cottage since we've been married for the past thirty odd years,' she corrects him. I wonder if perhaps they've both forgotten I'm here. 'You never come here unless you're forced to these days. What's going on?'

I should maybe excuse myself or else pretend I need the loo or something. This is very awkward. Rusty keeps rubbing his red beard, which up close I notice is flecked with little speckles of silver. With the frosty atmosphere between him and his wife, I'm surprised he has any red hair left at all.

'I came to check on – erm, I just came to – actually I could ask you the same question, Marion,' the man continues. 'What are *you* doing here?'

I'm hugely impressed by his evasion skills.

'I'm checking in my guest,' Marion says, tucking her short hair behind her ears again.

'But we don't let the cottage out at Christmas.'

'Yes, yes, I know that, but I've made an exception just this once. This is Charlie. He's a friend of Niall, one of our regulars, not that you'd know any of them, and so I've made an exception, just this once. He will be here for Christmas.'

The man's face twitches, and then all our eyes turn to the window as a third car pulls up outside. I remember I still haven't let Max out of my own vehicle, so I try to make my way past and rescue him while the two owners sort out whatever is bugging them, but the man is blocking the doorway like a panting guard dog.

'There may be a *slight* problem with that,' Rusty says, wringing his hands. 'You see, I happen to have made the same exception, just this once. I too have booked in *my* guest, and she has just arrived.'

'*Your* guest? Rusty!'

'Well, I didn't know you were taking a booking over Christmas, did I?' Rusty answers her quickly under his breath. 'Maybe if we communicated a little bit more instead of—'

'No, that's not good enough,' says Marion, her own voice rising as his drops. She folds her arms. 'How dare you go behind my back? This is just typical of you, Rusty Quinn. Typical!'

I hear a car door slam outside as they continue to argue in front of me. Very quickly my therapy tactics kick in and I can't help but give my tuppence worth.

'Sorry to interrupt. I know we've only just met but it sounds like *both* of you have gone behind each other's back?' I blurt out. 'This might be a lack of communication, but it seems to me it's on both sides.'

Rusty and Marion glare at me then glance in each other's direction in acknowledgement that this may indeed be true, but I can tell neither one is about to budge. Just at that moment the other guest arrives on the doorstep.

'Oh, hello again,' she says to me, looking utterly confused, which now makes four of us. 'What's going on? I thought I was meant to keep this a . . .'

'Rose?' says Marion with a look of, to put it mildly, horror. 'What on earth?'

'Er, hello Marion. I wasn't expecting a welcome committee,' says the flummoxed newcomer.

Rusty puts his hands to his head while Marion pushes her tongue into her teeth, looking at the ceiling in disgust. 'This is very, very embarrassing,' she scolds as her face almost folds in frustration. '*Very* embarrassing indeed.'

It's the lady from earlier. The one with the yellow umbrella, the dodgy car and the oil streaks smeared on her cheeks. The coat that was once perfectly blue is now a very dirty shade of grey around one pocket, but her lipstick is still perfect, and she still looks like she's stepped out of a different era.

'I think you've some explaining to do,' Marion says, shooting her husband a stern glare, her eyes darting around us like they are squatting flies. 'What on earth is *she* doing here?'

Rusty displays the diplomacy that his wife lacks.

'OK, let's not freak out,' he says gently, rubbing his weather-beaten hands together. He smells of diesel. He paces the floor beside me. 'Right . . . OK . . . right, why don't we all go inside and see exactly what we can do about it?'

'I think that's a really good idea,' I agree.

'I'll put the kettle on,' says Marion, marching ahead into the kitchen. 'But Rusty, *you* are making the tea.'

'I could murder a coffee,' says the glamorous lady from earlier who is already taking off her coat.

'I wouldn't push it if I were you, Rose,' whispers Rusty, which makes the new arrival roll her eyes. 'Let's all keep this nice and calm. Nice and calm.'

He looks at me and blows out a long, deep breath that seems to come from his toes as he makes his way to the kitchen behind his wife, who I can already tell takes no prisoners.

I think I like this Rusty character, but despite how nice he might be, there's no way I'm giving up this cottage because of a double booking.

I've been living for this. I need it or I'll crack up once and for all.

I'm not giving it up for anyone.

Minutes later the four of us are sitting by the dancing fire in the fussy floral living room of Seaview Cottage, and the tension makes it feel like the walls are closing in around us, so much so that the palpitations I haven't had in a few weeks are starting to jump around my chest again – the perfect reminder of why I booked this solo getaway in the first place.

I'm too exhausted to argue much, so I've stayed relatively quiet so far. Not that I could get a word in even if I tried as Marion and Rose battle it out from cream sofa to blue sofa. It's a tactic I've learned in my years as a therapist: listen first, comment later.

'*And* I've travelled *all* the way from Dublin with a very lively and impatient dog,' pleads Rose as she addresses the room, giving a very convincing case for why the cottage should be hers for Christmas and not mine. 'I've had a hellish journey. I've been tested to my limits. Where did *you* come from?'

Oh, she's asking me.

'Belfast,' I tell her.

'So, practically down the road, then,' she replies, as if she's just scored extra points.

'It's not a distance competition,' I say, unsure if I mean for her to hear it.

'Maybe not, but being here is the only way I can survive Christmas so I'm willing to use distance to raise my stakes,' she says. 'My coat is probably ruined. My car broke down a few miles out of town and I've been stuck on a roadside for at least half an hour in the pouring rain. Now, after all that, you're telling me I'll have to go back home again?'

'I'm not telling you anything,' I say, feeling my own engines warming up now I've heard her plea. 'All I know is I'm staying, so—'

I'm tempted to say, *and I was here first*, but I know it sounds childish so I don't.

'I'm sorry, Rose, but you simply can't stay here,' says Marion before her husband can reply. Her lack of empathy is a surprise even to me, given Rose's sincere and rather convincing story. 'Rusty has gone right over my head, so it looks like going home is your only option unless you want to try and find somewhere else nearby. I can give you a few numbers?'

'Numbers are no good to me at this late stage,' Rose replies, sounding deflated though clearly not defeated. 'I'd already tried everywhere before I tried here, but there isn't as much as a hotel room free this side of Christmas, never mind another cottage that welcomes dogs.'

Marion has the grace to let out a sigh.

'Look, this is a very humiliating case of a double booking which is simply not up to our usual standards,' she says, 'which is why I deal with things around here and not my husband. I'm sorry, I really am, but I'm afraid there is no other option, unless Rusty has an answer?'

Rusty raises his eyebrows, then looks to the ceiling. In fact, he looks like he can't wait to get out of here.

'Didn't think so. I'm sorry, Rose,' says Marion. 'I really am. I can assure you that this won't be taken lightly.'

'Well – I suppose that's it then,' says Rose, biting her bottom lip and shrugging her shoulders. 'I can take defeat. I'm not that proud nor am I so desperate as to beg, so I'll get back on the road before the weather gets any worse. Thanks for trying to fit me in, Rusty. Some other time, eh?'

'Oh, Rose.'

Rusty looks like he might cry now. He stands up.

'It's OK,' she tells him. 'I really hope I haven't caused a storm between you two over this. It was only a last-minute decision for me to come here, so I guess I'll make my way back to where I came from. Thanks anyway. Have a great Christmas, everyone.'

She stands up, wedges her stained coat under her arm, fixes her puffy dress and, with her head held high, she makes her way towards the living room door.

'Unless . . .'

Oh, here he goes again. Charlie, the hero and saviour of the day. Just leave it.

'What?' asks Marion, her hands on her hips.

'Unless?' asks Rusty.

'Unless we share the cottage? As in, we both stay?' I suggest, realising I haven't thought this through for more than a split second. 'Is that an option? I mean, it would take some choreography to stay out of each other's—'

'Share?' Marion echoes with an outburst of very polite laughter. '*Share?* Charlie, darling, I haven't even shown you round yet properly!'

'True, but—'

'No, no, no. There's only one bedroom so there's no way you can share.' Her face is stern now. 'And, most importantly, you don't even know each other. I don't think this is what either of you would want, is it? You came here for comfort and solace, not to shack up with a stranger.'

Rose holds my gaze for no more than a second but it's long enough for me to catch a flicker of something which is far from the confident, independent woman I encountered earlier on the roadside, or the brave front she is putting up now as she is being sent back to Dublin.

'Thank you, but Marion is right,' she says, her voice strong and confident, a stark comparison to what her sparkly green eyes give away. 'You have a lovely stay, Charlie. It's a special place here and you're very kind to offer to share. But you're lucky to have found it first. Enjoy.'

I glance at Rusty who stares at his unlaced boots.

'Bye Rose,' he says as he slowly ties them, but she's already gone.

Moments later I hear Rose's car engine starting up on the third attempt outside. She leaves graciously, without a hint of malice or sarcasm. I can't say for sure that I'd have done the same.

'We need to talk,' Marion and Rusty both say at the same time.

Rusty looks like he is about to blow a gasket now, while Marion is pacing by the window with her arms folded.

'I'll just go and get my bags.'

I slip outside, feeling just a little bit guilty, and I'm followed closely by Rusty who jumps into a pick-up truck and makes a speedy exit, all spinning tyres and exhaust fumes in his wake. I look in through the window of the cottage where I see Marion dab her eyes in the mirror that hangs over the mantelpiece.

'Come on, boy, let's get you in and warmed up by the fire,' I say to Max who has been more than patient as we ironed out our uncomfortable start here at Seaview Cottage. 'None of this is our fault and we're here now. We may as well enjoy it.'

Max bounds out from the front seat where I'd left him, and races towards the open cottage door, giving me a moment to stop and take this all in properly for the first time.

As I watch the snowfall sprinkle down onto the thatched roof, I sense this really might be a very special place, just as Rose said it was.

I close my eyes and hear the rush of the wild sea which, according to the online cottage description, is just a stone's throw away. In reality, I expect it is more of a short stroll. As much as I try to absorb my new peaceful surroundings, I can't stop myself imagining Rose driving all the way back to Dublin, away from this magical place.

I know first-hand the kind of sadness that brings someone to book a Christmas break alone. I wonder what her story is. The more I think on it, the stronger my urge to chase after her. I imagine flagging her down, convincing her to stay no matter how much it's against both of our intentions.

But then my phone vibrates and the illusion shatters. It is Helena, of course.

Are you there yet? What's it like? How's Max getting on? I'm waiting for pictures!

Send me some soon, please.

Did you really like my outfit? I might change it if you don't.

Sod it.

I'm very sorry you lost out, Rose, but I really do need to be alone this holiday. Some you win, some you lose.

Now, it's time I got to try one of those warm home-made scones.

Chapter Three

Rose

I manage to make it to the cattle grid at the end of the bumpy lane, leaving my hopes and dreams of Christmas at the cottage behind, before I burst into the inevitable tornado of tears that has been welling up inside me.

I knew this was too good to be true. Seaview Cottage may be out in the middle of nowhere but it's lodged deep in my heart. It's a place that holds so many memories for me.

Don't be bitter, John, I remember my mother saying to my dad all those years ago. I agreed with Mum, but after what I just witnessed, now I'm more pushed to take my dad's side.

Still in the family, my arse. You'll see. Time will tell. There'll come a day when we don't get as much as an inch near that cottage. Those days are gone now.

My father is a man of few words, but the older I get, the more I realise he chooses his words of wisdom and shoots from the heart.

I'm just a hop, skip and a jump from my childhood home where my parents and sister are planning a perfect Christmas without me, and for a moment I contemplate swallowing my pride and making my way to join them. Do I really have to spend Christmas alone for the third year running?

Yes, I do.

I don't deserve to have it easy at this time of year. I'm not ready to get into the festive spirit like I used to, nor should I even contemplate it.

If Michael is to lose out on all the celebrations, then so will I. Now that he's gone, Christmas will never be the same again. It's not a punishment, it's a fact. If it weren't for me, he'd still be here, and that's something I have to learn to live with, though it might take forever.

I no longer 'do' Christmas.

Yet as I drive into the village my Granny Molly once brought us to, I imagine my family discussing plans for dinner, school nativities, 'secret Santa' presents back at our homely farmhouse, and my heart sinks into my stomach.

I'm thinking of a gold and silver table setting this year. I've made some new Christmas candle logs. The older ones were getting very tatty.

My mother says the same thing almost every year as she plays her all-time favourite, 'O Holy Night', on repeat. No matter where I go, no matter who I'm with, if I hear that song I'm transported to my mother's kitchen.

Jude's mum is sending over one of her prize pavlovas. She's even doing a banoffee for Dad. Isn't she just the best!

My sister has a picture-perfect two-point-four family complete with in-laws who are cloyingly sweet. Even though she doesn't compare her life to mine out loud, I know she looks at me and sees a terrible mess. She must do because it's true.

It's a glorified Sunday dinner, for goodness' sake. Write me a list of what you need at the shops, and I'll get it. And don't be buying too many sprouts. Sure no one even likes sprouts and they end up in the bin.

My dad, at almost seventy-five years old, is as predictable as a rainy day in Ireland. He's so cute and full of wit at the same time, he's a sharpshooter with his tongue, and he secretly loves food shopping.

If he doesn't have to *cook* the food, he'll go to the moon and back to find it.

Our Rose's eyes light up when she hears the children singing carols. She always loved to sing herself, even though she has a voice that sounds like a cat screeching.

My mother again . . . it's always been an endless source of jokes in my family how I love to sing but can't, yet it doesn't stop me singing or humming even though it should.

My eyes sting.

I drive through the main street of this festive little village, where children skip past, marvelling as it snows on their way home on what I'm guessing is the last day of school before the holidays. One little boy puts his tongue out to catch the snow-flakes, which has a domino effect and soon they're all at it.

'Oh George.'

I reach out for comfort, but even George is sulking in the passenger seat beside me, looking up at me with the saddest eyes.

'I'm sorry,' I say out loud. 'How many times do I have to say I'm sorry? I'm sorry, OK?'

I apologise, not knowing who I'm apologising to this time. To my dog? To Michael? To my family? Or to myself for how my own life is working out?

Michael and I often joked how we were living the dream, but the dream is over now. No more New Year Resolutions on the banks of Fanad Lighthouse where we'd feel like we were on top of the world. No more planning to travel the globe together. No wedding, no family, no nothing.

Yet to the outside world, I've been doing just fine.

I've created a whole new life in Dublin. I've been doing my best to start all over again. I've been trying so, so hard not to 'move on' or 'get over' his death as I don't believe there's such a thing, but to keep on living and be happy again like he'd want me to.

Yes, I can deliver award-winning speeches.

Yes, I can clinch shit-hot marketing contracts from under your nose. But at the end of the day it's just me dressed up as something I'm not, pretending to be braver than I really am, all lipstick, powder and paint and a broken soul wrapped up in cheery smiles and vintage clothing.

Behind the mask, it's just me and my dog, alone in a world I can't find my place in. And although that may be all right for some people, it isn't for me. I'm aching inside for . . . I'm aching for connection, for friendship, for company, and most of all I'm aching for the love I had with Michael, to let me feel that again in my life, just once more.

My phone rings so I pull in at the side of the street just across from the café with its steamed-up windows and twinkling fairy lights. I'm hoping it might be Rusty on the phone, or Marion who may have come up with some sort of last-minute idea for where I can spend Christmas.

But no, it's Carlos.

I shake off my misery, sit up straight, flick back my hair and step into character.

'Hey love,' I sing, and when I catch a glimpse of myself in the rear-view mirror, I see that I'm even *smiling*. My eyes are bloodshot from tears, my insides are crawling with fear and yet I'm smiling. When did I become such a good actor?

'Rose, Rose, my beautiful Rose.'

He sings down the phone to me.

'Everything is fine here at work, so don't panic. I just need to hear all about it,' he says with a burst of energy that never simmers. 'I'm in the office here up to my eyeballs in the Rainey account and it's boring me to death. Is it just as you remembered it? Has it changed at all? Tell me everything!'

'About what? The Rainey account?'

'No, your Granny Molly's ancestral cottage,' he exclaims. 'Donegal! Fanad? The little slice of heaven you've escaped to?'

Ah, of course.

'The cottage, well it's not my Granny Molly's cottage any more, you see,' I say, trying to buy myself some time to explain. 'It's . . . it's an Airbnb now called Seaview Cottage, and . . . yes, well it's – it's . . .'

'Rose?'

'Yes?'

'Are you all right? You sound like you're still in the car. You didn't get lost, did you? I thought you knew that place so well?'

I quickly turn the engine off, determined to hide the truth for fear that he'll try once again to convince me to ditch my last-minute plan that didn't work out and join his family for Christmas. No offence to Carlos and his lovely dad, but I can't think of anything worse than trying to be all things merry and bright.

'Oh, no, I *am* here – I'm in the car, yes, you're right. I was just out grabbing some groceries,' I mutter, closing my eyes and cursing myself inside for telling lies. 'You know, mince pies, shortbread, chips and dips, the works. It's a lovely walk into the village, but it's also just beginning to snow here. As beautiful as it is to look at, I don't fancy slipping and breaking my ankle on my first day.'

I force a laugh and hear my colleagues chatter in the background at the other end – our designer Mia's distinctive infectious giggle and our copywriter Rory's husky voice as he entertains her singing Christmas carols. They're seeing each other on the sly, I just know it, even if they've denied it for years.

At least I'm not the only one living a big fat lie.

'Ah, Rose, you're making me green with envy which is exactly what I'd hoped for,' says Carlos. '*Verde de envidia*. It's lashing rain here in Dublin. Grey, murky, horrible, sleety and wet. It would depress a dolphin just by looking out at it. Go on. Tell me more. I've hit a creative slump on this account, so I need some inspiration. Tell me exactly what you see right now.'

I close my eyes and giggle at Carlos. Depress a dolphin? That's a new one, even coming from him.

I try to look out through my car windscreen and realise that even if I did want to tell the truth I couldn't, as a sprinkle of snow is now covering the glass like a thin veil of white cotton. So I use my own, always vivid, imagination.

'Well, the smoke is billowing from the cute little chimney of the whitewashed cottage,' I tell him, as he almost melts on the other end of the phone. 'There's a big roaring fire in the hearth and I can see the orange flames dancing from where I sit outside.'

'Ah, you're killing me.'

'The garden has the daintiest little pink stone pathway up to the red front door, covered in snow for now, of course, and there's even a thatched roof. There is no sound, except for the hoot of an owl and the gentle rush of the distant seascape which you can see from the front door.'

I feel a tear trickle down my face.

'Wow!'

'Everything is going exactly according to plan,' I lie. 'Now, get back to work, sunshine. I came here for peace and quiet, not to hear about the Rainey account, no offence.'

'Says the lady who brought her laptop?'

'I did. What can I say? I might need to check in for my own sanity before you all shut off for the holidays.'

'Oh, before I go, Maeve and Yvonne have been quizzing me as to where you've gone. And I ran into your other friend,

Sophie, at the bank of all places and she was saying she'd pop round to see you. They're not being nosey, just concerned. What should I tell them?'

'Tell them I've run away with Bradley Cooper.'

'Again? Didn't you say that last year when you pulled the curtains and pretended you didn't get their texts over Christmas?'

'Possibly. Ah, I don't know what to tell them, Carlos. They know me by now. Just tell them I'm off home and I'll text them when I can.'

'OK, OK, just double-checking the script,' he says. 'We all love you, you know that?'

'I know you do,' I whisper, feeling tears sting my eyes.

'And I wish I could teleport to that Donegal hideaway and give you a big Carlos snuggle. But you're going to have a wonderful time. I can feel it in my bones.'

The only thing I can feel in my bones right now is the bitter cold, but I can't tell him that.

He makes another joke then hangs up, leaving the sound of the squeaking wipers and George's impatient panting my only company.

I put my head in my hands on the steering wheel, before letting out a stifled scream, wishing that all I had told him was indeed true. My car is facing in the direction south to Dublin, the snow is getting thicker on the ground, yet I've no idea really where I'm going. I can't bear the thought of my own usual surroundings at Christmas back in my nice townhouse, with my cosy lifestyle and my empty heart.

I reach my hand down with my head still touching the steering wheel and blindly turn the ignition to start the car to make my way home to the grey, miserable, sleety city rain, but then I sit up quickly when the car chugs and spits a little, just as it did when I was leaving the cottage earlier.

'Please, no.'

Then it cuts out with a splutter, just as it did at the cottage earlier too.

I try again and it does the same. First a chug, then a spit, then a splutter, then out. My palms sweat even though I'm beginning to shiver with the cold from outside. I can see my own breath. I say a prayer. A real prayer and not a made-up one, which confirms I'm truly beginning to panic inside.

'Third time lucky?' I say to George, who lets out a groan in an unconvincing vote of confidence. 'Don't panic, it's fine.'

And so I turn the key again, but this time there isn't so much as a whimper or a cough never mind a splutter from the engine.

This time there's nothing. I try again, and again, and again. But nothing.

Just silence. Then a scrape that sounds painful.

Ouch.

'Is this some sick joke?' I whisper, gripping the steering wheel. A blanket of snow clouds over the windscreen now that the wipers have screeched to a halt after a false start. I stamp my feet, both in bad temper and to try to warm them up. 'Give me a break, karma, please, I'm begging you. I get it. I don't belong here. I don't deserve the comfort of the cottage.

I shouldn't have come near Donegal at Christmas, but please just let me get home, wherever the hell that is these days.'

I try once more but the car just squeals as if it's angry at me too.

'Eugh.'

I pull my coat from the backseat and climb outside into the flurry of snow that is no longer picturesque but is now instead a proper pain in the ass. A thick puff of smoke greets me when I lift the car's bonnet, stinging my eyes for good measure, and the engine is roasting hot even though I'd only been driving a few minutes before Carlos called me.

This isn't good.

I mean, I can tackle some basic mechanics when it comes to cars. I know my way around an engine, it's in my blood, but this – this is way above my station.

'Please, please, *please* . . .' I beg, regretting instantly the basic insurance policy I took out, which doesn't include road-side assistance.

I live in the city for goodness' sake. It would have been a waste of money, even the broker said that. I barely need to take my car anywhere as it's more hassle than it's worth, not to mention expensive to pay for parking.

In Dublin I can walk to most places, or just jump on the DART, or hail a taxi if I ever need to go somewhere a bit further out. I don't think they even *have* taxis in this part of Donegal.

I slam the bonnet closed, resisting the urge to kick the tyre on my way past. I open the passenger door and George jumps up and out of the car to greet me.

'I'll sort this, George, don't worry,' I tell him, stroking his damp fur and trying to convince myself at the same time. 'I can sort it. Plan B or C, or whatever plan comes next is only a thought away.'

I clip his lead to his collar, grab my purse from the dashboard and carefully cross the road to the village coffee shop where I plan to gather my thoughts and consider my next move.

It's a pink building that says 'Sean's Scones and Bakes' in swirling gold text above the door – a new owner since I was last here many moons ago. I push it open as an old-fashioned bell announces my arrival.

'You look like you could do with a hot drink, and fast,' says the white-haired, pink-cheeked man behind the counter, who I don't like to assume but I'd place my bets might be Sean himself.

I shiver as the sticky warmth inside shakes me up against the cold. The place smells like hot-cross buns and chocolate which is enough to warm my soul, if only temporarily.

'Yes, please.'

'Car trouble?' he asks and I nod. 'I was watching you and was *just* about to go out to see if I could help in any way when I saw you crossing the road towards me. Bet it's freezing cold out there, isn't it?'

'Yes, it's freezing. Literally,' I inform him with a polite smile. Talk about stating the obvious.

I don't believe he was going to leave his warm café, not for one second, and nor could I blame him, but his gesture of assistance reminds me of how Charlie, the now very cosy and warm resident of Seaview Cottage, stopped to help me earlier and how I smugly shooed him away. I'm not so smart this time.

'I'll have a cinnamon latte, please,' I tell the man who is now wiping condensation from the window. His hands make a squeaking sound, and he stares across the road at my car again with squinted eyes, his hands on his hips now as he shakes his head. I take off my coat which is already soaked through.

'Have a seat and I'll bring you your coffee. And some water for the dog too.'

I realise that George and I have just plodded our wet feet and paws inside his cute little café without even checking if it was dog-friendly, but so far the man seems pretty cool about my companion. I'm the only one here, after all, so it's not like anyone else is going to complain.

'One steaming hot cinnamon latte just for you, my dear,' announces Sean moments later, and in true Donegal style, he pulls out the seat beside me and sits down for a chat. 'So, can I help at all? Now, I must admit, though I bake great cakes and buns, I've absolutely no idea about cars, I'm afraid. However, I do know a man who knows *everything* about cars, so I can call him if you like?'

'Oh no, I don't want to bother anyone in this weather,' I reply, wishing he would just let me think for myself for a second, or at least enjoy my coffee before I tackle my pretty major problem of being stranded in rural Donegal.

Sean pulls a frown.

'So you're going to fix the car yourself, then?' he asks.

I laugh at his tone. It's like something my own father would say to me.

'I wish I could fix it myself,' I tell him, holding the tall glass of coffee with both hands. 'I actually do know quite a bit about cars, but not at this level . . .'

'So let me get my friend to look at it,' he says, chuckling as he goes for the phone.

'If he doesn't mind . . . I'd be forever grateful.'

'Enjoy your coffee and relax, love. We'll get you sorted, don't worry. Don't worry at all,' he says, holding his back as he shuffles off.

I watch him disappear towards the back of the shop, then I look at the time on the clock above the door and close my eyes in despair. It's almost four in the afternoon. There's no way a mechanic will even look at my car at this stage of the day, never mind get me back on the road by tonight.

I feel a wave of panic prick my skin and my breath shortens as Sean potters back and forth behind the counter, his words on the phone a muffled haze in the background against the hum in my ears that warns me a panic attack might be near.

I can't let this happen. I won't let this happen. I am in control. I'm a business owner, a homeowner, a successful city navigator. I'm not going to crumble just because I'm stuck in my own home county in the snow with nowhere to stay and a dog who is depending on me to find us a bed for the night. Am I?

'That's that sorted then. He's on his way here now,' Sean tells me with a wide smile that shows his slightly yellowing tombstone teeth. 'You'll never believe it, but he was in town already getting something for dinner at the butcher's. He was at the till when he took the call, so he'll be here in under a minute.'

'Thank you. That was speedy.'

'We may be easy-going around here, but when it comes to helping each other, we always go the extra mile, pardon the pun,' he says. 'Now, I don't want to get your hopes up, but if Rusty Quinn can't fix your car, then no one can—'

'Rusty Quinn? Did – did you say Rusty Quinn?'

'I did, my dear, yes.'

'Aren't there any other mechanics around here?'

'You know him?' asks Sean in surprise, then his face changes. 'You don't look like a local if you don't mind me saying. We don't see fancy frocks like that around here very often, and I assumed with the Dublin car registration that you—'

'I'm not local, no. Well, I am in a way but I'm originally from—'

And then it's too late.

The bell jingles above the door to announce we have company and Rusty's mouth drops open when he sees me. I can barely meet his eyes as my cheeks flush.

'You didn't get too far, did you, Rosebud?' he says, giving me a cheeky smile, and my heart stings a little. I haven't been addressed by my childhood nickname in a very long time and it hits me with a blast of nostalgia.

'Not to worry,' he says with a wink. 'We'll get it sorted. Give me the keys and I'll go take a look.'

*

'So, this is the dog you mentioned in your email to me?' Rusty says on his return a few moments later.

His gravelly voice soothes me instantly.

'We didn't get a proper introduction earlier at the cottage. I never thought you were the dog type?' he says, sitting down.

He tilts his head to the side as if he's seeing me properly now, like our earlier meeting at the cottage was all a blur or didn't really happen. I tug my dress over my knees and sit up straight.

'Neither did I, but people change,' I say, meeting his eyes with trepidation. I feel my lip quiver and my legs go weak as my mind goes back in time. 'We can all change, Rusty, can't we?'

He bites his lip and nods slowly, then looks away. I swear I see his eyes glisten beneath his oil-covered navy baseball cap.

'We can, love, but only if we need to and only if we want to,' he says when he looks back at me again. His familiar eyes tug at my lonely heart. 'Some of us are simply unique, and it would be a sin for someone with a heart like yours to ever change.'

'Thank you.' My voice cracks.

'How've you been? You know, I couldn't guess how many times I've been meaning to call you but—'

'You're my cousin, Rusty, not my keeper. Life goes on, eh?' I whisper, recalling how many people have said that to me since Michael died. 'I'm coping, I guess. It's just Christmas that gets me right by the throat and pins me to the ground, so I figure I'm best on my own instead of being like a damp squib around others.'

He shakes his head and holds my eye.

'It's OK to ask for help, Rose,' he tells me, with his own voice breaking a little too. 'We all need a little help sometimes. I've always told you to call on me anytime you needed to. In fact, my heart lifted when I saw your email and you asked to stay in the cottage, but then . . . Anyhow now, about the car . . .'

'Look, I don't want to get you into any trouble, Rusty,' I say. 'I shouldn't have come here. It was typical of me. Whimsical and romantic, thinking that coming here to be alone would be better than another Christmas in Dublin away from it all. I was wrong. It's not meant to be.'

Rusty leans forward as I speak, resting his elbows on the table, and I smell a waft of tobacco mixed with mint which instantly takes me back to my childhood. He looks like my dad did, back in the day.

'I know how much you love it here.'

I take a deep breath.

'I really do.'

'And I wish I could offer you a room for the night at our house . . . but things aren't good at home and that's putting it mildly.'

'For the night? What do you mean, for the night?'

He looks at me like we're not on the same page.

'It's your car alternator, just like we thought it was.'

'Yes,' I nod, loving that Rusty and I are talking car parts just like the olden days, but not loving the way he's not going to be able to fix it as soon as I need him to.

'Well, there's no way I'm going to get car parts at this time of the day,' he says, 'so with that in mind, it looks like young Charlie up the road is going to have to move over in the cottage for at least tonight, OK?'

'No.'

My eyes widen and my head involuntarily shakes from side to side.

'Yes.'

'No, Rusty, honestly that's not fair,' I say, putting my hands up in defiance. 'There's no way I want to disturb that man again. He doesn't need any of my nonsense piled upon him when he's here to get away from whatever his own drama is.'

'But—'

'And what would Marion say if she knew I was staying after her total refusal to even discuss it?' I continue. 'She'll crucify you. No. Honestly. I'd rather sleep on the street in the snow than cause you any trouble, and that's no exaggeration.'

Rusty leans back and lets out a raucous laugh.

'You know what, Rose, I believe you when you say that,' he says. 'You're a Quinn, just like me. Stubborn as a mule. But it's my cottage at the end of the day, and you are my family. If I say you're staying for the night until I get you back on the road, then there's no one – not Charlie, not even *Marion* – who will argue against me. Now drink up and let's get you warmed up and settled in for the night.'

Marion has never forgiven my family since there was a big row about who should get the holiday cottage after Granny Molly died. My dad told her that for an outsider, she'd far too much to say on the matter.

My dad didn't hold back and Marion went hell for leather in return. I wasn't even in the room, but from Marion's reaction to my surprise arrival earlier, I can tell that she still holds a grudge against me for it.

'I'm really not sure about this,' I mutter.

But Rusty just shrugs.

'Well, I'm afraid we don't have much choice, cousin dear. So just get some food, a good night's sleep and I'll have you back on the road as soon as I can tomorrow.'

I try to think of another option but for once I don't have a Plan B. I'm sorry to hear that Rusty and Marion are having problems, but from what I witnessed earlier at the cottage, I'm not overly surprised.

'It's just for one night, I suppose . . .'

'It's just for one night,' Rusty agrees. 'Now, we need to make a move before the snow gets any heavier. Looks like we're in for a stormy night ahead.'

'You will be in for more than a storm if Marion finds out about this,' I say as we cross the road to Rusty's pick-up truck.

He just chuckles and shakes his head.

'Ain't that the truth, Rosebud. You know us all far, far too well.'

Chapter Four

Charlie

I have my phone on silent.

I know that's cruel, but she keeps calling me, every few minutes.

We discussed how she's not having turkey this Christmas because her friend Mary is vegetarian. She thinks she is going to turn vegetarian as of today – though might have a tiny bit of ham with her dinner.

Then we discussed her new shower gel. She loves berries and so naturally needed to call me to tell me she got some dewberry shower gel today, which apparently smells just as good. I promised that if I see any dewberry-scented stuff in Donegal, I would get it for her.

And then she asked if Max is missing her. And if I'd heard from Rebecca. She said she wishes Rebecca was with me for Christmas.

Oh God, so do I.

I hope I'm not being selfish. Maybe I am being selfish.

I adore Helena. I really do. But I just need quiet right now. I want to listen to the clock tick, to the dog snore, to some classical music or the light wind rustle outside and forget this gnawing pain inside of me.

In fact, scrap that. I just want to listen to the silence and absorb all the stepping stones that got me to this very moment. How did it come to this, just me and my dog in Donegal at Christmas? How did I get here? How did my potentially perfect life, if such a thing exists, end up like this?

I miss my daughter. I miss her little hand in mine, her face looking up to me. I miss picking her up from school, and hearing all about her day. I miss her temper tantrums and how she'd tell her mother one thing and me another just to get her own way.

I need her in my life.

But those wants or needs, whatever they are, are pushed to the back of my mind at least for now when the owner of the cottage, Rusty, turns up again all a fluster. He is very sorry. He has a favour to ask. It's just for one night. And that's a promise.

'No, no, I don't mind at all,' I tell Rusty, feeling my stomach swirl and my head thump as I stand in the hallway. I really wish he'd step inside to let me close the door so I can keep in the heat, but he insists he isn't staying.

'I really appreciate this, Charlie,' he says as the snowflakes catch his beard. 'I'm as perturbed as you are over this mix-up. Well. Maybe not, but you know what I mean.'

He does look very sorry.

'If it's only for one night, I'm sure we can manage,' I tell him as he blows into his hands. 'Are you sure you won't come in?'

'I'm not staying. I'm already late with getting back home.'

'OK, well, I've had a good look around the cottage and, as your wife rightly said, it's only made for one person – or two if they're sharing as a couple. There's only one bed, so I guess I'll—'

'Rose is adamant she'll take the sofa,' he insists, and I get the vibe that he isn't in the mood to argue. 'She's very understanding and very, very embarrassed, as I'm sure you can imagine. I've promised I'll have the car going by tomorrow and if not I'll . . .'

He trails off and looks over his shoulder, back to his pick-up truck where I see Rose staring ahead as the snow drifts down more heavily. I know absolutely nothing about her, yet I feel sorry for her again, just as I did earlier.

'It's fine, I'm fine with this for one night, but after that . . .' I tell the man who looks like he really could do with some peace in his life right now as much as the rest of us. 'Look, we'll manage. It's no problem whatsoever. Let me help her in with her luggage. It's fine. It's just one night.'

I can hear my ex, Clodagh's voice again in my head.

Yes, help the lady with her luggage. Pretend it's all OK even though it isn't. Whatever you do, don't say how you really feel, Charlie. Don't say how much you really wanted to be alone. Tiptoe around a stranger's problems, but bottle up your own.

Max barks in Rose's direction, and it's then I see the giant ball of fluff bouncing around in the front seat beside her in the pick-up truck.

Ah.

'Yes, there's the small matter of the big dog too,' says Rusty. 'Look, I'd take them both to my own house to stay but things are – well, let's just say this might be the lesser of two evils. I'll make sure you're properly reimbursed for all this inconvenience, Charlie. I'll knock this night off the bill, OK? Just one night.'

'Just one night,' I echo, nudging the man back towards his vehicle and to the woman who I know is probably as annoyed about this mess as I am right now, even though I'm doing my best to hide it.

I know I offered this very option earlier, but now that it's happening, it's not how I'd envisaged my time here, especially not my first night. I was just about settling in. I'd piled up the fire with smouldering turf, I'd poured a glass of red wine and I'd taken the huge decision to put my phone on silent to avoid any further disturbance. Yet now, even before I've cooked my first meal here, I'm asked to share my space with a total stranger.

You bring this all upon yourself, Charlie. That's what you get for always trying to save everyone and everything. Save it for your day job.

I hear Clodagh's voice again which makes me even more determined to shake off my self-pity and just get through this rather bumpy start to my peaceful getaway.

'I'm so very sorry,' Rose tells me when Rusty is gone and it's just the two of us in the living area with our two dogs who are sniffing around each other cautiously. It's not a very big space, just enough room for the two sofas which are covered in too many floral cushions, a coffee table piled with magazines and a TV in the corner, all set on an old-style terracotta tiled floor. 'I won't even speak. I won't utter a single word if it makes it easier for you.'

'I don't expect you not to speak.'

'I just need some rest and some warmth, and I'll be out of your hair as soon as Rusty gets my car sorted tomorrow,' she says, doing her best to make light of it all. 'Pretend I'm not here, if that's possible. I'm totally mortified.'

As if I could pretend she isn't here when she looks like she has just stepped out of the 1950s, and has a large black and white shaggy dog panting around her.

'Are you hungry?' I ask, knowing it's what my late mother would want me to ask under these unusual circumstances. 'I brought some basics like rice and chicken and vegetables. Enough for tonight, at least. You can help yourself and I'll go to the bedroom upstairs if you prefer, so you can make yourself comfortable.'

She is still wearing that ridiculously stained overcoat which is probably best suited to a dry-cleaner if not the bin at this stage, though it does look insanely expensive. She is dishevelled and the way she sighs as she looks around tells me this is equally if not more painful for her than it is for me. She is in some sort of emotional agony; I just know it. I can also tell that she's doing her best to hide it.

'I'm . . . thank you . . . I'm OK for food, but thank you,' she tells me, taking off her coat at last. Our eyes meet fleetingly, and I sense a pain that radiates from deep within.

'I was going to cook something shortly,' I say again. She really does look like she's fighting back tears.

'No, thank you,' she whispers. 'I'm deeply embarrassed at having to disturb you again like this. You're very kind.'

We stand in front of the blazing fire while the clock ticks in the background, the wind rustles outside and the darkness of a Donegal winter settles like a thick blanket. Rose looks paler now than before, and not quite as confident as she was on the roadside when we first met. She isn't a lot younger than me, I'm guessing. And something tells me she really did need to come here just as much as I did, though I've no idea why that might be.

'It's such a special place,' she says, taking in her surroundings. 'You're going to love it here.'

I want to ask if she's been here before, but I've a feeling that might set her off as she battles with whatever has brought her here in the first place. We couldn't look more different if we tried as we stand opposite, sussing each other out. Rose is all bloom and colour yet her mind is far away, while I feel muted in comparison in my loose grey T-shirt and jeans, overgrown dark hair and bare feet. If I'm rock 'n' roll, she's swing and jazz – at least on the outside. I feel even scruffier than usual beside her.

'Have a seat. Here. I'll take your coat,' I say, realising I should have suggested this a lot earlier.

She hands me the coat. She sits down, then stands up again.

'I'd love a shower if you don't mind?' she whispers. 'I'm cold to the bone. You see, my car broke down again and—'

'Yes, Rusty was saying,' I interrupt, sensing from her tone that she's already fed up talking about it.

She smiles very apologetically.

'I'll just . . . I'll just go and have my shower.'

'Yes, of course. Now, the bathroom is down the hallway to the right but you have to be quick before the water runs cold,' I tell her, but she knows the way.

I hear the door close and I lift my glass of wine and my book and go to the bedroom upstairs where I will lie in wait for the chance to cook later. Not the evening I'd planned by any stretch, but I can do this. I open the book and try to read under the light of a fringed bedside lamp with Max who is already snoring at my feet on the deep spring mattress.

And so this is Christmas, I sing in my own head.

Buckle up, Charlie, I tell myself. You've come up against much more uncomfortable situations than this.

I close the book almost immediately and let out a deep sigh. This is not ideal at all, but at least I still have the kitchen to go to where I don't have to disturb the stranger who is staying with me.

I offered her food. She said no.

I'll just stay out of her way until morning. Surely it won't be all that hard to do.

Chapter Five

Rose

Well, this is awkward.

I strip off in silence in the tiny old-style cottage bathroom with its squeaking toilet flush, floral curtains and timber floorboards, afraid of making too much noise and disturbing my unexpected host.

He seems nice.

A bit stiff and scruffy, but very handsome at the same time with his full mouth, chiselled cheekbones and strong features. Not that any of that matters to me.

He's polite, I suppose, but his blue eyes look like he carries the weight of the world on his shoulders. Maybe he does? He was having a glass of red wine by the fire with his dog by his side, reading his book when we turned up and disturbed him.

I'm totally mortified.

I step under the shower and turn the heat up full blast, knowing that time is against me before it shoots me with cold water. I smile as I remember it from years gone by, and although that would be annoying to most, to me it's the little edges of this cottage that make it so endearing.

I bet it will annoy Charlie though. He seems like the organised type, or is that just me jumping to conclusions from first impressions? Oh, I bet I'm right. I bet he has the table set in the kitchen for his evening meal, which he'd already planned out in his head and had timed to perfection.

He looks a bit Italian in some ways, even though his accent is distinctively Belfast and, as I let my mind go into overdrive, I imagine that he has knowledge of lots of secret recipes handed down through generations, never to be shared with strangers like me.

As I stand beneath the hot water, feeling the heat soothe my bones, I wonder how the hell did this happen? I feel like I'm in some sort of disaster movie and I'm waiting for the director to shout 'cut' and it will be all over. Or maybe it's just a bad dream? The water turns ice-cold, reminding me that it's none of the above.

Yes, Rose Quinn. You are indeed in your late Granny Molly's holiday cottage for the first time in years, with a stranger, when all you wanted was to lock yourself away for Christmas and face the world once again when it's all over.

I step out of the shower, hearing the floorboards creak above me. This cottage must be at least a hundred years old, and I can just hear what my dad would say if he were here.

If it were mine, I'd have fixed the shower after all this time. I'd have oiled the doors too. I'd have decorated it very differently if it were ours. Marion has no taste at all. She talks the talk, but does she walk the walk? No, she does not.

My tummy rumbles as I quickly dry myself off. The towels are soft and fluffy, which brings me back to staying here as a little girl on cosy autumn nights when school was out for mid-term.

Granny Molly would make soups and stews on the stove in the kitchen. She'd sing as she cooked, then she'd call me to taste her offerings, each dish even more delicious than the last.

I haven't eaten properly all day and although I said I wasn't in the mood for food, I'd murder a nice dinner right now.

I take a moment to look at myself in the steamed-up mirror.

What a terrible mess I've got myself into. This place is riddled with memories of happier times. So much for moving forward. I could kick myself sometimes at how I just do things without thinking them through.

I'm spontaneous to a fault, I know that, but while it works for the best in the workplace where I can let my creative spark lead the way, in my personal life, I'm just wading through treacle from one day to the next, lost in a fog of grief and pretence.

But this Christmas . . . if I can just get through this Christmas, it will be another milestone without Michael passed and I can try to focus on all the good I have in my life. I have fantastic friends in Carlos, Maeve and Yvonne. We do hot yoga, we have a book club, we have nights in front of the telly with wine and cheeseboards, we go for walks on the weekends. We've even been known to hike in the mountains. I have a great job, I have a nice home.

I just need to learn how to deal with Christmas again.

I wipe the condensation off the tiny square mirror above the sink and run my fingers down the tracks of mascara on my cheeks. I'm convinced all my tears must have formed little fine lines on my face after all this time. I long for the day when I find peace in my heart, once and for all.

With Michael on my mind, I spot Charlie's cologne on the bathroom window and can't resist a quick smell.

The scent is woody, just as Charlie smelled earlier, but my heart sinks when I find it's a world away from Michael's familiarity and warmth. He preferred stronger, fruity cologne. It's manly, it's attractive but—

Oh God.

I close my eyes and inhale this stranger's scent, then realise I'm being a little bit creepy and set it right back on the windowsill. What am I *doing*?

Michael's gone and he isn't coming back. And it wasn't my fault. It wasn't my fault.

I will repeat these words for as long as it takes for me to believe them, even though that might be forever.

No matter what Evelyn, Michael's mother, said in the past to reassure me, no matter how many pep talks I have with my sister and my closest friends, I will always, always wonder what if . . .

I hear a floorboard creak from upstairs, which makes me wonder what Charlie is doing up there, imprisoned in the bedroom with his book and his wine when he was meant to have the whole run of the cottage by now.

Everything belonging to him is set out neatly along the windowsill in order of size. Moisturiser, face wash, shower gel – all the same organic brand – and a damp bamboo tooth-brush which looks like it has already been used on this visit.

I'm just about to snoop a little bit more when a bark from George on the other side of the door stops me.

'Coming now, George,' I say just above a whisper, but my voice only makes him bark even more. 'Coming, George. Two minutes. Good boy.'

But still the barking continues.

Oh please, George.

I dry myself extra quickly and hear a door close which I assume is from the kitchen. So much for staying in his room for a while to let me settle. How am I supposed to leg it to the living room where I've set up camp on the sofa? All my clothes are in there.

And still George barks. Then Charlie's dog joins in, and I can't wait any longer. I should really make a run for it to try and stop the noise.

OK, I can do this.

The kitchen door is to the left of the small hallway, the living room is to the right and the bedroom is up a narrow flight of wooden stairs by the front door. I didn't think he'd be down so soon.

I open the knob on the bathroom door which always clicks so loudly no matter how you try to do it, and George jumps up on me, all clumsy, hot, breathy pants. Grasping my towel for dear life, I shimmy past him and Max, who is now running around in circles literally chasing his own tail and yelping in excitement. The kitchen door is closed, thank goodness.

With my feet still damp, I tiptoe quickly across the hall-way, open the living room door and pull it to, letting George in with me in a bid to lessen the noise.

It worked. No more barking.

Charlie's brown and white springer spaniel has settled after a few yelps now that George is out of sight, so I set about getting changed into my cosy, oversized fleecy winter pyjamas.

And then I smell what I assume is garlic frying in butter . . .

I'm so hungry I could cry. I sit down on the sofa, wondering if I should turn on the TV as a distraction. I'll cook something for myself after he's done. Yes, that will keep my mind and my belly in order. I've got some pasta and ready-made tomato sauce in my bag, and some pre-cooked spicy sausage, which happens to be George's favourite too. Even though I know I shouldn't, I always share a little bit with him.

I imagine Charlie in the kitchen right now.

There'll be no ready-made sauce on his menu, I'm guessing. He was barefoot earlier in his jeans, so he probably still is, his dark brown hair all outgrown and dishevelled and his tortoiseshell glasses still on with the makings of a light evening shadow on his face. He'll be sipping his red wine, stirring up a feast in the pan, smelling like a dream if that cologne is anything to go by, while I sit in here waiting and waiting for this moment to pass.

I must wait it out, yes. Then, when I hear him go back upstairs, I'll quickly make my sad instant meal and hopefully fall into a deep slumber by the fire.

I hear music. Classical music. I shake my head in surprise.

Chopin? What a dark horse you are, Charlie.

I wonder what he does for a living. Despite his rock star looks, with his taste in music and how super organised he is, I'd bet he's an accountant or a teacher. Even though he had been in this living room for a couple of hours before I got back with Rusty, there isn't a thing out of place.

I look around me. My shoes are on the floor, my coat is over the back of the sofa, my small case lies open as if it's yawning on the other sofa and my wet towel is strewn across the arm of the chair.

I wonder if he's tried to figure me out in the same way. No, he seems way too preoccupied for that.

As the waft of spices drifts under the door and the hunger in my belly threatens to consume me, I brush through my wet hair, tie it up in a bobble and switch on the TV to take my wandering mind off what has brought Charlie to Seaview Cottage in the first place.

Whatever the reason and whoever he really is, I guess I'll never get to find out.

Tomorrow morning can't come quick enough so I can leave him to get on with it. But where do I go then?

I've absolutely no idea.

Eight Days to Christmas

Chapter Six

Charlie

I spend my first early morning on the wilds of the blustery beach at Ballyhiernan Bay with Max after a healthy breakfast and a surprisingly solid sleep, almost forgetting that I'd company in the cottage at all.

With the wind in my hair and an icy breeze catching my breath as I walk along the foam and swirl of the water's edge, I find myself battling with an overwhelming feeling of regret that I've been smothering for too long.

Already, the time and space away from the norm is doing exactly what I'd hoped it would. I wanted to face up to my own realities here. I wanted to face my fears. And although I don't want to close the latest chapter of my life and pretend it never happened, I do need to forgive myself a little more for my own sake. I need to practise what I preach, which is exactly what Niall said before he sent me here.

Niall has been by my side since as far back as I can remember. We did primary school, secondary school and even university together. Now he's my accountant and although

I wind him up about his quotes and sayings, I'd miss them if he stopped.

No need for the inspirational quotes, kid, I'd told him when he came to me with the news that the cottage was mine over Christmas. He was on some sort of roll with his famous sayings, proclaiming something about how holding on to anger is like holding a hot coal expecting the other person to get burned.

I'm already a walking cliché as it is, thank you. The therapist whose own life is falling apart.

The lonely divorcee facing Christmas alone, added Niall.

We weren't married, I reminded him.

The fixer who can't fix himself, said Niall, sipping on a beer in my kitchen.

That'll do, I told him, knowing his humour was only an attempt to shake me out of my slumber. *I'll go to Donegal to get away from it all if you think it's the right thing for me, but I mean it. This is the last Christmas I'm going to skulk around like this. After this year, it's business as usual, whatever that may be.*

He held his fist out for me to 'bump' which made me roll my eyes in return. Niall, as much as I love the guy, has been on way too many training courses where he's been encouraged to 'reach out' and to 'think outside of the box' for my liking, but I wouldn't change him for the world. When my parents died less than a year apart, each of them having fought a heart-wrenching cancer battle, he was the first person through my door, and now that Rebecca has gone to live far away, he makes sure to call me every single day. He begged me to bring Helena and spend Christmas with him and his wife and family, but I don't want to take his generosity too far.

Go and clear your head, champ, he told me, when I said I'd planned to escape to Donegal instead. *Sometimes good things fall apart so better things can come together.*

I shot him a *very* lengthy stare for coming out with that one.

I arrive back to the cottage expecting to see Rose up, packed and ready to leave, but the living room curtains are still drawn. There is no sign of life. At least, not until her dog goes bananas at the sound of me and Max coming into the hallway.

It's well after nine and she still isn't up?

And that damn dog. For something so big and dopey, he really does have a deep bark that would wake the dead.

'George, that's enough, old boy. Hush, please,' I hear Rose mutter to him when I stop by the living room door. 'You'll wake up Charlie and Max. It's too early for so much noise.'

Early?

I've usually half a day's work done by now. Should I shout a hello? Ask how she slept? What exactly are we supposed to do in this surreal situation? I cough, just so she knows I'm in the vicinity. Then I cough again, just for good measure. This is very strange.

I heard her moving furniture late last night after she crashed around the kitchen making what I gathered from the splashes of orange sauce around the cooker this morning was some pasta dish, but this morning the house was silent again.

I wonder if she is as nervous with this as I am.

I cough again, just in case. Sometimes I like to do things in threes. Sometimes I fear I've been around Niall for too long with his traits and ways of doing things just for luck.

Max circles around me where I stand in the hallway then shakes his coat, making me scramble for the towel I'd left by the door for exactly this moment. I dry him off quickly, then take off my woolly hat and black rain jacket before sitting down on the stairs to take off my boots and socks which are sodden through and through.

We walked further than I'd intended, leaving the beach to skulk around the village, taking in the sights and sounds of the little main street which is decorated with snowflake lights on lamp posts and old-fashioned multi-coloured bulbs that string across in a zig-zag.

Those decorations must be almost as old as I am. A lot about this place is like time stood still. What era exactly I'm unsure of, but I guess that's what makes it so magical. The people here live for a friendly chat, a helping hand or a kind ear. It's the type of place where you still see old men smoking pipes outside the pub with a newspaper tucked under their arm as they put the world to rights. It's a slower pace of life and I plan to savour every second of it.

On the way back to the cottage, a little robin skimmed over my head by the river, so close I'm sure its feet almost landed on my mop of hair, and the way it made me jump reminded me I'm very much still alive, even though sometimes I do wonder.

That's a sign loved ones are near, Helena reminded me when I sent her a photo of it perched by the riverbank.

I wish you were nearer now, she said, accompanied by a tear-faced emoji. That almost killed me.

I'll see you soon, I replied, and then I waited until the robin disappeared.

I stopped in at Sean's coffee shop where he was able to tell me all about the drama yesterday with Rose's car, and how he saved the day by contacting Rusty who is the best mechanic this side of the county border. I get the impression that not a lot happens around here at all if that's all he had to talk about.

'She's running from something or someone,' Sean told me with his arms folded. 'She's got this great façade going on, but a very sad look about her. Very pretty, smart too, and friendly for sure, but I can tell when someone is running from something. Mark my words.'

'Aren't we all running from something, Sean? Aren't we all?'

I let him rant on, jumping to his conclusions while I did the same in my head. Despite Sean's grand summary, I have my own theory about Rose, and a lot of it comes down to years of listening to other people's problems in a professional setting.

She's masking something mega, yes; I know that for sure. There's a reason for her coming here, but it's anything but straightforward. She certainly seems distracted, and there's a sense of chaos that surrounds her.

For a start, she's messy. The spaghetti sauce on the cooker was one thing, but the way she stacked the saucepans back in the cupboard would drive anyone insane.

Plus, she's loud without even realising it. She hums a lot for someone so badly out of tune. I know I'm no Pavarotti, but boy, I could hear her from upstairs last night when I was going to bed.

I'm still standing in the hallway mulling over our brief experience of sharing this cottage when Rose opens the living room door and finds me frozen in thought. She is wearing fluffy pyjamas which wouldn't look out of place in the Antarctic and her thick, dark hair is bunched up on top of her head in what Helena calls a 'pineapple'.

'Oh, good morning,' I splutter. 'Er, sorry, I don't mean to be in your way. I was just out for a walk.'

'Morning, Charlie,' she replies, then skulks towards the bathroom with her trusty companion in tow. 'Hopefully Rusty will get here soon and I'll be out of your hair. Thank you again for letting me stay.'

She closes the bathroom door which clicks loudly, leaving the slobbering ball of fluff barking after her.

'Would you like a coffee?' I ask her above the barking, but she doesn't hear me.

I take a quick peek into the living room and rub my forehead when I see how it looks like it's been hit by a mini tornado.

Two magazines lie on the floor along with blankets and cushions dotted across the terracotta tiles. Her suitcase lies wide open, leaving nothing to the imagination, and is that an overflowing make-up bag on the armchair? I close the door and try to blank the whole scene out of my head. She'll be gone soon, and I can finally make this place my own again.

'Come on, Max. Come on, George,' I say to the two dogs. 'How about I let you both out to the back garden to explore?'

Max bounces towards the kitchen but George chooses to totally ignore me and slumps down on the floor with his head on his paws, waiting on Rose by the bathroom door. Ah well, seems like he is as distant as his owner.

Hopefully Rusty arrives soon and then I can relax here at last.

Chapter Seven

Rose

I deliberately dodge Charlie for the next hour by camping out in the living room with just a coffee and George for company, staring out the window longing for Rusty to come to my rescue.

'Rapunzel, Rapunzel, let down your hair,' I mutter to the dog. I really do feel like a prisoner. Charlie is in the kitchen, listening to a podcast or something through his headphones but I bet he'd rather be in here by the fire. I've invited him to do so, but he politely refused.

So far, we've managed a conversation about the weather (*there's more snow on the way*), the price of fuel (*extortionate*, we both agreed) and the beauty of Donegal (*there's just something about being by the sea and so close to the guarded eye of the Fanad lighthouse*).

I then made an excuse to go pack my bags for Rusty's arrival. I've been sitting here for what feels like forever, like a damsel in distress waiting to be rescued.

I have never been a damsel in distress, no matter how lonely and sad I've felt over Michael, and nor do I ever intend to be.

This really sucks.

There's barely signal on my phone here, the Wi-Fi is touch and go to put it mildly, and even though I've managed to set up Netflix on the TV, the snow is interfering with the signal too much to make it worth fighting with, so for now all I can do is sit here and wait.

But when Rusty eventually does arrive, I can tell by his tone of voice and the way he sniffs, then looks at his feet, then rubs his chin, that the news is far from good when it comes to me making my great escape.

The three of us are standing in the kitchen of Seaview Cottage as the dogs chase birds in the back garden through the blanket of snow that has now settled outside.

Well, I should say *Max* is chasing birds while George just watches on, his big whooshing tail swinging to and fro, but there's no way he's getting stuck in. At least one of us is happy around here.

Charlie, meanwhile, looks like he's very slowly swallowing nails as he drinks his coffee waiting on Rusty's big announcement.

'The g-good news is that the car *can* be fixed, so that's a relief,' says Rusty, waiting for a reaction he doesn't get. I hold my breath, knowing the bad news is on its way. Rusty always stutters when he's nervous, so I think I know what's coming. 'The *bad* news is that the p-part I need for the engine – well, it's tricky to find for your car considering its age, but . . .'

'Tricky?'

'I'm looking online as well as my usual suppliers,' he finishes quickly. 'I *will* get it. It just might take a wee while longer to arrive, that's all.'

Charlie sets his cup down on the worktop and the delph hitting the wood makes Rusty jump.

'How *much* longer?' he asks. His full lips are open and although he looks sulky and unimpressed, his striking features wouldn't look out of place on the cover of some high fashion magazine.

'It could take quite a while.'

'How long is quite a while?' asks Charlie.

I have to say something.

'I'll check out bus times,' I chirp.

'You can't take a dog on the bus,' says Rusty. 'Plus, that would be a four-hour trip.'

'Right, well, I guess I'll just have to wait a while.'

'When I say quite a w-while . . . I'm not hopeful for this side of Christmas to be honest,' Rusty stammers, biting his lip.

'*What?*'

My eyes widen.

So do Charlie's.

'W-well, there's a major backlog in supplies and everything is slow at this time of year.'

I see Charlie's jaw clench, before he exhales. He almost looks as if he might punch something. I feel a bit dizzy.

'How about . . . how about you drive me back down to Dublin, Rusty?' I suggest, pacing the floor as I speak. 'I'd pay for the fuel and your time, and you'd be up and down in one day, or you could . . . you could even stay the night to break up the journey?'

Rusty rubs his chin and scrunches up his face, looking at the floor and avoiding me and Charlie all the way.

'Sorry, Rose, you know I would if I could,' he whispers.

'Rusty, please?'

'I've already mentioned . . . things aren't good at home with me and Marion right now,' he says, as if the words are being forced from him, 'and without going into any more detail, that's putting it very mildly.'

I stop pacing. I'm out of ideas already.

'So, it's not a good time for me to go away,' he explains. 'Not to mention the weather. It's not ideal driving conditions either. Sorry, love.'

We stand there, all three of us blankly staring at the floor in silence until Charlie launches his attack.

'Well, I'm not sure what options are left, but if you don't mind, I came here for a break and I'd really like to get on with it,' he says, with more than a pinch of anger in his usually mild-mannered voice. 'This has been an absolute shambles since I got here.'

Ouch.

'So, if you two don't mind quickly coming to some sort of arrangement and sticking to it, I'd really appreciate it.'

'We're trying to,' says Rusty, his own voice a little bit clipped as he pushes back his shoulders. He isn't tall compared to Charlie, but I've a feeling he's well able to stand his ground amongst the big boys. 'This was a *double* booking, don't forget.'

'I know – and mistakes happen. We're all human. I know you were equally looking forward to staying here for Christmas, Rose.'

Charlie takes a deep breath, holds his forehead and shifts from one bare foot to the other. What is it with him always in his bare feet? It's cosy in the cottage, yes, but it's the middle of winter.

'Why don't you just stay, Rose?' says Charlie, rinsing out his cup now and putting it on the dishrack. 'I'd offer to leave myself but quite frankly, even this unconventional arrangement is more appealing than going home. And I can't be bothered with any more of this faffing around and wasting time.'

'Excuse me?'

He lifts the cup before it gets the chance to drain, dries it as he speaks and puts it back in the cupboard, pushing the handle to the right to match the others.

'Just stay until your car is sorted, but I'll expect a further discount, Rusty.'

'Of course, I can honour that,' says Rusty. His eyes light up. He stands up straight, as if he's just been offered a long-awaited lifeline.

'And I'll pay half of it, of course,' I say quickly.

The air feels lighter. Rusty is already offering Charlie a handshake.

'Are you sure?' I ask him, even though I don't really know how I want him to reply.

He pauses.

'Yes, I'm sure,' he says, rubbing his forehead.

Rusty brightens up.

'Well now, that's very generous of you, Charlie. This won't be forgotten,' he says.

'But there's only one bed . . .' I remind them. 'Actually, never mind. You have it, Charlie. I'm good with the sofa. It's actually quite comfy and—'

'No, no, we'll draw up a set of, well, let's call them house rules, to avoid any unnecessary clashes,' says Charlie. 'Just so we can move around each other easily.'

I still feel like I'm intruding.

I still don't know if this is a good idea, or what we're getting ourselves into.

'And I know I can be a bit messy, so I'll do my best to keep the place tidy, I promise,' I say before *he* says it to me. I always talk too much when I'm nervous. 'Rules are good. We can make up some rules for sure.'

I want to agree wholeheartedly with everything so we can all hurry up and get on with things, just as Charlie suggested. In truth, I don't know whether to feel terrified or excited about what lies ahead.

'Now, I don't intend to be here a lot during the day, if that helps. I want to explore a bit, and then in the evenings . . .' I continue.

'I go to bed very early so I won't be around most evenings,' Charlie interjects. 'I'm a morning person.'

'Well, you're the opposite of me, then. Gosh, this could be easier than we thought.'

Charlie smiles, even though I know he doesn't want to, which I hope is a sign that deep within that sultry, dark exterior there's a sense of humour somewhere.

I haven't felt like laughing in a very long time, but sometimes, just sometimes, I do see the lighter side of things. I'm getting better at that, even though I'm not sure I should be yet. I'm forever measuring stupid milestones against my grief as if there's some timeline on when to laugh again, or to stop crying, or to stop missing someone. But that doesn't exist, does it?

Rusty claps his hands and rubs them together, clearly delighted that we have come to some sort of a plan for the days ahead.

'Great,' he says. 'And I'll do my best to find the part for the car before Christmas. Now, that's that then . . . right . . . I need a cigarette. Or a whiskey, or both. I'll leave you both to it. Er, good luck.'

'Thanks, Rusty,' I say to his back as he bolts for the door.

I'm not even sure if this is for the best. I needed to be alone at Christmas. I needed to forget about it all, not be cooped up in this cottage in the middle of nowhere with a stranger, yet for some reason I'd rather do this than head back to Dublin where there's too much reality to face up to.

'You can thank Charlie, not me,' Rusty says with a grin. 'You're a good man, Charlie. You'll be heavily reimbursed, even for future stays if you decide to come back here again. You OK, Rose?'

I pause. Am I?

'Yes, I'm OK,' I tell my cousin, whose tired eyes make me yearn to take away all his discomfort and whatever personal hell he is going through right now.

'You know where I am if either of you need me. I'd better get home. I'm late already.'

He tips his hat and leaves Charlie and me standing in the poky kitchen, neither of us sure what we've just bought into.

'Are you sure about this?'

Charlie doesn't answer, but gives me a nod and a slight smile.

I think I'll go and take George for a walk to give us all some space.

Chapter Eight

Charlie

Rose is at the sink wearing yellow Marigolds, quietly scrubbing the pocket of her oil-stained coat when I join her in the kitchen around an hour after Rusty's grand departure.

We've been playing some strange game of cat and mouse since then, with her taking George for a walk even though the heavens had opened with snow, and me playing hideout in the bedroom as if I'd lose some points if we found ourselves in the same room at the same time.

To be honest, I don't know what I was thinking of, suggesting Rose could stay, but there weren't too many other options.

Clodagh's words that keep popping into my head might be right for once. If only I could stop myself from trying to fix everyone else, I just might find a way of fixing myself, which is what I came here for after all.

I'm a sought-after counsellor, I'm a good father, I'm a good friend. But my heart is in tatters, despite my brave front. I need to find a way of accepting the changes that have come my way like a freight train since this time last year. If I'd known it would be the last Christmas with the most important person in my world, I'd have taken absolutely nothing for granted.

You don't know what you've got 'til it's gone. That's my motto.

I hear Niall's voice in my head now, which makes me shiver. I'd mocked him, instantly recognising 'his' motto as the lyrics to 'Big Yellow Taxi'. But Joni knew her stuff, that's for sure.

Rose is humming gently to herself as she scrubs her coat, which is both endearing and annoying at the same time. She quite simply hasn't a note in her head.

I cough to try and subtly interrupt.

'Sorry to disturb you.'

'Oh hi, Charlie,' she says without looking my way. 'I know, I'm a terrible singer, sorry.'

For a split second, I fear I may have expressed my thoughts out loud.

'I must remember I've company,' she continues, before going back to her scrubbing. 'It's usually just me and George all the time, so he's probably used to it, or else he's a lot harder of hearing than I've realised, but I'll do my best not to make your ears bleed.'

She seems nice. Light-hearted. Humble even, which makes the sheet of paper I have in my hand feel like overkill now. I've spent the best part of the last thirty minutes jotting down some house rules to try and make our unexpected joint stay in this tiny cottage a bit smoother, but now I wonder if there's really any need.

'It's just . . . well, I've jotted a few things down which might help make our time here a bit easier,' I say, and thankfully she doesn't look too surprised. Her green eyes are heavy with mascara, her lips are a deep shade of red as usual and she wears an electric-blue cardigan tied around her waist which draws my attention, but within seconds the Marigolds are off and she is looking my way.

She blows her dark fringe away from her eyes. Endearing or annoying? I'm taken aback that I'm no longer sure.

'Are you a teacher, by any chance?' she asks, knocking me off my tracks.

'Why do you ask?'

She shrugs.

'Just you seem very, very organised. I mean that in a good way. I must confess, I'm not very good at following rules – generally I'm the one who makes them, which naturally means I can break them – so I hope your conditions aren't too . . .'

Her tone is light and jokey, but I've decided it will be much less complicated if we don't get too familiar.

I came here to give my mind a break, not to make a new friend with my unexpected housemate. In fact, the last thing I need is to get cosy with a stranger this Christmas, which I'd imagine is the same for Rose too. I've a lot of figuring out to do, and I need a lot of head space over the next while.

'I'm not a teacher and they're not conditions, just suggestions,' I reply, determined to keep this swift and to the point. 'Look, I'm sure you did too, but I wanted to come here to be *alone* for Christmas, so the first suggestion I've made is that we don't feel any pressure to be familiar or friendly.'

'Oh. Of course,' she says. 'And yes, likewise. I wanted to be alone too.'

There it is again – that look of deep pain. Her eyes glisten. She looks away. I want to ask if she's OK but I've got to keep my distance. This is not my job. She is not my problem.

'Good,' I mumble.

I refer to the page where I've written down *keep conversations factual and minimal, and only when required.* It seemed a good idea when I was making notes upstairs but now it feels cold and over the top. But anyhow . . .

'So, I'm Charlie, you're Rose,' I continue, gesturing to each of us as if we're on some cheesy game show. 'The dogs are Max and George.'

She raises her eyebrows and nods along.

'If we have a problem, we contact Rusty or Marion,' I read, then I look up at her. 'We don't need to know anything more than that on a personal level, do we?'

She looks a tiny bit taken aback, shifting from one blue leather ankle boot to another.

'I suppose we don't.'

I swallow. I'm tempted to scrunch up the paper and forget about it all, but then I remember why I'm here. I don't need a new room buddy. I need peace and quiet. I need this Christmas to be nondescript, to come and go, and to get plenty of rest and sea air. I don't need or want company.

'Now I was also thinking we could swap phone numbers, so if anything major does happen to do with the cottage, we can drop a message since we're likely to be doing different things at different times of the day?'

She is staring at me now, her mouth slightly open, as if I'm a mumbling freak which, let's face it, I probably do resemble. Her face is puzzled.

'So . . . what you're saying is that you'd prefer if we *message* each other instead of – instead of talking? Is that what you're saying?'

Gosh, it does sound a bit over the top when I hear it back. But I'm sticking to my guns. There's no need for small talk about the weather or the price of fuel or how lucky we are to be in such a beautiful location.

We need to keep it almost professional. It's an agreement. It's a contract of sorts, to make sure there are no hiccups in what has become a very surreal situation.

I nod. 'Well, yes. Exactly.'

She laughs. I don't think for one second she is finding it funny. I think she's finding it a bit ridiculous.

'Is that OK with you?' I ask. 'Look, I know it probably seems a bit cold, but I think boundaries will be useful for us both. It'll help us give each other the space we came here looking for.'

'It's totally fine,' she says, picking up her phone from the worktop. 'Boundaries are good, I guess. And it is a tiny cottage. OK, shout out your number and we can text each other if an emergency comes up.'

She thinks I'm an asshole.

I relay my number. She rings it to make sure she has it right. She does.

'Anything else?' she asks, one eyebrow raised and the twitch of a smile on her lips that hints that she's mocking me.

'The tap's dripping.'

I noticed the tap was dripping into the sink behind where she's standing as soon as I walked in here. She didn't turn it off properly. I did my best to ignore it, but I can't.

She glances back towards the sink, rushing to turn it off.

'Oh. Whoops, I didn't even notice – sorry. I'm not exactly off to a great start, am I?'

She has a sense of humour which I'd normally find very appealing, but again, I'm not even daring to go there. We are strangers who have been thrown together in a unique way at a very sensitive time of the year and we must keep our distance.

'It's OK, no big deal. Just a waste of . . . anyhow, never mind.'

This feels very cringey.

I glance back down at my hand-written list. Maybe I should ask her for some of her own suggestions now? Or do I wait until I'm done and then let her put in her own penny's worth? No, I'll just keep going now I've started.

'OK, so I like to shower twice a day, once in the morning around six a.m. and then again in the evening around nine before I go to bed.'

'Cool.' She yawns into the back of her hand. 'Sorry, excuse me. Gosh, I didn't realise I was so tired. I don't mean to be rude.'

Her yawning makes *me* yawn which in turn makes me a bit uncomfortable. We laugh, then we stop laughing swiftly.

'Anyhow.'

'Yes, go on.'

She nods at the sheet of paper. I know I sound a bit nit-picking in all this. I know it isn't exactly exciting or riveting conversation, but I need to push through and then we can both move along and keep out of each other's hair.

'This is just so we don't clash,' I continue. 'So, I was thinking that if we took turns to get in basics like bread, milk, butter, et cetera, it would save doubling up and would leave more room in the fridge.'

'OK.'

'I'll get one of those magnetic whiteboard things and we can mark up each time whose turn it is to grab the essentials.'

She lifts an apple from the fruit bowl and crunches into it quite loudly, then talks as she chews.

'What about sleeping arrangements? I take the sofa as offered?'

I pull out a chair from the kitchen table and sit down, poring over my list as she speaks. I've a pen in my hand just in case she comes up with something I've left out, but I think that I've covered everything.

'Well, yes, I'll get to that in just one second, but first please know overall that I'd like to respect your personal space and in return, I'd like you to respect mine,' I reply. 'Now, what time do you usually eat dinner?'

'Gosh, I'm not sure.'

'Roughly?'

She frowns in thought.

'I tend to just eat when I'm hungry, to be honest, Charlie,' she replies. 'Which I know probably isn't much help, but I'm more of a snacker than someone who sits down for a proper meal. My cooking skills aren't my greatest asset, and that's putting it lightly.'

'A *rough* time, even?'

'Er, around six? Look, I'll stay out of your way at mealtimes best I can, I promise,' she says, leaning on the worktop. 'You said you're a morning person. I'm a night owl. We'll take turns to get basic food stuff in and we'll communicate by text message or via your whiteboard thing. After that, I imagine the rest will fall into place. We'll be like ships in the night in no time.'

Her eyes sparkle as she speaks. I watch her move around the kitchen, and I know I could easily enjoy getting to know her better. But that's the opposite to why I'm here, so I'm sticking to my guns.

She throws the apple core into the pedal bin and puts her gloves back on, then begins tackling the stain on her coat again.

'I would really like to use the hot tub but I'll give you plenty of notice,' she says, glancing back at me as she scrubs. 'I can't believe this cottage has a hot tub now. How *en vogue*! I know it's bitter cold out, but I've this vision of sitting beneath the stars and gazing up at the night sky. It gets so dark here at night. I think that's the only thing I really would like to do, but I'll write the time on the whiteboard so we don't clash.'

I have a thing about stars too, but I won't mention that. The last thing we need is to find things in common.

'OK, great. Now, on to the big one. Sleeping arrangements,' I say over her gentle humming, which she stops almost as soon as she starts, as if she's remembered again that we're strangers and that it's just a tiny bit annoying. I think it might be a rather unbearable version of a well-known Christmas hymn I've heard before, but never in this way.

'OK, I don't expect to have the bedroom to myself every night, so I was thinking if you take the sofa bed again tonight, then you have the proper bed upstairs for the next two nights?' I suggest.

She is going to scrub a hole into her coat pocket if she carries on.

'You sure? That means a lot of changing of bedclothes,' she says without looking back at me. 'But yes, that sounds fair. Thank goodness one of us is organised or we'd be bumping into each other in the bedroom.'

She laughs, just a little, but I do my best to keep a straight face.

'Apparently bicarbonate of soda is a good way to remove oil from clothing,' I suggest as I watch her battle it out with yesterday's unforgiving stain.

'Bicarbonate of soda?'

'It might be too late but it's worth a try. Looks like an expensive coat.'

She stops and stares at the coat as if it's almost too good to be true. Then the rubber gloves come off again.

'*Bicarbonate of soda?*'

'Yes, you know, baking soda. I remember my mother doing it once. Or was it my aunt?' I try to recall where I've heard it from. 'It works, believe me.'

She turns away again and strokes the coat like she is remembering something, or maybe a time she wore it somewhere special.

'You're sure?'

I search the cupboards then set a small tub of bicarbonate of soda down on the worktop beside her.

'Thank you,' she replies, smiling as she stares at the little tub in wonder.

We stand side by side, perhaps a little bit too close. I step away immediately.

There is no denying she's very attractive. Her dark hair is soft and wavy, and she has this strange way of looking at me like she can read my mind.

'Isn't this blurring the boundaries a little?' she asks, raising an eyebrow. 'I thought we were going to communicate by text and only in emergencies?'

She smiles when she says it.

'You're right. It is.'

'That was meant to be a joke.'

'I know, but we both came here for solitude so let's make sure we get it,' I respond, going back to business-like mode. 'Now, I've cleared some space in the bathroom for your stuff, and I was thinking the wardrobe upstairs could be shared, just to keep the living room tidy. I'll take the left side, you take the right.'

She closes her eyes for a second.

'Ah Charlie, honestly,' she says.

'We only need to discuss this once.'

'Yes, and then we text the rest,' she replies. 'So, on that note, I think I'll go and make a start on moving in properly if you don't mind. Thanks for all your efforts. I'm sure we'll work it out just fine.'

She sounds exhausted.

'If you've anything more to contribute as we both settle in, feel free to—'

'Send you a text,' she says, holding up her phone. 'Even if I'm only in the next room or upstairs, I'll make sure it's only emergency contact from now on.'

She goes to walk away, but I call her back quickly.

'Rose?'

'Yes?'

'Are you finished with your coat?' I ask her. She's left it on the draining board and I'd really like to make some lunch soon.

'No, but I'll try out the bicarbonate of soda later. I think I'll go and unpack. It's been a long morning.'

She lifts the coat and glides out of the kitchen, leaving a trail of damp on the floor, perfume in the air and me with my list at the table as both dogs lie on the floor by my feet. George gets up to follow her. Max looks up at me with a tilt of his head.

'Don't panic,' I tell him, leaning down to ruffle his coat just as he likes me to. 'It's just teething problems. Wait and see.'

Chapter Nine

Rose

The little village that sits just half a mile away from Seaview Cottage calls out to me in the late afternoon after I've unpacked my belongings, and with every step I take in the snow, it feels like I'm walking back in time.

Granny Molly told me the story of how her father built the cottage many years ago with his own hands, every stone placed with tender loving care at a time when money was tight and things were so much simpler.

She'd take us here as children, my sister Sarah and I dressed in matching coats in winter or dresses in summer, and she'd show us off to everyone who so much as glanced our way.

I'm not sure yet if being here is healing or hindering, but for now I'll push through and hope that whatever is meant to be, will be, during my unexpected return.

Maybe that's why I was guided here in the first place. I don't usually believe in fate, but my grief has pushed me in every possible direction as I try and grapple with my new-found reality, and I'm open to any signs that will help me find my way through.

One day I was being whisked away on a surprise romantic trip here on Christmas Eve, the next I was planning a funeral.

'Life is like a journey with no map to guide you,' I say out loud to George who tiptoes beside me in the light fall of powdery snow. 'But we're doing OK, yeah, George? I'm doing my best to see that we're doing OK.'

I stop and breathe in the cold air, taking in the beauty and comfort of my surroundings. This place used to be my playground. These winding grey roads, the dips and turns, the wilds of the valleys that lead to the ocean and down to the lighthouse where I made my childhood wishes, so many of which did come true.

I feel my shoulders relax and my jaw loosen. This is my favourite place in the world. This is the place where I'll always feel like I belong.

Michael loved it here too.

We'd visit Fanad Lighthouse every year and make up the most ridiculous New Year Resolutions with the wind in our hair, paper cups of coffee to warm our hands and steam from our breath chasing the air as we looked out over the majestic expanse of Lough Swilly that stretches for miles across to Malin Head, the most northernly point of Ireland, and out into the Atlantic Ocean.

This year, I pledge to drink no beer until St Patrick's Day.

Michael's first resolution every single year, and always the first to be broken. He did Dry January once and I bought him one of those cheap medals with a ribbon to congratulate his efforts.

This is the year I'm going to learn how to speak a second language.

That was always my starting point, and so far I've taken up French, German and Italian at a very basic level, but it was enough to let Michael know that when I put my mind to something, I usually meant business. His mother, Evelyn, was very impressed. She always said I was such a good influence on him, which made him roll his eyes to the heavens.

I often think of Evelyn. My mother tells me she doesn't mix at all any more. She still prefers to grieve alone, taking no calls and no visitors. I wonder what she'll do this Christmas, alone now that both her son and her husband are gone. Every year my family invites her to join them, but every year she turns their invitation down, just like I do.

I take a deep breath and inhale the new surroundings which I'm hoping will lift my spirits, and at first glance they really do.

A frosted, bushy Christmas tree is perched proudly outside the dainty little sandstone chapel in the village, and it draws me closer to take a better look.

It has a life-size re-enactment of the Holy family outside by the Christmas tree, all set on a bed of straw, while festive carols are piped through a crackling sound system.

The various poky little shops, all painted in bright colours, are lit up with a golden, welcoming glow. It may only be four in the afternoon, but it's already dipping down dark and as the snow falls softly down on shoppers, many of them scurry for the Lighthouse Tavern, a cosy pub with traditional Irish music most evenings if my memory serves me right.

I haven't been here in a long, long time.

'Your face looks familiar,' the lady in the craft shop tells me as I browse around her impressive range of stationery, handmade cards and decorative bits and pieces which have me salivating when I think of what I could do with them.

Let Rose loose in a craft shop, and she'll make you a home in no time.

'I used to spend my summer holidays here, but I haven't been around these parts in many years,' I say, trying to focus on what the shop has to offer more than what its owner has to say. 'I must admit, I've a bit of a spring in my step just walking down memory lane.'

My family history is rooted in Fanad, so I'm not surprised I'm recognised even though many moons have passed since any of us were here, but I don't want to strike up too much conversation in case Rusty hasn't yet told Marion that I'm staying here and it gets back to her. As quaint as this area is, walls have ears and people talk. The last person I want to bring trouble to is Rusty, though I feel it might already be too late.

I feel bad for their marital problems, but it's not my place to comment. Marion is prickly with me, I can sense that, so it's best not to rock the boat by getting in any way involved. When Rusty's father inherited the cottage through a silly raffle-type agreement after Granny Molly died suddenly with no proper will . . . well, let's say some bridges were burned forever.

'How much for these?' I ask, holding up some scented pine cones.

I only came in here for a look around. It's not like I'd planned to get into the festive spirit by buying things, but I'm already being swept along by the atmosphere and warmth of the store.

'Aren't they sweet?' says the shop assistant. 'They're just two euros for three. My daughter made them. She's been able to turn her hand to anything since she was a teenager. I was the same before my arthritis kicked in.'

'I was the same as a teenager too,' I reply as my mind rolls back to Christmas at home when I used to be that girl. I was the one who went hunting in the forest for berries and holly. I used to spend hours making pretty decorations out of nothing. I gulp back tears. How I wish I could find that girl again. How I wish I could even get a glimpse of her once more.

I don't think she's gone away totally, but she's been taking a long break. My sister Sarah says my humour still shines through sometimes to show the old me, but I fear it's just a mask to hide what's really going on. Even how I joked earlier, ever so slightly, with Charlie. It was once so instinctive, but these days I wonder if it's just a nervous reaction when I try to make someone laugh.

I used to be the funny one. I used to be the life and soul of the party, the one with all the ideas, the one who loved Christmas.

I reach for a basket.

I slowly lift some of the scented pine cones and put them into the basket, and my heart gives a leap. What am I doing?

I only came in here to pass some time, but I can't help being whisked up in the sounds, smells and warm Christmas atmosphere.

There are bunches of fresh evergreen and holly in the window, perfect for making up colourful Christmas wreaths . . . I feel a rush run through my veins. There are multicoloured ribbons in silver, red and gold. There are little ornamental robins, there are gingerbread and cinnamon candles, and when I lift one to my nose, I'm instantly taken back to when this time of year filled me with gladness. I think of my mother's handmade decorations with a pang.

Decorate the tree for me, Rose, I hear her say as she so often did at Christmas. *No one can decorate the tree like you can.*

And then she'd sip a glass of cream liqueur, she'd put on 'O Holy Night', and she'd watch me with the same pride as a parent would watch their child if they'd just won Olympic Gold. It was our little moment, every year for as long as I can remember. 'O Holy Night' and the simplicity of decorating a tree for my mother. I suddenly realise I've been singing or humming the tune, albeit badly, since I got here.

I beam as I walk around the little shop, my heart beating in my chest with the thrill of all that's on offer. It's like the clock is speeding back in time and I can't stop myself.

My basket is already almost full of candles, holly and ribbons, glitter spray and a collection of cute mini-Christmas trees which are pre-lit with speckles of twinkling gold. I don't know what I'm going to do with all this stuff, but everything I touch takes me back to happier times.

Could I decorate Seaview Cottage with this lot? Would Charlie like that, or would it upset him if he's wanting to avoid Christmas? I can decide later on, but for now I'm experiencing something wonderful inside and it feels so good.

'Just shout if you need any help,' says the lady.

'I will,' I reply, as I glide around the shop, smelling and touching and closing my eyes with glee. I'm like a child in a candy store. I'm like my sister when she looks at her children. I'm like my mother when she hears Elvis Presley. I'm like my late Granny Molly let loose in a fancy boutique. I'm like my dad when he sees us all laughing together.

I'm in my element.

I glance out the front window to see George patiently waiting on me by the door. He isn't like most other dogs. He doesn't need to be fixed to anything, nor will he dash out onto the street. He is always happy to wait and to simply be by my side, so I know he'll come to no harm even though I'm taking a lot longer than I'd planned to in here.

'Oh my goodness, what's this?'

There's a little wooden music box for sale which gives me goosebumps when I open it, hoping it might play 'Love's Greeting', a delicate tune that reminds me of happy times here in this village with my Granny Molly, but it plays *The Nutcracker* instead. For a brief, delicious moment I think it might be the same music box as she had, but it isn't. It's beautiful, but not as beautiful as hers, so I put it back on the shelf.

There's so much to choose from. Sixteen-year-old me is in Christmas heaven.

I go to the till with my basket full of goodies. The scent of Christmas fills my senses and I know if the lady is nice to me at all, I might break down and cry. I need to stay strong. My emotions are sky high.

'This is a beautiful little nook you have here,' I say, hoping to keep my mind focused in my usual way, which is to talk my way through it. 'I could easily spend all my holiday allowance on candles and frosted pine cones.'

I've no idea where I'm going to put all this stuff, but I'm so overcome with nostalgia that I can't resist. I'm taking it as a sign. Up until now, the very thought of buying anything festive would make me feel sick.

'Are you OK, lovely?' the lady asks me, but I can barely respond as my breath catches in my throat.

There's a warmth in her voice that soothes my broken heart. Her name badge says 'Lorraine' in a fussy, swirly font that the marketer in me wants to ask her to change to something simpler.

'I'm fine,' I reply, but my eyes are giving me away. I stop. I wonder. I'm caught up in this hazy daze of limbo where I don't really know if it's Christmas or it isn't. And yet, here I am with a basket of decorations that I don't even know what I'm going to do with.

'You're not fine at all, are you?' Lorraine asks me. Her kind, motherly approach almost knocks me off my feet.

'I'm just . . .'

'Go on.'

'Well, it's been . . . it's been a few years since I felt like buying anything like this. I've been avoiding Christmas for a while.'

She nods like she's heard it all before as she carefully places all my decorations into two brown paper bags. Then she pauses.

'My mother always said that Christmas can be the happiest time of year now, but then the saddest time of year when we meet it next, eh?'

I nod in agreement. A tear threatens to escape. I beg it not to.

'Your mother is a wise woman,' I say, my voice cracking. I take a long breath.

'Take your time, be kind to yourself and you'll get through it.'

I nod.

'I know I will.' I close my eyes.

'Oh, love.'

'Yet here I am in a little shop in a village I once loved buying decorations again,' I say with a nervous laugh. 'I wasn't expecting this at all. Sorry, I'm a bit overwhelmed.'

She doesn't shy away. I don't know why I blurted all of that out to her, but it felt strangely OK to do so.

'Just always do whatever feels right for you and take each day as it comes,' she whispers to me as another customer enters the shop, gasping in admiration at all its delights, just as I did some minutes ago. 'There are no rules, nor is there any rush on grief, my love. And just the same, there is no right or wrong time to smile again after we lose someone close. So, never be afraid to smile again, please remember that. If something or someone makes you smile, then mark it down as a very good day.

You deserve many more good days, and you will find them. You'll see.'

Oh God, I think I'm going to break down in front of her just as I feared I might.

I breathe.

'I like that. I'll remember your words. Thank you.'

I marvel at how such a small step in a new direction has made me just a little bit stronger, even if my emotions are on edge right now.

I pay her with my card, then I lift the two large paper bags from the counter, glancing to where George waits in the doorway.

'Happy Christmas,' she calls after me. 'And I mean that sincerely. I wish you a happy Christmas.'

'I'm Rose,' I say in return, and I open the door to leave with a fuzzy feeling inside of me. 'Rose Quinn. Happy Christmas to you and your daughter too.'

Her eyes light up as the penny drops.

'Ah, of course you are,' she says with a knowing smile. 'You have your Granny Molly's impeccable style and her beautiful green eyes. I should have known. It's so lovely to meet you, Rose Quinn.'

'And you too, Lorraine. Happy Christmas.'

'The white chocolate and raspberry scones are just out of the oven. I made a few extra. You're welcome to try one.'

'You're spoiling me, Sean.'

Sean tilts his head to the side, his notepad in hand and his pen in mid-air. The café is buzzing now, in stark contrast to the empty version I visited just a day ago.

'For purely selfish reasons. I like to see George coming through the door.'

'Gee thanks. And not me?'

He chuckles and puts his hand on my shoulder.

'I'm teasing you, of course. Now, a cinnamon latte like before?'

'Yes, please.'

'Just like before. My pleasure, my dear,' he says as he shuffles away, mumbling to himself. 'I'll get some water for your gentleman friend. We mustn't forget about George. Some water and a treat for good old George and a coffee and scone for the lady.'

The place is full up with cold and hungry revellers, and I pull myself together after my unexpected shopping spree, but my phone bleeps to announce a text message just in time to distract me from sinking further into the past.

I've left the key under the mat.

It's Charlie.

I've also asked Rusty to get us another key so we don't have to share. He said it's the least he can do. He'll put it in an envelope and drop it through the letterbox later.

Charlie is on top of his game as always, which gives me a surprising sense of ease and comfort, despite his list of rules. I've felt so much at sea over the past few years, yet already after just one day back here in my happy place, I'm breathing again.

Thank you, I type in return. I set my phone back on to the table, but it bleeps again.

> Got some fresh bread and milk too. Whiteboard is on the fridge for any food-related messages.

I laugh out loud at his sincerity, which is rather sweet, but I can't resist nudging him just a little when I notice something.

Do you always use full stops at the end of your text messages? I reply, childishly.

I hope I haven't offended him. I'm just poking a little. I'm still giddy from earlier, but hopefully the coffee and scone will bring me back to earth again gently.

You don't miss much, he writes back straight away. Have a good day!

And then another one.

> Exclamation marks are used frequently too, which might be equally irritating, so apologies in advance!!!

So, he does have a sense of humour after all. I could grow to like Charlie and his comforting ways, but I know it isn't part of the deal. We need to keep our distance.

Sean arrives with George's water bowl and sets it carefully on the floor, spilling a little as he bends down.

'Whoops-a-daisy. Someone was thirsty,' he says, looking very pleased with himself as George laps it up. 'Nice to see you smiling, anyhow.'

I raise my eyebrows.

'Who, me or George?'

'You, silly,' he replies. 'Not being nosey, love, but you were grinning away at your phone just now, which is lovely to see.'

'I was?'

'Yes, and it really suits you to smile like that,' he tells me. 'I'll go fetch your coffee. Won't be long.'

Chapter Ten

Charlie

I press Clodagh's number on my phone and rub my hands together as I wait for my daughter to answer my call. I've been counting down the days, hours and minutes until this moment and now that it's here, I feel like I might burst with anticipation.

It's pitch dark outside. The snow is falling heavily and I'm sitting by the fire in a quiet pub, the Lighthouse Tavern, with a bowl of mussels and a pint of Guinness in front of me for Dutch courage.

It's Friday at last.

To be more precise, it's 6 p.m. on Friday at last, which means it's time for my weekly FaceTime call with my most beautiful girl.

My Rebecca.

The screen lights up with a photo of Rebecca and her mum, both wearing sunglasses and pink floppy hats, smiling in the Tenerife sunshine, a world away from me.

Let's keep it to one weekly chat until we get her settled in, Clodagh told me. *It's not good to upset her in the run-up to*

Christmas by seeing you too often. Give her a chance to acclimatise then we'll come to another arrangement.

I breathe slowly. A little faster than usual, but then there's nothing usual about this whole sorry set-up. Since Clodagh and her new husband, who she seemed to only have met five minutes ago, decided to whisk my seven-year-old daughter off to a new life in a foreign country, my whole world has been turned on its axis.

Rebecca doesn't keep me waiting. She picks up on the second ring. Oh God, she's been waiting for this as much as I have.

'DADDY!'

My nose twitches. My eyes sting. She's already lightly tanned and her blue eyes sparkle as she speaks, her little lisp fading as her new front teeth push through. Her olive skin, which she gets from my side of the family, has taken nicely to her new life in the Mediterranean sun, even though it's winter. And as much as I try to deny it, she already looks so different to the little girl I said goodbye to six weeks ago when she boarded a plane for a new life far away from home.

'Look at you!' I whisper, as my vision goes cloudy.

I blink. I don't cry. I will never cry in front of my daughter.

'Hello, Daddy!'

'Oh Rebecca, baby. It's so good to see your pretty face again at last. How are you? Are you—'

I want to ask if she's looking forward to Santa but the words stick in my throat.

'It's only eight days till Christmas but it's so sunny here, Daddy. It's so weird.'

'No snowmen then?'

She giggles and puts her hand over her mouth. Her tiny nails are painted turquoise. She used to love me painting her nails. Sometimes, when I wanted to make her laugh out loud, I'd let her paint mine too.

'A snowman would melt here, silly,' she replies with a frown. 'There's a grotto at the supermarket but Santa is wearing shorts so he's not the real one. His beard is light and he's far too skinny to be Santa.'

I inhale her every word.

'Have you spotted any elves over that direction?'

She purses her rosebud lips.

'I'm not sure the elves know I'm living here yet, but Mum says they'll know by the time Christmas comes. Do you think they will, Daddy?'

'I'm sure they'll find you, darling. Santa knows everything, and the elves are always on the ball if a child moves house, so don't worry about that at all.'

How can I not be part of this? I used to have these conversations daily with my little girl when she'd light up as I told her stories all year round of talking animals, wild adventures of made-up characters and my own childhood memories. But the excitement of Christmas was always the best story fodder of all, and we'd while away hours chatting about the antics of Santa and his elves.

How can so much change in so little time? Her mum and I haven't been an item for years but we'd a tight family unit in place, meaning that Rebecca always came first. Christmas was always spent together, so we both could never miss out on the magic of these innocent years.

Girlfriends came into my life, Clodagh met some nice people along the way too, but Christmas was always ours to spend with Rebecca. Until Rob came along and swept them both away for a new life in the sun. Before I could get to know him well or even take in his big plans for my daughter, they were gone.

'Tell me more. What else have you been up to?'

My heart is thumping with the ticking of the clock. I already don't want to say goodbye, yet at the same time seeing her is tearing me apart from the inside out. I've never known pain like this. Maybe this is heartbreak? Is this how it feels when your heart is broken into pieces?

'Um . . . I got a new wetsuit and, er . . .'

She pauses for thought, her blue eyes looking upwards as she thinks.

'Any new friends yet?'

She lights up.

'Yes . . . well, no. Not really. I did make one new friend but he's only here on holiday,' she tells me. 'But Mum says I'll make lots of new friends once I start my new school after Christmas.'

'Of course you will, baby,' I say, wishing I could reach into the phone and give her a hug.

'Are you sad, Daddy?' she asks me. 'You look a bit sad.'

I bite my lip and then force a smile. Even the sound of her sweet little voice is enough to make me weep.

'No, I'm not sad at all, sweetheart, I've just something in my eye,' I say quickly.

'Like an eyelash or something? Remember when that happened to me and it came out by itself like you said it would?'

'I remember,' I reply. I remember everything.

'You need a haircut,' she giggles. 'It's so long.'

I ruffle my hair, pulling it forward, and she laughs out loud.

'Oi, I think I suit it like this. What do you think?'

'No!' she squeals. 'Get it cut!'

'I want it to grow as long as yours,' I joke. 'How can your hair be so long already?'

Her eyes widen as she gets to talk about one of her favourite things. She tips her head back like she always does to make her straight brown hair seem even longer than it really is.

'I want to be like Pocahontas. Look, Daddy, it's nearly to my waist.'

I feel my stomach twist. Even the creamy pint of Guinness and the bowl of steaming hot mussels can't distract me from my favourite face.

'Oh, guess what?'

'What?'

'Good guess!'

She rolls her eyes and giggles.

'Just tell me, Daddy! You don't need to always say guess what.'

'OK, I've been dying to tell you this,' I announce proudly. 'I've downloaded an app to help me learn Spanish so I can keep up with you when you go to your new school in the New Year.'

'Cool!'

My heart crushes in my chest. I touch her face on the screen again, and the distance between us feels so real. The day she took her first steps comes to mind. The day I taught her to ride her first bike. So many firsts still lie ahead, yet I'm going to miss them all.

'And maybe I can even still help you with your homework? We can Zoom to do it together. We'll make it happen, I'll make sure of it.'

I spot a plush, very expensive-looking Christmas tree twinkling behind her on the polished tiled white floor of her new home. I try to ignore her mother's feet walking past in the background, but my blood boils at the sight of Clodagh, even if it's just her feet in her whole new world. I do my best to shake it off. I've already said all I have to say about her decision to make her big move to Tenerife, especially leaving just before Christmas.

'I can't imagine you speaking Spanish, Daddy,' Rebecca giggles.

'Oh, really? Well, I can already speak Italian and a little bit of Irish, remember?'

'I do remember. OK, maybe you *could* learn it,' she replies, tucking her hair behind her ears to show off tiny new stud earrings. 'Rob's already taught me hello, goodbye, dog and cat.'

'That's kind of him.'

Rob is ahead of the game as always. I'm so glad that Rebecca is totally unaware of the pain I'm feeling right now.

'Me, Mummy and Rob are all learning ten words together every week so that when I go to school, I've got a head start,' she explains.

Me, Mummy and Rob.

I force a smile but my heart cracks a little bit more with every attempt I make to be fine with this situation. He doesn't miss a trick, good old Rob. Always at least ten steps, never mind ten words, ahead of anything I have to offer when it comes to my seven-year-old daughter.

I'm always the last to know about everything she does now that Rob is on the scene. Rich kid Rob, with his fancy house in the Canaries, who has whisked my only child away to a place where she doesn't understand the language or why it's sunny at Christmastime.

It will never last, Niall told me as soon as he heard of Clodagh's whirlwind wedding and plans to pack up and go, all within months. *Wait and see. Too much too soon is never a good thing, believe me.*

It's not that I wish my ex any unhappiness. I just wish she'd stayed in the same country so we can co-parent our child.

'Where are you?' Rebecca asks me. 'Where's Max? Is Helena with you?'

I bite my lip as my eyes sting again at the thought of the long stretch to Easter when I'll see Rebecca again in real life.

'No, darling,' I sigh. 'Helena is staying at her own place this Christmas so it's just me and Max here.'

'Can I see him?'

I flip the phone screen to show Max snoozing by the open fire.

'We're spending Christmas in a very pretty cottage in Donegal,' I say quickly, hoping that seeing Max doesn't make her homesick. 'It's in a place called Fanad where we used to take you when you were very little. Do you remember?'

She does a double-take.

'Is that near the lighthouse?'

'It sure is,' I reply, marvelling at how she forgets nothing. 'It's just a short walk from the lighthouse.'

'Cool.'

'Yes, it's very cool. It's freezing, actually.'

She rolls her eyes at my attempt at a joke, then goes quiet.

'Are you and Max . . . are you there by *yourselves*, Daddy?' she asks, her eyes wide. 'Not by yourselves at *Christmas*? Why did you not bring Helena?'

I choke back emotion at her concern, plus I've no idea how to explain it to her. Why *did* I not bring Helena?

'Well, I . . .'

Her lip trembles.

'I don't want you to be on your own, Daddy,' she whimpers. 'Not at Christmas. Not ever.'

'No, no, don't worry. I'm not staying on my *own* at Christmas,' I say, quickly lifting my tone of voice to calm the tears that are filling her eyes. 'I have Max.'

'But he's just a dog.'

'Ah, now Max is more than just a dog. He's my buddy.'

'But he can't talk to you.'

I need to think fast. I know by her face that she's close to tears.

'Well, there's a very nice lady called Rose who is staying at the cottage too,' I add, not sure where I'm going with this one. 'And *she* can talk to me.'

I flounder at the irony. I've made a rule that we don't actually 'talk'.

'She has a lovely black and white dog called George, so both Max and I have company. George and Max are already great friends. So, no need to worry. We're not on our own at all here.'

When I say it like that, it does sound quite idyllic, even though my cosy description couldn't be further from the truth. I haven't seen Rose since this morning. So far, we've been doing very well to keep out of each other's way.

'Is Rose pretty?'

My eyes widen.

'Um, yes, she is very pretty,' I reply.

'Is she a *new* friend?'

'Yes, she's a new friend.'

'A new *girlfriend*?'

'Er, well . . .'

I'm stumped by her question but I don't get the chance to say anything at all. Rebecca is already shouting an update on my life to the rooftops.

'Mum, Daddy has a new girlfriend called Rose and she has a dog called George!'

'Rebecca, no, she isn't my new girlfriend,' I say, trying to keep up. I see Clodagh's feet walk past again but this time they stop. 'She's a new friend. Not a girlfriend.'

'That's nice,' I hear Clodagh say to our daughter. 'Now, we need to go soon, Rebecca, so say goodbye to Daddy and let's get you ready for the beach. Rob is taking the boat out for the evening.'

The boat. Why am I even surprised he has a boat? Rob has everything.

'But I'm not finished talking,' Rebecca chimes. 'I have to tell Daddy about my new earrings and—'

'They're very pretty, honey.'

Here we go. The big goodbye is on its way again.

'It's time, Rebecca,' says Clodagh. 'We want to be there to see the sun set.'

I close my eyes and count away the seconds as my blood pumps through my veins. Four minutes and thirty-five seconds. Is that it? Is she for real? I've waited all week for this call and she can barely give me five minutes with my child?

I bite my tongue for Rebecca's sake. I always bite my tongue for Rebecca's sake.

'But I don't want to hang up yet,' says Rebecca. 'I want to see where he's staying and I want to see Rose and George.'

I hear muffled conversation in the background. I see Rebecca's eyes dart to and from the camera as her mother fusses some more and I know if I do too it will only make this whole moment worse.

Deep breaths.

'Run along and have fun,' I tell my daughter, desperately trying to ignore the knot in my stomach and the words that threaten to trip off my tongue to Clodagh, who always seems to have the upper hand when it comes to my relationship with Rebecca. 'We can catch up again very soon. Tell Mummy to please keep sending me photos.'

'But—'

'Rebecca!'

'I posted all your presents before I left,' I tell her, hoping to divert her fears, 'so maybe when they arrive you could ask Mummy to let me know?'

She gasps and her eyes that were just now filled with sadness light up, which makes me happy too, even if our call is cut short.

'My presents? Thank you, Daddy, you're the best!'

I don't feel like the best, sitting here with our dog at my feet without her.

'I love you, Rebecca,' I say, trying to swallow the lump in my throat. 'I love you so much, don't ever forget that.'

This is too hard. My heart is aching right now in a way I never even thought was possible.

I can't bear to spend Christmas without my daughter.

'I love you too, Daddy, to the moon and back and round the world a million times.'

I nod, unable to repeat the words we would say to each other every night when I used to tuck her into bed. How have I gone from seeing my daughter every night of her life, to then twice a week to now only being able to see her on a phone screen thousands of miles away? How did I let this happen?

She hangs up the call and I stare into the dancing flames as Christmas songs jingle in the background and a bunch of old men laugh on high stools at the bar.

Just another eight days and all this festive fuss will be over, I remind myself. Then it's the countdown until I see my baby girl again.

Christmas will come and Christmas will go, but at least I can go back to the cottage where I can hide away and just pretend it isn't happening.

When the song 'Fairytale of New York' strikes up from the one-man band in the corner, and the few revellers at the bar decide to join in with the iconic sounds of Shane and Kirsty singing, I know it's time for me to try and get out of here.

There is no fairy-tale ending to my Christmas this year. Clodagh and her new husband with their boat and their sunsets have made mighty sure of that.

Chapter Eleven

Rose

As late evening comes around, every one of my fingers is red raw from twisting and bending metal coat hangers to make a Christmas wreath for the front door of Seaview Cottage.

With a mix of berried holly and bushy fern, I've added some gold ribbon and some battery-operated lights which twinkle and glow, making the place feel more festive already from the outside in, which is so far from what I ever intended.

Carlos called earlier, and I was glad that this time I was able to be a lot more honest with my surroundings.

'So, Maeve and Yvonne are totally off scent. They're happy to know you're up north with your parents but are already planning a post-Christmas Secret Santa gathering since we didn't have a chance to get together before,' he chimes, as I listen to him on loudspeaker. 'Everything is calming down at work, but I can see you're logging in every morning, which is so unnecessary.'

'It is for my own sanity. I've a fifteen-minute curfew and I'm just being nosey,' I replied, as I fixed a new set of batteries into another string of lights.

'And in other news,' Carlos said, 'I've a date tonight but I'm not going to bore you with the details as it will probably fall flat on its face as always. My love life is like a pancake. A gluten-free pancake for that matter – I simply have bad taste.'

'Ah Carlos, you're too hard on yourself,' I told him, while secretly acknowledging he wasn't far from the truth. No wonder we are such great friends. We are both hapless.

'I'll keep checking in so you're never alone for too long,' he told me before he headed off for lunch. 'Text me if you're lonely. You hear?'

'I hear!' I replied and pushed away the idea of my three friends huddled together over a cosy pub lunch in Dublin, where no doubt they'd be talking about how they didn't know what to do with me any more.

Now, with a warm glass of mulled wine in my hands, I stand back to admire all my hard work this evening.

The smell of cinnamon and gingerbread fills the air from the candles in the hallway, an evergreen garland decorated with robins and tiny red and silver baubles lines the mantelpiece in the living room, and another is wound around the banister that leads upstairs.

I've scattered mini trees in coloured pots around the various rooms, including the kitchen, where I've also added a deep red tablecloth and a candelabra, which I've slotted candles into.

Everything feels so much more seasonal already. Although I may not be in the mood for celebration this year, decorating the house has kept me occupied. It's an unexpected baby step forward to finding myself again, and I'm very pleased with the outcome.

'So, George, what do you think? Do you think Santa will pay us a visit here in Donegal?' I ask my canine companion. 'It may be a little bit too remote, even for Santa, but we can always live in hope.'

George responds by wagging his tail. I've no doubt he knows exactly what I'm saying. He can always pick up when I'm feeling low or when I'm excited about something. He even knows when I need some space or when to stay out of my way on the rare occasions I'm not in the mood for cuddles.

I used to always be in the mood for Christmas too, but when I picture Christmas Day here with no presents and no fancy dinner, no family board games and no snoozing off the turkey by the fire with a belly full of pudding and a few too many glasses of wine, my heart sinks.

I plonk down on the sofa as the lights twinkle around me like tiny dancing stars and the flames in the open hearth keep up with their tune. Even though I'm delighted on the outside with all my handiwork, I still can't seem to fix myself, nor can I change the past.

It's like a sea of darkness, a strange stillness that reeks of anxiety and the sound of silence that deafens you from within.

I am alone and it's suffocating me.

I lift my phone and scroll through the names I've collected through the years. I can't tell my sister I'm here. She would be on the doorstep in a heartbeat demanding that I come home. And I can't go home in case I bump into any of Michael's friends or extended family, which would make my grief even darker. I can't call Carlos or he'll tell me off for not switching off and enjoying my time away.

And then I come to his number. I scroll past it and then I scroll back to it.

I've never had the strength to delete it. My thumb hovers over his name.

Michael.

But what would happen if I called his number now? Would it ring out when my name appeared? Would it go to his voicemail? Would I hear even just a few seconds of his warm, familiar voice just one more time?

Does anyone even have his phone still? What if some stranger has his number now? Or maybe Evelyn kept it . . .

Charlie's arrival stops me from hitting 'dial' and finding out, which is probably a good thing.

I drop my phone onto the sofa, but a WhatsApp from Charlie makes me pick it up again quickly.

What's with all the decorations?

Oh dear.

I thought you were here to forget Christmas like I am . . .

He is literally on the other side of the door. Why can't he just come in and talk about this instead of this stupid text only arrangement?

My own mood crashes to the floor.

I thought it might cheer us both up, I reply.

Wrong, he writes back. You should have discussed this with me first.

Really? I breathe slowly through my nose. Talk about an over-reaction . . .

The tip worked by the way, I say, in a bid to change the subject swiftly.

The what?

The bicarbonate of soda on my coat? The stain is gone so my coat lives to see another day.

I wish you'd messaged me before decorating the place.

I hear him rummage about in the kitchen, pulling out pots and pans and muttering to himself as he does so. I feel claustrophobic and confined in this living room now that he's back. Gosh, I didn't honestly think I'd done much harm with a few fairy lights here and there. It took me ages to make that wreath on the door.

I'll be using the kitchen for the next hour to cook a late dinner, he tells me in his next text.

My eyes sting with tears. He's being a prick, but I don't want to argue with him. I don't have the energy, nor do I want to make matters worse.

Yes, I should have let him know what I was doing, but it's not like I'd planned it. I surprised myself more than anyone when I found myself lost in the moment that made me feel good about myself again.

Now, I just feel stupid.

Work away, Charlie. The kitchen is all yours.

I press send, switch on the TV, search through Netflix and snuggle down to watch *Home Alone* for the hundredth time in the hope it might make me feel better. It was a family favourite when I was growing up and I need some comfort now.

As I lie down on the sofa, pull a fleecy blanket around me and fluff up my pillow, I can't help but feel sorry for myself. It was a giant leap forward for me to find the urge to make decorations like I used to, plus the conversation with Lorraine in the craft shop really filled me up inside.

But I feel silly and selfish now that I've had my knuckles rapped by Charlie. I should have been more sensitive to his feelings since we're both sharing such a tiny space.

The bubble is burst. The brief glimmer of festive cheer is gone. I pick up my phone and message him one last time.

I'll take everything down by morning.

I must have fallen asleep during the movie.

I wake with a crick in my neck, remembering how I'd dreamed that an evil version of Macaulay Culkin was chasing my sister Sarah and me while tugging a huge Christmas tree behind him.

I long to tell her so, but I know if I message her now I'll get the usual plea from her to come home and spend Christmas with my family, when I've made it very clear that I'm not ready for that just yet.

If she knew I'd come to Granny Molly's cottage, she would have a fit.

Sarah knows how much I need space at this time of year, so she doesn't push, but if I give an inch then she'll try to convince me to walk a mile. I really do miss her so much.

My latest message from her was just today, in a very vague check-in as she knows I go underground at this time of year.

You OK? We miss you.

All good, I replied, with a close-up photo of George wearing tinsel on his collar. I was careful not to give away any of the background as my sister could spot this cottage and its surroundings in a heartbeat.

The TV has gone on standby and the only sound in the cottage, apart from the ticking clock above the hearth, is the muffled sound of Charlie's deep voice from the kitchen. He must be on the phone, which is no mean feat considering the mobile reception here is glitchy to say the least.

His voice comes closer as he moves into the hallway, I assume, for better reception.

'Yes, I can hear you now,' he says, sounding a lot jollier than he was to me before. 'Yes, that's better. It's nice to hear your voice too. So, what were you asking?'

I tug the soft blanket beneath my chin with one hand and scramble around to find the remote control for the telly with the other. I didn't intend to fall asleep so soon. It's only just past ten so no doubt I'll be up half the night now, though I am a little bit peckish.

'Yes, I have lots of decorations up in the cottage, so it's very Christmassy,' I hear Charlie say now.

Really?

He has lots of decorations up?

The smell of his night-time cooking fills the cottage, mingling in with the smouldering turf from the fire beside me. I should really top it up before it goes out, but I'm intrigued now to know who he is talking to.

I sit up a little on the sofa, dropping the remote back onto the floor where I'd just found it.

'There's a handmade frosted wreath on the front door made up with lights and gold ribbon,' I hear him say. 'Yes, lots and lots of twinkling lights around the banister and on all the picture frames.'

Seriously?

'I'll send photos, of course. And in the hallway, there are candles that smell like cinnamon and gingerbread – you'd love them.'

I'm very confused.

'It's all very festive and cheery here, so you've nothing to worry about. I'm managing just fine.'

I slowly sit up straighter, hoping that George doesn't bark so I can hear some more of the conversation. Who the hell is he talking to? And where did he suddenly get all this newfound Christmas spirit from? He hated the decorations just a couple of hours ago and now he sounds like an enthusiastic interiors vlogger, or someone who's had a personality transplant.

'Yes, I had a few pints earlier before dinner *and* I spoke to Rebecca too, which was lovely. She misses you,' he continues, sounding very cheery and very un-Charlie. 'Did you like the photo of the village Christmas tree? Yes, I thought you'd like that one. The manger is very special.'

He pauses. I can hear my own pulse in my ears as I strain to listen.

'I miss you too, Helena,' he replies softly.

Oh . . .

'But I'll be home before you know it and we have so much to look forward to in the new year . . . I know, I know you do, darling.'

He speaks so tenderly. I know nothing about the man, really, so it's very strange to hear him talk like this to someone from his real life.

'Now, I hope you haven't opened your presents early – I know what you're like, and there are still a few days to go . . .'

He pauses and laughs in a way I haven't heard him do before, but then our conversations have been very stilted and minimized to date.

'I love you too,' he whispers. 'Enjoy your day tomorrow and tell the girls I say hello.'

More laughter.

'OK, I'd better go. Max needs to go outside before it gets too late, and you know I'm usually asleep by now. I'll call you tomorrow. Bye darling, bye.'

Why isn't Charlie with his girlfriend at the most wonderful time of the year? Maybe Helena is in a foreign country and they can't travel to see each other, or maybe she works as a nurse or doctor and is tied up for Christmas. Or maybe he's having an affair, and he's running away from reality just like I am.

We're clearly in very different situations, but perhaps Charlie and I have a lot more in common than we first thought.

I hear him call Max and they make their way upstairs, giving me space to make a dash to the kitchen for a quick snack from the fridge.

I switch on the kitchen light, almost tiptoeing in case I disturb him. But when the room lights up, the first thing I notice is the scrawl on the magnetic whiteboard fixed to the fridge door.

He has left me a message that doesn't involve bread or milk, or any food supplies for that matter.

Sorry about earlier. I'm a bit of a Grinch these days. Your decorations are lovely. Thanks for trying. Sorry for being a dickhead. Charlie.

Oh.

I'm a bit flummoxed to say the least. So he does have a heart in there somewhere.

I pull the marker from the clip beside the board, wipe his message off and write my own message so that he'll get it in the morning.

Apology accepted. Even the Grinch was misunderstood, I reply. *Have a lovely day.*

Seven Days to Christmas

Chapter Twelve

Charlie

I didn't mean to sleep so late, but even Max is still snoozing when I eventually do wake up, so maybe we needed the lie-in.

I could blame the few drinks and the big dinner I had when I got back from the pub for keeping me up until almost eleven. Or the fact that the book I've been reading has disappeared from my bedside locker. I like to read before I sleep – I always have – but last night I found myself scrolling through my phone, which did more to keep me awake than knock me out.

I'm sure the book will turn up at some stage. I'll ask Rose if she's seen it, though I'll have to tread carefully. I suspect I was a bit too sharp with her last night over the decorations. I did apologise on the whiteboard, but maybe I should have done it in person.

Shit, I feel awful now.

The more I looked around me at the effort she'd made, the guiltier I felt at being so tart, but it was unexpected to say the least. I really believed she was as anti-Christmas as I've been feeling coming here.

I check my phone to see the usual string of missed calls from Helena and throw myself down on the bed again.

I'm not able to switch off at all like I'd hoped to while I'm here.

Last night's call with Rebecca knocked me for six, and the guilt of leaving Helena for Christmas is never far away. Then there's this insane living arrangement with Rose who I've managed to unintentionally offend already over something as silly as a few twinkling lights and candles.

What's happening to me? Am I turning into some sort of grumpy old man who hates everything and everyone?

Max stretches out his paws and opens his eyes slowly. I find watching him wake up soothing and it makes me feel a little bit better.

'I suppose we don't have to get up at a certain time if we don't want to, eh? We're on holiday after all. Well, at least we're supposed to be.'

Max obviously fully agrees as he curls into a ball at the bottom of the bed and drifts off to sleep again, but when I close my eyes, I imagine Rebecca playing happy families with her new stepdad on his luxury boat as the sun sets behind them, learning more new Spanish words with him and laughing as they sail. I see him giving her a 'gold star' then patting her head as she grins up at him.

I try to think of how I'd advise my clients if any of them were to be in this position. I'd probably say to think of the child's happiness even though you're feeling broken inside.

Yes, I would try to divert their agony. So, I do just that for myself.

I picture my daughter's smile with the wind in her hair as she sails, and this does ease the ache in my heart a little bit. I visualise her toothy grin, her long dark hair and her sheer sense of wonder and innocence.

She seems happy, so that should make me happy too.

I'd better get up and shower, but before I do, a text from Niall stops me from making a move just yet.

Your to-do list whilst in Fanad, he writes to me.

It can be quiet there in winter, but don't be lonely. Keep busy.

1. Drive out to Glenevin Waterfall if the weather allows it
2. Sit by the famous Fanad lighthouse and inhale the ocean. So good for the soul!
3. Meet the locals, say hello to everyone you meet in the Lighthouse Tavern
4. Take some photos at the Great Pollet Sea Arch, even more beautiful under the dark sky and stars
5. Marvel at the amazing views as you drive along the scenic Mamore Gap – it will make you feel alive!

As Albert Einstein said: 'A table, a chair, a bowl of fruit and a violin. What else does a man need to be happy?' You get the drift! Call me if you need to. You've got this.

I laugh out loud at Niall's words of wisdom, tailed off as usual by a quote or two.

But I know he's right. I didn't come here to mope.

And maybe Rose is right. Maybe trying to deny it's Christmas is just making it harder for us both. I can't deny that the decorations are beautiful. Rose has great talent and taste, even if I couldn't admit that last night. I was too busy feeling maudlin after my brief encounter with my daughter so far away that I couldn't see any joy, nor could I bear to see how the rest of the world can carry on regardless.

I do wonder why she's here, but I'll never cross the line to ask her. That's the sort of thing that friends confide in one another, and if I can't 'do' Christmas, I certainly can't 'do' new friendships either.

Rose seems nice and I didn't mean to offend her, but the last thing I came here for was company.

'I'd better go shower,' I say to Max, wondering again how I've come to talking to my dog as if he can hold a proper conversation. 'But I'll take you outside to do your morning business first. Come on then.'

Max bounds down the stairs ahead of me. I must admit the smell of cinnamon and gingerbread in the hallway is rather pleasant, and dare I say, even a little bit comforting too. It is nostalgic, a reminder of happier times with Clodagh and Rebecca.

My own childhood Christmas memories couldn't be more different, filled with resentful silence at the table, and my parents' drink-fuelled arguments. When Rebecca came along, I was determined her Christmases would not reflect mine. That I would embody everything good about Christmas and shine it back onto her.

Until now. Now I just want quiet and to pretend it's simply not happening. Not without her.

I tiptoe past the living room and let Max out, hoping we don't disturb George who in turn would wake up Rose, and I go to the kitchen expecting to see the usual carnage from Rose's late-night mulled wine and midnight feast, but to my surprise everything is clean and tidy.

I need coffee before I hit the shower, so I put on some soft classical music whilst I flick on the kettle. As I wait for it to brew, I spot a note on the whiteboard on the fridge, which makes me smile.

At least she isn't going to hold a grudge. That would be awkward.

'Oh, I didn't hear you up. Sorry. Excuse me. I just need some water.'

Rose saunters into the kitchen, pale-faced and smudgy-eyed in her fleecy pyjamas. She goes to the sink and fills a pint glass of water. I don't speak. Neither does she. Now *this* is awkward.

I glance her way as I wait on the kettle but there is no eye contact. Should I say something? I mean, I know I set all of these rules to make sure we don't become too familiar, but should I greet her good morning now that our paths have inevitably crossed?

I meet her eye at last on her way out. She waves a silent, sheepish hello. I wave back.

Her pale cheeks are now flushed but her exit shuffle is quickly interrupted by Max, who leaps into the kitchen with something in his mouth that makes Rose squeal.

'That's mine!' she says, holding her glass of water in mid-air. 'Max, give me that right now!'

Oh no. This has gone from awkward to mortifying at record speed.

Max has a turquoise lace bra in his mouth and is having great fun playing chase now that Rose is trying to get it off him.

'Max! Max, put that down right away!' I shout, knowing I may as well be talking to the wall as Max bounces from side to side, under the kitchen table, behind chairs and into any corner he can find. Anywhere to avoid our reach.

He isn't listening, of course. He thinks I'm playing.

'Max! Max, come here immediately!' I try again.

'Don't pull it from him!' Rose tells me. 'That cost me a fortune!'

But just as I'd have predicted, the more I chase Max, the more he runs away from me. He bobs and coils around the kitchen as George barks beside Rose, who thankfully is now laughing at the sight of me chasing my dog with her underwear in his mouth. He makes for the kitchen door and I've no choice but to run around the house behind him, begging him to drop it. He leads me upstairs at lightning speed, where I eventually corner him under the bed. The bra is thankfully discarded on the bedroom floor and at last the game is over.

'Max, you don't *do* that!' I scold, and he has the grace to look briefly sorry for his actions. 'You don't take other people's belongings!'

He buries his face in his paws as if he can't take my scolding while I stand up and get my breath back.

'Rose?'

I can hear her laughing to herself downstairs.

'You can come up here and get your belongings, Rose,' I call down the stairs, having decided that it would be very inappropriate for me to touch a stranger's underwear, even if my dog has just had it in his mouth. 'Rose?'

'My belongings? Can't you bring it down with you?' she shouts back at me. 'It's only a bra, Charlie, it won't burn you.'

She is finding this highly amusing, which I admit is better than her going crazy over it. I know that in a few minutes I probably will find it amusing too, but I've tried hard to establish strict boundaries, and this is about as far from them as I could have imagined.

I bend down and pick up the bra with two fingers, holding it at arm's length and trying not to look at it too closely, but as I walk down the stairs my eyes divert towards it as if they've a mind of their own.

It's a rather fetching colour, I must admit. It's made of lace and mesh . . . and I should really stop looking at it. Rose has a unique look with how she dresses and presents herself, so I'm not surprised at her glamorous choice of underwear.

What am I even doing? Why am I even thinking about this?

'Sorry about that,' I say when I eventually reach the kitchen after what feels like a marathon walk.

I reach out without meeting her eyes and maybe I'm imagining it, but I do believe she deliberately takes her time to reclaim the bra from me, as if she is enjoying my humiliation.

'You're such a rascal, Max!' Rose says to my dog, who now is willing to show his face again. Her attention only makes him want to play more, and then George joins in.

I feel my cheeks flush, but then her mood changes like the flick of a switch and her face turns to horror. She sniffs the bra and holds it out in disgust.

'Well, this is going to need a wash,' she says, horrified. 'He's peed on it.'

Max senses trouble as he runs under the kitchen table and George barks in support of his owner.

'If it's ruined, I'll reimburse you in full,' I shout over the renewed bedlam. 'Just send me the bill.'

She shakes her head and blows out some steam.

'Would you like the bill sent by text message?'

'Sure. That's how I roll.'

I don't know what else to say. Rose opens the washing machine door and throws in the soiled bra, then slams the door shut and mutters to herself as she adds detergent to the top drawer, then selects a delicate wash. Delicate, indeed. I quietly call Max with a light whistle and we are just about to make our escape upstairs, both very sheepish and embarrassed, when Rose calls me.

'Charlie, can you come back down a second?' she asks.

It's on the tip of my tongue to ask 'what now?' but I remember I'm already on the back foot, so I return to the kitchen.

'Yes?'

'I have . . . I have a confession to make, and I think now is a good time to come clean.'

Oh.

'Really?' I have no idea where this is going.

'Yes, really,' she says. She licks her lips and stands up tall. 'To be honest, I wasn't going to tell you at all until tomorrow, but now that *your* dog has probably ruined a very expensive item of mine, I may as well come clean about *my* dog. And it's too much to explain in a stupid text message or whiteboard note.'

'Go on.'

She takes a deep breath and just goes for it.

'Yesterday while I was caught up in making the decorations, George made his way up to the bedroom.'

'And . . . ?'

'And I'm so sorry but . . . well, he made mincemeat of your book.'

'*What?*'

'The one on the bedside locker,' she continues. 'He's a lazy sod most of the time but he does like to chew things if they take his fancy, so there's no other way to say this. He shredded the book to pieces.'

Now it all makes sense.

'I was loving that book! I was wondering where—'

'I ordered a new one to this address for you this morning, so hopefully it will be here by tomorrow. I'm so sorry! Dogs, eh?'

Well, at least I'm not going totally round the bend. I spent ages last night looking for that book in every corner of the bedroom.

'I suppose this makes us even,' I say to Rose, as beads of sweat form on my forehead even though the house is only just about lukewarm at this time of the morning.

My head is spinning a little.

'I suppose we are, yes.'

'Or the dogs are even. But either way, let's draw a line under this and move on with our arrangements.'

'Exactly,' she says. 'Back to texting. And late-night notes on the fridge door.'

For a few seconds we stand there like two gladiators in a ring, staring at each other with our mouths tight and our stance tighter, then the washing machine lets out a loud whoosh which makes us both jump.

I look at the bra, whirring around on its own in a blur of turquoise lace. It is a very nice piece of underwear, I must admit.

My eyes catch Rose's. She smiles with a look that goes right through me, like a bolt of lightning. I blink, trying to unsee the images that are now running through my head. I tell myself it's only the unexpected encounter with her soft touch and her underwear that has stirred me up like this.

'I'm going to go have a shower,' I mumble to Rose, who is now fetching a cup for her own morning coffee as if nothing happened. 'The coffee can wait. Have a lovely day.'

Chapter Thirteen

Rose

When Charlie finally leaves the cottage after breakfast, I spend the day reading a juicy romance by the blazing fire with George by my feet, glad to be swept up in a fictional world where old memories are in another faraway parallel universe, if only for a few hours.

Every now and then I'll think of the whole bra episode and I'll giggle to myself, remembering the fearful look on Charlie's face, and the desperate attempts we are both making to stay out of each other's way.

You'll be glad to know I don't need reimbursement. It's as good as new after the wash.

I don't want any tension between us, so I thought I'd put his mind at ease. I've no idea where he is today, but it's a lot easier when we're not here at the same time. In fact, the peace when I'm here alone is glorious. The fire is lit, a flurry of snow sits on the windowpane, and with only a snoring George and the tick tock of the clock, I'm finally beginning to unwind and enjoy my time here.

My phone bleeps. It's Charlie.

Great. My dog likes bras, yours likes books. They both have excellent taste.

The afternoon slips in and I enjoy some hot soup for lunch, and after an enjoyable stretch of the legs around the forest I'm back by the warmth of the fire with my book, but I can't concentrate. My mind drifts back to a memory I've been desperately avoiding of how Michael and I had dreamed of spending a romantic weekend here, but I'd never got round to making it happen. I never had the courage to ask Rusty if I could stay here until now, but I know it would have been perfect.

I imagine how we'd have laughed, cooked and danced in the kitchen. I imagine how we'd have shared meals around the little wooden table, how we'd have cosied up in the local pub or by the fire in the cottage, locked away from the world as it snowed down outside.

Some days it seems like he's been gone forever. Some days it feels like only yesterday.

George barks at a bird on the windowsill which is enough to shake me out of my daydream, and when I follow his gaze outside I notice how the sun has already melted most of the snow today, which means I really should go out and get some more fresh air instead of staying here cooped up indoors with only my over-running imagination for company.

I haven't ventured down to the lighthouse just yet. I'm not ready to do so, as I know once I walk around I'll be overcome with memories of happier times with Michael.

It was a tradition we'd stumbled upon one New Year's Eve when we'd set off on a road trip on our first year together. We kept it going every December 31st after that, for two more years until our time together was up.

'My Granny Molly used to come here to put the world to rights when she was little,' I'd told him, and it sparked off an idea to share some of our own resolutions.

The following year we made a little ceremony of it, all wrapped up in our winter woollies with a shot of whiskey in a hip flask to keep us warm. I remember the bitter cold wind stinging my fingertips as I rustled in my bag for my own handwritten resolutions while Michael waited with his in his hands. His writing was so individual, and I knew he'd spent quite a while preparing his with the greatest thoughts and intentions.

It was a humble tradition, but it was ours. I've never been back to the lighthouse since Michael died, but I'm going to go there in his honour before I leave Donegal. It's the least I can do.

I wonder where Charlie has gone to spend his day.

Maybe he has some sort of mysterious connection to this place too, or maybe he has friends who live nearby that he can go and visit. He'll be glad to have use of the living room and the fire for a change this evening, even if it means giving up the bed. I notice he changed the sheets already before he left, and has opened the windows to let some fresh air in.

Maybe he's off for a secret rendezvous with Helena for the day. But no, he said he would see her when he got home, so that can't be right. I wonder where she lives. I try to imagine his type. I bet he goes for smart, studious girls who are highly intellectual and say the right things at the right time.

But anyhow, it's none of my business and I've my own day to fill and make the most of.

'Fancy another ramble around, George?' I ask the dog, who jumps to attention with a wagging tail. I miss having the car. Without it I'm limited to how much we can explore while we're here, so apart from walking around there's not much else to do.

Unless . . . unless I could cycle?

I remember how there used to be an old bike in the shed for visitor use, and even though I haven't ridden a bike in quite a while I wonder if I could manage a quick ride around the forest. I've planned an evening in the hot tub beneath the stars and an early night in that comfy bed which I'm so looking forward to, but first I need to blow off some cobwebs.

Yes, a cycle would be fun.

I race upstairs, change into some comfy soft leggings and a hoodie, then I go out to the little brick shed which has a red tin roof and a proper barn door to have a root around. It smells of paint and petrol from the lawnmower that sits neatly against the wall. Shelves are filled with pots and tubs holding everything from screws to small tools, and an old box of washing powder that has faded in the sun. Sure enough, right at the back, pinned behind a stack of old baskets, there is a battered yellow bicycle with a matching helmet hooked over the large handlebars.

After some careful manoeuvring, I push the bicycle outside onto the grass and listen as the chain squeaks and squeals a little to begin with before the oil kicks in. By the time I get it off the grass, it moves along the gravel smoothly.

I remember this bike.

I was on it during youthful, happy, sun-kissed summer days when I rode around the forest with the wind in my hair and not a care in the world. I wonder if I could relive that feeling today. Could I go back to the days when I was welcomed here, before this all happened, and my life came crashing down around me?

'I'm sorry, George, but I'm going to have to leave you here for just a little while,' I say, feeling immediately guilty. Charlie never leaves Max here alone. At least he hasn't done so yet.

He whimpers and tilts his head to the side.

'George, really?'

Another whimper.

'OK, OK, you can come with me then, but stay by my side as always, won't you? I hope you can keep up. Don't say I didn't warn you, George.'

I put on the helmet and fix it round my chin which sends George a bit crazy as he doesn't recognise me at first, but I won't be put off by his fussing. I'm looking forward to this little adventure. I know every nook and turn of the forest, so there's no way I can get lost, particularly as the snow has almost melted away. It looks like it always did, and I'm excited to relive my youth on a bicycle ride around a place I love so well.

I lock the doors of the cottage, making sure to keep my key in a safe place to avoid the wrath of Charlie, and I set off – a bit wobbly at first – in the direction of the forest that lies behind Seaview Cottage.

Boy, this really does bring back memories. I tilt my head back and bathe my face in the winter sun as George trots along beside me, his panting the only sound in the air apart from some distant birdsong. This is heavenly. This is the reason I came here. This is fate. This is the feeling I've been chasing for so long, so far away from the rat race of Dublin, so removed from clients chasing results or number crunchers needing answers on the spot. Being here is a million worlds away from phones ringing and late nights at my desk or having to be dressed for occasions and putting on a brave front. Being here feels so close to being at home.

I let tears stream down my face, unsure if they're tears of sadness or happiness, or a mixture of both.

I feel like screaming so I do just that amongst the dizzy heights of the trees above me, knowing there is no one near enough to hear me. It feels so liberating, so refreshing just to let it all out. I can scream if I want here. I can cry if I want here.

I scream again, and just when I'm about to breathe in this momentary sense of escape, George runs out in front of the bike.

I'm forced to brake suddenly, which sends me tumbling onto the ground, and the heavy steel crossbar of the bike lands on my hip with a thud.

Now I scream again, but for a very different reason.

'Ow! My leg! George, you silly boy!'

His big dripping tongue hangs out of his mouth and I want to shake him for ruining my moment of tranquillity, but more so for making me fall off the bike onto a bunch of twigs that feel as though they are piercing every inch of my lower body.

I try to push the bike off me but its weight is digging into my thigh and the pain sears through me. Thank goodness there is no one else around to hear me moan and groan where I lie in melted snow, my leg injured along with my ego, which has also taken a bashing. George tries to lick my face in sympathy, but I shoo him away, not in the mood just yet for his apology.

I slowly climb up from the wet ground, my leggings sticking to the grazes on my knees. I lean on the bike for support then limp my way back to the cottage, which takes what feels like an eternity. It's dark by the time I make it back. Tears are silently rolling down my cheeks and the pain in my knees is a good match for how sorry I feel for myself.

'For once I was managing to forget all my sadness,' I say out loud to George, pushing along the bike, even though I know by now the culprit has forgotten any part he had to play in my fall. He's much more interested in sniffing out his way home. 'I was lost in another place, somewhere far away from all my troubles and from the pain I caused so many others. I was finally, *finally* feeling just a tiny bit of solace amongst the madness, but no, Rose. No, you aren't getting away that lightly. You need to suffer just a little bit more. In fact, let's give you a bruised hip and two grazed knees just to remind you that you're not out of the woods yet when it comes to your purgatory.'

'Are you talking to George or to me?'

I jump.

This is all I need. Charlie has obviously just arrived back at the cottage seconds before me and I didn't even see him by his car as I pushed the bicycle past him.

'I'm talking to myself, don't mind me at all,' I reply, with more than a hint of bitterness in my tone. 'No point trying to talk to anyone else around here, is there?'

'Wait a minute, Rose. Are you OK? What happened?'

I stop and lean on the handlebars for support. I'm so, so glad to get back here at last.

'I fell off the bike in the forest. No big deal.'

I wipe a tear from my cheek with the back of my hand, doing my best not to sob as I speak. I'm thankful it's dark and hopeful that Charlie won't notice my tears of self-pity.

'Oh, I'm sorry to hear that.'

I see how he bites his lip. He smirks a little.

'Don't you dare laugh,' I say, feeling a rush of anger as I sense his eyes on my legs. 'You look like you're going to laugh, Charlie, but it's not funny.'

'I'm not.'

'I hurt both my knees and my hip is throbbing.'

Charlie holds his hands up.

'I'm not laughing!' he says in earnest. 'Here, let me take the bike. You go inside and get warmed up. You're soaked through.'

I hand over the bicycle and limp indoors, passing the hot tub on my way. I was really looking forward to spending an evening under the stars now that the snow has stopped falling at least for a little while.

I make my way to the living room where there are no traces of Charlie's bedroom arrangement for tonight apart from a pillow and a duvet which is neatly folded in the corner on top of a wicker basket. I plunge down onto the settee and try to straighten out my knees but they sting so badly. The sensation brings me right back to my early days when I had a similar tumble off a bicycle and my mother told me I was much braver than my older sister, who always screamed from the rooftops if she'd as much as a paper cut to deal with.

I lean down and begin to roll up my leggings, one leg at a time, wincing as I pull the material up from where my skin is grazed.

'Can I help?'

Charlie stands over me, already equipped with a small red first aid box in hand.

'I don't think it's as bad as I . . . oh, it's not pretty, is it?'

'It looks sore for sure.'

My knees are scorched with glaring red stripes dotted with gravel and mud, and they look a lot nastier than I'd thought, which almost takes my breath away. I never was good with blood and cuts, no matter how brave Mum says I was.

Charlie bends down on his knees on the tiles and opens the plastic box, then takes out bandages, scissors, cream, tape and some disinfectant wipes.

'Good old Marion,' he says, as I sit there wondering if he is going to let me get on with this myself at any stage. 'I found this kit under the sink just now. It has everything you need.'

'Thank you, that's very kind,' I say, looking down at his mop of hair as he cuts the bandage to size. 'If you want to just give me that, I can take care of it myself.'

He doesn't seem to have heard me, or else he's choosing to ignore my independence.

'Now, this will sting a little but it's so important to get it cleaned,' he says, taking a wipe in his hand. 'You ready?'

I don't think I can speak.

'You're going to clean it for me?'

He looks puzzled, as if I've asked him a very tricky question.

'You're in pain, right?'

'Yes,' I nod. I feel tears well up in my eyes again and it's nothing to do with the pain I'm in. It's the opposite, in fact.

'Then let me help you.'

I nod again and he curls his hand so gently behind my left knee, then dabs around where I'm cut as I do my best not to jump or hiss too much from the sting. His hand is cold but it's his touch that sends shivers right through me.

'You've done this before?' I say, swallowing back a wave of emotion at how careful he is being right now. 'Ow.'

'Sorry,' he says, glancing up my way. 'Yes, many times, but not in a long while. Let's just say my parents sending me to Scouts was one of their better ideas.'

'You were a Boy Scout?'

'A long time ago,' he says, moving on to my right leg. 'You've a nasty scratch here for sure but it should heal up quickly once it's cleaned and dressed.'

He examines my knee further, his hand hooked around the back of my leg again, and within a few minutes I'm wrapped, bandaged and feeling better already.

'Thank you,' I say, still a bit perplexed at how he went way above my expectations to help me just now.

'You're welcome,' he says with a shy smile.

He stands up, the first aid box, neatly packed up, in his hands.

'You'll be right as rain by tomorrow, wait and see.'

He takes my hand and helps me off the settee and I can feel his eyes on me as I shuffle past and out into the hallway.

'Would I be pushing it if I asked for a fireman's lift up the stairs?' I shout back, thinking I need to say something to shake off a moment of tenderness I haven't experienced in a very long time. 'I'm joking – before you answer.'

'Yes, you would be pushing it,' he calls back as I make my way up the stairs, one sorry step at a time. 'That's my good deed done for today. We can go back to texting now.'

I smile to myself as I take one stair at a time, and when I do make it to the top, I can hear Charlie rummage around the kitchen, which reminds me how hungry I am now that the shock of my fall is slowly wearing off. I am *so* hungry, yet I don't have the energy to cook, or even stay standing. No way.

I strip off my leggings, wincing with my eyes closed as they catch on the bandage and pull at my skin. I throw them into a corner, knowing their destiny is in the bin, and I slowly lie down backwards on to the bed, ignoring George's paws that tap me for attention. If his paws brush my knees, I'll scream.

And then I smell food cooking from downstairs. Ah, really, Charlie? Are you trying to kill me?

George sniffs the air too and I feel bad for him as his food bowl is all the way downstairs. I simply didn't have the strength to take it up for him, so just like me he's going to have to wait another little while to be fed, or however long it takes for me to be mobile again.

'My poor knees, George. Don't you feel even a little bit guilty? 'Cos you sure don't look it, mister.'

He totally ignores me, obviously sick of my moaning already. I sink into the pillow.

'Man, that feels good,' I whisper as I stretch out on the bed. I may be in pain but at least I have room to manoeuvre and stretch out instead of curling up in the foetal position on the sofa, as I have the past two nights. Poor Charlie has that ahead of him. Let's see how tidy he keeps the place when he has to camp out there.

And then comes the waft of garlic, slinking up the stairs under the door, which makes my stomach grumble.

I text Carlos to see how his date went in a bid to try and distract my empty belly.

Disaster, he replies instantly, which makes me giggle, even though it probably shouldn't. Totally catfished again. He said he was middle-aged, which is vague but acceptable. The man looked like my da, only a paler Irish version. I HATE internet dating.

I warily open a message from my friend Maeve, who as always is soft and gentle in her approach, which makes me feel bad for not being upfront and honest with her and Yvonne. I've only known them a few years since I moved to Dublin, but they took me under their wing after we met at hot yoga and the rest is history.

Hold tight, Rose, I know this time of year sucks for you. You've got this.

Her words could easily make me cry, but hunger is my overriding sensation right now.

My mouth is watering. I can't stop it. I try and guess what might be on Charlie's menu this evening, but my stomach almost hurts at the thought. My tastebuds tingle.

But I just have to suck it up and take a good rest for now. The pain will eventually subside and then I'll hobble downstairs and put a frozen pizza in the oven. Maybe with some oven chips, because I'm feeling sorry for myself. And lots of vinegar and ketchup.

My tummy growls out loud. The dog growls too.

'We'll get you some food very soon,' I say to George, who has now made his way up onto the bed and seems to be enjoying the extra space as much as I am. 'Tomorrow I'll go to the butcher and get you a nice juicy bone – how does that sound? Even though you tried to put me over the handlebars earlier, I forgive you. Tomorrow we will dine in the finest manner, I promise. But for now, we will wait until Charlie is finished. He's normally very fast, I can at least give him that.'

As my voice trails off, I close my eyes and try to distract my mind from the culinary delights from downstairs, but in less than fifteen minutes I hear footsteps coming up the stairs and I freeze on the spot.

I'm lying on top of the covers in only my underwear and with two bandaged knees on display as well as everything else Mother Nature gave to me. I have to say she was particularly generous in the boobs, hips and belly department, which may look good in the right light, but certainly aren't for a stranger's eyes at this moment.

Charlie might have forgotten something from the bedroom, but I doubt it – he is so meticulous, there's no way he'd leave as much as a sock behind.

'Rose?'

He knocks the door ever so gently and I pray he doesn't walk in. Oh my word – I need to cover up and fast! He wouldn't walk in, would he? No, he wouldn't.

'I'm not decent,' I whimper, with one eye closed as if that's going to make a difference to what he sees if he does dare to enter. 'Please don't come in.'

I hear him laugh a little.

'Are you OK?'

'Yes, thank you, I'm fine,' I say. 'A wounded ego and two sore knees but I'll be all right. Thank you again for looking after me so well. It was very kind of you.'

My words are met with silence, and I wonder is he still there.

What is he *doing*?

'Charlie?'

I take the far end of the duvet and gently wrap it over the top of me, nudging George quickly out of my way to cover myself up, just in case.

'Listen, Rose, I know this is breaking all my own rules, but . . .'

I wait again. What is he up to?

'I'm . . . I'm not sure if you've eaten yet this evening, and if you have I won't be offended. But in case you're hungry I've left you some pasta here on a tray by the door,' he says eventually. 'Don't eat it if you don't want it. No pressure.'

Oh my . . .

'Food? For me?'

More silence.

'Yes, Rose, food for you.'

My eyes prick with tears again.

'It's nothing fancy,' he says, and I can imagine him pushing back his hair as he speaks. 'It's a lemon pasta with parmesan and some parsley I found in the herb garden beside the shed. Oh, and I seasoned it with some black pepper, which I hope you don't mind. It's simple, but tasty. And I brought up George's food bowl too as I know he'll want to stay near you.'

Simple, but tasty. And he brought food for George too?

I could honestly cry. In fact, I do cry. Hot tears spring to my eyes and roll down my cheeks onto my pillow.

I swallow hard. I try to speak but I can't. I'm in so much pain and I'm so hungry, yet I can't even get the words out to thank him.

He made me food. He bandaged me up so tenderly and now he has made me food. No one, and I mean *no one*, has done anything like that for me before, not since my mother did when I was a young child.

I hear Charlie's footsteps cross the landing and I try to get my breath back, but the tears keep trickling at this double gesture, so I lift my phone and with my hands shaking, I text him instead.

Thank you, Charlie, I write even though I can barely see the words through my tear-blurred eyes as I type them. I really appreciate your kindness.

I peel myself off the bed and steady myself, then shuffle my way across to the door. I open it, peeping around to make sure he is gone. I'm still in no fit state to be seen, especially not now with puffy eyes and tearstained cheeks to match my pitiful state.

I look down at the floor and my hands go to my face when I see the steaming hot bowl of goodness waiting for me, the parmesan melting into the pasta, a pale golden delight. Beside the bowl is a slice of glistening garlic bread on a plate and a small glass of ice-cold white wine.

'You're an angel,' I whisper.

My mouth is watering as I savour the aroma of garlic and lemon which now fills the air.

I bend down slowly, the pain in my knees already subsiding as my heart almost bursts with joy, not to mention how delighted my empty stomach is. I take the tray into the bedroom, shuffle back for George's bowl too and then I prop up some pillows so I can lean back and enjoy this very welcome and unexpected feast. I take the first forkful and close my eyes as I savour the sumptuous flavours I've smelt from a distance since I got here two days ago.

I'm so touched. I'm in agony, but I'm happier than I've been in a very long time when Charlie replies to my text message.

Buon appetito, Rose! Get well soon.

So, he *must* be part Italian, then. I had a feeling he might be the first time I saw him – and this pasta all but confirms it.

The zing of lemon awakens my tastebuds, the garlic bursts with flavour and the tagliatelle melts in my mouth. I may be in pain but I'm also smiling from ear to ear and floating in food *paradiso*.

Six Days to Christmas

Chapter Fourteen

Charlie

Niall wakes me with a phone call just after nine in the morning, which is early for him but unusually late for me to be still asleep.

It's daylight outside, which I haven't woken to in a very long time, and as I reach down onto the living room floor for my phone, still half dozing as I answer, I wonder how I managed to go into such a deep slumber.

Ordinarily by this stage of the morning I'd have had a shower, gone for a run and dealt with a few emails, having checked out the daily news with a full plan for the day ahead. In fact, I'd probably be finishing up with my first client as a lot of people like to squeeze in a session at my office before they hit their own workplace.

'Were you asleep?' asks Niall, sounding just as flabbergasted as I am. 'Sorry, man, I forget that some people are already off for the holidays. I'm working from home today and the kids are wrecking my head as school's out already. So, how's it all going up there in Fanad? Not too quiet for you, I hope? I know you've been to County Donegal loads in summer, but it's different in winter. I love it.'

I stretch out, feeling cramps in my legs that wake up with me, then I yawn and sit up, trying to rotate the crick in my neck away. Lying on this sofa is not ideal for anyone over six foot tall, but I must admit the heat of the fire was nice to fall asleep to, even if it's chilly in here now.

'Fanad is a special part of Donegal. You were right about that,' I tell Niall, stifling a yawn. 'It's been years since I slept past six in the morning – and that's two days in a row now. I'm already a changed man.'

Niall laughs in agreement.

'Yes, that's the slow pace of life on the north coast and the power of a good blast of sea air, my friend,' he tells me. 'Good stuff. So, are you talking to yourself yet? It is isolated at Seaview, but that's why we love it so much. I guess you've the dog to keep you company, which isn't so bad.'

It's on the tip of my tongue to mention the whole double-booking fiasco, but I decide to keep that element of things to myself, at least for now. Niall and his wife were so elated when I got booked in here on their recommendation, considering Rusty and Marion don't normally take reservations over the festive season. I don't want to take away from that. I know they've been worried sick about me lately since Clodagh took Rebecca away to Tenerife, so I'll keep it all positive as far as they're concerned.

'Yes, Max is keeping me company so I'm absolutely fine,' I say, ruffling Max's ears as he comes to me at the sound of his name. 'We've been for a few walks on the beach and in the forest, we've checked out the pub and visited some of the little shops nearby. It's such a peaceful place and just what the doctor ordered.'

'And the beer?'

'I've had a few, yes, which might be the answer to my snoozing so late. The Guinness is good for sure.'

'Ah, I'm so jealous,' says Niall and I can almost imagine him licking his lips at the thought of a cool, creamy pint by an open fire in the Lighthouse Tavern. 'And have you spoken with Rebecca yet?'

I smile at the sound of my daughter's name.

'We FaceTimed, yes,' I tell my lifelong friend. 'Briefly, but for long enough to see that she's happy over there so far, which is the main thing, I suppose. I can't thank you enough for helping me get away from home for Christmas. I don't think I could have coped being there without her.'

Niall pauses for a second.

'You've given me some sound advice down the years when I was going through tough times, Charlie, so I wanted to do something for you in return,' he says. 'Call me crazy, but I always think there's something almost magical that happens at Seaview Cottage. I hope you come back at least with a clearer mind and a way forward.'

I await his punchline with a smile, knowing it's on the way.

'Great things happen when we least expect them.'

That's my boy. He never lets me down. I do my best not to be cynical in my response, but I freeze when I hear Rose's footsteps coming down the stairs.

She is singing, which makes my eyes widen, and my heart races a little faster with Niall on the other end of the phone.

'Well, anyhow, yes, so far, so good,' I say loudly, doing my best to end the conversation and drown out the noise in the background. Rose is lilting now to a part of her song of choice as she obviously doesn't know the words and she isn't keeping it down at all, but then she probably doesn't expect me to be here at this time of the morning.

I'm on the edge of the sofa, wearing only my boxer shorts, and I've a feeling she's about to—

'Oh! I'm sorry! I thought you'd be gone by now.'

Niall hears her. It would be very difficult not to.

'Who is that?'

I don't know who to answer first, Niall on the phone or Rose who stands in front of me, or if I should I try to calm down Max who is now yelping with joy at seeing his buddy George.

Rose closes the sitting room door quickly, taking both dogs with her, and I sigh with relief, but it's too late. Niall is on the ball.

'Was that – Charlie, you old devil! Who's the lucky lady? Ah, kid, I'm over the moon for you. Sadie and I were so worried about you up there all alone for Christmas.'

He holds the phone away and shouts to his wife before I get the chance to explain.

'Sadie! Charlie has a new lady friend with him.'

I can't stop him. Between him and my daughter jumping to conclusions, I've no defence.

I hear Sadie's sweet, familiar voice in the background. 'That's the best news! We can settle now, or at least you can stop wondering if he's coping on his own up there.'

I was best man at their wedding, and if Niall is like the brother I never had, she's almost like my sister. I know they've both my best interests at heart.

Niall comes back to me.

'Look, don't even let me hold you back one second, my friend. I'm seriously over the moon. In fact, that's made my whole Christmas already.'

'It's not like that, really,' I say as quietly as I can. I don't want Rose to hear any of this. 'It's just there was a mix-up with—'

'No need to explain. Your mix-ups are your business, kid. OK, I'd better go 'cos Sadie is dragging me shopping today once I finish work, but hey, we're thrilled to bits for you. I'll have a pint in your honour later. This is so good. Catch up with you later, Charlie. No wonder you're in bed until this time of the morning. Guinness, my arse. Enjoy!'

He laughs heartily as he hangs up, leaving me no time to explain the truth to him, so I lie back on the sofa and decide to start the day all over again.

Rose is still singing in the kitchen. She's playing cheesy Christmas songs and I close my eyes, unable to hide the smile that creeps over my face. Why am I smiling? I hate Christmas songs and she is the worst singer I've ever heard in my whole existence – and I've heard some dodgy voices down the years.

I put my head in my hands and squeeze my temples.

As much as her messiness annoys me, her clumsiness can be irritating and her singing is enough to make my ears bleed, I have no choice but to admit that Rose has a certain charm which I'm beginning to get used to in a tiny way.

But I need to reinstate the rules I was adamant we stick to in the first place. From today on, I'll do my best once again to keep my distance.

To become any more familiar would be a recipe for disaster, and the last thing either of us need.

Yesterday was a one-off because she'd hurt herself. Today, it's back to business as usual.

Chapter Fifteen

Rose

So much for not being here much during the day.

That's two mornings in a row where I've woken to find him still here, which is not exactly how we'd planned to manage this arrangement, *and* he was barely dressed which was, I must admit, a bit of a sight for sore eyes first thing in the morning.

His tanned skin and the muscles on his arms did make me do a double-take, not to mention those damn tattoos, but then a healthy tan and buff body isn't something I'm used to in a man. Michael was quintessentially Irish in his colouring with a, well, *regular* body that only ever burnt in the sun. He was more cuddly than chiselled, but I loved that about him – and he certainly didn't wear his boxers as tight as Charlie does. I did try not to look, but my eyes wouldn't listen.

I turn the music down as I wait for the kettle to boil, my mood shifting gears now from the high of a new morning here at Seaview Cottage where I've planned to explore so much more. This is my third day here and after yesterday's tumble off the bicycle in the forest, I plan to be a little less adventurous today, but I also want to make the most of my stay by absorbing all there is to love about this place.

I want to visit the lighthouse as soon as I feel strong enough. I want to taste Guinness by the fire in the pub. I want to sing carols by the Christmas tree and I want to – I want to learn to laugh again. Properly laugh, where I feel it in my toes and in my ears and in my belly. I want to live again. As cheesy as it sounds, I just want to be me again. No pretending, no masking, just me.

That's probably way too much to ask, but it does no harm to dream.

'Sorry, I'll be out of your hair in a few minutes,' says Charlie, who thankfully is dressed now, as he pops his head around the kitchen door. 'Just wanted to say that. I'll, er – actually, I'll leave you to it. Pretend I wasn't here. Pretend I'm – OK, I'll be off.'

Pretend he wasn't here? Well, that's a lot easier said than done as the sight of his semi-naked body is now etched on my mind no matter how much I try to 'unsee' it.

'Thanks again for yesterday,' I call quickly before he disappears.

'Oh, that was nothing,' he says, avoiding my eyes. 'It was honestly no big deal. I hope your knees are better today. Have a good one.'

I call after him again.

'Charlie, it's fine if you want to grab breakfast before you go!' I say, feeling I need to be a bit more appreciative. 'I'm just having some toast and a quick—'

But I hear the front door slam before I can finish my sentence. He's already gone as if I've scared him off, or maybe he just doesn't want to be too familiar after all.

Maybe he prefers to keep his distance, despite his kindness last night.

And maybe that's for the best.

I spend the day out by the coast, taking a lengthy walk with George, reflecting on why I came here to Donegal.

But no matter how much I let the winter sea batter my face or the wind knot up my hair, and no matter how much George yelps with joy as his paws hit the water, my mood dips with every step I take along the wild shores of this place I've always known and loved so well.

And then I see it in the distance.

The lighthouse in all its glory. It's a sight that never fails to make my heart lift with joy. Its whitewashed walls gleam in the winter sun; the sea-green doors, the tiny windows, the rush of the foam on the waves below – I can't stop myself. It's time. I need to get closer.

I walk with Max down the winding roads, past damp grey stone walls, through sleety puddles that line our pathway, and my heart is beating in rhythm to my steps.

With every step I take, my childhood days come closer to meet me, and I leave civilisation behind, in a place where time always stands still.

I can see my Granny Molly's smiling face coming towards me. I hear her sweet voice telling me the famous story of how, centuries ago, a ship hit the rocks at Fanad and two hundred and fifty souls perished, with only the ship's parrot surviving.

'A pirate?' I once asked, my eyes like saucers. I can still hear her laughter.

'No, a parrot,' she told me. 'A bird. After that, the light-house was built to prevent any further atrocities.'

I cried when I first heard this story as a little girl, and as I make my way closer to the iconic tower, I feel those early emotions return.

I see my mother skipping along here too with the wind blowing in her hair, telling Sarah and me to be careful as we peered over the stone walls and down onto the swirling water that crashed against the rocks below. It was a sight that filled me with magic then, and it still does again and again, no matter how many times I've been here.

I find a seat on a picnic table from where I inhale the dramatic views. I smile to myself as I relive the carefree, innocent days when coming here was the highlight of my whole summer.

It's raining now, but I barely notice. This viewpoint will always soothe me no matter what the weather.

My mother would happily spend hours of summer here with us, looking out for ships in the distance. She'd point out the protective beam of light spilling onto the sea, and how the angry waves would beat off the rocks but the lighthouse would still stand tall and strong, guiding the boatmen and looking after itself always. We'd try to spot dolphins. We'd take solace in the wild, northerly point that made us feel on top of the world.

George puts his head in his paws, not bothering to budge when I throw a stick for him.

'You are the laziest dog in the world, you know that,' I tell him. 'But I wouldn't change you. Do you know how special it is here, George?'

George tilts his head and gives out a squeaky groan which makes me want to scratch his ears as I tell him the story of the shipwreck, just as my Granny Molly told me time and time again.

I stare out at the lighthouse and the wild waves that crash below it. Everything around it is, as always, chaotic and turbulent, yet it stands so serene and strong with its light shining from within, giving guidance where it's needed, just as my mother used to tell me.

It's only been a few months since I saw her last but I miss her so much right now that my heart aches, and I know that she's longing to have me home for Christmas.

But I don't want to ruin her Christmas. I don't want to take away her joy of this time of year, a time that until three years ago was always filled with celebration and family love.

I'm giving this time of year back to them all by staying out of their way.

I close my eyes, letting the blustering wind take my breath away, and I do my best to ignore the tears that stream down my face. I seem to have cried a lot since I got here, with both physical and emotional pain, but maybe that's what I need. Maybe I need to let it all out instead of swanning around Dublin like I'm the woman who has it all.

George cuddles in by my side, which ironically makes me feel even more alone. I have so many missed calls from my mum. I have ignored calls from my dad, but he can barely speak to me in person any more, so why is he putting himself out to call me on the phone? I know he blames me for Michael's accident as much as I do myself. He adored Michael.

I have voicemail messages from them all which I simply can't listen to. I have texts from my sister, but I can't bring myself to read them as Christmas comes closer. I desperately want to run to them, but I need to stay away from them for all our sakes.

I imagine them calling and calling me. I wonder when they'll give up trying, when they've heard my faux-happy message more times than they need to.

Hi, you've reached Rose. George and I have left the bright lights of Dublin for Christmas, but we'll be back in action in the New Year. Have a good one! Go easy on the turkey!

But no one apart from Carlos knows *where* we are this Christmas. No one knows that our destination is so close to home, yet far away enough to keep me invisible. No one knows that I'm in this majestic place that was once my playground when I was a little girl, where I was always reminded of how wonderful our world is.

Now, with six sleeps until the biggest family day of the year, I still don't know if I'm doing the right thing by choosing to spend Christmas alone. I don't know if by coming here I'm taking steps forward or taking steps backwards in time. The wind catches my throat and I gasp back tears of regret and sorrow for how it's all turned out.

I shake my head into the blustering clifftop wind, trying to erase the darkness that comes towards me now like a freight train. I hear Michael laughing again, that night when he picked me up on Christmas Eve to come here.

I hear the sound of Slade on the radio, I smell the smoky scent of the second-hand car he'd recently bought and I feel the sense of dread scoop out the pit of my stomach as I anticipate the moment we were heading towards.

He wouldn't tell me where we were going. He'd only say it was the end of one chapter in our lives and the beginning of the next one.

But that chapter was the end of Michael's story.

As if in slow motion, I see my hand reach over to hold his. I see his eyes look down at our hands for just a split second.

I cover my ears now as the inevitable crash of metal comes back to me so clearly that it crushes my eardrums. My head bangs from side to side off the window, off Michael, off the window again. I'm reliving the horror once more in the sickening technicolour I haven't seen in so long. I smell burning. I hear glass smashing, the crunch of metal on metal, the rattle of my brain as we tumble to our destiny.

To Michael's destiny.

To mine too.

I distracted him. What if . . . ?

'Are you out there, Michael?' I shout out as loudly as I can towards the water below me. 'I just wish I could hear your voice one more time.'

It's so windy and the rain is pouring down now, so no one can hear me, not that I'd even care. Not that there's anyone else around.

'I'm so sorry, Michael. I'm so sorry we didn't get to make all our dreams come true.'

I try to stop my tears with the back of my hand. I fall to my knees and I sob into the rain.

What was I thinking?

I should never have come here. It's too painful.

Charlie was kind yesterday, kind in a way that filled me up, but today I'm empty again. I'm alone in this world and that's never going to change, no matter where I go. No matter who I'm with, I'll still feel alone without Michael.

I should go back to Dublin. This is all too much. I should give the cottage over to Charlie, get out of his way and go back to Dublin where I can wallow in my own misery without dragging anyone else down with me.

A double booking is a double booking and he got here first. I stand up slowly, my legs soaked through. My knees are stinging as the bandages stick to the scrapes and scores from yesterday. I lean on the picnic bench and then bend down again to grab George's lead.

He's really all I have. I've never felt so alone in my entire life as I do now.

'Come on, George,' I sniffle, taking my dog by the lead. 'Let's find our way back to Dublin. I can cope better there. I'm so sorry for dragging you here. I'm so sorry for everything.'

I struggle back towards the village as the rain soaks me through, blending in on my face with the salt of my tears.

I'll go back to the cottage and pack up my things. I don't care if I have to *walk* back to Dublin. I'm going to find a way out of here. I'm going to face up to the fact that I shouldn't have come back. It's gone. My family Christmas memories are gone. Michael is gone. I can't go home to my family. I just need to let Christmas slip by and then I'll get on with my life when there's no festive fuss, no expectation to play happy families, and no reminder on the calendar of how miserable and alone I am.

Nothing and no one will ever to be able to take that feeling away.

Half an hour later, with my cheeks flushed pink and my whole body dripping from the rain, I stop and breathe out when I see Charlie's car is back at the cottage already.

It's dropping down dark so I guess that's expected, but I don't want to talk to anyone. I just want to text him my farewell and go.

Hopefully he is still in the mood to stay out of my way to let me pack up and figure out my next move.

I put my key in the door and stand on the mat inside where I take off my coat and shiver as the warmth of the cottage clashes against the tight cold on my face. I hear him in the kitchen, and then I pause.

It isn't his usual crescendo of classical tunes that he cooks to.

Hang on a moment . . .

Is Charlie, who hates Christmas, who didn't want to hear anything to do with this time of year, listening to my mother's favourite Christmas song? The one I've been humming or singing since I got here?

I stand here in the hallway, frozen in time as well as freezing from the walk back here.

Hearing the song hits me hard and I sob like a baby, not stopping when Charlie comes into the hallway, a tea towel over his shoulder and a smile on his face which turns to dismay when he is met with the state of me.

'Rose, what happened? Are you OK?'

I shake my head. My mouth drops open and I try to speak but I wouldn't know what I want to say even if I could find a way to get the words out. How can a song bring back so many happy memories yet instil such a wave of sadness at the same time? Will I ever get to relive those days and spend Christmas with the people I love again?

Charlie watches me aghast as I go into the bathroom. I turn on the shower and strip off everything to do with this mind-boggling day as quickly as I can.

I want to go home, but not to Dublin. I want to go home to my family for Christmas, but I can't.

And I need to accept that I simply can't do it, once and for all.

Michael is dead. He's never coming back, and I can't ever face going home for Christmas again, no matter how much I long to.

Chapter Sixteen

Charlie

I don't see or hear from Rose for the rest of the evening, so it's a surprise when the silence of the cottage is interrupted by a knock on the door just as I'm settling down by the fire with my wine and my novel which arrived in the post this afternoon.

I sent Rose a quick text to say the replacement book had arrived after George's mauling of the original. I do my best to make her feel better by referring to how we don't know each other's surnames even though we've been sharing a house for three days.

Hi, this is Charlie the Holiday Occupant, Seaview Cottage. The book arrived. Thank you. I hope you're OK?

But she didn't reply at all.

Maybe she's gone out and I didn't hear her? Maybe it's her at the door? Maybe she slipped out for a while and forgot her key, which, let's face it, wouldn't be out of character.

I wonder if she has eaten much today. She doesn't seem to eat a lot or cook a lot either for that matter. She seems to live on toast and ready meals, and the longer we share this cramped space, the more I wonder what's really going on in her world.

Here we go again, Charlie. Just butt out and mind your own business. It was your big idea not to speak to each other as far as possible, so don't go breaking the rules after you've set them. You always want to have it both ways, but that's not how life works. You must choose one way or the other, not have your cake and eat it too.

As I hear Clodagh's taunting and mocking voice in my head, I can't help but toss around possibilities as to why Rose was so upset earlier when she returned to the cottage in such a state.

Maybe I should have made more of an effort to speak to her instead of pretending I couldn't tell she had been crying and going back to my cooking? But she didn't exactly leave me much room or time to communicate. She didn't seem in the mood to talk to anyone, never mind me and my texting rules.

Regardless, I've left a chicken casserole in the oven with a note on the fridge whiteboard to help herself should she decide to come downstairs at any stage of the evening, though I've a feeling she won't. That's if she's even here at all.

I go to the door half expecting to find her there, but instead I'm greeted by a woman who is almost unrecognisable with her raincoat hood up and a scarf that covers most of her face. She pulls it down to greet me.

It's Marion.

'Sorry to bother you, Charlie, but I was passing by, and I just wanted to make sure you're settling in well. Do you need anything?'

Passing by? No one 'passes by' Seaview Cottage unless they're heading towards a dead end or a field full of sheep.

'Hello, Marion. Gosh, come in out of the rain. It's lashing down,' I say, standing aside. Marion seems glad of the offer. *Where the hell is Rose in this weather?*

'Sorry to disturb you.'

'Not at all,' I reply. 'Come in by the fire. I was just reading and chilling out – and to be honest I'd no idea it was such a treacherous night outside. How are you?'

Marion's eyes glance around the living room which makes me glad I did a quick tidy up earlier. Sleeping in the bedroom upstairs is one thing but camping out in the sitting room and trying to keep it relatively tidy isn't quite so easy. I think back to the first day I saw Rose's tornado effect on the living room and can understand why it looked that way. I wonder where she is.

I see my phone light up where it sits on the arm of the chair and I know it's rude, but I lift it to see if it's a reply from Rose. Surely she isn't out there wandering around in the rain again? She has no vehicle, so wherever she is, she's on foot.

But it's not Rose. It's Helena. It's another missed call, which makes seven from her today.

'Now, I really don't want to intrude on your time here, Charlie, and I wouldn't have come inside at all if it wasn't raining so heavily outside,' Marion continues.

I put the phone down and give her my full attention to see her eyes now squinting slightly when she sees the pile of blankets and a pillow stacked on one end of the sofa. She seems puzzled.

'So, is everything in working order for you? Do you have enough . . ?'

I wait for her to finish.

'Enough?'

She doesn't answer, but instead her eyes seem stuck on my makeshift bedding and they won't seem to pull away.

'I was going to ask if you were OK for firewood and . . .'

'Yes?'

'Is the bed upstairs OK, Charlie?'

'The bed? Yes, it's very comfortable. It's perfect. Why do you ask?'

'Good,' she replies with a frown. 'Sometimes the cottage does get a little damp and cold at this time of year, but I hope you'd say so if that's the case?'

I go to open my mouth to explain but something tells me to pause and think on my feet. She thinks I'm sleeping on the sofa out of choice . . . oh dear. The penny drops in my head.

She doesn't know Rose is staying here. Rusty hasn't told her.

'No, no, the cottage isn't damp or cold at all,' I say quickly, staring now too at the blankets and pillow. 'You see, well . . . well, I fell asleep by the fire last night with old Max at my feet, so I just thought it might be best if I was prepared in case it happens again tonight. It's a very cosy room.'

I don't want to get involved in Rusty's marital disputes, but I feel a strange urge to protect Rose, which surprises me. Marion throws her head back and then nods as if it all makes total sense now.

'Ah yes, of course it is! It really is a very cosy room indeed!' she agrees, as if I've paid her a compliment of sorts. 'I deliberately tried to make it so with the floral cushions and throws I chose, and the warm creamy colours. Rusty wanted more blues in this room, but I got my way in the end.'

I've no doubt about that.

'And you know sometimes, between you and me, I've been known to come here of an evening and take advantage of the warmth of the open fire and the peace and quiet,' she says. 'It makes me nod off too. We don't have a fire at home. Just oil heating. It's not the same.'

'It's not the same at all,' I say, really hoping she'll leave, but she hasn't finished yet.

'It's good to enjoy your own company sometimes. I do wish I could do it more often.'

She seems caught up in a trance now, but then she slowly meets my eyes again.

'Well, anyhow, enough of my maudlin rambles. I've been thinking of you here all on your own for the past couple of days,' she says, 'and I do know that you want it that way, but just in case you *did* want something to do, our Christmas Fayre in aid of homelessness is on at three tomorrow afternoon in the community hall.'

'Ah, lovely.'

'It's like a mini indoor Christmas market with charity proceeds,' she says with a beaming smile. 'You know, with stalls and a carol service and they serve some delicious mince pies, which I'm in charge of.'

She pauses at that. I can't think what she is expecting me to say in reply.

'Wonderful!' I exclaim with wide eyes. She pushes back her silver hair and her eyes twinkle, followed by a modest shrug. She looks right into my eyes now.

'They ask me back every year. It's kind of *my* thing.'

'Huh?'

'The mince pies. Marion's Mince Pies.'

I'm not sure if it's the fire crackling, the fact that Marion doesn't appear to know that Rose is here and that she might arrive back at any minute, or my fear that there may be a slight hint of flirtation in Marion's manner that both battles and unnerves me at the same time, but I feel a layer of sweat cover the back of my neck.

'Excellent! Three p.m. tomorrow, then?' I say, praying that she'll hurry up and make a move. 'It's a date, then! A date for my diary, I mean!'

'It's a date!' she replies with a giggle, fluttering her eyes once more before making for the living room door at last. 'There's normally a bit of a jolly in the pub afterwards with a few tunes and lots of craic. Rusty isn't interested in going at all. In fact, he isn't interested in much these days, but I'll go if you fancy a drink and some company?'

'Me, with you?'

I feel a bit dizzy.

'Oh, not like that, Charlie,' she laughs, but I'm not so sure. 'The Fayre is always a bit of a milestone. It's a sign of Christmas kicking off in the village so there'll be lots of us local folk there. There's Edith who does a crochet stall, there's Hannah who makes cakes, and lots, lots more. I do hope you can make it. Oh, and bring your lady friend too if she happens to pop by again.'

I'm puzzled now.

'My lady friend?'

'I was chatting to Sadie.'

'Sadie?'

'Your friend Niall's wife?' she says with delight. 'She and I have grown quite close over the years. It was Sadie who gave me a glowing review on your behalf, so—'

'Ah . . .'

'Some people around here might say I'm nosey, but I only wanted to see if you needed anything. And to invite you personally to the fayre, of course.'

'I don't have a lady friend here, Marion.'

'No?'

'It's just me and Max.'

Shit. I wish I hadn't opened my mouth. I should have just left it all to her and Sadie's imagination, because when she gets to the hallway she stops again.

This time, she freezes. And it's probably my imagination but the air suddenly feels cold.

I follow her gaze to a radiator where Rose's bright yellow raincoat and stripy scarf from earlier hangs over to dry.

'But then, whose—'

'Sorry?'

I stumble and mumble some incoherent sentence which makes absolutely no sense whatsoever, but Marion is mumbling too. What is it about this narrow hallway that makes it the scene of such awkwardness?

'I knew it . . .' she says, as if a rather large penny has just dropped in her very investigative mind. 'It's Rose, isn't it? I've learned that my gut instinct is never wrong. I knew it. How dare he! How dare *she*!'

She keeps staring and mumbling under her breath, though I can't make out what it is she is saying, which means both of us now are mouthing the most awful gibberish. I want the ground to open and swallow me. I want to tell her none of this is my business. I want to tell her that I believe her communication with her husband is dangerously dysfunctional and to leave Rose and me to get on with our break while they sort their problems out.

But I don't want to rock the boat more than it's already rocking. I sense that in Rusty and Marion's world, there's a storm brewing. I want nothing to do with it.

'It's not the sharing of the cottage that bothers me, Charlie,' she says, breathing in through her nose and out again. Her face twists, her breathing becoming more rapid as it all sinks in. 'But I would never, ever have agreed for Rose to stay – it's not her, but I would never have allowed any of her family to – oh, I've said enough already. I hope this terrible hindrance hasn't ruined your visit, Charlie. What a mess. It's all just a terrible mess. She shouldn't *be* here.'

'It hasn't ruined my stay at all, believe me,' I say, though I'm not sure she is even listening. 'What do you mean, you would never have agreed for *Rose* to stay here? Why not?'

She puts her hood up again, fixes her scarf over her face and mumbles something inaudible.

'I'll see you tomorrow at the Christmas Fayre,' I call out to her as she marches like a woman on a mission down the pathway in the rain. 'Bye, Marion.'

She lifts a hand and waves without looking back, then I watch her climb into her car and roar off as the rain pelts down onto the babbling brook in the near distance.

Poor Rusty.

I wouldn't like to be him this evening, not in a million years. But more importantly, what's Marion's big gripe with Rose? And most important of all, where the hell *is* Rose?

I'll send her a text again to see if she replies. It's not my place to worry, but after how upset she looked earlier, I can't help but feel concerned.

Chapter Seventeen

Rose

The Lighthouse Tavern was already busy when I got here about two hours ago just before another outburst of rain.

Now, as a small group of musicians squeeze into a corner marked as 'reserved', I'm hoping that hearing the lilting sounds of the fiddle, guitar and banjo with a few Irish ballads thrown in for good measure, not to mention the bottle of wine in front of me, will take my cares away, if only for a while.

I don't know why those flashbacks came to me earlier.

I've spent a fortune on therapy to make sure they don't, but grief can be as unpredictable as the waves on the ocean.

One foot in front of the other, isn't that what Carlos always says? One step at a time all the way.

I called Carlos from my bedroom earlier as soon as I knew the coast was clear and Charlie was out of earshot before I escaped to the pub.

It was so good to hear a familiar, reassuring voice and although I didn't plan to tell him about the double booking, when I unexpectedly found myself filling him in, he loved how I've decided to stay and at least feel a little bit closer to home by being here in Donegal.

'Is he hot?'

'Carlos, trust you,' I laughed in response. 'Can you be serious for once?'

'I just need to visualise him so I can feel totally in the loop with this vital and very out of the blue information. Is he hot? Describe . . .'

'Tall, dark, nice physique. Is barefoot most of the time,' I replied. 'Oh, and he cooks really tasty food and has tattoos. Cool tattoos. And has a girlfriend called Helena who calls him a lot.'

The phone line went silent.

'Carlos?'

'I think I just swallowed my tongue,' he says eventually, so I let him get his breath back before we return to serious mode.

'If this guy is playing Christmas music when just a couple of days ago he was mad about decorations, maybe you're both helping each other without even realising it?'

That's better. Carlos does make me laugh a lot, but behind the humour he always also has words of wisdom to share when I push him for some.

'It was definitely a huge bolt out of the blue to hear him listening to my mother's favourite Christmas song,' I told him. 'Before that, I was set to get out of here and thumb it back to Dublin if I had to.'

Carlos seemed to find the idea of me thumbing a lift hilarious. He knew as well as I did that was never going to be an option.

'Well, it was inevitable that the lighthouse would stir up emotion, Rose. But maybe next year you'll drive that extra sixty miles home to your family,' he said. 'Go gently. You've suffered immensely since you lost Michael. Go easy on yourself, please.'

So that's what I'm trying to do. I feel better after a good cry, a hot shower and a chat with Carlos. I also strangely feel better at the thought that maybe, just maybe, I might have helped Charlie take a tiny step forward in acknowledging it's Christmas. And I can't help but feel festive cheer as I look around the Lighthouse Tavern.

I'm snuggled into a small booth now with George resting under the table by my feet, and if it wasn't so noisy in here, I'd imagine I could probably hear him snore. Like me, he's happy to be warm and dry after earlier when we were both soaked to the bone.

After a tasty bowl of chowder, I chatted with some locals and some fellow holiday makers, including an American family who spend Christmas here every year. They help at the fayre which takes place tomorrow, I'm told.

There's a couple from England, Stacy and Chris, sat near the bar. They're on their first visit to Donegal which allowed me to gush about everything that's so beautiful about being here.

'It's so dark here at night,' Stacy exclaimed as they enjoyed a pint of Guinness each. 'I've never seen a sky so dark and the stars so bright. Wow. It's such a perfect place to switch off and forget the world.'

'And leave the fuss of Christmas for others,' Chris added.

So, it's not just my dad who says that.

'We live in a big city, so this is like stepping into a totally different world here. We love it.'

Their earlier enthusiasm, and now as I watch them look on in wide-eyed wonder as the traditional Irish musicians strike up a tune, reminds me why I've always loved it here.

It's not only the majestic, breath-taking scenery of Fanad; it's not only the easy-going pace of life here; it's also the people you meet in tiny pubs like this.

People who, like me, are hoping to escape from the rat race even for just a while, be it in the summer or spring, or during the winter months when more layers are needed to go outside. I adore summer here, but in winter the fresh air and crisp wind give that extra kick that cleanses the soul.

I marvel at how the revellers are packed in together here, perhaps thirty people maximum, all smiling with ruddy faces and clapping along in time with the music. Everyone is dressed casually and comfortably. There's no one bothered about how they look or thinking of fashion in here. Even the bar staff look happy to be working, their famous Irish *'céad míle fáilte'* so tangible in the air, creating an atmosphere that simply doesn't exist in city bars where no one cares to ask who you are or where you're from.

This is the type of place where, excuse the cliché, everyone wants to know your name. I've ditched my usual skirt and tights combo for leggings and a hooded jumper, my kitten heels for cosy, fleeced-lined boots, and my red lipstick for a more natural look – and it feels like I'm stripping off all I was pretending to be.

I'm not Miss Bright and Cheery like I've pretended to be in Dublin. I haven't been in a long time. I'm broken, I'm wounded, but I'm determined to heal. And to do so, I'm going to take life at a slower pace for the next few days, facing up to whatever comes my way.

I'm dreading Christmas Eve. But I'll cross that bridge when I come to it.

It's too busy and noisy in here now to hold a steady conversation, but no one seems too bothered as they allow their bodies to get caught up in the uplifting music, all attention on the musicians who are respected in a way that comes so naturally. I'm engrossed and absorbed. I'm entranced and enthralled.

'I'm trying to think of something to say to you, but everything in my mind sounds cheesy, so I'll just say hello.'

I can barely hear what the stranger at the next table says over the music, but I soon realise he isn't going to give me much time to respond as he keeps talking. He wears a long, evidently brand-new camel coloured coat which is the same colour as his hair. It's the same colour as his face too, I notice, and he is very, very tall. He pulls his stool closer to where I sit.

'I'm Billy,' he says, his bushy blond eyebrows moving as if they've a life of their own.

'Hi.'

'I'm here on holiday. Do you come here often? OK, there I said it. I told you it would sound cheesy.'

He leans in, a little too closely. I lean back as he rambles on – something about a divorce and the power of being by the sea and how he's never been before, and how he's been told he needs to get out more.

As he talks, his warm breath hits my cheek no matter how much I try to keep my distance. It's hot and cramped in the pub, but Billy isn't getting the hint at all that I'm a tiny bit uncomfortable right now.

My eyes scan the small room and are drawn magnetically to the door as it opens and another thirsty customer stoops under the door and squeezes past people on their way to the bar. He's wrapped up in a coat, scarf and hat that will no doubt soon be shed when the heat of the fire and the atmosphere takes over.

I watch him as he greets strangers with a smile and a nod. His back is to me now. He is tall and broad-shouldered in a strangely familiar way, and when he takes off his woolly hat and runs his hand through his dark hair, I feel a sharp intake of breath.

It's Charlie.

He glances around and catches my stare before I've time to look away, then he slowly raises his hand to acknowledge that he's seen me. He takes out his phone and within seconds my own phone bleeps.

There you are.

I reply even though Billy is still in my ear.

Hello. I can see you.

I know you can. And I see you've got company. Just saying hello.

I crack a smile and my heart lifts, yet I don't understand why. I see him look around, then he signals to me to question if I want a drink. Billy backs off from my table, getting the message that I'm not interested in small talk when it's so noisy in here.

I shake my head and lift my glass of wine to show Charlie, wondering why my cheeks feel like they're suddenly on fire. I take off the hooded jumper, glad I've a baggy T-shirt on underneath, and when I'm sure he isn't looking my way I blow on my chest, determined to cool this unnecessary flush that has swept over me unawares.

There's an empty stool beside me which I know is the only one left in the whole place, and that makes my heart thump. Charlie makes his way over, shuffling past all the applause and the swaying audience who are too caught up in the music to notice him.

'Sorry,' he says, pointing at the stool. I try to avoid eye contact and top up my wine, determined not to make this a big deal.

It isn't a big deal. We're sharing a holiday cottage for goodness' sake, so it's no issue to sit so close to each other in a public place, is it? Plus, it's not like we must communicate at all if we don't want to.

And for a good while, we don't.

Charlie sips on his pint, then takes off his coat just as I'd anticipated would happen sooner rather than later. He is wearing a black shirt, the one I saw in his closet, and I stare at my glass when I find myself noticing how he unbuttons it to loosen his collar when the heat of the pub takes over.

I feel a little bit dizzy. I blame the wine. And the fire. I glance again at his side profile, but he barely acknowledges I'm here now as he settles into the famous warmth of the Lighthouse Tavern.

A friendly old man who sits next to me says something in my direction, but I've no idea what it is so I just smile and give him a thumbs-up sign which seems to satisfy him as a response. We spent ages earlier talking about everything from the commercialism of Christmas to the awful weather we're having, and he taught me a lot about how he lives off grid, but now it's impossible to keep any sort of conversation going as the music has taken over.

I'm quite happy to sit here and say nothing. It's nice to just take it all in.

Charlie, who hasn't turned around since he took off his coat, lifts his phone and punches in a message which allows me to sneak a quick glance his way. He's probably messaging Helena. He's smiling as he types, and then he sets his phone on the table beside mine. Mine lights up, I don't think anything of it at first until I see his name on my screen.

Is he texting me from where he is sitting less than a metre away? It makes me a little bit giddy, I must admit, especially since his expression hasn't changed, nor have his eyes diverted in this direction.

I thought you'd drowned in the rain, his message says. Good to see you're dry and safe.

When I look up, he still isn't looking my way, but instead is po-faced and focused on the music.

No need to worry. You're not my keeper.

I press send. He casually turns and spots the message. He opens it, then types a response.

Correct. But I won't apologise for being concerned. You were upset earlier.

This jolts me a little.

I'm fine now.

Glad to hear. You've got an admirer, I see?

I glance across at Billy, who is all smiles and eyebrows in my direction. Oh Lord.

That's Billy, was chatting to him earlier. Friendly guy.

This time Charlie doesn't reply. He just taps his hand on his leg in time to the music as if I'm not here. His concentration on the tunes allows me a moment to study him more closely. I sit back in the booth, feeling George stir by my feet, and discreetly admire his profile.

He is a very handsome man, and though the pub was a very nice place before he arrived, it looks a lot nicer with him here.

His light stubble, which he rubs now with his fingers, has already turned my head more times than I care to admit to myself back at the cottage. I keep getting flashbacks of his semi-naked body on the sofa this morning. I notice his nose, bent slightly in the middle as if it has been broken more than once, and the tattooed arms that look like they could hold you tight and take all your pain away.

Why am I thinking this way? It must be the wine loosening my imagination.

We have never had a full, proper conversation, yet his act of kindness last night is one I simply can't ignore. In three years I haven't deserved kindness, or at least that's what I've always believed. In Dublin I'm living a big fat lie, so if someone is nice to me, it doesn't ever sink in.

Back there I never let my mask slip. I'm Rose Quinn, digital marketing champion, colourful and bright. Being here is the closest I've felt to my real self in a very long time.

But even Charlie isn't seeing the real me, nor do I know the real him. We are only skimming the surface of each other at face value, and maybe that's a good thing. It's like we are both a blank page, ready and able to start again with no judgement and no torrid past. How I wish life was as simple as that, where we could all press delete and refresh and start again.

He didn't have to help me when I fell, yet he did. He didn't have to make me dinner last night after I fell, yet he did.

But I don't want to look at him in this admiring way either. I'm not meant to look at him this way. He's a stranger. An accidental stranger, who I was never supposed to meet. Not to mention the fact that he has a girlfriend who he is clearly besotted with and who he calls to say goodnight.

I don't have anyone to wish me goodnight.

How can I be envious of such a simple gesture? Imagine someone loving you so much that they call you just to say goodnight.

I shouldn't be looking at him this way.

Still, it does no harm to admire from afar, as my mother used to say.

'There's nothing wrong with looking at the menu,' she would coo when we were teenagers, and she was in a boisterous mood. 'It doesn't mean you have to order.'

She'd have me in stitches at weddings or on holidays and she'd spot a good-looking man when Dad was well out of earshot. Sarah would feign horror, but I'd stir it up and join in with Mum on her admiration of some unsuspecting passer-by.

Sarah would go into a strop, telling her that Dad was so much nicer and we'd both wind Sarah up more, but deep down I know Mum never had eyes for anyone else. She often spoke about how the stars aligned when she met my father on a rainy winter's night here in Donegal. She spoke of how something clicked in that moment, and they never looked back.

It was like a fairy tale. It was magical. And it always got me thinking of how some people get so lucky, meeting the one they'll spend the rest of their lives with. Although not perfect, they make it work and still claim to love each other no matter how much time goes by. How do some people find all of that, and yet others, like me, end up with heartache after heartache, again and again?

My phone bleeps once more.

Your wine is almost done. I need another pint. Can I get you one?

His words lift my heart and I quickly punch in a response.

I'll have one for the road and then I'm leaving. Thank you.

I look up and find Charlie staring in my direction and our eyes lock for a second. He surely is a kind soul deep down as well as gorgeous. I also find it very funny that he is still sticking to his rules and texting. I know he's doing it now more for the fun than to keep up the walls we've both built around each other.

He comes back with our drinks eventually, after a lot of squeezing past the gathered locals and holiday makers to get to the bar. When he sets my drink down on the table and takes his seat back on his stool again, I can't resist joining in and texting one more time.

Cheers, I write.

Sláinte, he replies, and we both laugh a little as we deliberately avoid any other form of communication for the next half-hour while we enjoy the music, but in the corner of my eye I can still feel Billy's gaze on me. I don't find him creepy but he is keen, that's for sure.

'Great music,' he says, leaning across again. I try a thumbs-up like I did with the older man earlier, but it doesn't seem to satisfy him. 'Are you from around here?'

I shuffle in my seat. I wish Charlie would look around. I don't need to be rescued, but I do need an excuse to fend off Billy's attention, even if he's just being friendly.

'No, I'm on holiday too. I hope you enjoy your stay,' I reply, even though I don't know if he can hear me. It seems to work as he nods his head and goes back to drumming his hands on the edge of the small round table next to him.

I should probably go. I'm feeling just a tiny bit of a glow from the wine, and the last thing I want to do is cross the line with alcohol when I've to walk home alone.

'Wait,' Charlie says as I squeeze past him a little too closely, but it's not like I have a choice. This place is packed. Another man takes my seat like a vulture pouncing on his prey, so even if I wanted to change my mind, I couldn't sit back down again.

I raise my eyebrows, wanting to stick to our arrangement as much as I can. Minimum communication.

'Are you leaving already?'

'Yes,' I reply. 'Getting tired. Thanks for the drink.'

'I can walk with you?' he says, looking up at me from where he sits. He glances over towards Billy, then back at me.

I am suddenly aware of every breath I'm taking, and every breath that he is taking too. I'm afraid I misheard him, so I lean down and put my ear in his direction. Oh my God he smells so good. His hair brushes the side of my face. He leans up slightly, touching my arm, and I feel his breath on my cheek.

'I'll walk with you if you want me to? It's dark out there and I'm finished up now.'

I've stared at him more than I should have tonight. I've got lost in his kindness and lost in this music more than I should have. I've drunk too much wine, and I'm seeing him in an all too familiar light at this very moment. I've felt something every time he caught my eye. I also sensed him looking at me a little too often, even though I know he was trying not to.

But I am tipsy, tired and vulnerable. I fear he might be the same.

'It doesn't matter,' he says when I keep him waiting too long for a response. 'You have George. But I'll be a bit behind you. Bye, Rose.'

He lifts his glass and my stomach lifts too.

'Bye, Charlie.'

I take my dog by the lead, apologising repeatedly as we push past everyone to reach the door. When I get outside, the rain has stopped and the sky is lit up with what looks like a navy blanket dotted with a million diamonds.

I keep walking, Charlie's simple offer to accompany me echoing in my mind until I reach the bumpy lane that leads only to Seaview Cottage. I walk a bit up the lane, then I pause to admire the sky, my head tilted back in wonder. I must stand for longer than I realise because soon I hear footsteps which I know can only be his. No one else uses this lane.

'You don't get to see this in the city.'

I turn around to see him slowly approach.

'The dark skies of rural Ireland,' he continues. 'It's more than magical, isn't it?'

'It's so pretty.'

'No glow of streetlights to take away from the stars, no light pollution to block the view. Just raw, pure beauty, as if the sky is being itself here.'

My heart is beating a little bit faster than it should.

Maybe I'm like the sky when I'm here, dark but slowly peeling back the layers of life to try and be myself.

Maybe I'm just drunk.

'Look,' he says, pointing into the distance. 'If you look way, way over there you'll see the faint green glow of the aurora borealis, the northern lights. So beautiful. Yet so, so far away.'

He stares at me, as if he wants to say something more, but he doesn't. I follow where he points to and sure enough in the distance is an image I've only ever seen in photos or on the television.

'That's . . . that's spectacular,' I reply in a whisper. 'I see pinks and purples too. It's magical.'

We're standing so close together, and for a split second I think I feel his arm around me, but it's just my wine-fuelled imagination.

'No interference, no artificial brightness, nothing to mask its true beauty,' he whispers softly. 'Sometimes we're all too busy to stop and appreciate moments like this, and then we miss them entirely. Sometimes we run too fast and forget what it's like just to walk a while. To take life in. To savour it. To enjoy it. God, I love it here.'

I take a deep breath and briefly close my eyes.

'Me too.'

'That guy in the bar,' he asks, in a change of tone. 'Was he coming on strong? Maybe I'm wrong. Maybe you know him? If it's none of my business, just say.'

I'm touched by his concern, though I'm not sure if it reads as that or if he's . . . is he jealous?

'I'm a big girl,' I say with a smile. 'I think he was just being friendly.'

'Cool. Just checking.'

We walk again slowly, step in step, back to the cottage without saying another word. But I hear every single breath he takes and I'm acutely aware of my own too. Our feet crunch in tandem along the pink pebbled pathway that leads to the red door of Seaview Cottage, both rustling in our pockets for a key.

'Got it,' says Charlie, and we step inside where Max comes bounding to meet us in the hallway. I lean down to greet him just as Charlie does and we almost collide. Our eyes meet.

'Right, I'll get out of your way then,' I say to him. Now that we're back at the cottage, it doesn't feel right to start chatting. I'm aware of the routine by now. I know the rules. Plus, I'd put the hot tub on before I left today and I plan to sample it beneath the stars at last, if only for a few minutes before bed.

'Come on, Max, I'll let you out to do your business,' he says, leading his dog into the kitchen and out towards the back door. I slip into my swimsuit in the bathroom, pull on a heavy towelling bathrobe and slippers and make my way outside, bracing myself against the cold when I step out of the cosy cottage and back into the crisp night air towards the hot tub on the deck.

My knees sting a little from my fall when I tentatively step into the steaming bubbles. I immerse my whole body in the warmth, then I lean my head back and stare up at the velvet sky.

This is the life. This is bliss. I breathe in the silence of the night, only slightly disturbed by the hum of the hot tub bubbles and the gentle hoot of an owl in the distance.

I don't know if it's this sense of freedom as I lie back with my arms outstretched across the edge of the tub, or if being outside in a swimsuit on a cold winter's night with the contrast of temperature is so thrilling, or the drinks I'd had earlier, but I feel giddy and glowing.

Then I open my eyes slowly to see Charlie and Max make their way across the garden from the forest behind us.

He sees me.

Our eyes meet from a distance. He breathes heavily. His hungry eyes are on my glistening skin for what feels like much longer than it really is.

Oh God.

He smiles and my heart lifts. Then he waves, I wave back and he goes inside.

It's time I was in bed.

Moments later, I shower, brush my teeth then go upstairs, where I lie down with George at my feet. I turn over and pull the duvet up under my chin, knowing I'll sleep very well tonight after a beautiful evening, still feeling Charlie's eyes on me from earlier. I know I want to savour that look, even though I shouldn't. I reach across to the bedside locker to put my phone on silent like always, but just as I do I see a message come through.

Goodnight Rose.

Two simple words. Three simple syllables. Yet enough to take my breath away.

Goodnight Charlie, I reply, then I put my phone back in its place and close my eyes into the warmth of the cosy cottage with the sound of the sea in the distance seeping through the open window.

Maybe it's the wine that makes me smile as I sink into a warm slumber, but I doubt it. It's Charlie. And I can't deny it for much longer.

Five Days to Christmas

Chapter Eighteen

Charlie

Max bounces around the hallway like he's on a springboard, thinking he is coming with me as soon as he sees me putting my coat on, but I'm popping down to the Christmas Fayre this afternoon, just to show my face. There's no way I could take him in there. Somehow I'm not sure a springer spaniel, a host of excited children and a range of carefully laid out stalls would mix well together, so I'll have to leave him behind on this occasion.

I'm not even sure a Christmas Fayre is what I need right now either as I've been avoiding all things merry and bright, but it's for a charity close to my heart – plus it might be nice to keep things sweet with Marion, so close to Christmas. I don't want any of us getting turfed out amidst a domestic between her and her husband over the cottage.

'I can't take you with me this time. I'm sorry, old buddy,' I explain to Max as he tugs at the lead from where it hangs on a peg in the hallway. 'You're making me feel very guilty. I'll make it up to you later with a long run on the beach, even though I know you'll be fast asleep by the time I come back after all our adventures this morning.'

I lift an umbrella, but just as I'm about to walk out the door I hear my phone ring out from my pocket and my heart skips a beat. I sigh, assuming it's Helena. It's only been twenty minutes since her last call, so she's due another soon.

I try to ignore it but I can't, and when I look at the screen, I'm glad I did because it isn't Helena this time.

It's Clodagh.

This is unexpected.

Seeing her name on my phone literally stops me in my tracks. She never calls me unless it's about Rebecca, so I automatically fear the worst.

My eyes go foggy and I feel dizzy. I go to the front door to take the call as Max pants and wags his tail impatiently, but when I swipe across the screen to answer the phone, it's not Clodagh's face staring back at me.

It's Rebecca herself and she is crying her heart out.

'Baby! Rebecca, what's wrong?' I beg. 'Where's Mummy? What's happened to you?'

I hear Rose come down the stairs in the cottage, so I step outside into the cold, hoping she'll make herself scarce if she hears I'm on a call. I've been out all day hiking with Max in the Glenveagh National Park, taking in the magnificent Poisoned Glen walk. I came back, had a long hot shower and was feeling quite good in myself for the afternoon ahead until this out-of-the-blue call from my daughter has taken the wind from my sails.

'Daddy!' she sobs, unable to get anything more out as she catches her breath.

'Rebecca, tell me!'

'I – I – Daddy, I just want to go home,' she says, as tears stream down her beautiful face. 'Please let me come home, Daddy. I don't like it here in Tenerife any more. It was just like a holiday, but now I miss you and I want to go h-home to B-Belfast to you and Max and—'

A huge knot forms in my stomach. I feel the blood pump through my veins and I can barely breathe.

'Rebecca . . . Rebecca, darling, it's just a few days until Christmas, so I need you to be very brave,' I say, even though I'm not feeling very brave either, 'and know that I'll come and see you as quickly as I can. You're doing so well. Where's Mummy, Rebecca? Can you tell me?'

I pride myself at being very calm in most situations, but my tolerance is tested on a new level when I see my daughter crying on the other end of a phone when in a different country, and there's very little I can do to help her.

'Everything is so-so different . . . I'm scared of it all, Daddy, I don't know the language even though I'm trying my b-best and it's scaring me. I want to go home.'

At that I hear Clodagh's voice in the background coming closer and closer. When she realises Rebecca is on the phone she takes it from her, looks into the camera and paints on a smile as she flicks back her long dark hair.

'Charlie! Oh, hi!'

'What's going on?'

'Nothing! She's fine!' Clodagh says quickly, wearing the same fake smile she always does when she's trying to brush over something as if it's no big deal. 'Everything's fine. She's just a bit bored today, that's all.'

'Clodagh, she's not fine,' I say through gritted teeth. 'She's not just bored. She's in hysterics. Has something happened?'

I need to stay calm.

'No, nothing has happened. This is typical of you to jump to some far out—'

'Oh, and it's not typical of you to have jumped into moving her into a different country only months after meeting someone? I'm concerned for my daughter who has just called me in tears . . .'

Clodagh is making eyes at me which I know means to keep my voice down.

'Well . . . well, we're all finding it a little bit tough right now,' she says, shooting signals to let me know Rebecca is still listening. 'But it's just because everything is new, isn't that right, Daddy? It's just because everything here is new and it's almost Christmas, so emotions are high. Christmas is different here. Not better, not worse, but different.'

Emotions are high? Of course they're high. They've been high since the day she whisked my child from under my nose like I didn't have a say in the matter and took her to a different bloody country against my wishes.

But I don't say any of it as I know my daughter is upset enough without me tearing into her mother.

I need to keep my cool. Think of the child.

'Yes, it's all very new, I suppose,' I say to Clodagh even though I really want to explode. I don't even want to talk to her. 'Now, can you put Rebecca back on, please?'

I can feel every pulse point in my body throb. I pace the front pathway.

'No, I don't think that would help, Charlie.'

'Daddy!'

My heart stings.

'Clodagh, put her on the phone, please!'

'No, Charlie, this is *not* helping.'

I clench my left hand into a fist and squeeze my eyes shut to try and release some tension.

'She wants to talk to me. She's upset.'

'She'll be even more upset if she sees that you're upset,' Clodagh tells me, her voice rising a few octaves. 'Now, it's better for us all to acknowledge that, yes, there'll be good days and bad days while we settle into this new way of life. Rebecca knows that. She's doing so well.'

'Rebecca,' I call out so my daughter can hear me. 'Rebecca, darling! Daddy loves you and will see you very soon, OK? You stay brave. Send me lots of photos of everything you do, and I'll send you some too. You can call me anytime you want. It doesn't have to just be once a week. Do you hear me, Rebecca?'

I can't help it. I'm staying as calm as I can, but if Clodagh won't put the child on the phone then I'll shout it out so she can hear me.

'This is *not* helping,' Clodagh says firmly. 'We agreed to stick to calls only once a week for now to avoid exactly this. You're fussing, and fussing doesn't help anyone.'

'I'm not fussing! This arrangement is *bloody* ridiculous, Clodagh. Our child called me from your phone in distress!' I say, doing my best to keep my voice level. 'Christ, this is hard for me too, you know? Can you imagine how you'd feel if Rebecca was in a different country from you at this time of year – or any time of year for that matter? I asked you to wait until after Christmas. You should have let us have one last Christmas together. I told you this would happen. I knew it would happen.'

Then Clodagh hangs up. She fucking *hangs up*, and I want to kick something so badly.

'Fuck!' I say as loud as I can, forgetting that Rose is probably in the vicinity. It takes all my willpower not to throw my phone away, so instead I march around the side of the cottage, down to the bottom of the back garden until I can go no further unless I go to the forest, and I stand there with my eyes closed, willing my heart rate to slow down.

I want to scream. My lip trembles. My eyes sting. I haven't cried properly in years.

'Charlie?'

I hear Rose's voice from the kitchen door and I raise my hand to let her know I hear her.

'It's fine,' I call back, hoping and praying she gives me some space like I did for her yesterday when she was upset. 'All good. I'm fine.'

I thankfully hear the back door close, followed by George barking from inside the kitchen. I'm grateful that Rose didn't push me for answers. After last night, when some sort of tension – *attraction* – seemed to build between us caused by too much alcohol, I've been staying out of her way deliberately. I've enough on my mind without getting to know or like a stranger I'm forced to spend Christmas with. I could easily find comfort in Rose. I'm sure I could probably fall for her too, especially last night when she looked so beautiful in her casual clothes and that smile that gets me every time. But I'm too raw right now, and so is she.

I take a few deep breaths and clutch my phone, almost squeezing it in my hand. Man, this hurts to my very bones. I feel so helpless. Maybe I should jump on a plane and just go to see Rebecca? But no, that wouldn't help matters in the long term. Plus, Clodagh would go mental.

I try to think rationally and switch my mindset into a practical mode where I can see things as if I'm looking from the outside in. Yes, that's helping.

I try to look at it from a bird's eye view, even though I'm drowning in emotional agony right now.

Think practically, Charlie. You're always in way too deep. Don't absorb everything so much; you're like a sponge, taking in everyone's feelings and emotions to heart. Think for yourself. Think of the bigger picture and decide from there.

For once, Clodagh's voice in my head is right on the money. As much as my ex drives me insane, she is all in all a very good mother. Yes, that's a better way to look at it. She is usually calm and reasonable when it comes to parenting, which I am too, but I can also err towards the emotional and impulsive side, going into full protective mode if I think my child is hurting.

If she is in pain, I am in pain.

If she's happy, then I'm happy.

But she isn't happy. She wants to come home. I know it's an inevitable bout of homesickness as Christmas creeps closer. Yet hearing her say it and seeing her tear-stained face when we're so far from each other is incredibly hard to bear.

Max, as always when I'm in a bit of a spin, is right by my side. As I stand with my hands on my hips and my head tilted back, trying to focus on breathing this pain out, he jumps on to his hind legs and puts his front paws on my thigh, then tilts his head to the side and looks up at me in solidarity.

'You miss her too, don't you, pal?' I let out a long sigh as I stroke his furry brown and white ears. 'We both miss her so badly. It's cruel.'

He slumps down onto the cold, wet grass. I squeeze my temples, breathing in some more fresh air as I wait for this crippling anxiety and frustration to subside. But minutes later it's still not working. I feel like I need a drink to numb the pain – and I know a few whiskeys would soon make me forget the world – but I also know that would only make it worse. Been there, done that many times in the last few months. I'll go and distract my mind by doing something practical, just like I would tell my clients to.

There's nothing else I *can* do.

'Sorry, Max, but I need to go. I'll make it up to you later, I promise,' I say to the dog. 'I'm going to see what's happening at the village hall. I need to get away from reality before I totally lose my marbles.'

I check my phone to see a text from Clodagh.

She's well settled. I know this is hard, Charlie. I'm taking her swimming now. Try not to worry.

Try not to worry . . . that's a lot easier said than done when you're thousands of miles away from your only child.

At least she had the grace to update me. She didn't have to, I suppose. However, deep down I know that as much as I'll try not to worry, it's going to take a lot of distraction and a whole lot of jolly festive feelings to get my daughter off my mind this time.

When I go back through the kitchen, I see a note from Rose on the fridge.

I'm here if you need me.

I stop and stare. I close my eyes and breathe. It's a very nice gesture, but I need to get out of here before I explode. I just scribble a simple *thank you* beneath it then grab my coat and hat, and head out of the front door.

The fresh air does me the world of good and my head is a little bit clearer by the time I reach the village hall, which is a hive of activity from the outside in.

People of all ages, from newborn babies dressed as pixie elves and reindeer, to elderly folk decked out in Christmas jumpers of all colours of the rainbow, are the height of Christmas cheer. By the time I step inside, even if my own inner mood is much more heated and hellish than 'ho, ho, ho', I find myself getting swept along on the wave of festivity.

They have a chocolate fountain by the entrance which instantly reminds me of Rebecca and how she loves to dip strawberries into the warm, running liquid yet always ends up with most of it on her face. Schoolchildren, most of them around her age, run around with tinsel on their heads, while their parents fuss over cake stalls. There are several arts and crafts displays which, to be fair, are quite impressive. I pick up a snow globe from one of the stalls and shake it, watching the tiny coconut flakes fall on a snow-covered cottage against a deep blue sky. Again, it makes me think of Rebecca and the innocence in her eyes at this time of year.

I put it down again as if it burns me. In a way it does. I can't believe I'm even here at all. So much for avoiding Christmas – though I need distraction from the vision of my daughter crying her heart out to come home.

I browse around some more, greeting locals who whisper and stare, obviously not used to too many strangers at a community event like this. The smell of cloves and freshly baked shortbread fills the air, the sound of carol singing floods my ears and, whether I like it or not, there's a feel-good factor here that couldn't be extinguished if I tried.

This is working. This is good. I can feel my heart rate slow down and the fog in my head settle.

'I'm Charlie,' I say to one pleasant-looking lady behind the craft table. 'I'm staying at Seaview Cottage for the holidays.'

She nods and folds her arms with pursed lips.

'Ooh indeed! I heard there was a double booking at the cottage,' she says with a whisper, like it's the hottest gossip in town. It probably is. 'Marion is fuming! Especially when she heard who you're sharing with. One of Rusty's . . .'

She stops, which makes me wonder where she was going, but then she picks up again.

'Oh, I'd say poor Rusty got an earful, but then it doesn't take much these days,' she continues. 'They're constantly bickering, those two. Would make your head spin.'

I don't indulge in idle gossip. Never have, never will, but of course the lady's comments have piqued my interest when it comes to Rose.

'I have to say, we're managing absolutely fine,' I say, hoping to quash any ridiculous rumours of some big drama. 'In fact, it has worked out much better than we could have imagined. Rose is a wonderful house guest. We're—'

'Father O'Leary!' the woman gushes, interrupting my attempt at unravelling the grapevine gossip. I glance to my side to see the parish priest, who appears to be almost like a celebrity around here, but each to their own.

Then a music box catches my eye. It's a small walnut box, and when I open it a tiny ballerina angel twirls round and round to the sound of a very familiar tune. I recognise it instantly, the gentle melody reminding me of the story behind the tune, where the French composer gave it to his bride-to-be as an engagement present. 'Salut d'Amour'. I think I must have learned about this in school.

'I'll take this, please,' I say when the woman comes back to her pew. She watches as the priest moves on, doing his rounds and congratulating everyone for such a fine job.

'Of course,' she replies, and puts it in a heavy paper bag, along with a couple of chocolate treats she gives to her paying customers. 'It's a very romantic little tune, isn't it? You know, I found that in a car boot sale years ago. I knew someone would like it one day.'

'Sorry?'

'The tune in the music box. For someone special?'

I don't respond to her question. I know exactly who I'm buying it for.

'No, it's just a tune that I recognise, that's all,' I tell her. 'No biggie.'

'So, no trouble at the cottage at all, then?' she asks with bulbous eyes, then pushes her glasses back on her twitching nose. 'Well, I mean it's hardly ideal to be sharing with a stranger at Christmas, is it?'

'It's fine,' I say as I take my change. 'No trouble at all. Thanks for this. I'll make sure it goes to someone special.'

I wink at her, just for boldness, and when I turn away, pleased with what I've picked up so far on my travels, I spot someone waving at me in the distance under a sign that reads: Marion's Mince Pies.

She looks very excited to see me, which is a relief after her swift departure from the cottage last time.

I suppose I should go and say hello.

Chapter Nineteen

Rose

I make my way down to the village hall for the Christmas Fayre, leaving George in the cottage with Max for the first time, which I hope doesn't cause carnage when they're home alone.

The fayre, just as I'd expected, is packed with families and couples from near and far, some queuing up at the far end of the hall for Santa's Grotto and a lot of children running amok, weaving their way in and around pretty little stalls that are bursting with Christmas cheer.

'Some mulled wine, Rose?'

I turn to see the smiling face of an older lady. I've never seen her before.

'I hear you're staying at the cottage? Oh, you're the picture of your Granny Molly. Mind you, I wouldn't mind being cooped up with *him* if I was thirty years younger.'

She hands me the paper cup of warm red wine and nods in the direction of a rather dishevelled Charlie, who appears to be overseeing a stall across the hall. He's the last person I expected to bump into here.

He's made his feelings very clear about how much he wanted to hide away from Christmas, yet yesterday I found him listening to 'O Holy Night' and now this? I pretend I don't see him as I browse around the other stalls, but then he catches me looking his way. If I'm not mistaken, his face brightens when he sees me.

I wave across to him, wondering if a wave in public counts as breaking the rules.

He raises his eyes upwards to indicate the sign on the wall behind him and I nod slowly when I see that he's been roped into looking after Marion's stall. He sends me a text.

Help.

I look his way and can't help laughing. Marion's little helper, I write back.

Please buy one. My sales skills are nil.

I laugh out loud again and make my way over to him.

'Before you ask, I'm only looking after it while she goes and sorts out some sort of crisis that has arisen at the children's art corner,' he explains, leaning his strong, muscular arms on the table. I try not to look at them. 'I think some kid got a bit carried away with the glitter.'

He smiles. Those dimples.

'Ah, I see,' I say, feeling the weight of the huge elephant in the room. In fact, a small herd of elephants, to be precise.

He knows I was a mess yesterday, but he doesn't know why.

I know he was upset earlier, and although I did pick up on the fact that he has a young daughter who he is breaking his heart over, I don't know any more than that.

And then there's the small matter of how we walked home together last night, shared a moment under the stars and texted each other 'goodnight' for the first time, which made me feel like something had changed between us.

I don't know what it was, but it was something.

'Wine,' he says, as if he's been reading my mind.

'What?'

'Too much wine, beer and emotion last night. No need to overthink things.'

Well, that's the ice well and truly broken in that department.

'Of course,' I say, running my eye over the mince pies in a bid to avoid his face. My own, I fear, might be flushing.

'So, are you just going to stare at them or will you try one?' he asks, but just as I'm about to lift one I look around to see Marion strutting towards us, smiling to herself as she marches, but then she sees me and her face turns sour.

'Maybe later,' I say to Charlie and before he can question my decision, I make a quick exit over towards the Santa Grotto where a group of parents and children are waiting impatiently in a haphazard queue, all under the guidance of a very cool young elf who is taking none of their nonsense.

'It's not the real Santa,' I hear one of the youngsters say to her mother, who glares at her to be quiet. 'I can see his ginger hair under his hat, Mam! Since when was Santa ginger?'

She has a point.

Santa, who seems to be doing his very best at being a good listener, sits on a painted park bench with a post box beside him. The small area is surrounded by a white picket fence, a yellow brick path that leads to where he sits and various ornamental reindeer, owls, snowmen and a rather annoying oversized train set which is playing 'Jingle Bells' on repeat. It's not the worst effort I've seen, and I have to say Santa looks rather jolly amidst the commotion.

To my surprise he gives me a wave. I wave back, slightly cautiously.

'I hope you're on my nice list, Rosebud!'

It's Rusty. I shake my head and laugh out loud.

'For a change,' I say, feeling very proud of him and his important role.

I watch on for a few seconds, allowing myself to soak up the excitement of the awaiting children, and the enthusiasm of the helpers who have pulled this community fayre together. Women and men in hi-vis vests go around with charity buckets, and I notice that each stall has one placed for customers to donate some change in aid of a well-known homeless charity. Sweet wafts of sugary treats fill the air, a small group of carol singers entertain the masses, and an inflatable snowman provides a popular photo opportunity. All in all, it's very heart-warming and festive.

I glance towards the mince pie stall where Marion is now engrossed, all giggles and eye flutters up at Charlie. She keeps touching his arm and laughing out loud, fondling her hair. She is also wearing a rather fetching shade of pink lipstick which is very unlike her.

I feel he is trying desperately to make his escape, but she has him well and truly in her clutches. From a distance it looks like he's doing a great job at playing along, but I can't imagine he's in the mood deep down for any of this commotion.

Marion is on a roll though, introducing him to everyone who comes their way as if he's a prize for the raffle, and everyone who comes their way looks like they would gladly buy a ticket.

Charlie from the cottage, I hear some locals whisper. *Isn't he a babe? He's staying there for Christmas.*

I feel eyes on me too and realise we are most definitely the talk of the town, but Marion is making it very clear that she found him first.

I've nothing against Marion whatsoever. In fact, in days gone by, she and I got on quite well until she and my dad tore each other apart over the cottage, but that's not really my fault or business. Anyhow, I admire how involved she is in her community, but I think it's fair to say that the feeling is no longer reciprocal. If looks were daggers, I'd be dead by now. And that's putting it mildly.

'She's doing it to annoy me, I know she is,' Rusty whispers when I bump into him later as I enjoy a paper cupful of hot chocolate, marshmallows and cream with a chocolate flake. It was served up by the most delightful crew of costumed local actors who told me all about their up-and-coming pantomime. Cinderella herself insisted on making me their 'Snow Queen Special' and I can guarantee it has enough excess calories to go right to my already voluptuous hips – but it's Christmas and I'm practically spending it alone so I don't care.

'You really think that's all for your benefit?' I ask, even though I could already guess the answer. 'I thought she was trying to make *me* jealous, but if so, she's wasting her time.'

'Nope, it's all for me,' says Rusty, smacking his lips together. 'Oh, she knows how to do it in style. I was sweltering in that Santa suit, trying my best to be jolly for the kids when all I wanted to do was tell her to catch herself on. We're not teenagers any more. There's no need for silly mind games.'

I don't like to say it, but I don't think Rusty has anything to be concerned about. Marion is a very attractive lady, and a popular one too, but I doubt if she's on Charlie's radar. He has enough on his plate from what I overheard earlier, plus she is at least twenty years older than he is, I'd guess.

Nonetheless, it's hurting Rusty and that's what matters most.

'Gosh, Rusty, are things really that bad with you two?' I ask him. 'I never thought I'd see the day. I remember you two being love's young dream.'

'Me too.'

Rusty watches his wife in the distance as she does her thing, busying around the stalls, checking if anyone needs extra cash or wants to empty their charity collection boxes, while Charlie is still stuck minding her stall. It's no surprise that her mince pie sales are now flying. From what I can see from here, they're mainly being bought by women who are taking the opportunity to ogle the handsome stranger who is serving them up with a delightful smile, and even posing for a few selfies.

'She's all over him like a rash,' Rusty says, his sad eyes glistening. 'Like, he's young enough to be her son.'

'Hmm, just about at a push, but he'd make a nice toy boy,' I tell him. He raises his eyebrows to insinuate that I'm not helping matters.

'Thanks for that vote of confidence. Mind you, if she sees me sitting here with you it will only add fuel to the fire,' he continues, his eyes jumping around and his left knee shaking with nerves. 'Ah, I'm finding the whole thing exhausting, Rose. She's raging I let you stay in the cottage. Especially that I didn't tell her the change of plan.'

I knew I'd come into this somehow.

'Wait a minute. So, you didn't *tell* her?'

He shakes his head.

'Nope.'

'Ah, Rusty.'

'I think I was being stubborn, if truth be told,' he says, fidgeting as he speaks. 'I was trying to make a point that it's not always her way or no way, but boy, that has backfired spectacularly. She's barely speaking to me at all now.'

We both sip our drinks and try not to stare in the direction of the mince pie stall, where it all seems to be happening. One woman in a very fetching Mrs Claus outfit which is barely suitable for a family event, has her arms wrapped round Charlie's neck and is planting a bright red kiss on his cheek for a photo. I catch his eye as he wipes it off with the back of his hand and my own face goes red in response. My face can't lie, and I can't deny that I did feel a slight nip from the green-eyed monster. I'm a bit like Marion. I need to catch myself on. I don't own him.

'I do understand how she'd be upset by me not telling her,' I say to Rusty, doing my best to divert my eyes in any direction other than Charlie's, 'but if you need a strong defence, it was really *Charlie* who let me stay. You only just suggested it, even if you didn't give him much wriggle room to say no, but Marion doesn't need to know that. You could just claim it was his idea, full stop.'

Rusty's forehead wrinkles into a frown.

'But what were the alternatives?' he asks me, his ginger beard catching some of the cream of his own Snow Queen Special as he sips from his cup. 'Leave you out in the cold, literally? You're my own flesh and blood, Rose. If you were a total stranger, I still couldn't have left you stranded.'

I put my hand on Rusty's arm as a gesture of thanks for his loyalty.

'Mind you, Marion would have probably welcomed in a stranger over me, not that I'd blame her after some of the words that were exchanged back in the day. It was brutal.'

He doesn't respond for a second. He knows all too well that's the truth.

'It was brutal indeed, but it's my family affair, not hers. And on the same page, our marital problems are exactly that,' he concludes. 'Ours. Not yours to be bored with. Now, on another note, how are you and Prince Charming getting along at the cottage?'

I laugh at the idea of Charlie being charming. But then I remember he is. He's very charming indeed which is why I need to keep my distance more than ever.

'I'm still waiting on that car part, so I'd say you're here for another while,' says Rusty.

'I was thinking that anyhow.'

'Sorry, Rose, but I did warn you it wouldn't be this side of Christmas. So is everything going OK for you both? How've you been getting on?'

My eyes magnetically move again to Charlie as I ponder my answer and my face creeps into a smile as I recall some of our encounters over the past few days. Where do I begin?

'Well . . . you could say that we're equally irritated by it all, and equally playing some sort of silly avoidance dance which is kind of working,' I reply, doing my best to sum it all up so far. 'It's been interesting, I have to say.'

'Oh . . .'

'But then I fell off the bike the other day, he helped me bandage up my war wounds and he made me dinner. He left it at the bedroom door.'

Rusty takes a step back and looks me face to face.

'Uh oh . . .'

'What?'

He laughs and slaps his thigh.

'Rosebud, you're smitten!' he says, his face lighting up. 'Ah, it's like the circus has come to town. All the women around here are going gaga for him, but I should have known this would happen. Two fine-looking youngsters, tucked away in a cottage with no one around to bother them and then, boom!'

'No, Rusty, no, no. Slow down, it's not like that, and we're hardly youngsters. Look, I know absolutely nothing about Charlie so far, not even his surname. In fact, the only thing I do know is that he has a young daughter somewhere out there who he is missing terribly, and a woman called Helena who seems to call him, and vice versa, an awful lot. So it's not what you're thinking at all, and it never will be.'

Rusty rolls his eyes and stirs his drink with the chocolate flake which is quickly turning into a melted mess. His Santa duties are done, having been rescued for the final hour of the fayre by a younger, much leaner model who I must say doesn't seem to be having the same appeal. Meanwhile, the cool elf from Rusty's shift has been replaced by a much rattier female version who sounds like she'd be better placed in charge of a prison than a children's Christmas grotto.

'If there's a woman and a child involved, then stay far, far away,' Rusty warns me, shooting me a warning glance. 'Don't get your fingers burnt, Rose. That's all I'm saying on the subject. Be careful.'

Oh, here we go.

'You've no need to tell me that,' I remind him quickly. 'I'm not some sort of marriage wrecker, Rusty. Do you think I'd even go there? Not a chance. Besides, Charlie and I barely talk to each other.'

He does a double-take.

'What do you mean, you don't talk to each other?' he asks. 'He makes you dinner, but you don't *talk*?'

'No, we don't talk unless we must. We communicate by text, or we leave each other notes. It's one of our house rules.'

'You're kidding me!'

'I'm not,' I reply, knowing it sounds as strange as it really is. 'It was his idea. We text each other if need be, and we stay out of each other's way as far as possible. The dinner was a one-off gesture as I was genuinely hurt. My knees are still a bit—'

'So, you've never had a conversation? In four days?'

'Bits and pieces, just,' I say, realising it's the truth. 'Well, we walked home from the pub when we were a bit tipsy last night. He pointed out some stars and the northern lights and – yes, that's probably the most time we've spent in the same place at the same time since we got here. It was nice. I think.'

'Rose . . .'

'It's cool! It was no big deal, I swear. We'd sat beside each other in the bar beforehand for ages and barely said a word, so the brief stargazing was hardly romantic. Anyhow, our four days of minimum conversation arrangement, it's working. We haven't had a row or really annoyed each other – or at least I don't think we have . . . yet.'

'Ah, well I've heard it all now,' Rusty says, in amazement. 'You two sound as bad as Marion and I.'

'How?'

'All picture, no sound. We don't talk to each other either.'

He laughs even though I know he doesn't find it funny.

'Oh Rusty.'

'In fact, every time we do talk, it turns into a full-blown argument, so it sounds like your arrangement is better than mine. Ah, I don't know. Relationships, eh?

He stands up with a sigh and I notice a shake in his hands as well as in his voice. I've never noticed that before.

'I hope you're OK?' I say as he goes to walk away, but he comes back again and leans down towards me.

I think I know what's coming.

'I'll be grand. Now, I know you're going to tell me to mind my own business,' he says, 'and feel free to tell me to do just that, but since you're only about fifty minutes away from your parents' house . . .'

I point my finger in his direction with a smile.

'Mind your own!'

'I must ask,' he continues. 'I'd kick myself if I didn't. Would you not go home for Christmas?'

'Oh Rusty, don't, please.'

I'm more serious now. I put my head in my hands, but he keeps going.

'I know I couldn't drive you all the way to Dublin, but I *could* drive you to see them before Christmas Day. Now, I've said what I wanted to. The offer is there if you want it.'

I slide my hands down my face and look up at Rusty whose pleading eyes touch my soul, but I just shake my head slowly. A lump forms in my throat.

'You know why I can't do that,' I reply. 'And please don't go against my decision by telling anyone from home I'm staying here. You said you wouldn't. Please don't let Marion tell them either. Promise me, Rusty. I just need one last Christmas alone.'

He shrugs and holds his arms out wide.

'But you're not alone, are you?'

'You know what I mean,' I say. 'And it's not like I'd exactly planned this arrangement, is it?'

'No,' he replies. 'OK. I won't mention it again. Your secret's safe with me if that's what you want, but I can't speak for Marion . . .'

'Oh no.'

'Let's not even make it seem like a secret to her,' he whispers. 'That way, she won't feel the need to get in touch with anyone if there's no big agenda.'

'Thank you.'

'It's the best I can come up with,' he shrugs. 'I said I wouldn't tell a soul and I won't. You know I'll always go that extra mile for you, Rose.'

He holds my gaze.

'It was nice seeing you here today and it's good to know you have my back,' I say with a light smile. 'One day I'll repay you for your kindness, I promise.'

He scrunches up his face, drains the last of his hot chocolate and throws his cup into the bin.

'I'd better go and get ready for the big clean up,' he says, and then he saunters off, taking a tiny piece of my heart with him.

Thank goodness for family. Rusty's as close as I'm going to get to my own this Christmas.

*

I make it back to the cottage before Charlie does, which is a relief as I can't be bothered awkwardly skirting around each other, and after a walk with George and Max in the forest, I take my time getting ready for the evening which I plan to spend eating something nice at the Lighthouse Tavern before it gets busy, followed by a few drinks with the locals, and an early night.

Rusty's words earlier about going home were like a knife in my heart. It's one thing avoiding calls and blocking the whole 'going home' option from my own mind, but hearing it from Rusty has taken it to a whole new level.

My parents are in their mid-seventies now, my niece and nephew are growing up fast, and I know I can't hide away forever when it comes to family gatherings at this time of year. I would have an excuse if I lived in a different country, but I don't. And here I am, closer geographically than I've ever been at this time of year since Michael's accident and the pain and grief that followed it.

I take out my phone, check it for messages and put it away immediately in case I'm tempted to listen to or read any recent correspondence from my family. Their efforts have simmered as the days have passed, which I'm grateful for, and I can just imagine them wondering where I might be on my impromptu holiday to escape Christmas.

Sarah will hedge her bets on somewhere hot, like the Canary Islands, but only because she likes the sun and would probably choose it for herself.

Mum will wrack her brain trying to work out *who* I might be away with as well as where I'll go. She'll delve deep into the possibility of old school friends from over twenty years ago, or the nice girl, Patricia, who I met at university and who moved to London never to be heard from again. Or she'll hope and pray that I've laid the ghost of Michael to rest and have met a decent man in Dublin who has taken me to Paris or Rome in some happy ever after.

Dad, on the other hand, will keep out of it all, saying *'it's up to Rose what she does and who she does it with'*, and then an argument will blow up as to how that attitude didn't exactly work out in anyone's favour this time two years ago. And he'll say I shouldn't have had a few drinks before we left that night, even though Michael was sober and driving. And Mum will say it was supposed to be a celebration. And didn't Michael *bring* me the champagne? And didn't everyone have a glass knowing what was coming? And that it was an accident. It was an accident.

I leave a note for Charlie on the whiteboard in the kitchen.

I've walked Max and George both. Have u good evening.

Then I put on a floaty red maxi dress, funky flat gold boots and a light sweep of lipstick, feeling the urge to get dressed up just a little bit. When I know the dogs are safe and happy inside, I lock the door and head to the pub where a glass of red wine and a tasty dinner has my name on it.

Despite this never-ending inner claw at my gut, the freedom and pace of life in Donegal is sinking into my bones.

And when I allow it to settle there, it feels so good.

*

Should I go for the seafood chowder again, or try out the fish and chips? Or the macaroni cheese?

Now I know that I'm probably going to be staying here for Christmas Day, my mind is totally focused on food glorious food and how I can fit in a festive feast, even if I don't have anyone to share it with.

'I'm going to have to go for the chowder again,' I say to the waitress who served me up the same here less than twenty-four hours ago.

'It's very popular so I'm not surprised,' she says, taking my order down with pen and paper. There are no fancy tablets here like I see in Dublin restaurants, which is strangely refreshing. 'I love your dress by the way. Red is your colour.'

'Thank you,' I smile. 'That's very kind of you to say so.'

As the days roll by, I really am beginning to relax here now. I'm glad I visited the lighthouse when I did. I'm glad I let out all that emotion early in my trip. I feel a lot lighter for it, pardon the pun.

And now that I know I'm here for the duration, I've decided that by hook or by crook, I'm going to make sure I eat well in the run-up to Christmas, or what's left of it. So when the chowder arrives, I savour every single second of it.

It's a delicate golden colour with chunks of salmon, prawns, mussels and cod. The homemade wheaten bread soaks up the buttery juices and, just like yesterday, it's a delight to see some baby boiled potato chopped up in there too. I'm in food heaven. It's full of garlic and goodness, its warmth hitting the bottom of my stomach. I close my eyes and savour every flavour. There's simply nothing like sea-food when you're so close to the Atlantic.

'Everything OK?' asks the nice young waitress. 'Can I get you more bread?'

'Oh, yes please,' I reply, almost salivating at the thought, and for a brief second I feel lucky and content to be able to sample such pleasures.

I may not have anyone to share gifts with, or any family members to laugh and bicker with, or anyone to pull a cracker with. But I can still rely on good food to keep me company.

But then I think of that again.

'I don't even have anyone to pull a cracker with,' I whisper out loud. The thought of this stops me in my tracks, and my moment of ease is gone.

I put down my cutlery to let it sink in.

I don't even have someone to pull a stupid cracker with. Suddenly, images of myself in old age come to mind where I'm sitting at a festive table, with all the trimmings and a cracker that can only ever be ornamental as I've no one to share the moment with. How many years of Christmas alone do I have in front of me? And how many people across the world face up to this every year, not out of choice, but out of circumstance?

I'm young, I know that, but when Michael died my future plans died too, so it's going to take a long time to create a new vision of what I'd like to lie ahead.

He and I had planned to travel the world together in all seasons. We'd planned to spend Christmas in Bali, summer in Mexico, and we'd fill our weekends with city breaks to

Paris, London and Rome. We would live our very best lives. We'd make so many memories our photo albums would be bursting, and our passports would be stamped like memory books we could look back on forever.

We'd create our own traditions for different times of the year. We'd make each other birthday cards rather than buy them. We'd write poetry as gifts instead of splashing cash on presents we didn't need, and we'd always make sure to greet each other good morning and good night, no matter what our mood was like.

We had so many dreams, but that's all they turned out to be. Dreams that didn't come true.

'Rose? I was hoping we'd bump into you again. Do you mind if we join you?'

It's Stacy and Chris, the friendly English couple I met last night.

'Have a seat, of course,' I say to Stacy, who doesn't have to be told twice. 'It's so nice to see you again.'

I push the remainder of my chowder to the side, my appetite now gone as a fantasy fog slowly clears to let me see the truth. I have company though, so I need to snap out of it.

'Oh no, sorry. You're still eating. We'll grab a stool by the bar.'

'Yes. We'll do that until you finish,' says Chris. 'In fact, I'm going to nip to the bathroom first.'

I dab the sides of my mouth with my napkin.

'Honestly, no. I'm all done. Bag a seat for him while you still can,' I say to Stacy. 'This place just gets busier every time

I'm here, so you mightn't be so lucky in a wee while. I'm finished. Promise.'

'Were you at the Christmas Fayre?' asks Stacy and I nod in response. 'Wasn't it just a delight? I bought so much stuff I don't know how I'm going to fit it all into my suitcase.'

The pub is filling up quickly as some other faces I recognise from the Christmas Fayre begin to arrive, all thirsty and high on festivities after what seemed like a very successful event.

They arrive full of chitter chatter and praise – *Didn't the tombola go down a treat? The grotto was so well managed this year. Susie O'Hare's craft stall was a sight to behold. And all handmade! Did you try Hannah's cakes? And the mince pies were to die for as always.*

I wonder if Susie O'Hare is the lady I bought the cute 'forget-me-not' picture frame from. Its moon and stars design caught my eye as I was leaving. When I examined it more closely, she took great pride in informing me how she'd made it from scrap wood she'd found in her late father's shed. It was too pretty to pass and I thought myself lucky to snap it up before anyone else did.

'Can I get you a drink?' Chris asks on his return. He takes off his coat and hangs it on the back of his chair. 'White wine?'

'Thank you,' I reply. 'That would be lovely.'

Then, just as Chris's back is turned, Stacy leans across the table, her face bursting with excitement to tell me whatever is on the tip of her tongue.

'Chris will murder me for telling you, Rose, but I believe in passing on a compliment,' she whispers.

'Oh, me too. Go on,' I say, feeling this must be my lucky night.

'Now, do you remember yesterday evening he was chatting to a guy at the bar while I was fussing over your gorgeous dog?'

I don't, to be honest, but Stacy doesn't give me room to respond.

'Well, the guy was asking who you were in a very admiring way, and he's just walked in. Look! He's chatting to Chris again. Rose, he's lovely.'

I do my best to discreetly look towards the bar, past all the coats and bobble hats who are trying to find a seat, and then I see who Stacy is talking about.

He wears a long beige woollen coat, a white shirt and has sandy hair which looks like it's been freshly cut in time for Christmas. He is smart and very clean-cut. He looks friendly, I suppose, but he is most definitely not my type.

It's Billy.

'Well, I'm very flattered,' I say to Stacy, as the waitress who admired my dress earlier clears the table. 'Oh, Chris is bringing him over. Oh.'

'I've a terribly big mouth,' Stacy giggles. 'Chris says I can't hold my—'

'Rose, Stacy, this is Billy. I've asked him to join us for a drink. Hope you ladies don't mind?'

I open my mouth but nothing comes out, and before I know it, Billy has taken off his camel coat and is in the seat beside me with a pint of beer in hand, telling me again all about his recent divorce and how he came to Donegal to forget about it all for a few days, and now that there's no music to distract us, isn't it great to get chatting properly.

Sweet Lord above, help me.

And again, despite my efforts to be polite to Billy, I'm barely listening because Charlie has just come into the bar and I can't think straight. He must have gone back to the cottage to get changed because he's now wearing a navy shirt and fresh jeans that hug him in all the right places. His hair is damp from the shower, and as usual he fills the room. There isn't a woman in the place who doesn't look his way.

'Isn't that the guy you're sharing the cottage with?' whispers Stacy. I nod. 'Jeez, Rose. No wonder you've hardly given poor Billy a sideward glance. He's a dish.'

She giggles like a schoolgirl. I do my best to stay po-faced. I try to focus on my present company, but my eyes give me away. They are trained simply to follow him as he finds his bearings, looking at his phone, pushing back his wavy hair, smiling to greet people he doesn't know.

Thanks for walking Max. Most appreciated.

He's texting me. The sound of my phone and the words on the screen distract me.

No problem

I type the response quickly and set my phone down as if it's on fire. I hate texting in company, but I don't want to ignore him either. He is with Marion and her cronies from the Christmas Fayre, who look like they've just won the lottery, but Charlie's eyes are skirting around too as if he is looking for someone.

Is he looking for me?

He sees me. I wave.

He waves back.

He smiles at first but when he spots Billy by my side again he looks away quickly and busies himself at the bar, tapping a beer mat as he waits for his friends to find a table. I can't quite read the expression on his face as he stares up at the television that broadcasts a TV music channel with the volume turned down. Now his hands are in his pockets. Now, they're back on the bar. Now he is biting his lip.

He looks my way again.

He looks away again. Billy is still talking. I'm still barely listening because I can't. I feel a pull, like a crazy tug, a magnetic urge to be near Charlie. I've no idea why.

Too much wine and beer, I remember him saying. Yes, that's all it was last night and it's all it is now.

We are just strangers who are sharing a cottage. We have no obligation to be physically close to each other outside of that.

'This is Charlie,' I hear Marion coo to anyone who will listen. 'Yes, he's staying at our cottage.'

Our cottage. Huh. It was my Granny Molly's cottage until Marion got her claws into it over some stupid raffle.

She puts her hand on his arm, showing him off as if he is her own prize property. And now he's taking off his coat, laughing and joking with his new-found friends. He sits beside them, leaning in, giving them his full attention, including the lady who was dressed in the Mrs Claus suit earlier.

So I do my best to give my new-found friends the same attention, even if boring Billy is already sending me to sleep with his tales of woe.

I could top his anytime, but I can't be bothered. I'll finish this drink and then I'm out of here.

'Can I walk you to the door?' Billy asks me when I bid my farewells.

I glance for Charlie. He is already looking my way.

'You're very kind, but I better race on. Goodnight, every-one. Enjoy the rest of your evening.'

'Or I could take you for dinner some time?'

I look at Stacy who might spontaneously combust.

'Lovely to see you again, Rose,' says Billy, leaning in to give me a kiss on the cheek. 'Maybe you can let me know?'

'Sure,' I reply swiftly. 'That's kind of you to ask. I'll let you know.'

I can't get out of here quickly enough.

Chapter Twenty

Charlie

'Sorry to be a party pooper, but I'm going to call it a night. Cheers for everything, Marion. I'll see you again soon.'

Marion does her best to stop me, offering beer, wine, champagne, anything I want, but I'm having none of it.

I won't deny it.

I feel like I need to scarper from the pub as soon as I see Rose leave, mainly because my head is fried after being pulled like a rag doll from Marion's clutches towards Julie, the local librarian who has at least changed out of her racy red and white suit before joining us in the Lighthouse Tavern for drinks after the fayre.

For the last hour, Julie has insisted on taking numerous selfies with me, apparently to show her friend in New York who loves Irish men, so eventually I quickly make the excuse that I've accidentally locked Rose out of the cottage. Leaving half a pint of beer behind, I quicken my step, hoping I'll catch up with Rose along the way.

And now here we are.

'Oh, hi,' she says, stargazing just like we did at this very same spot last night. 'I was hoping to see the northern lights again, but maybe I'm looking in the wrong direction?'

Her multi-coloured woollen scarf is tucked up around her chin, and the pink bobble hat she is wearing clashes totally with the red dress that skims along her ankles – there's always something with Rose that makes her whole look less than perfect, yet perfect for her.

'You're on the right track, but it's a bit cloudy tonight to see it, I imagine,' I say, looking into the distance.

'Pity.'

'There'll be other nights,' I remind her. 'It's going to snow quite a lot tonight by the looks of it. Did you have a nice evening?'

She glances at me as we now stroll together, her eyes puzzled at my question.

'Hang on a second. Are you – are you striking up a *conversation* with me?' she asks, her voice lilting in surprise. 'Like, an *ordinary* conversation and not one about the cottage or the rules? Or are you loaded up on too much wine, beer and emotion again?'

We walk in a rhythmic step about a metre apart as she guides us along the darkened lane with the torch light on her phone, dodging puddles as we go.

'I only had two drinks, but speak for yourself,' I respond, taking the dig at my earlier comment on the chin. 'Nice to see you making new friends. You looked like you were enjoying yourself.'

'As did you,' she says, jutting out her chin now. I bite the inside of my lip. The moonlight is shining down from where it sits over the bay, far enough in the distance to see its full shape clearly but not close enough to light up our path.

'I was a bit suffocated to be honest,' I say, hoping to break the tension that hangs like a fog in the air.

'Suffocated?'

'Yes, Marion was literally stroking my face at one stage,' I say with a laugh, 'and don't get me started on that Julie woman. She was on my knee as if she was in Santa's grotto. I had to make an excuse to use the loo.'

'She sat on your knee? I hadn't noticed.'

Oh yes, she had. I know she had because I saw her looking at that exact moment.

I stop walking, but she marches on with pace now, so I follow quickly to catch up as snow begins to fall.

'I thought I *saw* you noticing,' I tell her, knowing I'm pushing it but I can't resist. 'I kept checking my phone, waiting on some sort of funny remark from you.'

'I was looking at the clock on the wall behind where you were sitting.'

There was no clock on the wall behind where I was sitting, which makes me grin. I can feel Rose beam too without even looking at her.

We reach the cottage gate and I walk behind her up the pink gravel pathway, our boots crunching beneath us in the freshly laid snow.

'So, why didn't you come over and say hello to me, Charlie?' she says, a little pinch in her voice. 'You know, like normal people sharing a cottage would? We *can* be civil to each other in a public place . . . or were you too afraid of Marion to do so?'

My mouth opens as she wrestles with the key in the door. This has taken a bit of a jack knife.

'What? Why would I be afraid of Marion? I didn't want to . . . we are trying to keep our distance, aren't we?'

Now she stops.

'Seriously, Charlie? Grow up.'

She marches inside the cottage.

'And I didn't want to disturb you as you seemed engrossed in that guy with the long detective-style coat and the swept back hair. Beige Billy.'

Rose tilts her head back and laughs as she leads the way into the hall, taking off her coat and hanging it over the bottom of the stairs on her way past.

'Beige Billy!' she giggles.

I automatically lift her coat and hang it up on the proper stand just as I do with her hat and scarf when she sets them on the radiator. I take off my own coat, shivering as the heating clicks in when Rose gives the switch a thump. Seconds later we're both greeted by our forever enthusiastic canine friends, who so far don't seem to have done any damage in our absence.

'Sounds like you were keeping a very close eye on *my* company when you even know his name?' Rose suggests, making her way to the living room where it's her turn to sleep tonight.

'There was a clock on the wall behind where *you* were sitting,' I tell her.

'Touché!' she says in return. 'So, you know Billy, then?'

'I met him a few nights ago when I was in the pub.'

'Well then, you should know that he isn't totally beige.'

'You think?'

'I don't think. I know,' she says. 'He's asked me out to dinner.'

I feel a gut punch which I try to ignore.

'How lovely.'

'Indeed.'

'I'll let the dogs outside before bed.'

'Good idea. Goodnight, Charlie.'

We hold each other's gaze as my stomach swoops and I do my best not to let my face give away what's going on in my head.

'Goodnight, Rose.'

She closes the door and I walk outside into the cold night air, staring out into the forest as the dogs sniff and bounce and pee into the already frosting grass.

It looks like we're in for another thick snowfall overnight, but right now all I can picture in my head is Rose and Billy chatting over dinner on their forthcoming date.

In my mind I hear her laughing at his jokes, I see their hands touching across the table, I see her smile as they send and receive messages just like we do.

I feel a bit queasy.

I'll go inside and stick on the kettle then get the dogs back inside. Maybe a hot cup of tea will help me settle for the night. Maybe I should offer Rose a cuppa too?

No, I shouldn't. It's doing things like that which has led to me feeling this way about her and it must stop.

It's time I was in bed. Wine, beer and emotion is never a good mixture.

Four Days to Christmas

Chapter Twenty-One

Rose

The cottage is eerily silent this morning.

It's cold and ghostly. It's empty. It's just me and George and although that has been the case many times over the past week, I've grown quite used to seeing Charlie and Max here when I wake up every day.

But now for the first time I'm really feeling the quiet out here, and even though this is what I craved since I got here, it seems strange to be alone. I turn on some music on the old radio in the kitchen, tuning into the comfort of Donegal's local station Highland Radio which makes me feel a little less isolated. They're playing upbeat Christmas carols, but so far they don't faze me.

My mood has dipped, but what was I expecting when I came into the kitchen this morning? Charlie's classical music? Dodging around him while he made breakfast in his bare feet, calling for Max who is usually causing havoc with the starlings in the garden? Hearing him sing in the shower or just potter around upstairs?

Whatever I was expecting, it's not here and it's knocked me off centre.

'So, what will we do today, George?' I ask my furry old friend. 'But first things first before you answer, let's get you fed.'

I've a banging headache, so even before I see to George my first mission is to drink some water, but when I go to the fridge I see a note on the board.

So we're back to leaving messages and texts after last night's awkward walk home? The sight of his writing does draw me in, I admit.

I fed George. You were fast asleep. Have a great day, Rose.

I can't help but smile, so I wipe it off and write my reply.

Thank you.

Then I remember his words at the Christmas Fayre, and the smile disappears from my face. I didn't ask him to follow me home last night. He didn't have to leave his company for my sake, no matter how suffocated he was feeling.

I need to get out of here. I need a change of scenery or some distraction at least before I analyse and overthink every aspect of Charlie so far.

And then I remember I've no car. I'm stuck.

One thing about being here is that when you've walked the beaches, admired the views, drunk lots of Guinness and explored the forest, with no car there aren't too many options on what to do in winter unless it involves cosying down by the fire and watching a movie or reading a book.

I don't think I've the concentration span for that now.

It's all very well for Charlie. He can jump in his car for a spin with Max and go explore further afield, into the Glenveagh Mountains less than an hour away if he feels like it, or into the bigger town of Letterkenny to have a look around the shops.

My options are very limited.

I lift my phone as a wave of loneliness overcomes me.

It's four days to Christmas. I would dearly love to see my niece and nephew. I'd dearly love to see my sister. I could really do with some of her wise words right now, if only I could swallow my pride and go to see them all. I wonder if they are missing me as much as I am them?

You've spent two Christmas Days alone, Sis, Sarah said to me only last week in our last conversation. *Don't feel like you have to do another one for our sake. We want you home. We really do. Cry on my shoulder. You know I'm here for you.*

Yet when I explained how I simply couldn't face it, she was perfectly understanding.

I go into a folder of unread messages from Sarah on my phone, and my breath catches in my throat when I read them.

We miss you, Aunty Rose. See you after your holiday. Hugs to George. From Jack and Ada.

And then from Sarah:

Rose, somewhere up there, Michael is shining down on us all. Yes, shining. He would want you to smile and be happy. I just know he would. But do what you have to do to get through, always.

And finally:

Don't ever feel you've left it too late to change your mind and come home. Mum has enough food ordered in to feed the five thousand as usual. So even if you want to rock up Rose-style on Christmas morning with a bashed-out supermarket pavlova in a plastic bag, know that we'll welcome you with open arms xx

I put my hand to my mouth and let the tears flow. I cry out loud in a way I haven't done since Michael's funeral, but I'm laughing somewhere in there too. My sister never forgets. She knows me better than anyone else. She knows my whimsical ways and spontaneous flaws. Like the time I decided to go to America for Christmas when I was nineteen, only to change my mind and arrive home at the eleventh hour with a battered, soggy pavlova I'd scavenged from the corner shop discount aisle on Christmas Eve.

I plonk down on the sofa with George by my side.

Charlie's jumper from the night before lies uncharacteristically over the back of the sofa behind me. I close my eyes, inhaling his scent, and a strange sensation claws at my gut. It feels empty here without him.

Am I *missing* him?

I jump when my phone vibrates. It's him. Just when I was thinking of him, he has messaged me.

Shopping today. Saw this and thought of you.

I almost choke on my own breath. It's a photo of a rather fetching 1950s-inspired blue and white polka dot skirt with a matching belt. It's so me. I love it.

I can't resist a message back. I take a snap of his jumper, strewn over the back of the sofa which is so unlike him.

Saw this and thought of you.

He replies immediately.

Ha! What can I say? I'm finally making myself at home. Hope you are too.

I lean my head back on his jumper behind me and close my eyes. I hug my phone to my chest.

Who am I and what's going on? Where am I? I'm so in limbo right now. I'm so confused with how I'm feeling his absence this morning. I don't know where I belong.

And although a huge part of my heart still yearns for Michael, I fear that I'm falling for a stranger I've barely conversed with. But I can't be. It's too soon, surely.

I feel like I'm in some sort of empty waiting room, waiting to be called. Waiting to be told, 'Yes, Rose. You can live again now. You can try to laugh again. It's allowed. You can pass go, you've proved your sadness. Go and enjoy Christmas. Go and enjoy life like you used to.'

But there's no such instruction from anywhere when it comes to grief. It's like waiting on a train that never comes. It's like walking in fog. And maybe it's going to always be like this.

But Charlie . . . something about him has shown me different. Something about him has given me some glimmer of hope, like he's helping me to smooth over some of the tiny cracks in my heart.

The way he so tenderly bandaged up my battered knees. The way he offered to walk me home that first night from the pub, pointing out the stars and lights in the distance. The time he cooked me delicious food when I was feeling low and sore. How his eyes lit up when he saw me at the Christmas Fayre. Most of all, the way I couldn't concentrate on anyone else in the pub last night as soon as I saw him, and how he left his company to walk with me again.

And now he's thinking of me when he's shopping, when I know he's trying harder than ever to keep a healthy distance after last night.

Neither of us is ready to get close again.

So why am I thinking of him from the moment I wake up most mornings now? Even when he's not here, I feel his presence everywhere. I look around the cottage, I see him in every room. I go to the shower and I hear him singing to himself as he washes. I try not to think of him lathering up the soap, his tanned physique which I caught a glimpse of unexpectedly the other day now etched in my mind. I go to the bedroom to get dressed and see his clothes hanging in the wardrobe beside mine. I can't help but run my fingers along his shirts, touching the soft cotton that will hug his chest when he wears them. I see his book on the bedside locker. A glass of water he's been drinking from. I feel his eyes on me, heavy and longing, like when he came outside to the hot tub that night. In the kitchen he is everywhere, from his adopted favourite mug in the cupboard to his yogurt, cheese and cold meats with cute Post-it notes saying 'help yourself Rose' in the fridge.

And now that I'm here in the morning silence, I realise so is my Granny Molly. The memory of her wraps around me like a warm hug on a cold day.

I'm in a daze, staring out the kitchen window onto the back garden thinking of her, when I'm drawn to some blackbirds helping themselves to some seed from a net on the bird table in the garden. I'm transported instantly to a time when I wasn't tall enough to see out this window. She'd pick me up and point out the blackbirds, singing soft lullabies as she gently swayed with me on her hip.

In later years, when I'd catch her leaning on the worktop by the sink, lost in thought as she watched the blackbirds, she'd say to me:

When you're feeling all at sea, don't ever underestimate the power of the simple things, darling. Those are the things that can get us through the darkest days. Watch nature do her thing, listen to your favourite songs, talk to a kind friend, bake a delicious cake. These are the little things that will lift your spirits.

I close my eyes and I feel her so close to me. Maybe I could bake a cake today? I probably haven't baked a cake since I was here as a teenager.

But yes, that's exactly what I'll do.

Granny Molly used to love baking in this kitchen when we'd come to stay. She never lived here full-time, but the summer holidays she gave us in this cottage were legendary, from seaside walks to lighthouse visits and so much more.

And one of my favourite pastimes to do with her right here in this little kitchen was to bake chocolate cake. Is there anything more comforting than a slice of velvety chocolate cake with a thick gooey centre and layers of icing on top? I may not be a master chef in the kitchen, but I do remember how to bake Granny Molly's cake.

There is very little stuff left in the cottage to remind me of her. Aside from the practical things that have stood the test of time, there is very little of her personality here any more, so it makes me smile when I see on the top shelf of a cupboard all her baking essentials. I'm so glad Marion and Rusty didn't get rid of them when they took over this place. Yes, there they are. A mixing bowl, a cake tin, a whisk. It's all here.

She's still here.

Now, ingredients . . .

I pull on my yellow raincoat and my pink hat, then rush out to the corner shop with George alongside to grab some cocoa powder, granulated sugar, icing sugar, lots of chocolate, eggs, flour and butter.

I hurry back, turn up the radio, put on an apron and get to work to the sounds of some of my favourite Christmas carols. I whisk. I mix. I stir. I taste. I close my eyes to savour the rich flavour. I feel so much better already, like my heart is slowly filling up in a way it hasn't done in so long.

The simple things.

Within an hour, I open the oven door and carefully take out the cake tin to see my masterpiece. I'm feeling very proud. It's spongy, it's smooth, it's just right. I taste the icing I've prepared. Yum.

I drip melted chocolate icing over the top so that it runs down the sides, then I frost it with icing sugar and top with a sprig of holly.

I take a photo and I can't resist. I send it to Charlie.

'Ta daaaa. What do you think, Georgie?'

Yes, he looks quite impressed as he licks his lips with a very pink tongue when I show him the fruits of my labour. I can't stop smiling.

When you're feeling all at sea, don't ever underestimate the power of the simple things.

No truer words were ever spoken.

The doorbell rings and I race to open it, not knowing who to expect, but I'm feeling so high that I barely stop to wonder.

'Stacy!'

Bless her for remembering and for acting on what was a tipsy conversation last night when we agreed to meet up today.

'Some afternoon delights for after our walk?' she says, holding up a basket of cheeses, breads, chutneys and a bottle of red wine. 'Oh, you look surprised. Did you forget I was to pop by?'

'Of course not. I'm delighted! Come in. Your timing is impeccable,' I say, opening the door to let her inside. 'I'll put the kettle on. I've just made chocolate cake. You can be first to try it.'

For a day that started out maudlin and slow, I'm feeling so much better already.

The power of the simple things.

Granny Molly was right as usual.

Chapter Twenty-Two

Charlie

'Max! George!'

It's bloody freezing outside.

I call out into the still mist of the night, yawning as I do so beneath the navy sky. I rub my chin. So much for early morning rises and no late nights for me. Donegal is changing my body clock – not that I'm complaining, but it does take some getting used to.

Rose was fast asleep when I got back this evening. She was sleeping when I left this morning and now she's sleeping on my return, which a few days ago would have suited perfectly.

But now I can't help but admit a tinge of disappointment when I peeped into the living room and saw her sleeping soundly.

Do I miss her?

She looked so serene and peaceful, so I let George out to play with Max a while as I didn't want his barking and bouncing to wake her up when she obviously wanted an early night.

From the empty bottle of wine and two glasses by the sink, it looks like she had company today.

There's a selection of cheeses and chutneys in the fridge that weren't there before, some crusty bread they'd shared, and a rather spectacular chocolate cake with a note on the board on the fridge.

Heat it, eat it, enjoy. There's ice cream in the freezer. Hope you enjoyed your shopping. Rose

My stomach twists.

Was Beige Billy here for wine, cheese and cake? Did she bake him a cake? Wow.

I look at the kitchen table where I can picture them laughing and sharing food. I hear his dulcet tones whispering in her ear, his hand brushing hers across the table. Maybe they went for a romantic walk by the sea or in the forest with George?

I feel a bit sick.

Rose and I have been here for almost a week, and I've never had the balls to do something like that with her. In fact, I've avoided it completely through communicating with notes and keeping my distance, like running away to Letterkenny today so I didn't have to bump into her, yet when I got back her company was the first thing I longed for.

I'd better get the dogs inside.

'Max! George!'

I'm so confused. I'm not in the mood for cake, and it's nothing to do with the time of night. I'm not jealous, am I?

George brushes past me, all wet paws and shaggy damp fur, and makes his way into the kitchen. Max, as usual, never comes on the first call.

'Max, come on boy!' I whistle, which usually works by the third attempt. I expect him to come pounding around the gable of the house any second. I rub my arms, which are covered in goosebumps beneath my shirt. 'Max! Bedtime, Max!'

Oh, here we go.

I knew it would only be a matter of time until Max decided to explore a bit further than he's supposed to, and Marion did warn me about the garden not being totally dog-proof. The forest behind the cottage to Max is like candy to a baby, but I live in hope that he hasn't gone too far when I venture out into the garden in my T-shirt.

'Max?'

I hear running water in the kitchen. It's Rose. Shit, we've woken her up. George comes back outside to join me, then Rose calls from the back door.

'George, come back inside. You OK, Charlie? Why are you outside in just a T-shirt in the snow?'

She's wearing a T-shirt too which skims her thighs. Brilliant. I try not to look.

'Sorry if we woke you up. Max has gone AWOL so I'd better go and look for him,' I say, making my way back inside to put on a few more layers and begin a proper search. 'Of course, he's chosen the coldest night of all to do so. Why can't he be a good boy like you, George, eh? He does this at home sometimes too, as soon as he spots an opportunity.'

'Max is *missing*? Wait, you can't go looking for him alone,' Rose exclaims, her voice shooting up the scale in dismay. 'Give me two seconds and we'll come with you.'

I pull on a hoodie and a warm coat from the coat stand in the hall while she scurries upstairs to get dressed with George on her tail, but I'm still hoping that by the time Rose gets ready to face the elements of this very cold night, Max will have already made his way back home. He can't have got far. He's only been outside for a few minutes.

'OK, there's a torch under the sink,' she says on her return to the kitchen seconds later, already with her head stuck in the cupboard to fetch it out.

'Great stuff, Wonder Woman.'

'What?'

'Making cake by day, finding dogs by night.'

She puts her hand on her hip.

'What?'

'I'm joking,' I say, fearing my seeping envy of Billy might be showing. 'What I really meant was that you got changed very quickly. Like Wonder Woman.'

'Oh.'

'But no need to panic, honestly, he'll come back soon.'

'I'd rather he wasn't out there in the freezing cold,' she says, in a tone that shows she means business. She is wearing a yellow padded jacket, gloves, some heavy boots and the same bobble hat as before in her hand. 'And I've some dog treats in my pocket which might help. George only went missing once but I was told afterwards to always take treats to lure him back should it happen again. Your Max has a good sense of recall. It's important not to panic, just like you said.'

'I'm not panicking.'

She is panicking, if only just a little.

I smile with my lips closed and eyebrows raised as Rose takes over control of the search operation, reassuring me as she fusses and grabs more dog snacks from her own supplies and stuffs them in her pocket.

'You have a lot of energy for someone who was asleep only five minutes ago . . .'

'I never sleep this early,' she says. 'Must have been the wine. Come on, let's get searching.'

'You sure?'

'Yeah, I know the forest pretty well, even at night-time, so don't worry,' she says, fixing her woollen hat. 'We've got this. We'll find him in no time.'

I'm staring at her. I can't help it.

'What?'

I swallow hard. I shrug.

'Thank you,' I say, biting my bottom lip as if there's nothing more to say right now.

'It's fine.'

'You don't have to do this, but it's very much appreciated.'

'Come on, no time to waste,' she says, handing me Max's lead. 'The quicker we go, the quicker we find him. Come on, George. Let's go find your best buddy.'

We step outside, all three of us, and plod through the crunchy frosted grass in the garden until we reach the small gate that provides a shortcut into the forest behind the cottage, calling Max as we go, our breath visible in the black night air.

'So, he's done this before?' Rose asks as she swirls the torch light into the tree, her voice a bit breathless already. 'What a rascal!'

'Many times,' I remind her. 'Springers like to hunt so he'll sniff his way back, I'm almost sure of it. If it weren't so cold, I'd leave him to it.'

Rose is already a few steps ahead of me, calling my dog's name and reassuring her own dog George as she goes along the dirt path that's already covered in snow.

'Don't worry, Georgie. We'll find him. No need to worry at all, old pal.'

I can't help but watch her in admiration as she hurries along, talking to George. It's a bitter cold snowy night, and I know it's not everyone who would head out while on holiday in winter to look for someone else's dog. Especially one who has a tendency of going on adventures alone.

'We'll have Max home in no time,' she says when she waits up for me. 'He may have taken shelter somewhere out of the cold.'

'Hopefully, yes,' I say before stopping in my tracks.

As freezing as it is out here in the forest, as tired as I am and as jaded as I've been recently with everything that brought me here in the first place, I can't help but feel a warmth in my usually cold heart tonight. Since I saw her at the fayre, since I spotted her in the pub, and since we walked under the stars again . . .

There's no denying it any more. The warmth I feel in my heart tonight is all because of her. If only I'd the guts to tell her.

'You OK?' I ask Rose, as the tips of her glove-clad fingers hang on to the inside of my upper arm.

She is close to me now, and it's making my head spin just a little bit. The cold air makes our breath visible like clouds in front of us, and we step in sync as far as I can manage to keep my strides shorter.

'All good,' she replies, clinging on to my arm like her life depends on it. 'Just trying my best not to fall. Again. Me and this forest have a history of injuries now.'

'Don't be afraid to say if you've had enough of searching,' I reply. I take the torch from her and circle the long beaming light into trees on either side of our path, which show nothing but a false alarm which turned out to be a fox's eyes and heaps of snow-covered winter foliage. 'I've a feeling we could be on a wild goose chase out here and that we'll return with nothing but hypothermia. I'm also already dreaming of how I'll light the fire to get us warmed up when we get back to the cottage.'

'Good thinking. I'll dream of that too, then.'

'Imagine the heat on your fingers and toes right now.'

'And a big steaming mug of hot chocolate in your hands.'

'And warm, clean clothes that haven't been soaked through.'

'And the sound of jingle bells in the distance and the dulcet tones of Michael Bublé.'

'Ah, now you've just gone and ruined it,' I tell her, which makes her giggle. I have no doubt she intended to shift gears with that one. 'I'm trying to avoid Christmas songs when I can, which I have to admit hasn't been easy.'

Now it's Rose's turn to stop in her tracks. She looks up at me, the moonlight casting faint shadows across her face so I can only see her eyes.

'So, how come you were listening to "O Holy Night" yesterday then, Scrooge?'

I swallow. I look up at the sky. I look back at Rose.

'It reminds me of someone who, even though she doesn't know it, manages to gently lift my battered heart and make me feel a little bit better than she found it.'

She holds my stare.

'Oh.'

'Simple as that,' I say light-heartedly, though my statement is anything but.

'Well, I'm glad you have someone who makes you feel that way,' she whispers. 'You're very lucky.'

I nod.

'I know I am,' I reply. 'Right, let's get this search over and done with. Five more minutes and then we head back, what do you say?'

'I say I've probably got another five minutes in me, yes,' she tells me, taking my arm again.

'You're a superstar.'

'A superstar and Wonder Woman all in one night? I'll be getting a very big head at this rate.'

I don't answer her this time. I think I've said enough already as it is.

'Whoops-a-daisy!' she says seconds later, breaking my train of thought and letting go of George's lead as she stumbles again for what seems like the millionth time. She grabs my arm with both hands, the weight of her body pushing me back, which makes me drop the torch. We're both in almost pitch darkness, scrambling around with our hands to find it.

We knock heads.

'Ouch!'

'Sorry!'

She slips again. Then I do too.

'Oh, this is ridiculous,' I say, and we both burst out laughing. 'We're like a poor man's Torvill and Dean. Come on, I think that's a sign. Hold on to me properly and we'll make our way back to the cottage. I don't think we should risk even five minutes more. Max, you better show your face very soon to make this worthwhile!'

'I have to give in and agree,' she says, sounding defeated, but I know she's as cold as I am, not to mention injury prone in the ice and snow.

We stand up and brush ourselves off once Rose has found George's lead again and I've found the torch, and this time she links her arm into mine a little bit closer, her head just skimming my shoulder.

I feel my heart race. I sense my breath quicken. I'm aware of every movement of every limb in my body as the warmth of hers presses into mine.

We don't say another word but as we trudge along, I wonder if she's thinking the same thing as I am.

And when we get back to the cottage gate and she lets go, then makes her way across the garden in long, careful strides as if she is on stepping stones, my arms feel empty without her.

'Careful now,' I call out to her from behind as I watch her tread so carefully. 'It would be an awful shame to fall when we're so nearly there. Imagine having made it all this way back and then—'

She freezes on the spot, one leg spread out ahead of the other.

'You're making me laugh, Charlie, and that's not helping my balance,' she says, wobbling a little, before she keeps going again until she reaches the back doorstep safely as I follow a few seconds behind. 'Oh, I'm gutted we didn't find poor Max. Are you worried? I hope he's OK out there, wherever he is.'

She stands under the sensor light at the cottage door which illuminates her face, so full of worry and regret that we've come back empty-handed.

'Get inside before you freeze to death,' I say, pushing past her to open the door so she can make her way into the warmth of the kitchen. 'Max will come home when he's fed up chasing rabbits down snowy ditches, don't worry. He always does. Now, I don't know about you, but I fancy that hot drink we talked about to thaw out. Hot chocolate?'

'Sounds amazing,' she says, kicking the snow off her boots and then stepping inside. 'Tell you what, let's get changed out of these wet clothes and then I'll make us the hot chocolate. *You* light the fire.'

'*I'll* light the fire,' I say at the same time, and at that moment, I know we are already in danger of lighting fires in more ways than one.

And so does Rose.

Chapter Twenty-Three

Rose

Oh no, please don't let this be happening.

I can't let this happen.

My breath quickens as I heat up milk in a saucepan and stir in cocoa powder, watching the fine brown dust melt and turn the liquid from off-white to chocolatey in no time. I lean on the counter and close my eyes for just a second, wondering why everything I find in life that feels good is always so wrong for me.

Charlie feels the same way, I know he does.

I could tell when we were out walking how our bodies moved closer and closer on the way home. I was so glad to get to the gate so I could be forced to let go, but by the time I reached the doorstep I was missing his warmth already.

But I can't do this. Rusty warned me not to. I had no intention of feeling like this and I'm sure Charlie didn't either. I mean, of course he didn't! What about Helena, who he said he loves? And his child that I still know nothing about?

'Rose? Is something burning?'

Shit! The milk sticks to the sides of the pan and I scrape it just in time, filling two mugs and making sure I scrub out the saucepan quickly before it makes a mess that's impossible to clean.

I notice how I move so swiftly round this tiny kitchen where everything is at arm's length. I get a sudden wave of homesickness when I think of leaving here when the time comes. I don't want to go back to Dublin. I don't want to leave this bubble of loveliness. I don't want to leave Charlie and this wintry cocoon we are slowly falling into, but I should. I really should.

'All good, coming now,' I call back, popping some spongy pink and white marshmallows on top of the steaming milk, then I sprinkle over some flaked chocolate, thinking how I'd give the Snow Queen Special at the Christmas Fayre a run for its money when it comes to presentation.

I'm making an extra effort for him and it feels good to do so after all he has done for me. I pop a long-stemmed teaspoon into each mug, take a quick second to admire my work of art and then I make my way into the living room where Charlie kneels on the floor by the hearth in front of the dancing flames.

Oh, help me someone. I stop.

Then my jaw drops at the sight of him in his fresh, clean T-shirt and casual shorts watching every move I make with a welcoming smile.

Our eyes lock and I take a deep breath before making my way towards him, a mug in each hand, like I'm walking a tightrope. If I make my way across this room without spilling a drop, it will be an absolute miracle.

My heart skips a beat when I get near to him again.

'Come, sit down and get warm,' he says, carefully taking a mug from me and bringing it to the floor. I lower myself down slowly, curling my legs beneath me. I do my best to focus on the orange flames that dance a jig in the hearth beside him.

I want to reach across and touch his arm again, but instead I focus on gripping the mug of chocolate in my hands. His arms look so strong and inviting, but *I* must stay strong of mind at the same time.

He is not mine.

My eyes dart towards his phone which is sitting on top of the magazines on the coffee table beside us. It lights up and vibrates every few seconds, but he doesn't seem to notice.

'Don't you need to get your phone?' I ask him. He shakes his head slowly, keeping his eyes on me as he sips his drink.

'No, it's fine,' he replies. 'I can deal with that later. It's not important.'

'But it's late?'

'It's OK, it's not important right now.'

And I am? I want to ask. Oh please, don't let this be happening. I don't want to be anyone's secret. I don't want to be the cause of another woman's hurt.

'Are you married, Charlie?' I ask him. His face crumples into a smile.

'Is that what you're thinking right now?' he replies, pulling his legs beneath him to mirror my own stance. 'If I was married, do you think I'd be here spending Christmas in a secluded cottage with you?'

I put down my drink and warm my hands by the fire, all the time feeling his steely blue eyes bore into my soul.

'You're not spending Christmas with *me*,' I say, managing a smile. I shyly look away. 'We are spending Christmas here, together, alone.'

'Together, alone,' he repeats. 'Me and my big rules. Maybe it doesn't have to be like that? Maybe we could relax the rules a little?'

My eyes widen more than I intend them to.

'Relax them, how?'

'As much as I've fought against it, I like your company, Rose,' he tells me. My heart skips a beat. 'I know I'd kick myself later for not taking this opportunity to know you, in whatever way you're happy with.'

'You mean, talking instead of texting?'

'That's it,' he continues. 'That's exactly it.'

'So, no more whiteboard?' I ask him. 'I've grown quite fond of that.'

'Well, I've been resisting so far but my emojis are quite legendary,' he jokes.

'As is your cooking.'

'You think?'

'I do.'

He bites his lip. I nod.

Our hands are so close now on the floor. My fingertip is pulsating right beside his. I want to touch him, to pull him in, to feel his arms around me.

But I can't do that – not when I still feel he's hiding something from me. I desperately want to ask who Helena is, and why she keeps calling him. They might not be married, but that doesn't mean they're not romantically involved.

Why can't I ask him that one simple question?

Maybe because I'm so very afraid of the answer.

'You didn't have any cake yet, did you?' I ask him, hoping he'll taste possibly the one thing I can put in an oven and not burn to a crisp.

'It was late when I got back,' he tells me. He looks like something is weighing on his mind. 'It looks amazing.'

'Yes, Stacy gave it ten out of ten.'

'Stacy?'

'My new friend from England who I've met in the bar a few times,' I explain. 'She came to see me today. We had such a lovely afternoon.'

He lets out an obvious sigh.

'I thought you were with Billy.'

I splutter so hard I fear I'll spill my hot chocolate this time.

'Beige Billy? Ah, come on. Give me some credit, Charlie. He's a really nice guy but if I hear about his divorce one more time . . . no, I politely turned down his dinner offer. He's not for me at all.'

I cup the mug in my hands and lean back against the sofa, stretching my legs out so that they skim his – accidentally, of course.

'Wait a minute,' he says as he watches me. 'You look a bit smug right now.'

'Do I?' I can't hide it. 'You weren't – you weren't jealous of *Billy*, were you?'

He shakes his head but can't seem to find the words to deny it. He catches my eye but I look away, as my thoughts drift into a darker, all too familiar place.

'I'm not the happy person you think I am, Charlie,' I whisper out of the blue, staring at the hearth. 'I put up a front, but I'm not great company these days. I'm not very strong at all.'

He sits up straight.

'I'm sorry to hear that, but please know this is a safe space and you can talk about it. Without judgement. And talking might help. Is that why you're here, Rose? To feel stronger in yourself?'

I nod. I can barely speak for fear I'll crumble.

'I don't really know why I'm here. I don't know where to start, and I've no idea how to move on. I know it *looks* like I have moved on to everyone, but inside I keep slipping back to the start again. It's like two steps forward and one back. I don't even know why I'm telling you this. I didn't mean to tell you any of this.'

And now I'm sobbing like a baby, heavy, choking tears that make it hard to breathe.

'Come here, Rose,' he whispers. 'It's going to be OK. You're going to be OK.'

He holds out his hand and quietly takes me in towards him where we sit until my tears subside, holding each other by the fire with George snoozing on the sofa. There is so much going through my head right now. In a way I dreamed this might happen – earlier when we were walking so closely, and last night when we watched the stars. I've yearned for him to hold me properly and now here we are, yet it doesn't feel real.

I can hear his heartbeat in his chest. I can feel his breath in my hair. I grip my hands tighter around his waist, the softness of his T-shirt so soothing, and the brief smooth touch of his skin enough to make my own heart skip a beat. I promise myself I'll stop in just a few seconds. He isn't mine. He may not be married, but I get the sense that he isn't mine.

We lean into each other in blissful silence, the heat of the fire so soothing it could easily make me fall asleep in seconds if I let it. But I can't.

So I break away slowly, wiping my tears with the back of my hand, and I do my best to shake myself out of my pity party.

I shouldn't have let myself go like that, but there's something about Charlie that feels so familiar and safe. In his company I don't have to try to be something I'm not. I don't have to be Rose the ambitious businesswoman or Rose the life and soul of the party, when it's the last thing I want to be sometimes.

With Charlie, I am just me, like I've pressed the reset button and it's slowly kicking into action at last. Or is that just me being idealistic in my grieving, susceptible state of mind?

'Maybe you should get some sleep. It's been a long night,' Charlie says to me as he stands up by the fire. 'You're a good person, Rose. Maybe don't give yourself such a hard time, eh?'

'Thank you.'

'Use your time here to reflect and heal,' he continues gently. 'And if you ever feel like talking about it, I'm here. No more notes or messages. We can talk. You're stronger than you give yourself credit for.'

I stand up too, clutching the mug in my hands for support after letting my guard down to this virtual stranger.

'You think so?'

'Believe me, I know you are.'

'Thank you for everything, Charlie.'

We stand face to face, a force between us that is so hard to ignore. I yearn for his touch again. I feel colder apart from him.

'Your turn in the bed upstairs,' I remind him as I glance upwards, trying to lighten the mood. 'Enjoy.'

'Well, you've got the fire,' he says with a smile.

Those dimples . . .

'And I'll keep an ear out for the return of Max, the prodigal son,' I whisper, as he fixes the fire guard in place after throwing another few logs on for me. 'Thanks for listening and for being so nice to me. Again.'

He reaches out and touches my shoulders so tenderly with both his hands and my eyes fall in response to his touch.

'Goodnight, Rose. Sleep well,' he says, and I feel like my heart is going to burst. I open my eyes. We are both breathing slowly. His eyes look at my mouth and then back to my eyes again.

I think he is going to kiss me.

My God, I want him to – so much.

But I can't let him do that, no way, so I step back quickly and his hands brush off my shoulders and fall by his sides.

'Goodnight, Charlie. You too.'

He looks as crestfallen as I feel deep inside, but he doesn't try to make a move again or say another word to convince me, which I'm grateful for. He knows how vulnerable I am. He just doesn't know why.

And so I watch him leave the room, then gently he closes the door, and I crawl onto the sofa and hug my pillow tightly, wishing it could be him I was holding for the rest of the night.

I wish that I could allow myself to go with the flow and fall for a kind man like Charlie, a funny, gorgeous soul like him, without harming the memory of Michael. Without hurting the other woman in his life. I wish most of all that one day I'll allow myself to just be me and learn to love myself again.

Yes, that's my biggest wish of all.

Three Days to Christmas

Chapter Twenty-Four

Charlie

'You miss my breakfasts? Oh Helena, come on, you're an excellent cook too!'

This is verging on ridiculous, but I have to give her top marks on her creativity. Her latest reason for missing me is pretty far-fetched.

I have her on speaker phone as I cook this morning and I can't deny that she's making me smile as she grasps at straws to convince me to come home again.

'The breakfast at your place is just as good . . . ha, ha, no, I don't do anything differently, darling. I do them exactly like I showed you many times.'

Yesterday it was that she couldn't remember the password to her Netflix account and when I gave it to her, it still wasn't enough because the Christmas movies made her sad because I wasn't there.

Today it's about my breakfasts, tomorrow it will be about something else.

'Sausage, egg and bacon,' I tell her, even though she knows the ingredients off by heart. 'Mushrooms on the side.

Some soda bread to give it that Irish finish. And you know I always love baked beans too . . .'

'No baked beans! They make the bread all soggy!'

'See, you don't even like how I do them after all. Yours are so much better.'

I've a spatula in one hand, a tea towel over my shoulder, the snow is thick on the ground outside and all I need is for Max to rock up this morning, which I'm fairly confident he will very soon. I'm even listening to cheesy Christmas songs which Helena is choosing for me in some very amusing game she has come up with. And after a promise to Rebecca this morning in a very unexpected but welcome phone call from her, I'm doing my best to get into the festive spirit as far as I can now that the big day is very close.

I didn't tell either Rebecca or Helena about Max, who has been gone around nine hours now. I know my dog and I trust that he will turn up soon, but I can't deny that I'm beginning to feel a bit worried.

'Good morning. You look happy. Oh, sorry, you're on a call.'

Rose puts her hand over her mouth and makes her way back out of the kitchen as soon as she gets in, but I call her back. She's fully dressed, which is unusual for her at this time, and I feel a pang inside me when I think of her leaving for the day.

'No, no, come in and pull up a seat,' I tell her quickly. 'I'm cooking up a storm here. Do you want some?'

'Who's that, Charlie? Is that Rose?'

Rose makes a face and nods towards the phone where Helena's voice is piping through. I've propped it up against a teapot so I can move around freely while I chat.

'Yes, Helena, it's Rose. She has just come in for breakfast.'

'Hi Rose!'

'Hi Helena,' says Rose quietly while looking completely perplexed.

'Next song please, Charlie. "Rockin' Around the Christmas Tree",' chirps Helena. 'It's my new favourite. And play it a little bit louder so I can hear it better, please.'

I roll my eyes and guide Rose to a seat at the cute little round wooden table which sits by the window in a tiny offset of the kitchen. She seems very taken aback as she fidgets and scrunches up her pretty face.

'My sister and I are playing Christmas songs and she can be very demanding,' I whisper into her ear.

She turns her head up towards me from where she is now seated.

'Your sister?' she asks, bemused. I nod. 'Helena is your *sister*?'

'Yes,' I whisper out of earshot. 'This is my first time not spending Christmas with her and I feel guilty as hell, so I thought we'd play some music together this morning. You can join us if you want?'

Rose looks flabbergasted. I'm not sure if I've mentioned Helena before to her, but she seems surprised that I have a family member at all. We have so much still to figure out about each other.

'Alexa, play "O Holy Night",' I call to the device that sits on the worktop. Meanwhile, the sausages sizzle and the bacon spits and crackles in the frying pan.

'I'm swaying and dancing, Charlie! Are you swaying and dancing?' I hear from the phone which is set at a volume just above the music.

'I'm cooking, Helena. Rose will dance with you!'

Rose shakes her head and laughs, as if she is still in some sort of shock at the morning Christmas music party, but I'm not getting off that lightly with Helena.

'Dance *with* Rose, Charlie,' she says. 'Come on. Dance with me, both of you. It's Christmas!'

I can't count how many times she has said 'it's Christmas' since she called. It's sweet, even though it's very repetitive.

'Dance with Rose,' she calls again. My sister is very insistent.

I look at Rose, who looks like a rabbit caught in the headlights. I put the spatula down. I take her hand.

'Wait? What? I'm hardly awake,' she says with a smile. 'But I do love this song,'

'It's Christmas!' shouts Helena from the phone by the teapot. 'Dance, Rose!'

'We're dancing, Helena,' I call back to her and when I put my hand on Rose's waist and cup her hand into mine, she doesn't pull away like I thought she would. Instead, she moves with me, like we were made to do this together, and I can't stop smiling.

Remembering how she trusted in me last night, recalling how we sat together by the fire, so cosy, thinking of the warmth of her body against mine . . . It's ignited something inside me and I can't deny it any more. I want this time to last forever.

'So, Helena is your sister?' she whispers, raising an eyebrow as our feet glide around the small kitchen floor. She is smiling too. 'Helena is your *sister*?'

'Yes, who did you think she was?'

'Your *girlfriend*!'

'Oh, Rose,' I laugh, as her actions last night now begin to make sense. 'No, she is my sister and she's absolutely wonderful.'

I spin Rose under my arm and as she ducks under, her face lights up in a way I've never seen before. She throws her head back with a beaming smile as I pull her in towards me again and we waltz around the kitchen with the odd pause for me to move the food around the frying pan. When the music comes to an end, I expect Rose to rush away, but she doesn't.

'I must go now, Charlie!' shouts Helena. 'Mary is dying my hair today for Christmas and she's waiting, but that was fun! Call me later!'

'OK, I'll call you later, bye Helena!' I shout as Rose and I stand frozen, holding each other even though the music has now stopped and the only sounds are the sizzling of the frying pan from behind me on the cooker. Thank goodness it's turned on very low.

Rose closes her eyes.

'About last night,' she whispers, running the tip of her tongue across her lips.

'Yes?'

She breathes in and out so slowly now, I can see her chest rise and fall. Before she can continue, a loud knock on the kitchen window makes us both jump a few feet apart. I look out. It's Rusty. Talk about bad timing. We fidget and fix ourselves like teenagers caught in the act, and if Rusty saw anything through the window, he doesn't mention it.

'I've been knocking on the front door a few minutes now,' he says, coming in and standing by the kitchen door.

Rose looks like she might burst out laughing any second. I will too if I catch her eye.

'Sorry, Rusty,' I say, going back to the frying pan. 'We were getting into the festive spirit. How are you?'

'Have a seat. I'll get you a cuppa,' says Rose, already filling the kettle. 'You must be freezing cold. Looks like we're in for a white Christmas, eh?'

Rusty rubs his hands and blows into them, and George sniffs around and jumps up for attention, but it doesn't faze Rusty at all. He pats the dog's head as he speaks.

'No thanks, love. I'm not staying. But speaking of Christmas, I come bearing good news for a change,' he says, his eyes darting between Rose and me. 'Your car is ready for the road again, Rosebud. The part arrived in yesterday's post, and I've fitted it this morning so you're free to go back to Dublin if that's what you still want to do.'

He hands Rose the keys. She takes them as if she is handling burnt coals. I focus on the bacon and sausages in the frying pan and turn the heat down very low, matching the sudden dip in my appetite.

'Gosh, thank you,' she says after a brief silence. 'I wasn't expecting that at all. Gosh. Great news. Thanks, Rusty. Do you need a lift back to the yard?'

Rusty looks confused at Rose's lack of delight. I feel her glance my way but I can't look.

'No, no, I've a young lad waiting for me in the pick-up,' says Rusty. 'He followed me here in your car. It's not a day for driving, mind you, but I promised you I'd do my best to get you back on the road as soon as possible.'

Rose, realising he seems a bit deflated, springs into action and gives him a hug.

'Thanks, cuz,' she says, then she goes to the fridge and takes out her chocolate cake.

Rusty's eyes light up. 'Granny Molly's cake?' he says in surprise. 'Did you make that? Ah, Rose.'

His eyes glisten as she wraps three large slices in tinfoil and hands them to him.

'One for you, one for the lad outside and one for Marion. It might sweeten her up.'

She winks, then they both say in unison, 'Heat it, eat it, and enjoy.'

They hug again.

'It's been so good having you here,' Rusty says with a beaming smile. He rubs his ginger beard. 'Granny Molly would be proud of you. She wanted this place to be for the whole family, not just mine.'

The penny drops now I hear that Rusty and Rose are related. The way she knew her way around the cottage from day one. The tension with Marion, which must be from some sort of family dispute.

'Thank you for putting your life on the line for me,' Rose tells him, to which he chuckles in return. 'How much do I owe you?'

'For putting my life on the line? You owe me nothing for nothing,' Rusty replies, then interrupts her when she tries to argue. 'Happy Christmas, Rose. It's been my pleasure to spend time with you after all these years.'

They walk outside and I see her through the window, waving him off, then she returns and I hurry back to my cooking.

The pan sizzles as the inevitable hangs in the air now. The car is fixed. She has no reason to stay here any more.

'You OK?' I ask her. 'Good news about the car, yeah?'

'Great news,' she says. 'Great news about the car.'

She busies herself around the kitchen, wiping worktops that don't need cleaning, folding tea towels that were already folded. Then she stops and stares into space. She looks lost and lonely again, so vulnerable, just like she did last night by the fire.

I walk towards her and lean against the worktop with my arms folded.

'Does this mean you're going back to Dublin?' I whisper, almost afraid of her response. 'You don't have to if you don't want to.'

We breathe in sync. I close my eyes with dread of how she might answer.

'Do you want me to?' she asks.

'No.'

More silence.

'I think your breakfast is burning, Charlie.'

'Shit!'

I turn around and shake up the pan as Rose opens the back door and swings it back and forth to let the smoke out while I try to salvage the fry-up I'd so been looking forward to.

'I hope you like your sausages charred?' I call.

Her answer to my question is interrupted when we both gasp in delight at the sight of a very cold, very wet and shivering springer spaniel coming from the forest through the garden towards where Rose stands at the back door.

'He's home! Max, come inside, honey!'

Max greets us with a shake of wet fur that sprays across the kitchen, including over Rose, but she doesn't even seem to notice.

George joins us immediately, barking with delight, and the two canine friends sniff and rub noses and cheeks while Rose and I do our best to join in the action, petting their fur as they lick our faces.

'You little scamp! You had us out searching by torchlight in the snow, but you don't care, do you?' I say as I snuggle him.

I catch a glimpse of Rose watching me with tears in her eyes.

'How about I fetch a towel and take this old guy to the fire to get warmed up while you finish off your charred special?' she asks me, and we stand up in unison.

'Sounds good to me,' I tell her, our look lingering as we smile.

I hear Rose coo and marvel over Max's grand return as she dries him off. She has no idea how much her simple gesture to care for him means to me. I hope that someday soon she can see in herself what I've seen in her so far.

She is funny, she is kind, she is a beautiful soul inside and out. She is strong, she is smart and she is going to leave this place much better than when she arrived, no matter what happens between us.

She hasn't said so, but I don't think Rose is going back to Dublin just yet.

Chapter Twenty-Five

Rose

The dogs are gently snoring by the blazing fire, the snow is piling up outside and with my belly full and my heart about to burst I put down my cutlery and lean back on the kitchen chair, watching as Charlie finishes up his breakfast.

'I hope I didn't poison you,' he says, and I shake my head, then dab my mouth with a red napkin. So very festive. 'That wasn't my finest culinary achievement, I must say, but I was unexpectedly distracted.'

'It was delicious,' I reply. 'Even the choice of music as we ate together was perfect.'

He holds my gaze as we listen to the soothing sounds of an orchestra playing Christmas classics in the background, a very thoughtful compromise from his usual classical pieces and my more commercial sounds for this time of year.

It's already gone ten a.m., yet it's still quite dark outside and I notice how the windowsill is covered in at least three inches of snow.

'You haven't written any new rules or messages on the whiteboard in a while?' I say, trying not to laugh as I realise we've broken almost every one of them.

'Well, they weren't exactly rules,' he replies. 'I was just trying to . . .'

He stops.

'Go on.'

'To be honest, Rose, I was trying to make sure I did everything I could to keep a distance between us from day one,' he confesses.

'Really?'

'I mean, for goodness' sake, *look* at you,' he says in wonder, pushing his plate to the side. 'You turned my head from the moment I saw you on that roadside, and I'm sure you do that everywhere you go. I was afraid to get to know you. I was afraid to let you stay because I kind of figured that we're possibly both here for very tender reasons and getting too close might get in the way of what we each set out to do.'

I can't argue with that.

I was a vulnerable mess when I arrived here and I don't want to be leaving in the same fragile state of mind, but waking up to see Charlie in the kitchen each morning is something I'm getting very used to. I now know that he is single, too, but I'm not sure if I've even processed or let that sink in yet.

'And now?' I ask him. 'Where do we go from here?'

He leans across the table and puts his hand on my forearm.

'I've been thinking the same thing,' he replies softly. 'And I don't have any answers at all, so all I can say is that we do what we want to do, and when the time comes to go back to our own real lives, we make a decision then.'

'What happens at Seaview, stays at Seaview,' I say, but I know that he knows it might not be as simple as that.

'Sort of . . . just let's just be kind to each other and enjoy our time here together for now,' he tells me. 'I would never hurt you, Rose. Ever. That's one thing I'll promise for sure. And if it ever gets too much and you want to change the rules again, then one word from you and it's done. Deal?'

'Deal,' I say to him. 'And the same goes for you. So, we chill, then?'

'We chill,' he says with a hearty smile that's so adorable, I want to touch him more, but I don't for now. 'I think we can both live with that?'

'We can for sure. So, tell me about Helena,' I say to him, and he lights up again at the opportunity to talk about his sister who sounded so sweet on the phone. 'She must have quite a pull on you if she can convince you to play Christmas songs over the phone. The Grinch has seen the light.'

I reach for the teapot and top up our cups with more steaming hot tea.

'Hmm, it wasn't *quite* so sudden as that,' he replies. 'It's been baby steps over the past few days to get myself to acknowledge it's Christmas at all, but I'm slowly surrendering, let's just put it that way. You have influenced me a lot, in your own subtle and not so subtle ways.'

'You're talking about my singing, aren't you?'

'I'm not saying a word about your singing,' he laughs, and I pull a mock shocked face. 'You're a wonderful singer.'

'Now, you're lying.'

'You're a *confident* singer,' he replies, lifting his cup to his lips to hide a smirk. I have to say that Rusty and Marion have very good taste when it comes to the finer detail of Seaview Cottage. There is a small selection of mugs in the cupboard for everyday use, but Charlie has managed to find this very delicate, pale-blue bone-china tea set which makes our breakfast feel very special.

'So, Helena played a small part too,' I continue. 'It's nice to see you relaxing, no matter who or what is responsible. I've a feeling you deserve to.'

'Yes, I think I do. But Helena is a treasure,' he says sincerely. 'She is older than me by one year, but – well, we've been through a hell of a lot together and without getting too morbid on this very beautiful winter's day with such a wonderful breakfast companion, she probably saved my life more times recently than she could ever know. Between her and my dog, well, there were some days when I . . .'

His words stop me in my tracks.

'Oh, Charlie.'

He shrugs, bites his lip and then lifts his plate and reaches for mine, which tells me he has said enough for now. I hand it across to him before remembering my manners.

'No, let me, please. I'll wash up. It's the least I can do.'

He takes a deep breath and glances out through the window. I didn't expect our conversation to steer that way and I don't think he did either.

'You fancy a snowball fight in the garden?' he says as I'm filling the sink with hot soapy water, and I must admit

I'm impressed at his quick effort to lift the mood again and change the subject. 'I bet I can build a much better snowman than you can.'

I turn to face him and dry my hands with a tea towel, delighted to see him smiling again.

'Oh, do you now?' I ask him, wearing my game face. 'I'm not really the snowball fight type, to be perfectly honest, but I'll rise to your snowman challenge for sure.'

'You're competitive?'

'You better believe it, Charlie, boy. What's your surname by the way?'

'Sheerin. Charlie Daniel Sheerin, the first and last boy Sheerin of my family line. And yours?'

'Quinn,' I reply, picturing my dad's sweet face as soon as I say it. He always called me his golden girl. 'Rose Marie Patricia Quinn. Not named after anyone, but named three times nonetheless.'

'So now that we've cleared up that small matter, what's the prize for the winner of the snowman competition?' he asks.

'You'll have to wait and see,' I say, scooping some bubbles from the sink before turning to face him. I put some on the tip of his nose. He blows them away.

'OK, I'll meet you in the garden in five,' he replies, and as he leaves the kitchen I lean up against the sink, realising my legs have gone to jelly as the tension fizzles between us.

I lift my phone from where it sits on the worktop. I'm tempted to call Carlos and fill him in on how wonderful Charlie has turned out to be, but then I decide not to.

I don't want to tempt fate for a start, neither do I want to put pressure on anything to come out of this holiday haze we're now in, but most of all I want to savour these moments with Charlie all to myself for as long as I possibly can.

And I hope I can find my old self once again somewhere in between.

Chapter Twenty-Six

Charlie

'So, who's judging this? I mean, if it were up to me I'd say the snowman on the left has much more pulling power for votes than the one on the right.'

'You're biased,' says Rose, as we stand at the kitchen window, staring out at our individual masterpieces. 'I'll give you that he does look very stern and bossy, but the one on the right is much more stylish and glamorous. She's a she, of course.'

'Of course.'

It's just gone lunch time, Rose and I are each cradling a large mug full of creamy tomato soup, and the lane coming up to the cottage is a no-go area, so for the first time since we got here we can now officially say we're snowed in. I have to say, there's a sweet surrender about that feeling of going absolutely nowhere.

'They do look like they're having a conversation,' I muse as I take in the two very different characters in the garden. 'She is probably telling him off.'

'He is probably mansplaining something to her and deserves every word she says.'

'Do we call it a draw then?'

'You're so diplomatic, Charlie,' she whispers. 'I won fair and square. I mean, look at her lips – she's had fillers and everything. I went to so much effort.'

'I'm not so diplomatic as to hand you the winning title,' I say, folding my arms now as we both study our form out through the window. 'My guy has a moustache, which must add extra points. And he's wearing Rusty's old hat which I found in the shed. He's a bit of a dude, if I do say so.'

'We could call them Rusty and Marion,' Rose suggests which makes us both chuckle. 'That was fun, I have to say. But now what do we do? Not like we can go anywhere, is it?'

I look around the kitchen for inspiration. We could dig out a board game from a collection on the sideboard, or there's a deck of cards in the drawer.

'Movie and wine?' I suggest, and Rose looks at me like I've just handed her a winning lottery ticket.

'By the fire?'

I nod. 'With snacks?'

She nods too.

'You had me at movie and wine. Let's do this. I think I'll put on my pyjamas and get extra cosy. I'll be right back.'

A few minutes later, both Rose and I have turned the living room of the cottage into a cosy haven with blankets, pillows, twinkling lights on the mantlepiece and a roaring fire with two very chilled-out dogs taking up prime position on the hearth.

We have a bottle of red wine, two glasses, a bowl of crisps and dips, enough chocolate to feed a small family and Rose is flicking through Netflix to find a movie we can both zone out to, if it doesn't glitch like it has been with the low level of signal coming into the cottage against the thick snow.

She sits on one sofa, I sit on the other, and as it begins to drop down dark we decide to keep the curtains open to watch the snowfall. It couldn't be more festive if we tried.

'I'd never, ever do anything like this at home,' I say to Rose as we chat over the movie, just as I thought we might do.

'Me neither,' she replies. 'I head up a business, well, with a partner, so it's very hard to step aside and just be in the moment instead of dreaming up new ideas for marketing campaigns.'

'So that's where you spill out all that creativity?' I say to her. It makes perfect sense. 'You're the boss?'

'I'm the CEO. I'm one of the leaders of an amazing team,' she says, and I shrug. If that's the way she sees it, I guess it's a fresh approach.

'And what about you, then? What do you do when you're not staying in double-booked cottages over Christmas where you make all the local ladies go weak at the knees?'

Her teasing reminds me of Beige Billy, but I'll have to remind her of that later.

'I'm a therapist,' I reply.

'You're a therapist who suggests no communication?'

She is poking fun at me and rightly so. My cheeks flush slightly and I can't resist an eye roll.

'Yip, I'm the man who can sort out everyone else's lives, but who can't sort out his own,' I say, finally admitting to myself that's it in a nutshell. 'I listen to people's problems, I unravel them as much as I can and I send them down avenues they may not have thought of, yet when it comes to my own existence, I found myself on a road to a very dark place and it wasn't pretty. Which is why I'm here.'

Rose shifts her position on the sofa across from me and listens intently.

'You have a child?' she asks me. 'That day when you were upset, I figured it was a child you were worried about?'

'Yeah, I've a little girl. Rebecca. She's only seven. She's moved to Tenerife with her mum and her new stepdad and, well, it almost broke me. I was facing an awful Christmas alone, and my friend suggested I come here to get away from it all.'

'I'm so sorry,' Rose replies. She pulls herself up from where she was lying down snuggled in fleecy blankets. 'That explains so much, Charlie. That's heartbreaking.'

'It's not something I ever thought would happen, that's for sure, but life is life, eh? None of us know what's around the corner.'

We sit in silence as we both absorb these profound moments of getting to know each other. Being with Rose in this darkened cocoon, so cushioned from the outside world, makes it easier to open up and be honest with each other. It's like this state of enveloped enclosure brings out heightened emotions from deep within us that have been held inside for far too long.

'I know you're only just dealing with this fresh,' she says after some thought, 'but you seem like such a strong person. I imagine you're a great daddy too. You'll find a way of making it work. You all will. I know it's breaking your heart now, Charlie, but finding a new normal around it will just take time.'

'I haven't always been the good guy,' I confess to Rose as I look at the ceiling, and it already feels like a weight has lifted when I get to say that out loud.

'None of us are good all the time.'

'True, but I took what I had for granted,' I reply. 'I wasn't present enough in ways that I should have been, and everything that happened since then has been my own fault. I put supporting and pleasing other people before supporting and pleasing my family – work, socialising, drinking, sport, you name it. And then one day my ex said she was leaving. Her new husband Rob is very rich, and he whisked her and Rebecca away within the space of a few months.'

'Wow.'

'So, I launched straight into victim mode and stayed there for quite some time, drinking to make it all go away, punishing myself physically while thinking I was dealing with it like anyone would,' I explain. 'But then one day I snapped out of it. I realised that Clodagh had been begging me to change for years but I hadn't been listening. It takes a lot to admit you're wrong. It takes longer to forgive yourself, but like you, I'm nearly there, I think. I just miss my daughter so badly. That will never go away.'

'Oh, Charlie. We all make mistakes,' she reminds me. 'We're all just messed-up, selfish, crazy miracles who don't get it right all the time. We get caught up in bullshit, we take our eye off the ball, we get swept along with pleasure and forget who and what is most important to us sometimes.'

I take a deep breath. I watch Rose's features glow in the light of the fire.

'Being here has made me realise I can still be the person I want to be,' I tell her, only now understanding how true that is. 'Being here I can learn how to start again. I hope that you too can find the strength to start again if that's what you're looking for.'

She sinks back into the sofa across from me. We are closer than ever, and I want to touch her so badly.

'That's what I'm looking for, Charlie,' she whispers. 'That's what I want more than anything.'

Chapter Twenty-Seven

Rose

I glow from the inside out when I see the look on Charlie's face when he comes into the kitchen for dinner, after snoozing on the settee while I cooked.

My mother always preached that we should use our imagination when cooking from what's left over in the fridge, and although I'll never match Charlie's talent for cuisine, I'm very proud of the rather delicious meal I've made from fried chicken, a dash of cream, a generous glug of white wine and a mix of hearty winter vegetables. With some fluffy rice and savoury garlic potatoes on the side, it looks very impressive – as does the small round table which I brought to life with a centrepiece made from candles and glittering pine cones left over from my Christmas wreaths.

The lights are low, the room is warm, the food looks, smells and – I hope – tastes delicious. And to top it all off, I have the company of this wonderful man for another few days. I would pinch myself if he wasn't standing right in front of me.

'Well, aren't you the dark horse?' he says, pulling out a chair as I serve up. 'Rose, this looks and smells amazing. Chicken à la king?'

'I have absolutely no idea, but if that's what you want to call it, let's run with that.'

He picks up his cutlery, his eyes glued to the plate in front of him.

'Chicken à la Rose,' he jokes, shooting me a friendly glance before tucking in. I wait with bated breath on his opinion.

As I watch him from my seat across this dainty round table, I allow myself a moment to revel in a small but very satisfactory sense of achievement. Charlie has been so kind to me, and although I give out a lot of energy in my day job, doing my best to make my clients feel like they're in good hands, it's been a very long time since I did something as simple as cook for someone else with such care and attention.

I'm used to eating out with friends, or grabbing a sandwich on the run, but I'd clearly forgotten just how good it feels to prepare and then share a meal with someone in such an intimate, caring way. Someone I genuinely enjoy being around; someone who seems to bring out the best in me.

I'd forgotten how such a small gesture can fill us up, and how, with some effort, we can bare our souls on a plate to those we care about. Seeing the delight on Charlie's face as he enjoys the simple dish I've prepared makes me glow unexpectedly.

'This is magnificent. Honestly, Rose,' he says as he heartily tucks in. 'Wow. It's delicious. I honestly don't know when I was last cooked for like this. Thank you. I really appreciate it.'

I feel a warm and fuzzy rush inside as we eat together, locked away here on this magical snowy evening in December. As our conversation naturally flows, neither of us can deny that something big is happening between us and it's moving at lightning speed. We are falling deeper and deeper into each other's hearts.

'So, tell me more about your family, then?' Charlie says to me.

I launch in happily, telling him about my beautiful, selfless mother who I can only ever see as wholesome and strong, no matter what life has thrown her way.

I joke about my sister Sarah, whose relationship with her husband is cardboard cut-out perfect compared to my messy, inconsistent love life, but then my mood dips to a much lower level when I speak of my dad.

'My dad and I . . . well, we don't talk much any more,' I say, as a huge lump settles in my throat. 'He's the type of person who cuts no corners. If he has something to say he says it with no filter. Sometimes it's funny, sometimes it's shocking, but he feels so sad for me that he can barely look me in the eye these days.'

Charlie sits back in his chair. He looks so relaxed, so at ease, so unbelievably sexy and exotic in the flickering candlelight.

'Ah, Rose,' he tells me as he tops up our wine. 'We all love different people in different ways – that's what I think, anyhow.'

I'm all ears.

'For example, growing up, my mum was totally focused on Helena and unashamedly so,' he explains further. 'I may as well have been invisible as far as she was concerned, but then my sister had a car accident that totally changed everything.'

'I'm so sorry.'

He pauses. He swallows his food. He takes his time. The pain in his eyes is excruciating.

'She had a boyfriend. A lovely lad, Colin, and they'd been on their first proper date to the cinema. Helena had whiplash, they said, and Colin walked out unscathed, but a few weeks afterwards, she had what doctors called an ischaemic stroke because of a loss of oxygen to the brain. She was only seventeen.'

I drop my head and hold my temples, as I hear the crash of metal again. The scrapes, the screams.

'Rose?'

'I'm so sorry, Charlie,' I whisper. I reach across the small kitchen table and squeeze his hand. 'Poor Helena.'

He takes another moment before he continues.

'Her life has never been the same since. Nurses, doctors, occupational therapists and then sheltered care when she needed her independence. But Mum changed even more than my sister did, if that's even possible. It was like she couldn't bear to be around Helena. She couldn't cope with the change in her precious only daughter, and she hit the bottle big time to mask her pain. It was sad to be around. My father reacted in a similar vein, but I've no doubt they each loved both of us in their own way.'

I sip the white wine, feeling the coolness on my lips, and realising how easy it would have been for me to have gone down a similar route when it came to numbing my pain.

'You've had it tough, Charlie, yet you still give so much,' I tell him. 'You're a very kind person. And how are your mum and dad now?'

He smiles, but I can see the sadness behind it.

'Well . . . just to add the final nail to the coffin of my sad story, pardon the pun, but we lost them a few years after Helena's stroke. So, until Rebecca came along, Helena was my world. Every Christmas I make an almighty fuss over her with presents, the best food and a movie night sleepover at my house with Rebecca, but this year I just needed a break from it all. I needed headspace to get myself back into a positive place so that I can be the brother Helena deserves; the father Rebecca deserves. Does that make me selfish?'

'God, no,' I reply. 'I just heard you with Helena. You're the best brother she could wish for, so I'm sure one Christmas won't change that. She adores you.'

He lights up when I say that and goes back to his food, deep in thought now. For two people who seem so entranced by each other, it's strange to think this is the first time we've sat across from each other and had a proper, heartfelt conversation. With every word he speaks, I feel like I know him, and that I like him, just a little bit more.

'I've had to work a lot on myself so I can do a better job of helping others,' he tells me, having given this reply some thought. 'Yes, that's basically it in a nutshell. I've worked hard for a long time to get to where I am mentally, yet my daughter leaving the country has rocked my core. But I'm beginning to see things more clearly already about all of that, which is what I needed from this time out.'

He seems so strong, so self-assured and already a lot more at ease than the man I first met just a few days ago.

'And then you ended up here with me.'

He stares at me intently, taking me in, as if what I just said was too good to be true.

The classical music in the background seems to get louder and I realise that I can hear my own pulse.

'I wouldn't change being here with you, not for a million,' he tells me. 'I wouldn't change it for the world.'

Oh God.

There's a table between us, my candlelit centrepiece and a hot cooked meal, but he finds my hand and squeezes it and it's enough to send delicate shivers from my fingers to my toes.

'So where were we before I launched into my sob story?' he asks, his eyes cast downward, his long eyelashes blinking away the intensity of the moment we just shared.

'You were telling me about . . . you were telling me about how you believe different people show love in different ways when I mentioned my relationship with my dad.'

'Yes, that's how I choose to look at my own family background, anyhow. Don't get me wrong, I do sometimes have a moan about Helena's phone calls and dependence, but only to myself, or Max if he's listening.'

'You're incredibly loyal, then.'

He laughs.

'Thank you. Though I have been very selfish on occasion, too.'

I shrug.

'There's no harm in needing your own space sometimes.'

'You're good.'

I put my knife and fork down slowly. I've gone to a huge effort this evening and hoped it would be perfect. So far, so good.

'I've always felt like the black sheep in my family, but I don't think I've ever said that out loud before,' I tell him. 'I was a rebel while my sister was pure as the driven snow. She still is.'

'So you're unique, then,' he replies quickly. 'Unique is much more interesting than pure as the driven snow.'

I can't help but smile.

'I'm also a bit stubborn.'

Now he's smiling too.

'Challenging, you mean.'

'And I've never been good with money.'

'Generous to a fault,' he says straight off the mark. 'I could have guessed that.'

'Ha, thank you.'

'It's all about perspective,' he tells me, which makes my stomach flutter. 'We're all shaped and moulded in different ways by so many different things, Rose. You're creative and sparkly. You light up a room.'

'My boyfriend died,' I blurt out like an overflowing volcano. I didn't mean to spit it out like that but when people praise me in any way, I feel the need to tell them the truth. I don't want anyone thinking I'm something I'm not.

Charlie looks like he's been jolted.

'Oh, God. Oh Rose.'

'He died in a car accident when I was with him on Christmas Eve three years ago,' I say, feeling my throat close and my eyes sting. 'I vowed to spend Christmas alone since then, or at least until I feel I deserve to celebrate again.'

Charlie falls silent. I feel as if my words have just stabbed him in the heart. But now I've started I don't want to stop until Charlie knows the truth about me. I have so much to face up to. Being here is heavenly, but it's not real life and I'd rather he knew the real me, warts and all.

Charlie's eyes dart around the room and suddenly I feel very exposed. I feel like I've shed my skin in front of this wonderful man and that he's going to want to run away and never see me again. I wouldn't blame him if he did.

'Oh Rose,' he says, and I close my eyes waiting for him to backtrack on all the wonderful ways he was making me see myself just a few moments ago. 'You were in an accident with him when he died?'

'Yes.'

'What happened?' he asked gently.

'He died on the . . . he died instantly. He died on the scene,' I stutter. 'I called an ambulance, but it was too late. He was gone.'

I gasp so deeply it feels like I've been shot as I briefly see Michael's face in my head again.

'I screamed for him. I called his name. I reached for my phone and I couldn't keep it in my hands I was shaking so badly, but I somehow managed to press an emergency call button. It's still all a blur. It's still all a nightmare.'

I try not to cry in front of Charlie but the noises in my head start up again like a spluttering engine that suddenly takes off.

Michael's choice of music for our trip away, the cigarette smell of the car, the five o'clock shadow on his face, the way he clasped my hand and looked down at it as if for reassurance when lost in thought, the sound of the brakes screeching, the crash, the smoke, the silence.

Charlie takes his time. He doesn't rush in. He doesn't blurt out. He doesn't talk for the sake of talking. He just sits with me, holding my hand which is shaking now as I sob like a baby.

I wipe the streaming tears with the back of my hand. Charlie hands me a clean napkin.

'I think you've been really strong to have carried that weight all alone,' he says. He holds my gaze with such confidence.

'And that's why it's good to talk it through. In fact, sometimes the word strong is used when we simply have no choice but to keep going. We keep going, we are vulnerable but we are brave. Even the bravest of us need help, and that's OK.'

I push away my plate and put my head in my hands.

'Rose, look at me.'

But I can't.

I feel hot, and the thought of eating makes me nauseous. I push the food I'd prepared so carefully around my plate and for the first time since I got here, a wave of claustrophobia and panic sweeps over me, making me catch my breath.

'I – I distracted him, Charlie,' I confess, feeling real pain in my chest when I say it out loud. 'I put my hand across and took his when he was driving. I mean, who does that? Why did I do that? He took his eyes off the road for just a second and he was smiling because I did that but then—'

Charlie stands up from the table and comes around beside me.

'Rose, it wasn't your fault,' he whispers so gently, and this time I do look him in the eye. 'I hope you already know that, but if it helps, I will tell you again: it wasn't your fault. You have been to hell and back, and I am so sorry for your loss, but you are going to be OK. You really are.'

'But—'

I look out through the kitchen window into the bright night sky, a stark contrast to the usual darkness in these parts, all those tiny snow crystals reflecting the light of the moon. I think of the lighthouse, standing tall and strong as waves crash against it and chaos unfolds around it.

I know Charlie is right. I've always known this, but it's a comfort to hear it from someone else right now.

'It wasn't your fault,' he says, direct, but with a softness.

'I think my dad blames me. I'd had a few drinks before we left the house and he thinks I was being giddy and silly, distracting Michael when he was driving.'

Charlie closes his eyes.

'Has your dad said that to you?'

I shake my head.

'He's never said those words?'

I shake my head more.

'Rose, you have created a narrative that may not exist. You need to find out if that's what your dad really believes, or if it's what you *think* he believes. Does that make sense?'

I look up into Charlie's eyes and nod slowly. That makes more sense to me than anything I've ever heard before.

'I know it doesn't often feel this way, but we have control over our thoughts – we can choose how we speak to ourselves in our minds. Thoughts are just thoughts. Once you learn to control your thoughts, they no longer control you. You should talk to your dad, because his take on the situation might be far kinder than your mind has told you it is.'

'Yes,' I mutter in response. 'Yes, that makes total sense. Thank you. I'm sorry I ruined our first proper meal together.'

'You haven't,' he replies with a smile. 'Now, deep breaths and let's finish eating your culinary masterpiece, then we'll watch some more trashy TV on the sofa. But we can also talk about it more, if you want to.'

'Trashy TV on the sofa sounds good.'

'Thank you for being so brave and honest,' he replies. 'Today was perfect.'

'It was.'

'And right now,' he continues, 'I think you are even more wonderful than before, Rose Quinn. And that's pretty wonderful, believe me.'

Two Days to Christmas

Chapter Twenty-Eight

Charlie

Rose and I spend the morning hiking through the base of the snowy Glenveagh Mountains with Max and George, taking in the views and sharing stories and snapshots of our lives. We take selfies, we drink tea from a flask, and then we finish our day with a hearty lunch in the village of Kerrykeel, where oysters and Guinness are served to us with crusty bread in a cosy booth made for two. We also talk a lot more. Rose opens up about the night Michael died and the aftermath – how she ran to Dublin, a city so bustling she could almost feel invisible as she hid away from reality.

'We all grieve in different ways,' I remind her. 'That was what you needed to do at the time.'

I talk about Rebecca and no matter how much I try to ignore it, the pain of being away from her at this time of year is almost too much to bear. I need to stand up to Clodagh about the once a week contact and insist that Rebecca and I should be able to talk more often.

'Try and compromise,' Rose tells me as we make our way back to the car. 'Try not to act on impulse when your emotions are high. Christmas brings everything to the surface. I know it's easier said than done, but act with your head as much as your heart if you can.'

I'll do my best to remember that – it's the advice I would give to someone too, but it's often a different story when it comes to ourselves.

We are ruddy faced and tired with mucky feet after a glorious day. We've peeled back layers of our lives, but on the drive back to the cottage as Christmas moods go into overdrive on the car radio, I feel old fears seeping in again.

It's Christmas Eve tomorrow. I need to speak with Clodagh. I need to make some changes, and fast. I'm not having her dictate when I can speak to Rebecca over Christmas – or any longer, for that matter.

'Do you mind stopping at the corner shop on the way past?' Rose asks me as we approach the village.

I don't answer at first. My mind is racing with what I want to say to Clodagh.

'Charlie?'

'Sorry, yes, of course. No problem,' I mutter, rubbing my forehead. I let out a sigh. I can feel Rose's eyes on me. Her voice is full of concern.

'I just need a few things in the shop. Won't be long,' she says. 'Are you OK, Charlie? You look miles away.'

I'm biting my nails when I'm driving. It's a habit that used to drive Clodagh insane.

'Yes, yes,' I reply quickly, feeling bad for threatening to dampen the mood of our day.

'It's Rebecca, isn't it?' she asks when I stop the car.

I nod. I look out the window where the snow is being washed away by rain. I turn up the wipers.

'Give me a few minutes,' she says as she opens the car door. 'We can talk about it when I'm done.'

She puts up her hood, dips her head down against the elements and makes a run for it into the shop.

I lift my phone immediately. I need to say something to Clodagh right now. I can't go on like this, living under her weekly five-minute phone call regime. It's Christmas Eve tomorrow and I should be able to see and speak with Rebecca every day of the holidays if that's what me and my daughter both want. I can still see her tear-stained face from the last day she called me, and it makes my heart hurt.

'Charlie?'

Clodagh's reaction is as I expected when she answers, like a wolf in sheep's clothing with her polite voice that stings like a wasp when it needs to, but I won't back down, not this time.

'Hi Clodagh, I was hoping we could have a quick word.'

'I'm just . . . hang on. Yes, go on. What's wrong?'

'What's wrong?' I ask, already feeling my blood heat up. 'Has something happened?'

I take a deep breath.

'Nothing's happened, but I should be able to call you to check in on Rebecca at any time. I can't go on like this, Clodagh,' I tell her, my voice shaking as I speak. 'It's unfair on me and it's unfair on our daughter.'

'Now, Charlie, wait.'

But I'm tired of waiting.

'No, Clodagh, it's time you listened. Rebecca and I can't be held to ransom for your decision to emigrate. I'm her father. I'm a good daddy and Rebecca loves me.'

I wasn't planning on making this call so soon, but I have to stay strong. It's time I began to fix my own life as well as trying to fix others daily.

'I've told you many times. I don't want to unsettle her,' Clodagh replies in her clipped accent which usually makes me cower and back down when she reaches a certain decibel, but not this time. 'I see how upset she is every time you speak with her. You don't see the tears that follow. She's terrified of you being alone this Christmas.'

'I'm not alone.'

'She is like a little sponge,' she continues, ignoring what I just said. 'She absorbs so much even though she's still so young.'

'Which is exactly why she doesn't need these timetabled, stifled calls where we don't even get to say a proper good-bye because the conversation hasn't run its course,' I tell her, standing up for both myself and my daughter in a way I should have done a long time ago. 'This was your decision, Clodagh, yet it seems that me and Rebecca are paying the price when it comes to our relationship. It's not on. I will call her, and she can call me whenever it organically feels right from now on. No more watching the clock. No more scheduling what day it can happen. It's not a lot to ask, but hell, I'm not asking any more. I'm telling you. You told me you were taking Rebecca to Spain to live, now I'm telling *you* I can call her when I want and the same goes for our daughter. She can call her daddy whenever she needs to, not when you tell her she can.'

I see Rose make her way back from the shop, but I needn't worry about her reaction to my spontaneity as Clodagh hangs up before we come to any arrangement that isn't on her terms. As bloody usual.

I come off the phone drained from my head to my toes, but as much as it took from me, I feel empowered like I wasn't before.

I feel like I've found the clarity I came here to find, the strength I needed to voice my own wishes about this new arrangement which has knocked the wind from my sails, and the realisation that I don't need to be told what to do by Clodagh. I won't wait another three months to see my child. I won't wait for that perfectly timed phone call every Friday.

'I'm so proud of you for taking the stance you needed to,' Rose tells me as we arrive back at Seaview Cottage. 'Are you going to try to squeeze in a visit to Rebecca before the holidays are up, then?'

'Absolutely,' I reply, still shaking, but a rush of determination floods through my veins. 'There's no way I'm waiting until Easter.'

'You've survived this snow, so you deserve to put some sunshine on your bucket list for sure,' she says.

'Thanks, Rose. Sorry if I'm upset. I suppose it was inevitable as Christmas comes closer.'

As I drive up the lane to our secluded retreat, I hope this feeling settles now that I've said my piece, but I'd doubt it ends there.

Chapter Twenty-Nine

Rose

Charlie is quiet.

I cook dinner, I make hot chocolate, I pour some wine, I stoke up the fire but no matter what I do or say, it's like he's slipping away from me. He feels guilty that he's not spending Christmas with his sister, and devastated that he is away from his daughter.

There's no dancing in the kitchen this evening. There are no Christmas carols and no snuggling up with a movie. Charlie is reading his book by the fire. I am scrolling through my phone looking at friends' smiling faces, sharing happy family photos in which their children look fit to burst with excitement for Christmas Eve tomorrow.

In a way it's a comfortable silence. But then I look at the frown on his face as he turns the pages and I know that nothing he is reading is being absorbed.

He is heartbroken.

'I know this isn't going to blow your mind or rock your world, but I've a very small gift for you.'

I don't want to disturb or push him, but I feel it might be the right time to try and cheer him up, if even just a little.

'Ah, Rose. You're very kind.'

He puts his book down, takes his glasses off and gives me one of his million-dollar smiles.

'It's not much,' I add quickly.

I wait for him to open the wrapping. As he peels back the silver paper ever so slowly, my heart flutters and my eyes well up when I realise that after Christmas I don't know when I'm ever going to see him again. But for now, I choose to live in the moment. As a smile creeps over his gorgeous face, I know that there's nowhere else I'd rather be right now.

'You never cease to amaze me, Rose,' he says, holding out the handmade wooden picture frame which is decorated with forget-me-nots. 'How did you get those two rascals to sit for long enough to take this picture?'

'It was tricky, but dog treats work wonders. I had it printed yesterday when Stacy and I were out on our travels.'

'Rose, it's fantastic,' he says, shaking his head in wonder. 'I'll never forget the memories we made here. It's perfect.'

We both stare at the photo of Max and George on the door-step of Seaview Cottage, the smoke billowing from the chimney, the dancing orange flames from the open fire through the front window and a white blanket of snow thick on the ground. Max has his head tilted, so full of mischief and rascality, while George has his tongue lolling out of his mouth. But best of all, up above is the most beautiful night-time Donegal sky, peppered with the stars we looked up to together.

'OK, your turn,' he says.

'What?'

'Great minds think alike,' says Charlie, and he reaches down underneath the sofa to where he pulls out a small, neatly wrapped gift with a rose-shaped gift tag. 'I got this for you. When I saw it, I thought of you straight away. I really hope you like it.'

My first thought is the polka dot skirt he'd spied when out shopping, but Charlie's gift is a small box shape that is heavy to hold.

I sit up straight and tear open the paper much more quickly than he did just moments ago. When I peel it back it reveals the most delicately decorated, stunning walnut music box. I put my hand over my mouth.

'Open it,' he whispers.

I prise the lid open gently. As the tinkling sounds fill the air, a tiny ballerina twirls round and round in its centre and happy tears roll down my face when I realise the song it's playing.

'The song it's playing is called "Salut d'Amour",' Charlie tells me. 'I got it at the Christmas Fayre. Now, it's vintage, which is a fancy way of saying it's pre-loved and has a chip on the corner, but I thought it was timeless, just like you.'

I can barely find my breath as I find the chip in the corner he is speaking of and my heart thumps in my chest

'"Salut d'Amour". Love's Greeting . . .' I whisper.

'You know it?'

'My Granny Molly . . . When I'd stay here with her, she used to play this to me and my sister to get us to sleep,' I say,

344

watching the tiny ballerina go around and around as the soft tinkling sounds fill the room. 'This was hers, Charlie. This was her music box. I'd always wanted to find it, and now you have.'

Charlie's mouth drops open, almost as astounded as I am.

'I'd no clue,' he says, his face in a puzzle. 'But now you can listen to it forever, wherever you are, and remember our time here at your grandmother's holiday cottage, as well as those precious childhood days you spent here with her.'

I'm totally stunned.

I take a deep breath, then I put my arms around his neck and kiss him, tentatively at first, but as his soft lips part wider, our kiss deepens. The passion of this kiss is unlike anything I have felt before.

He wraps his strong arms around my waist and pulls me close, our bodies melding together.

The tune from the music box fills the living room where we have spent so many wonderful hours together. This moment is everything I've ever dreamed of – yet never dared dream of with him. It's natural, it's warm, it's me and Charlie the way we've wanted to be for days. I smell that woody aftershave up close and personal, I taste his skin, I am dizzy and I am drunk on him.

'I've wanted us to do that for such a long time,' he murmurs as he plants kisses up and down my neck, making me weak at the knees. 'You've no idea how many times I've had to stop myself.'

'Me too,' I whisper, and we make our way to the sofa where we lie together by the warmth of the dancing orange flames and release a tension that has been bubbling for far too long.

Much later, with a new warmth in my heart, I sip some wine in the kitchen as Charlie makes us a tasty supper of bread, cheese and olives. And then we fall asleep together, wrapped up in a feeling that we never want to end.

Everything is perfect at first.

I fall asleep in Charlie's arms with ease but when I wake just a few hours later with palpitations and see it's gone midnight, I know I'm not ready for this yet.

I dreamed of Michael, and even now I'm awake, all I can see is his face, his hand in mine, the sirens, the coffin, the wailing mourners, and all eyes on me.

For the fourth year in a row, this day makes my blood run cold.

I toss and turn in bed. I watch Charlie sleep and a wave of horror overcomes me. Instead of the handsome, kind man I've got to know so beautifully over the last nine days, all I see is a stranger. All I feel is betrayal.

It's Michael's anniversary. What have I done? What on earth am I doing here?

I wrap a blanket around myself, steal a pillow from the bed and tiptoe downstairs, praying the dogs won't let me down by waking up Charlie.

I make a bed up on the sofa and try to sleep, but the sounds and smells of that awful night come back to haunt me once more.

I hear the tyres screech and slide on the roadside. I smell the burning rubber. I scramble with the airbag, I struggle to breathe.

I call out his name. I reach for his hand.

It's still warm. I don't know it yet, but he can't hear me.

I don't know it yet, but he's gone.

I don't know it yet, but a glimmer and sparkle lies on the floor. I don't see it until a policeman hands it to me as I shiver under a fire blanket on the roadside.

'It's not mine,' I tell the policeman.

But then I realise it was going to be mine. Michael was going to propose. He was taking me to the lighthouse. He was going to ask me to marry him.

I'm going to be sick. I race to the bathroom and heave as the horror physically punishes me again, the bile burning my throat as all the goodness of the evening with Charlie leaves me. I don't deserve to be happy at Christmas. It's not fair on Michael.

Then in the still of the night, I get my suitcase from the back hallway. I tiptoe upstairs and quietly collect my clothes from the wardrobe. I put George into the car with all his belongings.

And before I go, I write a final message to Charlie on the whiteboard.

I can't be with anyone else. I can't do that to Michael. I have to go.

Christmas Eve

Chapter Thirty

Charlie

I stare at the words on the whiteboard, totally lost and confused.

I'm so sorry. Take care, Charlie. Thank you for being so kind and loving to me. I'll never forget you. Rose x

I can still smell her perfume in the air, I can hear her atrocious singing if I concentrate for long enough, but as I rattle around from room to room on my own all morning, it just doesn't feel right being here any more without her. What happened? What was so bad she had to leave?

I've read her note a thousand times over. I've tried calling her number but her phone is switched off. I'm worried about her. I can't believe she'd leave so coldly without saying a proper goodbye.

Is this it? Did she really leave on Christmas Eve? Without warning? With a note on the fridge after all we've discussed? After all we've shared?

She is grieving sore, I remind myself. And I can understand that last night might have left her feeling guilty – whether that feeling is warranted or not. But she could have told me, and I could have seen her off with a warm hug and wished her well. Anything would be better than this. This is empty and cruel.

I make coffee but I don't drink it. I try tea but it doesn't taste right. I turn on the radio, then I turn it back off again. I try to hold Max for comfort but he wriggles away to the window. He's looking for her too. He knows that something's not right.

I go to the bedroom and stare at the empty wardrobe. I lift her pillow and hold it close, doing my best to think of all the good things she brought my way. I refuse to think that the time we spent together was in vain. I'm a great believer in everything happening for a reason. Even the toughest life lessons that hurt are there to teach us something. It's what I tell my clients. So I close my eyes and I try to think of the positives.

Rose reminded me of the joy of making someone laugh, the magic of knowing when it was about me and when it was about her. She reminded me when to offer my arm to her and when to hold back and give her space. Of when to kiss harder and longer, or when to hug her without saying a word. She has taught me that it's possible to fall for someone again.

She also taught me to let go when I need to, and perhaps that time is now.

But it's not as simple as that, is it? I miss her already. I long for her smile and her presence.

I long for her, for everything about her. I know now that love doesn't care about time. It doesn't matter how long you have known someone. Love is measured in transformation, and the way Rose touched my heart is something that can never be taken away from me.

I walk the forest with Max and all I can think of is how she held on to me so tightly when we searched in the snow for my errant dog, who has no idea of the role he played in bringing us so physically close for the first time.

I go into the village but all I can see is the ghost of her on every street corner. I stop on the part of the lane where we stood beneath the stars, and when I get back to the cottage, all I can see is her empty chair which only intensifies my sense of loss.

I pick up the phone. I make a call I should have made before now.

I realise I don't want to be alone for Christmas.

I never really did.

Chapter Thirty-One

Rose

It's just gone 10 a.m.

I've been in my car for hours now with the heating on full blast, only getting out now and then to let George stretch his legs.

I don't know what I expected by coming here again today, but it's where I need to be so I can clear my head and think of where I want to go next in life. I can't keep hitting dead ends. I can't keep pretending. And I can't keep suppressing my feelings for Charlie, because I am punishing him as much as I'm punishing myself.

A bit of space and a change of scenery works wonders.

More wise words from my grandmother echo in my mind. She was right, as always. A few hours by myself here in my favourite place is already helping me think straight.

It's so quiet here. It is Christmas Eve after all, so everyone is busy with family life, getting ready for Santa tonight or for a big festive feast tomorrow. I think of my niece and nephew, so young and innocent, and tears prick my eyes when I imagine how excited they will be for the big day tomorrow.

They'll be in matching pyjamas, they'll go to bed extra early and they'll be far too high on anticipation to sleep. I'm missing them so much.

And then I picture Charlie, who'll have woken up well before now. I shouldn't have packed my bags and left that note. I can see that now. But grief pushes us into corners sometimes. It puts words on our tongues and pain in our hearts that make us react in ways we wouldn't have dreamed of before.

I so, so badly want to run to Charlie. I want to hide in the safety of his arms and never look back, but I need to be sure I'm strong enough to be the person he needs me to be in return. I need this space to think, to scream, to cry, all in the hope that I could accept that I'm allowed to be happy again.

And it's working already.

The sound of the waves, the memories I hold on to about this place, the strength of the lighthouse which never buckles under all its strain. It just quietly does its job every day, all year round. It is solid. It is timeless. It is a creature of outstanding beauty, yet there's nothing delicate about its bricks and mortar and steel. It's a tower of strength, quite literally, and I know I still have a similar strength inside of me too.

I've learned so much from my week with Charlie at Seaview Cottage. I've learned the power of giving in the simplest of forms.

I've learned the power of a hug from the right person at the right time.

I've learned how goodness is what people do, much more than what they say.

I've learned the joy in having someone who cares enough to wish you goodnight.

I've learned the importance of saying sorry, of showing up to apologise, even when it doesn't go your way.

I've also learned that by stepping out of our own lives for just a little while, we can see things from a different angle. We can learn to forgive ourselves for even the biggest mistakes. And that each of us have scaled mountains without knowing it.

I've learned that each day is a new start, a new chance, and a new time to start again.

I know that deep inside I am my own lighthouse.

I am hope. I am secure. I can weather any storm. I can stand tall and strong, no matter how the waves batter and crash against me, no matter how chaotic the world is around me, and no matter what challenges the changing elements of life bring my way.

I can dim my inner lanterns when I need to rest. I can shine brightly from within, and most of all I can beam my light for miles and miles to guide my own path and to help and protect others along their way.

I am my own lighthouse.

I turn on the engine of the car to leave at last, but just as I do so, something stops me. And then I see her.

A lonely figure walks past the car, towards the grassy banks and the white stone walls that line the drop of rolling rocks that lead to Fanad Lighthouse.

There's a familiarity in the way she walks, in how tall she is, yet her demeanour is so small. She stoops beneath a black umbrella, holding on to it with both hands, huddling under it as if she is clinging on to it for dear life. I haven't seen her in almost four years.

I couldn't face her, and I was told the feeling was mutual on her part.

It's Evelyn, Michael's mother, and the sight of her shuffling up the pathway towards her late son's favourite place is enough to take my breath away.

I slowly open the car door, leaving George in the heat of the car, and I follow her.

She doesn't hear me at first, so I call her name again.

'Evelyn?'

But she keeps walking.

'Evelyn! Wait, please. It's me. It's Rose.'

She turns round at last, so I quicken my step to greet her with open arms. I don't need to say anything more. It's raining heavily now but she shelters me beneath her umbrella. Michael used to joke how his mother was never a 'hugger', yet she clings to me now like a vine, but lets me go again almost as quickly as she started, then we link arms and walk slowly together up the slight slope to the lighthouse.

'What are you doing here?' she asks me softly. 'For Michael?'

I nod, biting my lip as my eyes burn hot with tears.

'Yes, for Michael.'

'I come here every year to remember him,' she whispers against the wind. 'Every year on Christmas Eve, I come here just for him.'

The way we are walking together reminds me of how we did the same at his funeral. My heart is thumping; Evelyn is poised and strong.

'He loved this place so much, Rose,' she tells me, even though I already know. 'He said there was a magic here on Fanad Head. A sense of time standing still, yet spectacular views that reminded him always of the beauty of the world. The vulnerability of humanity. I like to remember him that way. He was always so in awe of the beauty of the world, no matter what life would throw at him.'

I expect her to break down when she speaks of Michael so fondly but instead of crying, Evelyn turns to me and smiles.

'I've a lot to thank you for, Rose.'

I swallow back tears.

'You have?'

'I do,' she says softly, looking out towards Malin Head, a place that sits amongst rugged cliffs on this perilous ocean. 'Even though I've never had the courage to say it before, I need to thank you for so much.'

'But I thought you . . . I always thought . . . ?'

And then I remember Charlie's advice.

Thoughts are just thoughts. Once you learn to control your thoughts, they no longer control you.

We stop beneath the shadow of the lighthouse, the waves crashing onto the rocks below us. The rain slows down to a drizzle, the type that stings your eyes and soaks you to the bone, but I'm too enthralled with what Evelyn has to say to notice.

My heart thuds in my chest. I feel like falling to my knees in sorrow for this grieving mother, yet she wants to thank me? For what?

'You see, Rose, I've taken my time to process everything that has happened, and it hit me one day like it all made sense,' she tells me. 'Michael was so happy. He was the happiest I've ever known him to be.'

Oh God.

'You showed Michael more love in your brief years together than many people experience in a lifetime,' she continues, with a smile on her weary face. 'His final years were bursting with love, with smiles and with happiness and so many wonderful life adventures, all because of you.'

I choke back tears, but they aren't tears of sadness like they usually are. I feel a warm glow, as if the great memories of Michael are finally smothering out the horrific nightmare of the accident.

Yes. It all makes sense.

'We had some amazing adventures for sure,' I say to her, standing a little taller already here in the rain. 'We loved each other so, so much.'

Evelyn's eyes fill up now.

'Don't ever stop loving, Rose,' she tells me, shaking her head with a smile. 'For as long as you live, don't ever stop loving in the way you loved him. It's what we are all here for after all.'

Her words hit me right in the heart.

'We miss Michael, yes,' she says, 'but I know he still walks with me every day because someone like my son would never leave me, nor will he leave you. He was loved and he is still loved by so many. He's still in here, always.' She points to her heart through her heavy red waterproof jacket. 'So he's never really going away, is he?'

My hands are stinging with the cold, but I'm too absorbed by Evelyn's words to worry about the dropping temperature.

'And he left us both, me and you, with hearts so full of love that should always be shared,' Evelyn says. 'If you can find someone to love like that again, if you can find someone to keep sharing all the same laughter and happiness you gave to my boy, please don't waste it. He wouldn't want you to waste it. You have so much love to give. Don't ever hold that back, because my son would never want you to. When you show love to others, you are showing love to him.'

She hugs me, and lightly kisses my cheek.

'Thank you,' she whispers again. 'I'm so glad I got to say thank you.'

My face crumples as she shuffles away, leaving me standing in the rain under the heavy December sky. I watch her as she makes her way around to Michael's favourite viewpoint, a little bench that looks out onto the vast mouth of Lough Swilly, where she sits in the rain beneath her umbrella.

I sob the whole way back to the car park, but it's a different type of release after meeting Evelyn. All I can see now is Michael's smiling face, the joy he held when we were together, the fun we had and the love we shared.

Evelyn is right. Why would I stop loving like that? I never, ever want to stop. I can show Michael just how special the love we had was by sharing it in every way that I can.

George bounces around madly when he sees me approach the car. I throw my soaking wet coat in the boot, give my dog a fur-filled snuggle, and then I drive back to Seaview as fast as the winding roads will allow me to.

But when I get to the cottage, it is empty and locked up. Charlie has already gone.

Chapter Thirty-Two

Charlie

My playlist is blaring through the speakers in the car, my phone is on silent, and the roads are as quiet as I hoped they would be on my way back to Belfast. I need distraction, so I'm focused on the road ahead and the surprise I'm about to deliver tomorrow morning.

Helena isn't expecting me.

I called her supervisor, Mary, in the assisted accommodation block to say I was on my way home, and she secretly packed Helena's bag for tomorrow while she was helping in the kitchen for lunch.

'I didn't want to tell you, Charlie, but she's the only one here for Christmas Day,' Mary said when I called. My heart dropped to the floor when I heard it. 'Dermot's nephew is coming for him first thing in the morning and Frances is just away, so it would have been just me and Helena here. She'll be ecstatic when she sees you tomorrow. She's talked about you nonstop since you left.'

Again, I'm assured that everything in life happens for a reason. Had Rose not fled from the cottage this morning, my

362

sister would have spent Christmas with only her supervisor for company, and that would have never left my head for months and maybe years to come.

Even Clodagh's decision to take Rebecca away to Tenerife might turn out to be a positive thing in the long term. The experience of learning a new culture and language, perhaps? The character-building challenges of settling into a new country? A life in the sun that Ireland doesn't usually have to offer? I realise I'm being uber positive, but I don't want to go in any direction of darkness today.

Rose has made her decision. I am hurting to the core, but I need to keep going if only for my sister.

I also need to do some food shopping as soon as I hit the city. I'll get a small turkey fillet, some seasonal veg and some potatoes. I'll pick up a ready-made dessert. I'll be lucky if I can find any crackers on Christmas Eve, but Mary said she would try and seek some out as she knows as well as I do how much Helena loves all the trimmings on Christmas Day.

'We're on our way home after all,' I say to Max, who seems a lot more excited than I am to be on the road again. 'But we'll make the most of it, won't we? We'll have lots of delicious food. We'll have a few beers. We'll do our best to make sure it's a good one, just the three of us. Me, you and Helena.'

I battle to keep positive and control my thoughts on every mile of the road I travel, but I only have to blink to see her face again. I don't want to think about Rose and the Christmas Day we could have had together. Most of all, I don't want to imagine the pain she must be feeling right now as she faces Christmas alone, which I know is not what she truly wanted.

A pang grips my heart when I think of what she must be going through, and I ache to see her again.

I remember all the effort she made to make our stay special.

Her decorations still light up the mantelpiece at Seaview Cottage. The pine cones are still bringing the rooms to life with their seasonal scents. The candles still fill the hallway with cinnamon, vanilla and spice. And the forest-green wreath still lights up the cottage door.

Even Marion had to swallow her pride and admire the decorations when she called over to collect the keys and let me check out early. She and Rusty have made a pact to be kinder to one another over Christmas. They've been married twenty-five years, she said, and that was worth a little more respect and effort than either of them have been showing lately.

'I'd like to tell Rose I'm sorry for how I treated her,' Marion told me as I packed up the car, her chin jutted out just before we said goodbye. 'Maybe I'll pluck up the courage to give her dad a call and we'll try and fix those burned bridges once and for all. Life's too short to hold a grudge, especially when it comes to family.'

'I'm very, very happy to hear you say that, Marion,' I told her. 'You've a good heart. It would be a pity to hold a grudge over something as beautiful as Seaview Cottage.'

'You mean *Granny Molly's* Cottage,' she corrected me. 'I think it's time I gave this place back its proper name and allowed the people who should be here to enjoy it as much as we do.'

'I think you're absolutely right, Marion. Good for you, and good for Rusty. I have a feeling you're both going to be just fine.'

'Ah, we're two of a kind,' Marion told me. 'Two stubborn mules who don't know how good we have it behind all our huffing and puffing.'

'I'm delighted to hear that,' I told her with sincerity, before I bade her farewell.

As I drive now, I can still hear Rose's laughter as she slipped and slid that night in the forest. I can still feel her body so close to mine. I can smell her hair. I can hear her voice. I miss her so much it hurts, yet I'm thankful I got to know her at all, even if it was for a short, sweet blink of an eye. We shared more intimacy in those nine days together than I could ever have hoped for, and for that I'm so grateful.

I hope one day, when she is ready, that I'll see her again.

I lean across to flick the tunes when the steering wheel tugs to the side, so I hold it firmly, but it pulls again.

'Oh no. Oh, please no.'

I slow down. I let out a long breath. The snow is pelting down outside so this is the very last thing I need.

'Jeez, Max, is this my unlucky day or what?' I say out loud, but Max is chilling in the back seat, totally oblivious to my dilemma. I indicate left and snail along until I find a safe place to stop. We're just on the edge of the County Donegal border, not even an hour into our journey home, when I pull over and discover it's exactly what I thought it was.

A flat tyre.

Wonderful. This day keeps getting better and better.

The morning rain has given way to another snowfall, meaning the weatherman was right for a change. It looks like we're in for a white Christmas, which will certainly make Helena happy. She doesn't believe it's really Christmas if it doesn't snow.

I push the button for the hazard lights, pull my coat on and shuffle around to the back of the car where I fish a large golf umbrella from the boot, swearing to myself at the inconvenience of all this, especially in such horrible weather. I tug out the spare tyre from the boot.

'Just my luck for this to happen to me now,' I mutter as a car pulls into the lay-by beside me. The lights make me squint and when the kind stranger gets out, I don't get a chance to speak before she does.

'Can I help?'

I almost bang my head on the open boot at the sound of her voice.

'Not a good day for car trouble,' she says, 'but then, there's never a good day for car trouble, is there?'

I turn to face her, unable to disguise the wide grin on my face.

'I think I got it just in time,' I say, slamming the boot down with one hand and balancing the huge golf umbrella in the other. 'My tyre needs changing.'

I look her in the eye as she blinks back snowdrops that fall from her eyelashes onto her cheeks.

'You've got it all under control, then.'

'I have,' I reply with a coy smile. I walk towards her. 'You thought I needed help to fix a car because I'm a man, didn't you? What fooled you? Was it the—'

'Lipstick or the heeled boots?' we both say together, remembering our very first encounter. It seems so long ago.

'I'm really sorry for leaving in such a cruel way, Charlie,' she says. 'I imagine you're very angry with me, but I was so, so confused. I felt so guilty about how I've been falling for you, but now I realise I don't need to jump to conclusions about how I should feel or how others expect me to feel or what others think of me. Thoughts are just thoughts.'

I can't hide the smile on my face, nor can I control the warmth in my heart right now, even if we're standing in a flurry of snow on the side of a busy road. Rose is wearing the same blue coat again. Minus the oil stain, thankfully.

'I must have just missed you at the cottage before you left so I took a guess that you'd be heading home to Belfast, but I don't blame you if you never want to see me again.'

She is within touching distance now and all I want to do is hold her close to me. I can't think of anything I want more than to feel her body against mine.

'How are you feeling?' I ask, moving inches closer.

'I'm much better,' she tells me with a whisper. 'It hasn't even been a day yet and I've missed you. I'm sorry.'

'I've missed you too, Rose,' I say, gently touching the side of her face. Her lips move towards mine and her kiss warms me from the inside out.

This time there is no one and nothing in the world that could interrupt us. No guilt, no shame, no grief, no pain. Just us.

'So . . . should we do this Christmas thing together then, after all?' I ask as I kiss her forehead, then lighter butterfly kisses on her neck that make her eyes fall closed. I return to her lips and we kiss with more passion this time.

A blaring horn sounds from a passing truck and the driver shouts, 'Get some mistletoe, lovers,' which makes us smile and hold each other even closer.

'I think we should do this Christmas thing together,' she says. 'Thank you for forgiving me.'

'Thank you for following me.'

She looks at the car. The tyre is almost flat to the ground now.

'Doesn't the universe work in wondrous ways,' she says. 'Now, move aside and let me sort this quickly,'

'Sort what?

'The flat tyre,' she tells me.

'You?'

'Yes, me,' she replies, rubbing her hands together against the cold. 'Rusty taught me all I know about cars when I was just a little girl, so I can change everything from wiper blades to oil to a flat tyre by the time you'd scratch your head in wonder.'

I step aside and watch her in action. Thankfully, this time she takes off the blue coat before she gets stuck in.

Life with Rose, I can already tell, will always be full of surprises.

Christmas Day

Chapter Thirty-Three

Rose

I wake up on Christmas morning in a cosy cocoon, so warm I'm expecting to feel Charlie's arms around me, but instead my eyes open to the sound of the rooster crowing in the farm-yard outside my family home. I'm in my childhood bedroom, alone.

Charlie is the first person that comes into my head when I wake up, and when I check my phone, I can see that I'm already on his mind too.

> Good morning beautiful. Happy Christmas! I want to be the first to say it to you on the day itself.

I stretch and savour the simple words, holding the phone close to my chest. We spent far too long last night texting about how our respective evenings had gone as we each lay in bed. I was only too delighted to share with him just how wonderful it was to be properly reunited with my family for Christmas.

Mum is mad to meet you, I must have told him more than once. *It feels so right to be at home this Christmas.*

We both fell asleep cradling our phones like lovestruck teenagers and now, as I lie in bed with only the farmyard sounds so familiar to my childhood and the smell of a traditional breakfast fry-up coming from the kitchen, I long to be with him on this most wonderful day of the year.

I sit up under my pink and yellow floral bedcovers, and smile as I remember how Mum bought me these from a posh department store in Belfast when I was just a teenager. She was so proud of herself that day, declaring one day I'd be up and gone, but that these covers would always be here for me to sleep under when I needed them, and I can see now that her promise was true.

The next person who comes to my mind this morning is Michael, but not in the guilty, gut-wrenching, grief-stricken way I usually remember him. Today, I allow my thoughts to linger on the wonderful Christmas times I shared with him. I remember the happy times, the gifts we shared. I remember his laughter, his handsome face, and the way he always rolled his eyes at my singing efforts.

I think of Evelyn too, and hope that she can find peace in her heart today.

I hate to think of her all alone on Christmas Day. Mum assured me she extended her usual invitation but received the usual polite refusal. I can't thank Evelyn enough for the strength she gave me by helping me put my own future into perspective when I met her at the lighthouse.

Michael is gone, but we can still love him. We can still smile at his memory, and we can continue to share so much love for as long as we are here in this lifetime. Maybe one day

Evelyn will take up our offer to join us at our dinner table. I know that would make Michael very happy.

I pull on my dressing gown and some fluffy socks, then make my way downstairs, following the sounds of Frank Sinatra dreaming of a white Christmas. When I look out through the window I see that his dream has, for once, come true. The farm is like a winter wonderland, and I can't resist sending Charlie a quick photo of my view where everything is covered in pristine white snow for miles and miles.

'Happy Christmas, Rose,' my dad says when I enter the kitchen and I feel a nervous twinge when I realise that it's just the two of us in the same room at the same time, alone for the first time in what feels like forever. 'Fancy a fry-up?'

I see that George has made himself at home already, lying by the Aga, and almost moaning in delight at the constant heat that radiates from its coal fire.

'I'd love that, thank you,' I reply. 'Happy Christmas, Dad.'

I kiss him on the cheek, his spiky white stubble and the smell of Old Spice bringing me right back to my younger years when I'd wish him goodnight and feel like the safest girl in the world.

My daddy.

He nods his head towards a pot of fresh coffee in a gesture that tells me to help myself, and as I pour the steaming dark brown liquid into a mug, the smell of roasted beans fills my senses and takes me back to so many happy mornings around the breakfast table in our humble old farmhouse.

'Your mother's glad to see you home,' he says, as he lays out rashers of bacon on the frying pan. 'She insisted I go out and dig up another Christmas tree for the hallway, so there I was like an eejit at six this morning, in pitch dark down in the snowy meadow trailing up another tree on the tractor. Your box of decorations are waiting for you in the hallway.'

I gulp back a surge of emotion at the thought of my elderly father going to all that trouble, just so my mother can watch me decorate a tree like she always used to.

'Dad, that was a lot of work – and on Christmas Day too!'

He sighs in the way he always does. I used to think it sounded like he was saying 'Ah well.'

'You know what she's like at Christmas. She's missed you terribly these past few years,' he says, turning around with two platefuls of sausage, bacon, eggs, mushrooms and fried bread. 'We all have.'

Hearing that from my dad hits me right in the feels.

'Dad?'

He pauses, a plate in each hand. He puts one on a tray and the other in front of me.

'Can I ask you something?' I say, the words almost sticking in my throat.

I pull my dressing gown sleeve over my hand in a comfort gesture I've held on to since I was young, and I sit at the long wooden table that holds so many memories of happy times.

'The night Michael died . . . I know you said something about my drinking champagne and . . . did you think it was my . . .'

My throat dries up. I can't finish the sentence. I don't have to. My dad makes his way to the table, sits down beside me and takes my hand.

'Did I think it was your fault? No, darling. No! Where on earth did you get that notion from, Rose?' he says, his gravelly voice a lot softer than I've ever remembered it to be. 'I never blamed you. Not once. It never even crossed my mind, so don't ever let that cross *your* mind again. We all loved Michael, that's all. We still do. And we all love you – maybe even more now than ever, if that's possible.'

I can't speak so I just nod and wipe my eyes.

'That's so good to hear,' I whisper with my eyes closed. 'You've no idea how much I needed to hear that.'

Thoughts are just thoughts . . .

'Now, are you and Sarah making hot chocolate for the neighbours?' he asks me, swiftly getting back to business as only he can. 'The O'Neills will be twitching their curtains waiting for you once they get wind that you're home this year.'

My heart swells at his suggestion.

'I'll make sure we do that as soon as Sarah gets here.'

'Great. Right. I'll take your mother up some breakfast, then she'll be wanting to watch you decorate that tree,' he tells me. 'I suppose she'll be looking for you both to sing along to that awful song you both like.'

His eyes sparkle when he looks at me now, sitting at the table in my dressing gown having breakfast, just like I did for so many years of childhood on cold winter days.

He takes a few steps towards the door with the tray in his slightly shaking hands for my mother, and then he pauses and turns to me again.

'You'll never believe who rang me last night,' he says, throwing his eyes up to the heavens. 'And not before time. Mind you, I gave as good as I got back then . . .'

'Not Marion?' I say, my mood changing instantly. 'It's a Christmas miracle! Are you two speaking again?!'

He nods.

'We are indeed. She's changing the name of the cottage back to Granny Molly's *and* has invited me and your mother up to stay whenever we want. I might take her up on her offer.'

'You should, Daddy! That's brilliant news.'

He shuffles on a little and then stops again.

'It's really good to have you home, Rose,' he whispers. 'I mean that. It's so good to have you home this Christmas.'

And then he hums 'O Holy Night' as he moves on out into the hallway, his soft slippers now making a sound on the stairs as he brings my mother her Christmas breakfast, another ritual in our house that's as old as tea.

I can just about wait until he is out of sight before I let my head fall into my hands and take a moment to compose myself.

My dad said it was good to have me home.

I think that might be the best Christmas present ever.

Chapter Thirty-Four

Charlie

Helena has sent me at least ten photos so far this morning, all selfies, and all in various Christmas accessories such as Santa hats, elf hats, hairbands with stars and glitter – all of which did make me laugh out loud.

And then came her string of usual jokes by text message.

What do snowmen eat for breakfast? Ice Crispies!

What do you call Santa's favourite singer? Elfis!

It's just gone ten on Christmas morning and the world is very still and quiet, in a way I've never noticed before. Usually by this time, I'm swamped on the living room floor with Rebecca, buried in torn-up wrapping paper, trying to figure out what batteries fit which toy, and the whole universe is reduced in between the four walls of our existence.

But this year is a first year like no other. There's no flurried gift unwrapping, there's no tidying to be done, there's no fuss to be made. It's just me, Max and the silence of the snow-covered streets.

As soon as I woke up this morning after texting Rose, I made my way over to St Anne's cathedral and listened to the bell toll from the comfort of the car as Max bounced around in the backseat, still looking for George everywhere we go.

There was a comfort in the silence and then the sound of the bell. I savoured the quiet of the city on this peaceful Christmas morning. I took a moment to let everything pause, to stop doing, and to just *be*.

I thought of my parents, gone well before their time after cancer stole their future, and how although they were far from perfect, they did what they could to give my sister and me a good life.

I thought of each of my clients, many of whom are dreading Christmas just like I was, but for different reasons.

I thought of Clodagh and Rob with my darling Rebecca in Tenerife, who will today witness Christmas in the sun for the very first time. From my heart I wished them well, which is something I didn't ever think I would be able to do.

I thought of Rusty and Marion who were hanging on to their marriage by a thread but who now seem to have found a new lease of life, and I hoped they would enjoy the hamper I left on their doorstep before I went off yesterday. Maybe they'd even enjoy it together? I deliberately chose one of each item for the hamper: a bottle of wine, a block of smoked cheese, a pack of crackers, some grapes and a jar of chutney, and in my mind, I visualised them taking the quiet of today to have some long overdue conversations. Communication is key in any relationship, so who knows, maybe this and a few days off work might kick-start a conversation that's much needed between them.

I thought of Helena, my only sibling, my big sister who lives in a totally different realm of pure innocence and love. I only hope that I can keep on doing what's best for her, no matter what else life throws our way.

And I thought of Rose who would wake up this morning with her parents, in the one place she really longed to be this Christmas, surrounded by love and laughter at last. I hope she cherishes this morning with her family, and that she can now find peace in her heart. She deserves it all.

'And then there's you, my buddy,' I say to young Max, who probably doesn't realise what day it is. 'I've a huge, delicious bone for you to enjoy later today. You'll love that, won't you?'

He whimpers.

'Ah, you miss George,' I reply. 'I miss him too. But don't worry. We're going to have a lovely day, I promise. It's going to be special, just wait and see.'

So far, it's been a very slow, quiet Christmas morning, but I know it's going to be exactly what I'd hoped for. There's a strange, unexpected comfort in the stillness I've been lucky enough to experience all morning.

I've taken this chance to reset, to harmonise and to embrace all the clarity that comes with the art of doing nothing. I haven't felt lonely at all, because I know now what is important to me and what's not. I've learned to separate the nonsense from the core of my own being. I know now what I want and what I don't want. I know my who, and I know my why.

Rebecca called me first thing to show me her presents, which lifted my spirits immensely. Seeing her little face on a screen, so full of magic and childhood innocence, was a nice surprise.

'FaceTime me later, Daddy!' she squealed. 'Let me see what your dinner is like. I'll show you mine too, OK?'

'Of course, honey, just send me photos anytime you feel like it. I'd love to see every moment of your wonderful day.'

Even Clodagh couldn't pull against the joy of that phone call. It was all I ever wanted. My child and I had time and we had a laugh together on Christmas Day. It was never too much to ask in the first place, was it?

It's toasty in the car where I sit now, and there's something so peaceful about how quiet everything is around me.

Curtains are still drawn in many homes scattered along the street where I'm parked; some lights are on even though it's bright and snowy outside. There's life bursting at the seams behind all the closed doors, and I'm about to interrupt what's going on in one of the houses, I imagine for the best.

So, I do what I came here for. I pull on my woolly hat and get out of the car. I pick up the phone and dial her number, watching outside for the curtains to twitch when she takes my call.

'Charlie?'

'Yes, me again. Can you look outside? It's snowing.'

'I know it's snowing, Charlie! Of course it's snowing. It's Christmas, silly.'

'Look again.'

'Why?'

'Just look outside.'

'OK, I'm going to the window now.'

I hear her shuffle across the room, Mary's kind voice muffled in the background. I see her hand slip through the gap in the curtains and she pulls it to the side. And then I see her face. She squints at first in disbelief and then she lights up just as I hoped she would do.

'Wait a minute. Is that you? Oh my goodness, Charlie, you're here! Are you here, Charlie? Are you here for me?'

I run across the street to where she stands at the door in the sparkly green dress she bought especially for today, the one I've commented on at least a hundred times in photos.

She puts her hands up to her face and lets big fat tears roll down her cheeks. When I wrap my arms around her, I look to the doorway where Mary is crying too.

'Happy Christmas, Helena,' I whisper to my precious big sister. 'I just couldn't do this without you. I never have before, and I'll never try to again.'

She is talking ten to the dozen as usual, her voice muffled in the warmth of my coat, but when she finally pulls away, all puffy eyed and red faced, I know I've made the right decision to come and surprise her this morning.

'Happy Christmas, little brother!' she beams. 'This is going to be the best Christmas ever!'

And you know what, I think she might be onto something there.

'I couldn't agree more.'

Chapter Thirty-Five

Rose

'Ta-daaa!'

I stand back to admire my work of art as Mum applauds my efforts from her armchair, a glass of Bailey's cream liqueur and ice by her side. She looks as glamorous as ever in her red velvet dress, with her platinum hair trimmed around the nape of her neck and some oversized earrings that would give anything in my own collection a run for its money. The tree is sparkling, the mood is merry and our favourite Christmas song is on repeat in the background.

'I think we should sing even louder to irritate your dad,' she giggles, 'but yes, it looks like a fairy tale, just like it always does when you decorate, Rose. No one can decorate a tree like you can. I've said it every single year.'

I do a polite curtsey and follow her into the sitting room where Dad has lit the fire and left out some mince pies for us to enjoy.

'I don't know how I'm going to fit in dinner later,' I say, tucking into the warm, fruity middle of one of Mum's homemade pies. 'I forgot how much we eat when we all get together.'

'That's what it's all about,' Dad chirps as he shakes some more coal onto the fire.

Mum has been full of questions about Charlie since I got here, and she even interrupted our traditional sing-along while decorating the tree to ask even more. I told her about Rebecca in Tenerife, about his job as a therapist in Belfast, about how much he adores his sister Helena, and most of all about how his kindness made me see that I was still worth loving again. She cried when I told her that.

'He's calling me now,' I announce, holding up my phone for effect, but when I answer the video call, it's not Charlie's face I see, but Helena's.

'Happy Christmas, Rose,' she sings to me. 'Guess who picked me up? Guess who wanted to spend Christmas with me after all? Charlie!'

She wears a hairband with reindeer faces on springs, and a beautiful green dress. Her face is bursting with joy and her delight is instantly contagious.

'Oh, Helena, I'm so happy for you. I knew he wouldn't be able to stay away on a day like today.'

My heart sings.

'And guess where he's bringing me now? We're going to your house, Rose! I'm so excited to meet you,' she tells me. 'Charlie says you're even prettier in real life and that you're a brilliant singer.'

My mother laughs at the singing joke a bit more than she should. My father almost chokes on his mince pie.

'Oops, I forgot to say that Max is coming too,' Helena says quickly, as if I could ever forget about Max. 'We'll be there for around two?'

'The more the merrier,' Mum shouts from her armchair, lifting her glass in approval. 'I can't wait to meet you all. Love the reindeers, Helena!'

Helena squints and looks closer into the camera lens.

'There's no such word as "reindeers". It's just reindeer, even though there are two,' she says, nodding her head so they bobble and swing. 'Mary told me this morning.'

I burst out laughing then I hear Charlie's voice in the background. He shouts a hurried 'see you soon' and they're gone for now.

'Reindeers!' says my dad as he heads outside to check on the farm animals before our guests arrive. 'Who says "reindeers"? Even I know that much, holy Moses.'

Mum tries to respond but she isn't quick enough, so we just roll our eyes. When he's out of sight, I feel my mother's gaze on me, as if she's one more big reveal to make this Christmas.

'What?' I ask her cautiously.

'I have something to tell you,' she says quickly. 'I've been about to explode but I wanted to savour the moment.'

I shift in my seat.

'I'm almost afraid to ask you what it is,' I reply. 'Is it good news or bad news?'

'It's good news,' she says with a smile. 'I'm hardly going to deliver bad news on Christmas Day.'

'All right, all right, never mind savouring the moment. You've savoured it! Now tell me!'

She keeps me in suspense for just a little longer.

'Mum, what is it?'

She licks her painted pink lips then clasps her hands together and leans towards me.

'I've my own surprise visitor on her way to spend Christmas Day with us,' she tells me, her eyes wide with delight. 'I know how much you worry about her at this time of year, as she does you.'

'Mum, you're kidding me!'

She shakes her head. I can hear my pulse in my ears.

'Is it – is it *Evelyn*?'

'It's Evelyn, honey,' she tells me with glee. 'I think Michael is watching over both of you extra closely this Christmas. Isn't that such a turnaround after spending so long all alone? I can't wait to see her.'

I put my hands to my mouth and I momentarily lose my breath.

'Me too, Mum. Me too!'

Evelyn is joining us for Christmas. I think I need something stronger than tea and a mince pie to let that great news sink in.

Shortly after two on a snowy Christmas afternoon, Mum and Dad sit at either end of the long dinner table. It is, in my sister Sarah's words, 'a work of art', decorated with twigs I gathered from the garden, red apples neatly placed around some cream church candles, bunches of bright green holly with deep red berries and snowflake-shaped name places made from some recycled Christmas cards.

The candles are flickering, soft festive music plays in the background and the smell of succulent turkey, ham and an array of winter vegetables wafts from their neat arrangement on gleaming white plates.

'I could never have made up the table like this, not in a million years,' Sarah coos in admiration. 'My efforts extend to tacky tinsel and at a stretch, a few tealights. You've a real gift, Rose.'

'Well, you prepared all the food and there's enough to feed a nation,' I remind her. 'The cranberry sauce is outstanding.'

'Jude's mum made that,' she whispers. 'They were supposed to join us but send their apologies. I did do the rest.'

'Ahem,' says Dad from his perch at the top of the table.

We're all a bit squashed, but Charlie and Helena haven't stopped smiling since they got here, and I don't think I have words to describe how high I feel having them with us. And then there's Evelyn, who is quiet beside me, but who smiles every time I catch her eye.

'OK, Dad did the turkey,' Sarah announces. 'Isn't he the best!'

Everyone gives a cheer.

'And the stuffing!' he declares proudly. 'Don't forget the stuffing,'

'The stuffing is my favourite,' says Helena, giving my dad a playful nudge. They seem to have hit it off from the get-go, with Helena's lack of filter matching my dad's for once.

They've provided us with plenty of laugh out loud moments already.

The conversation flows, with Sarah's husband Jude intrigued by Charlie's job, and my little niece Ada can't take her eyes off Helena's blue and black streaked hair. Her younger brother Jack refuses to sit at the table, too busy having fun with Max and George on the floor, and with the Amazon Alexa being thrown demands every few minutes to crack out a special request, the atmosphere is crazy and busy, just as I'd hoped it would be.

'The gravy is *very* tasty,' I say to Mum, knowing it was the one thing she managed to contribute to today's feast. She reaches across to me and whispers, 'Charlie is quite tasty too,' nowhere near quietly enough. Sarah rolls her eyes.

'Don't let Dad hear you say that or he'll get jealous.'

Even Evelyn joins in and has a chuckle.

'There's nothing wrong with looking at the menu,' she says. 'It doesn't mean you have to order.'

Mum and I exchange glances and my heart glows at her cheeky grin, and when I see her scan the room with the widest smile, I know I'm so lucky to be able to spend this precious day with her and my father. Having Evelyn here is a bonus I could never have dreamed of.

'Do you mind if I take a quick photo for Rebecca?' Charlie asks me under his breath. 'Don't be afraid to say no, but I told her earlier I'd let her see us all together.'

'Of course,' I reply, with my mouth full of deliciousness. 'Didn't you say she wanted to see the dogs wearing Christmas hats? Here, let's pull a cracker and get that sorted.'

I lift a cracker, recalling how just days ago I feared I'd never get to do something so simple again, yet now I'm surrounded by so many willing participants. Charlie and I tug and wait for it to snap. Then we do it again, so that Max and George have a paper hat each. Young Jack, who is still on the floor, takes great pleasure in fitting them with the hats, after a brief discussion on who would suit red and who would suit green. I think my George is definitely a green. Thankfully Jack agrees.

Everyone is relaxed, the mood is light and there's no pressure to sit still or perform. We are drinking, we are eating and we are very merry.

I turn around and hold the phone camera up high, calling everyone for attention.

'Jack, look this way, honey! Max and George, you two scallywags too! Evelyn, Mum, Helena, Dad, everyone, say "Happy Christmas, Rebecca!"'

'Happy Christmas, Rebecca!' we all shout together, and when Charlie takes the phone to send the picture to his daughter, I can't help but notice that he has tears in his eyes.

'She'll be delighted,' he says, swallowing back the emotion. 'She won't believe it when she sees so many people around the same table at the same time. This is so special, Rose. Thank you for having us here. It really does mean the whole world.'

I rest my head on his arm for just a second, and Helena catches the moment in a photo of the two of us, our first photograph together. When she shows me it, my eyes are half closed, Charlie is blinking too and has his mouth open as if he's catching flies. It's horrible, but it's perfect. Soon, everyone is posing for pictures and I don't think I've felt this much joy in a very long time.

I send Carlos a few snaps to keep him posted and he replies instantly with a photo of himself and his dad, new crystal glasses in hand making a cheers gesture across a busy Scrabble board.

They both look very happy. *It's the simple things.*

'Rose for a song,' Dad calls out and everyone erupts into laughter.

'Oh, I don't think we're quite ready for that,' quips Evelyn, and I glow as it sounds like something Michael would have said. I close my eyes for just a second, and all I can see is his smiling face.

'Let's raise a glass to absent friends,' I suggest, and with happy tears in our eyes, our glasses clink in the air as we remember loved ones who are no longer with us at the table, but who are watching over us all this Christmas. Michael, his dad, Charlie's parents, and everyone who should be with us in body but who are very much with us in spirit.

'Thank you,' I whisper into Evelyn's ear. 'Thank you for reminding me that love lives on.'

'It's so good to see you happy,' she whispers. 'That makes me and Michael happy too.'

I put my arm around her and squeeze her delicate shoulders.

There's magic in the air. There's happiness everywhere.

It's Christmas and my heart is full.

Chapter Thirty-Six

Charlie

As darkness falls outside this wholesome family farmhouse, the party atmosphere slowly winds down too. Voices are hushed and the lively music from before is now just a background hum.

The open fire has sent both the dogs and Rose's parents off to a silent slumber in the sitting room, and Helena is in her element playing board games with Evelyn, Sarah and the children at the kitchen table while Rose and I finish washing up.

'I don't think I'll ever be able to get her away from here,' I say, watching my sister fuss and giggle over a game of Monopoly with her new-found friends. 'Honestly, Rose, we've had the best of days. I do think your dad and Evelyn are Helena's favourites though. She's had a ball. We've never had a Christmas like this before. We'll never forget it.'

Rose dries her hands on a tea towel and turns around to face me.

'Fancy a walk outside in the snow? Just the two of us?'

'Yeah,' I whisper. 'That would be nice.'

We wrap up in coats, scarves, hats and gloves in the hallway and slip out into the dark of the night with the moon glistening on the crisp snow that crunches beneath our feet. When we're only a few steps away from the house, Rose stops to look up at the stars, which brings me right back to our time at Seaview Cottage, or Granny Molly's as it's now rightly known.

'I don't want any of this to end,' she says, gazing upwards as snowflakes fall onto her nose and cheeks and eyelashes. 'I want to relive it all again and again and again. I know I'll never look at life in the same way after all the joy and love I've felt this Christmas.'

'It's been extra special,' I say, pulling her close, and we stand there for what feels like hours, just holding each other as the snow sprinkles down and happy voices spill out from the farmhouse. 'You're perfect, Rose, you know that? Just perfect. Don't ever change.'

'I'm not perfect,' she says. 'I'm—'

She steps back a little and I hold her beautiful, smiling face in my hands.

'You're perfect to me,' I tell her. 'You're funny, you're challenging, you're spontaneous, you're creative. You light up every room you step into. You make me want to be the best person I can be.'

I take a deep breath.

'I'm so glad we found each other,' she replies.

She smiles with her eyes closed and snowflakes fall onto her long, dark eyelashes. We kiss once more until Rose leans back a little and puts her hands on my waist.

We hold each other in silence but I know she's itching to say something. She looks up at me and flashes me a cheeky smile.

'Have you checked your phone lately?'

I frown in response.

'No . . . why?'

'Well . . . there just might be a very important text message waiting for you,' she says. 'I was going to buy another whiteboard but I figured my last message on there wasn't the best, so a text it is. Go on. Check.'

I'm confused, but I know Rose is up to something, so I put my hand in my pocket and fish out my phone. Sure enough, there's a text message awaiting my attention.

'Read it out so I can hear it too,' she says with a cheeky giggle.

I do as I'm told.

'Dear Mr Sheerin,

'Deepest apologies, kind sir, but there's been a double booking for your apartment for your four-night stay in Tenerife across New Year's Eve.'

I take a step back on the crunchy snow.

'Rose? I haven't booked a four-night stay . . . What is this?'

She just smiles. My heart rate rises. Could this mean what I think it means?

'Read the rest!' she tells me, her glove-clad hands clasped together as she watches and waits for me to continue.

'I can assure you this is not our usual practice, but your one-bedroom apartment has also been booked for the same few days by a Miss Rose Quinn, who is thankfully willing to overlook our mistake and share it with you.'

I read the rest of the message in silence, grinning from ear to ear as it all sinks in:

She does insist that no whiteboards are allowed on this holiday. But flirty texts are always, always welcome. And let loose on your emojis. You know you want to.

Happy Christmas, Charlie. We're going to see Rebecca next week.

Lots of love from Rose x

I blink and stare at my phone screen. Rose's message has left me speechless for a moment.

'You've booked us a holiday in Tenerife across New Year? To see Rebecca?'

'I sure have,' Rose tells me. 'But I'm not taking the sofa this time.'

I don't cry very often. It takes a lot to reduce me to tears, but Rose has well and truly got me this time. There's a lump in my throat the size of a watermelon.

'You better believe you're not taking the sofa this time!' I exclaim, feeling tears sting my eyes. 'Thank you, Rose. That's the most thoughtful, incredibly precious gift you could ever have given me.'

'Are you happy?'

'You better believe I'm happy!'

I pick her up.

I kiss her deeply under the light of the moon, and then we stroll hand in hand back inside to the warmth of the farmhouse where we shiver and dry out in front of the Aga in the cosy kitchen.

Max and George are playing with a silver Christmas bauble that has fallen from the tree, their paws touching and their noses rubbing as they scurry around the kitchen floor.

Rose's parents are in the sitting room snoozing off the dinner by the turf fire, holding hands, which is both endearing and inspiring. It makes me think of my own parents in heaven. I smile at the thought of them forever together.

Rebecca sends me a photo in response to mine from earlier. She is wearing a Santa hat, she has her thumbs up and has a cheery smile on her face, which makes me smile too.

And Sarah and Jude are making sure Helena and Evelyn are fully engaged with the kids in a never-ending, highly intense Monopoly session at the kitchen table. When I hear my darling sister giggle heartily, I'm reminded how it's one of my favourite sounds in the whole world.

Rose cuddles into me, wrapping her arms around my waist before we sit down to watch the rest of their board game play out, teasing that we'd like to join in even though it's too late.

I kiss Rose's damp hair as the snow flurries onto the windowpane, and after the most perfect few days together, we've another adventure in the winter sun to look forward to very soon.

There's magic in the air. There's happiness everywhere.

It's Christmas and my heart is full.

Acknowledgements

This book was sprinkled with a touch of festive magic from the very beginning, as the most wonderful things have seemed to happen over the twelve months or so since *This Christmas* began its journey into the world.

First of all I must thank my readers, who named the main characters in the story after a shout-out on social media which led to a flurry of suggestions and a very tricky job to choose my favourites. So thank you to the Armour family who suggested Charlie and Rose after their parents, to Sarah O'Donnell who suggested Rusty and Marion after her parents, and to Lynne Kelly for suggesting her niece's name, Rebecca. I've enough beautiful character names now to work on my next book too, so thank you all who put forward your ideas. I really hope those chosen enjoy seeing their loved ones' names in print!

Last summer, when I'd already written the first draft of *This Christmas* and while doing some tourism work for the Mid Ulster area, I stumbled across the most beautiful cottage, Rosehill House, here in my home county of Tyrone. Its thatched roof and green window panes reminded me of Seaview Cottage in this story, but it was only days later that I was told the owner's parents are Charlie and Rose – and they are the real-life couple whose names I'd chosen for my characters way before I'd known the cottage existed! What a coincidence!

And then in another twist of fate, later in the year when my sister and I took a very last-minute trip to Donegal in winter to an Airbnb she'd booked, my jaw dropped again when I saw the plaque on the wall of our accommodation – you've guessed it, 'Seaview Cottage'. Some things really are meant to be.

I adore County Donegal and all its towns and villages, but the Fanad Head area was new to me, so thank you to the lady who suggested I feature Fanad in my book. I met you at the Compassionate Communities event at the Seamus Heaney Centre and wish I'd got your name. My children and I had a great time in summer exploring the lighthouse inside and out, and of course we had to sample the chowder in the Lighthouse Tavern (yes, it's a real place) as well as admiring the views out onto Lough Swilly, the site of some very poignant scenes in Rose's story. The village in my story unfortunately is not real, so please allow creative license for that, but if you're ever lucky enough to visit Fanad Head, the lighthouse is a treat for all ages.

Speaking of villages, it really does take one to make a book like this come together, so thank you to my dream team who brought my words to life:

To Sarah Hornsley, my wonderful agent at Peters, Fraser & Dunlop for your confident, astute and truly personal guidance always; to Laurie Robertson, who looked after me so well while Sarah was on maternity leave; and to Katie Loughnane, my editor at Cornerstone, Penguin Random House, who always makes me feel so excited with her refreshing, creative ways and enthusiastic approach.

To Katya Browne (Assistant Managing Editor) and Jess Muscio (Editorial Assistant); to Hope Butler (marketing) and M-L Patton (publicity); to Olivia Allen, Evie Kettlewell, Mat Watterson and Jess Ferrier (sales); to Richard Rowlands and Barbora Sabolova (international sales); to Annie Peacock (production) and Lizzy Moyes (inventory). And a huge thank you to Lucy Thorne (designer) and Jennifer Costello (illustrator) who I'm sure everyone will agree brought the characters of Rose, Charlie, Max and George to life to the point of perfection on the cover. It's an honour and a delight to work with you all (and the illustrated Charlie is very handsome indeed).

To my aunty Eithna Vincent, to whom I've dedicated this book, as a token of thanks and acknowledgement of your efforts, your big heart, and the immense strength and love your showed to us in childhood when we faced our first Christmas without our mother. You set aside your own grief for your baby sister and battled through, making dinner for seven of us as well as your own family of eight. It was a Christmas full of mixed emotion, but thanks to you, it's a memory we can now look back on and smile as it brought us all together. Your generosity didn't end there of course, but you helped make a painful time a lot easier with your maternal heart. We all love you.

A huge thanks to the international booksellers and librarians who recommend my novels and continue to support me in so many ways.

To all the media and bloggers who help me spread the word for each new release. I fully appreciate every social shout-out, every column inch and every TV and radio broadcast that comes my way. Special personal thanks to *The Lynette Fay Show* (BBC Radio Ulster), *The Connor Philips Show* (BBC Radio Ulster), Pamela Ballentine and Petra Ellis at UTV Life, Will Scholes and Jenny Lee (*Irish News*), Maureen Coleman (*Local Women*).

To my writing students near and far, thank you for trusting in me to guide you with your own words. To my Write With Emma community which is going from strength to strength – thanks to Sean Quinn and his daughter Rose (yes, Rose Quinn – another coincidence!) with whom I have been working on building the Write With Emma community for the past few months; to Tanya and Sean Maguire, with whom I've built a global platform via The Player's Conservatory in Los Angeles. Thanks to everyone who supports me on Patreon by reading my short stories and thoughts, especially Ann McGlone. A word of appreciation also to Alex, AJ, Deanna, Denise, Elysse, Kathleen, Kim, Laura, Morgan and Stephanie – students who are now my great friends.

Thanks as always to my family, who do their best to still look excited after all these years when I talk about my latest novel ideas, and for understanding it's not just a job, but a true passion which makes all my hours at the laptop worthwhile.

And finally, my heartfelt thanks to you, my reader, who chose this book this Christmas. Like Lorraine in the craft shop said to Rose, it can be the most wonderful time of year and it can be the most painful time of year. I hope this Christmas finds you well, and if you've an empty seat at the table like most of us do at some point in life, I hope your heart is full in their name and memory.

You're all in my thoughts with the most heartfelt gratitude.

Take really good care.

Emma x

Granny Molly's Best Ever Chocolate Cake Recipe

Be like Rose and impress your friends with this delicious chocolate cake, from Granny Molly's recipe book!

INGREDIENTS
For the cake:
110g unsalted butter
180g dark chocolate, broken into pieces
310g plain (all-purpose) flour
520g granulated sugar
100g cocoa powder
2 tsp bicarbonate of soda (baking soda)
½ tsp baking powder
1 ½ tsp salt
3 eggs
235ml water
360g room temperature sour cream
2 tsp vanilla extract

For the chocolate fudge frosting:
200g dark chocolate chips
120ml whipping cream
30ml honey
12g cocoa powder
80ml sour cream

METHOD

For the cakes:

1. Preheat the oven to 180°C/160°C Fan and lightly grease and line three nine-inch round tins with parchment paper.
2. Melt the butter and chocolate together in a pan over a low heat. Once melted, pour into a large mixing bowl.
3. In a separate bowl, combine the flour, sugar, cocoa powder, bicarbonate of soda, baking powder and salt until blended.
4. Add the eggs, water, sour cream and vanilla extract to the butter and chocolate mix and beat until smooth.
5. Add the wet ingredients to the dry ingredients in the mixing bowl and beat together again until smooth.
6. Divide the mixture equally between the three tins and bake in the oven for 40 minutes, or until a skewer (or toothpick) comes out clean. Allow the cakes to cool for fifteen minutes before removing from the tins.

For the chocolate fudge frosting:

1. Combine the chocolate chips, whipping cream and honey in a saucepan and melt together over a low heat. Gently stir until all the ingredients have melted and the mixture is smooth. Pour into a mixing bowl.

2. Add the cocoa powder to the melted chocolate mixture in the mixing bowl. Once everything is combined, add the sour cream and whisk until smooth.
3. Leave the mixture to cool for 15 minutes, then whisk again until thick and fluffy in texture.
4. Spread a layer of the frosting between each cake layer, stacking them, and decorate with your choice of chocolate. (Granny Molly loved Ferrero Rocher, Kinder Bueno or seasonal berries.)

Please share photos of your masterpiece on social media and hashtag #ThisChristmas #EmmaHeatherington or tag me @emmaheatheringtonwriter on Instagram and Facebook or @emmalouwriter on Twitter. I'd love to see your creations!

Recipe kindly supplied by the real-life baking queen, Margaret McCrory. Thank you Margaret x